C000064980

NO MORE GAMES

A Novel

Gordon J. Brown

RED DOG
UK

Published by RED DOG PRESS 2023

First Edition

Paperback ISBN 978-1-915433-08-4
Ebook ISBN 978-1-915433-06-0

www.reddogpress.co.uk

*This book is dedicated to the Gigha Crowd. There is no need for names—
you all know who you are—and what you mean to me.*

Enjoy

The Conversation

'DO YOU WANT a job?'

'A job?'

'A job.'

'What kind of job?'

'We'll get to that.'

'Is it a good job?'

'That depends on your definition of good.'

'There's more than one definition?'

'In my world, there are many definitions.'

'Go figure. What do I have to do to get this job?'

'Listen.'

'Listen to what?'

'Me talking.'

'When?'

'When what?'

'When do I have to listen to you talking?'

'Now would be a good time.'

'I think I'd prefer tomorrow morning.'

'Why? Do you have something else to do tonight?'

'Funny. What if I don't want the job?'

'Then don't take it.'

'That easy?'

'That easy.'

'And am I qualified for this job?'

'Eminently.'

'Nice word.'

'I'm trying to expand my vocabulary.'

'You've been known to spend a lot of time in the library. People notice these things.'

'I like the library.'

'And do you actually read books there?'

'I read the classics.'

'And I thought you only masticated the extensive Mills and Boons collection.'

'I only masticate over the librarian.'

'You mean masturbate.'

'I know exactly what I mean.'

'And, apart from the librarian, is there another reason you are darkening the book shelves so often?'

'A desire.'

'A desire for what?'

'Catharsis. Retribution. Clarity. Forgiveness. All four?'

'And is that working out for you?'

'Not so much.'

'So why the job offer?'

'If I tell you a story, it will explain it all.'

'What kind of story?'

'A story central to my life. One that defined me. Made me.'

'That's some build up! You now have my attention.'

'But it's not a short story. No half-pinter. This is a full-blown night in the pub, shut out the rest of the world, let's take advantage of a lock-in, type of story.'

'And that's a problem, why?'

'Because I don't know if this is the right time to tell the story. Or if this is the right place.'

'I can't answer that for you, other than to say that the only right time to do anything is dictated by what happens after. A good outcome, and it was the right time. A bad one, and you screwed up.'

'Is that on page one of 'Philosophy for the Hard of Thinking?'

'It's on page two. Page one is given over to advising the reader not to share any of the book's wisdom with troglodytes.'

'And what does the book say about the right place?'

'That what really matters is not the right place, but the right person.'

'And are you the right person for me to unburden to?'

'I'm a terrible listener!'

'That could be a good thing. If I get going, you may want to tune out for parts.'

'Why? Are they too gruesome? Too shocking? Too erotic?'

'Too personal.'

'Are you scared I'll tell others your darkest secrets?'

'Would you?'

'Yes.'

'Even if I say to tell no-one?'

'Probably.'

'Do you always antagonise people that are offering you a life-changing job?'

'So now it's a life-changing job?'

'Totally.'

'And before I decide if I want this 'life-changing' job, I have to listen to you.'

'Maybe.'

'What does that mean?'

'What does maybe usually mean?'

'Can I ask, is all of the story going to be like this?'

'Like what?'

'A constant tease.'

'Sounds about right.'

'Okay, let's say I'll listen, at least for a bit. How does this story start?'

'How do all stories start?'

'At the beginning.'

'Not usually. This one doesn't.'

'When does it start?'

'A long time ago.'

'But not at the beginning?'

'It starts at the beginning of the story—but not the beginning of my life. It starts when I was twelve.'

'That's still a long time ago.'

'Yes, it is. And it all starts with a diary entry.'

'You kept a diary?'

'No.'

'I'm confused!'

'I was going to keep a diary, but gave up after the first couple of pages.'

'That shows real dedication.'

'I kept those pages. Do you want to read them?'

'Will it help?'

'Yes.'

'And after that?'

'I told you, you need to listen to me. So, are you sitting comfortably?'

'I'm neither sitting, nor comfortable, but please give me the pages!'

'Here!'

My Diary
16th January 1974

IT WAS MILKY who found the body. In the Woods. In our den. A *dead* body, he told me. Or as he said: a 'deed' body. Milky had come knocking on my door just after teatime. I thought he'd come around to cadge some food. He often did when his mum and dad had had a fight. After that, both would often storm out, leaving him staring at an empty cupboard and drinking tap water. That empty cupboard featured a lot in Milky's life. As mine.

I'd said to him, after he had gasped about the dead body: 'James Alexander Milkwood, you are a liar! You've not seen a dead body.' Milky lies a lot. But, to be fair, so do I. So do most of the people I know. Mum says it's a national sport amongst twelve-year-old boys in Simshill. Milky insisted he wasn't lying. Told me that I could go and look for myself. The fact that he was out of breath gave some credence to his tale. He'd obviously run flat out to tell me.

It was dark. Night comes early in Scottish winters. The Woods are a scary place at any time, but we went anyway. And Milky was right. There was a man's body in our den. And, to be fair to Milky, the man looked dead. He wasn't moving, plus, with no torch, we had no way to tell if he was breathing. I'd asked Milky what we should do. He said we should call the police. My dad's a policeman, but I didn't want to call him. There are things in our den that I didn't want him to see. And if we called any other police, my dad would go radio rental on me. Calling the police is a big no-no in our house. My dad tells me, regularly, that if he ever finds me down at the police station on Craigie Street, he'll leather the arse off me. *We sort our own.* It's what he says. I tell Milky this and he says we can't just leave a dead body in our den. We discuss moving the corpse, but neither of us are up for that.

When the man woke up, we both got one hell of a fright.

The Conversation

'SIMSHILL?'

That was my home as a kid,' I reply.

'In Glasgow?'

'Southside. You know it?'

'I do. And Milky?'

'My bestest friend in the whole wide world.'

'And you found a dead man that wasn't a dead man.'

'That's the gig.'

'I take it that this dead man that wasn't a dead man was the start of something.'

'Something that led me here.'

'Is that why you need to tell me about it?'

'I need to tell someone.'

'To gain what? Understanding, or is this a sympathy ploy that will bore me rigid?'

'Neither. But it will get you that job.'

'So, I get a job, but what do you get out of it?'

'To salve a wound that has needed tended to for so long that I've grown used to the pain. I live with the pain. And until recently, I actually thought I enjoyed the pain.'

'That's deep.'

'Deeper than you think.'

'And what brought all of this on now?'

'Self-help books.'

'So not the classics, nor Mills and Boon?'

'Actually, either would have been more enlightening. I got nothing from the self-help books themselves, other than a realisation that the more of them I read, the less helpful they were. And that was my moment on that fabled road to Damascus.'

'That self-help books are a pile of crap?'

'That self-help books only have one value in this world.'

'Which is?'

'They contain the word self-help. Or is that two words? Can never tell. The books are for shit. Full of advice that the writer doesn't believe. Or if they believe it, there is no proof their advice works. Or if they have proof it works, it's about as robust as using a pie-crust for a box to protect your nuts in a game of footie.'

'And this led you where?'

'That self-help is not about reading or listening—it's about talking.'

'Talking about what?'

'A confession. And confession is good for the soul.'

'It may be good for the soul, but I know a lot of people around here where confession didn't work out too well for them.'

'Do you still want to hear mine?'

'Do I need to wear a dog collar?'

'Whatever turns you on! All I ask is that you at least pretend to be engaged.'

'And there are no more diary entries to read?'

'No.'

'Well, feel free, my son. After all, we have a few hours to burn. So, pray begin and I will consider your penance as you speak.'

'As you wish, father.'

Chapter 1
'The Day It All Started.'

'JESUS, GINGER,' says Milky. 'He's not dead.'

The man rolls over and yawns.

'No kidding,' I reply.

Our den lay against the fence of a house, one of the many that lined the Woods. The den was an old badger set that Milky and I had dug out into a small cave two summers earlier. It was invisible to anyone, unless they stumbled right onto it. The wood it lay in was small, but big enough for us. It took you five minutes to walk from one end to the other. But there was a whole other world in there. The surrounding homes hemmed it in completely, with one small lane to let you get in or out. Mum thought the Woods were supposed to be covered in houses when Simshill was built back in the fifties, but whoever owned the land wouldn't sell, or wanted too much money, or liked trees. Some sort of something. The place was an oasis of imagination for the kids of the scheme back then, probably still is.

Anyway, whatever way you looked at it, the Woods were a boon to us local kids. A safe haven wrapped in houses. A natural play-area snuggled amongst the homes of Simshill. A safe-zone hidden away from the no-go zones of Castlemilk and the Valley that lay nearby. No-go zones for boys from Simshill in the early seventies, unless you wanted your head kicked in by the gangs that roamed there. Milky and I preferred to avoid steel toe-capped boots to the head if we could, so we played safe—and the Woods were as safe as you can get. That's if climbing fifty-foot trees unsupervised can be considered safe. Or finding strange men in your den.

The only light shining on the den comes from the orange glow of a lone streetlamp beyond the houses and, at this distance, the light is little more than a generator of faint shadows.

'We should go,' I say.

'Why?' Milky replies.

'He could be dangerous,' I say, pointing at the man.

'He doesn't look dangerous.'

'Milky, what would dangerous look like?'

'Dunno. But our stuff is in there. He might nick it.'

Our stuff consists of a metal bucket full of half-eaten sweeties, a few bottles of IRN-BRU and a small stash of scuddy mags.

'What are you saying, Milky? Do you want us to go in there and rescue the bucket?'

'I'm not saying that! I'm just saying he could take it.'

The man rolls over, moans and farts, sending out a smell that makes both of us cough.

'That's vile!' says Milky.

We stand back a little as the man farts once more.

'I tell you what' I say. 'Let's leave him here. Come back in the morning.'

'And our stuff?'

'Some sweeties and a few nudey mags. What's to miss?'

'What if he knows our mums and dads, Ginger? He could tell on us. My dad would lamp me for a week if he found those mags.'

'Milky, how would he know our parents?'

'Dunno. But he could.'

Milky was right, and Milky was wrong.

Milky was always right and wrong at the same time. It drove me mad. He was a master at saying one thing and, when his words transpired to be incorrect, he'd claim he'd said the opposite. He was right in that, of course, the man could have known our parents. The man could have known anyone or, if Milky was wrong, he could have known nobody. He could have been someone or no one. But all I was thinking was that whoever he was, he was in our den and it was getting late—and late wasn't good for my backside when I was expected back early.

'Milky, he can't know anyone. Why would he be sleeping here, in our den. if he did?'

We are now far enough from the den that we probably can't be heard, but both of us are still whispering.

'Ginger, we should ask him,' says Milky.

'Really. Ask him what?'

'What he's doing in our den?'

'And, Milky, where will that get us?'

Milky thinks on this for a second, scratching the wild clutch of hair that graces the barber's shears once in a blue moon.

Long hair was just about acceptable in school, as long as it wasn't too long. Milky's hair was the definition of too long, but his parents wouldn't pay for it to be cut. Save special occasions, his mum insisted on cutting it for him. When she eventually pinned him down, the result was a skinhead that would give a horse a heart attack. Milky avoided his mum's scissors for as long as he could. And then some.

But as Milky scratches his head, it's clear, even in the near dark, that he won't be allowed to go much longer before he's shorn.

'Dunno where it gets us,' he finally says. 'But we have to do something.'

The man passes wind again.

'Maybe someone should have a word with him about his diet,' suggests Milky.

'I think we should leave him alone!' I decide.

'And I say we should ask him why he's here.'

A stand-off. There was only one way to settle those in our world.

'First-On-The-Ground?' I say.

'First-On-The-Ground,' Milky agrees.

The rules of the game were simple. The first one to hit the ground lost the argument. Anything went. And if it was a draw, which happened a lot, we went again. All that mattered was that the first one to go down lost—and that was that. If I won, we'd leave the man in the den alone. If Milky won, we'd ask the man why he was there.

I stand back a little from Milky.

When we played First-On-The-Ground, Milky had a habit of striking fast. Milky was always a get in, get it done, and move on person. I was slower, more considered. That's why I usually lost. But, sometimes, my patience paid off. Milky was a few inches smaller than me and always went low.

As I step back, he puts his head down and charges. I barely see him coming in the gloom, leaping to one side at the last second, only to trip on an exposed root. My ankle bends. I throw out an arm and wrap it around the tree, squealing in pain.

I've no time to turn before Milky changes direction and is on me—hands around my waist. He lets all his weight fall on my middle, trying to drag me down. I have little choice but to go down with him, his mass too much for me to handle.

With the tree behind me, I push forward, ankle howling, tipping me on top. Milky realises that if he doesn't let go, he'll hit the ground first. He releases me, springing free like Tigger on caffeine. I struggle to keep upright, my ankle hurting like a hot pin to the eyeball. Probably twisted. I use the tree to keep me upright.

When Milky comes at me again, he tries to throw a punch. In the near dark, I don't see it, but I feel the edge of his hand clip my jacket. I throw my hand out, palm up. Caught off balance by the missed punch, Milky yelps as my hand catches his nose, hard. He tumbles past me.

I have a split second in which the back of his head is exposed. I lash out, catching him high with my knuckles. He spins to his left and crashes to the ground. I step back.

'Winnnnnner.' I whisper. 'I've won, so it's my call. We go home, let this all sort itself out in the morning.'

I sigh with relief.

Relief that lasts all of two seconds.

'What the…?' Milky says, as a voice, deep, gravelled, loaded with menace, rings out.

From within our den, the sound is followed by a shuffling and groan. A shadow rises up from the earth. The man is big. My dad big—then some. My father is six feet four, but this man has a good few inches on that. He's also wider across the shoulders. A giant is standing amongst us.

'Who the fuck are you?' he growls.

The light is poor. He can't possibly see my face, and with Milky on his front, still struggling to stand up, it's time to get the hell out of here before we can be recognised.

'Run!' I shout to Milky.

I turn to fly, and scream as my ankle revolts. I try to transfer the weight to my good leg, but my foot catches on the root that twisted my ankle in the first place. I tumble onto Milky. He curses as the pair of us end up in a ball at the feet of the giant, me trying to roll free of Milky, him pushing at my leg to release himself. I scream as he grabs my bad ankle.

A light blinds me. I close my eyes. Milky does likewise.

'Get up!' orders the man, a torch in his left hand pointed at us.

With Milky still tangled up with my leg, my ankle screaming not to move and the beam of the man's torch blinding me—the last thing I can do is get up.

'Now! Get up right now!' he orders.

Milky frees himself from me. I open my eyes, raise my hand to block out the light. Milky rises into the air as if he's just pressed the up button on a lift.

'Who are you?' says the man.

The torch beam moves from me and lights up Milky, who is being held off the ground by the man, a giant hand wrapped around the hood of Milky's anorak. I hear the sound of tearing thread as the hood gives way before Milky falls back to the ground.

'Jesus!' shouts Milky as he bounces on the ground. 'Mum will kill me, you idiot. This is the only jacket I have.'

I flip over onto my back, the cold earth pressing into my shoulder blades, taking as much weight as I can from my injured ankle. The man flicks the torch from Milky to me and back.

'I've hurt my ankle,' I moan to the man.

'You've ripped my anorak,' Milky whines.

'Who the fuck are you both?' he says.

'God, she'll go bloody nuts, will Mum,' says Milky, fondling the ripped hood. 'She'll leather my bum for a week.'

As he talked, he tugged at the hood. In the torch light I could see it was being held on by less than an inch of material. Milky was spot on. His mother would remove several layers of skin from his arse when he got home. And then repeat ad nauseum. She had a small varnished cane that she kept by her bed for just such occasions. I'd felt the end of it a few times. It could rip through cloth and cut skin with the keenness of a butcher's blade.

The man shifts the torch beam onto me again.

'I'm not going to keep asking,' he says. 'Who are you?'

'You were in our den.' I say.

'Your den?'

'Aye,' says Milky, still examining the torn hood. 'Our den.'

'So, the magazines are yours?' he asks.

'What magazines?' fires back Milky.

The man laughs. A deep resonant sound that rolls around the trees.

'It wasn't magazines when I was young,' he grins. 'It was pictures. Piles of glossy pictures.' Then he adds, his grin vanishing. 'So, this is your den? Who else knows about it?'

'No one, it's ours,' I say, still lying on my back, trying to assess how much damage has been done to my ankle.

'It's cosy,' he says.

'Who are you, mister?' asks Milky.

'Fucking none of your business, son. Who knows you are here?'

'Loads of people,' I lie.

The man drops the torch beam, playing it on the den.

'At this time of night, son? I doubt it. I don't hear any other kids up here. Too late, too dark.'

'Millions of people know,' says Milky weakly.

15

'Your arse,' says the man. 'It's fucking pitch black. Where's your light? There's not one in your den. What were you going to do? Eh? Contact the dead?'

'What are you doing here, mister?' Milky throws at him.

'Fucking nothing to do with you. Now both of you bugger off and say bugger all! I've seen your faces. I'll find you if you say a blind word. And if you do, I'll dump the porn on your mum and dad's doorsteps—with a note telling them where I found it.'

The thought of Mum and Dad finding the magazines is a horror movie that plays in my head regularly. But Milky has a different reaction to the man's words.

'No, you won't, mister,' says Milky. His voice gaining some strength.

'What?' the man grunts.

'You can't afford to have us tell anyone you are here.'

'What are you talking about, son?'

'You're hiding!'

'Am I?'

'Why would you be telling us to say nothing if you weren't? Anyway, why would you be sleeping in a hole?'

'Bright, aren't you?'

Milky was bright back then, smarter than me by a mile. He just lacked common sense at times.

'Mister,' he says. 'There's no way you are going to risk dumping scuddy mags anywhere. If you did, we'd blab. We'd tell them you were here.'

The man shines the torch straight into Milky's face.

'Okay, smart arse,' he says. 'The alternative is I can just batter your head in, stuff you in your den, bury you in the dirt and then piss on you for fun. Does that sound like a better idea?'

His voice cuts me to the core, and I see Milky's eyes widen in fear, his bravado gone in an instant.

'Feel clever now, kid?' the man says, taking a step forward. Milky does the only thing that makes sense. He turns and runs. And I would be with him if I wasn't still on the ground, if my ankle wasn't burning, if I wasn't close as damn to peeing myself.

'Mister, I'll not say anything,' I say, once Milky is gone.

'You might not, son.' he replies. 'But what about your wee smart-mouthed friend?'

'He'll not say anything.'

That was such a fib. There wasn't a blind chance that Milky would keep his mouth shut if he bumped into anyone on the way home. Milky loved being up front and centre with gossip. Milky was a classic shout from a distance type of kid. Mouth off and run. The threat of violence from the man would evaporate and, once the fear was out of sight, he'd start talking.

'But only if I get after him and shut him up,' I add.

'Then get your arse out of here, son. If he squeals a word, you both get it.'

I grab the tree. The man plays the torch on my legs as I pull myself up. He briefly lets the beam rise into the air. I catch my first real glimpse of him. He's unshaven. Heavy stubble across his face. His hair is greasy, thinning on top. His nose large and lumpy. He plays the beam back on me. I let go of the tree and try my weight on my bad foot. It hurts, but I can bear it. I hobble up the small hill towards the Wood's exit. After a few yards, the man kills the torch. My vision is little more than a spray of flashes and sparks. I wait for a few seconds. Letting my eyes acclimatise. My heart is still ripping along. I fully expect the man to walk up behind me, knock me back to the ground, sling me into the den, and start shovelling.

Then, despite my howling ankle, I run.
And run.

The Conversation

'WHO WAS HE?'

'Who?'

'The man in the den?'

'I'll get to that.'

'Why was he there?'

'I'll get to that.'

'Who did you tell?'

'I'll get to that.'

'Do you fancy giving me a cuddle and stroking my forehead?'

'I'll not get to that.'

'Pity.'

'Have you any other daft questions that could prejudice your job interview?'

'Does this story come with background music and sound effects?'

'Are you saying you're bored?'

'Not yet. I'll tell you when I am. Have you ever considered a podcast?'

'Sure, with the high-speed broadband we have in here and the access to state-of-the-art recording equipment, I was thinking of starting my own rival to the BBC.'

'Sarcasm isn't a good basis for a successful consumer programme.'

'Really? Who knew sarcasm wasn't to everyone's taste?'

'Funny.'

'So, do you want me to continue?'

'I take it you ran home to your mum and dad?'

'You have that right.'

Chapter 2
'Five Skelps.'

Skelp #1

I LIMP THROUGH the back door of my house to discover an atmosphere loaded to the gunnels with prime essence of parental post-argument. The give-away is the dead TV. Our telly is never off. It's why we rent the thing. All of them die of old age well before their time. The three-bar electric fire is also cold, the curtains are still open and the lights are off. Classic be scared, be very scared, signs. I think about wheeling around, heading back out, but that will just put me in the firing line. At the moment, while my parents are simmering in their own juice, there's an outside chance I can make it through the living room to the hall and get to my bedroom without taking any flak.

I'm wrong.

Mum. 'Where have you been?'

Me. 'Just out with Milky.'

Dad. Silence.

Mum. 'Where?'

Me. 'Nowhere.'

Mum. 'The Woods?'

Me. Silence.

Dad sits up, leans forward and slaps his hand across my backside. A full-on blow that stings. I leap out of the way as he sits back.

Mum. 'Room!'

I get the hell out of there.

My bedroom is cold. The single pane windows are bathed in moisture at the bottom. My one source of heating, a small fan heater, has been removed because I was overusing it.

'Electricity isn't free, son.'

My room was an eight foot by eight box with two single beds and a threadbare rug covering the no-man's-land between my brother's territory and mine. Deke was three years older than me, and got all the breaks. The favourite son. He'd been allowed to stay out late since he was ten. I was still on a curfew.

It's early, but if I'm quiet, I can read for a while—as long as I listen out for footsteps on the stairs. At the first creak of a stair, I'll kill the light and pretend to be asleep. Experience tells me that the resentment downstairs can easily overflow and catch me up here. I vanish into my book; *The Secret of Pirate Hill*—Frank and Joe Hardy trying to find an old Spanish canon. I love this time of the day, discovering a distant and exciting land, page by page. Pushing the world behind a thick curtain and closing it; muffling humanity for a wee while. Muffling my thoughts. Muffling reality.

I wake up the next morning with the book lying next to me on my pillow, Mum screaming up the stairs that I'm going to be late for school. I crawl from under the covers. The cold hits me like winter sleet. I run to the bathroom which is, if anything, colder than my bedroom, my ankle burning, but good enough for good enough. I wash my face, brush my teeth, shivering through the entire fifty-four seconds. I pull on my underpants, sprint down stairs and dive into the warmth of the living room. The electric fire is up and running. I can hear Mum in the kitchen. I think Dad's on early shift, so he'll be gone by now. My school clothes are lying on the couch. I dress. Mum appears, shoving a plate of toast and a glass of milk into my hands.

'You're going to be late,' she says.

The antique brown clock on the mantelpiece tells me that she's right. School is a fifteen-minute walk. I have less than ten. With Milky to pick up, that time could double. But he'll be long gone. He's not one for waiting. I slug the milk, stuff the toast in my trouser pocket, grab the plastic bag I use to carry my jotters and say goodbye to Mum.

I hit the outside world at full tilt. A wind from the north slices through my jacket as I run—the sprint more a way to keep warm than to get me to school on time. As I run, I wonder who Milky has talked to about last night. Once he hits the school playground, the man in the den will get a royal airing. My only hope is that whoever he blabs to thinks Milky is, as is his wont, making it all up. I zip down the stairs that connect our streets and hammer towards school.

This was my first year in secondary school. I wasn't the biggest fan. Our Primary School had one distinct advantage over its older cousin—a shortage of the nutter element.

My new educational establishment was littered with too many loons and not enough victims. My red hair marked me as a target, so arriving at school late was no bad thing. With the playground empty, the chances of getting picked on were smaller.

Skelp #2

I DON'T SEE Mr McGary. The sneaky git planked himself just inside the main door of the school, waiting on late comers. He catches me around the back of the head with a well-practised clip.

'Bannerman. Why are you late?'

There are three possible answers to this question. Say nothing, lie, or tell the truth. It makes no odds which I choose. I'm in for the strap, regardless. I could announce that my entire family had been killed in a blazing inferno, and I'd still get my hand warmed with leather. Three of the best for being late, six if I'm cheeky with it.

'Sorry, Mr McGary.'

'Report to me at break!'

Joy.

I trudge up the stairs to registration, drawing an evil look from Mrs Carol as I enter the classroom.

'Nice of you to join us, Robert!' she says.

I slip into my seat as Craig Brownlee tries to flick my hand with his ruler. I dodge it and sit down.

Milky was in a different class. After seven years of sitting next to each other in Primary School, the vagaries of the alphabet meant I now sat in 1A and he resided in 1E of King's Park Secondary School. A fifties built, three building, sharp-angled, concrete and glass award-winning complex. Award-winning was a joke. It transpired that the rooms in the main, three-story-high block breached some regulations for the amount of air that kids should have enjoyed when there was more than thirty of us to a classroom. And there was always more than thirty in a class. At least that's what Milky's Mum had told me. In addition, the PE block was supposed to have included a swimming pool. That had been binned when they found the whole building was sliding down the hill it was built upon. As a result, we had three gyms: boys, girls and, where the pool would have been, the big gym. All in all, we were short of legally required oxygen, but not on the space to keep fit. Anyway, back in those days, the first time I'd get to talk to Milky would be at playtime, or break as we had to call it. Calling it playtime marked you out as a kid, to the loons. And that marked you for possible violence.

My first class is double Maths. I hate the subject. Today is algebra and may as well be a lesson in World War II code. I've homework due. It's not done. Not through laziness. I'd looked at it when I'd got home two nights back and couldn't make head nor tail of the stuff. I'm planning to throw myself on the mercy of Mr Cruickshank, my Maths' teacher. If I plead ignorance, he might take pity on me and the worst that will happen is that I have to suffer five minutes of one-to-one with him as he tries to explain what can never be explained to me.

The bell rings out. The registration class empties into a heaving corridor. Around, above, and below me, a thousand plus kids are trying to get to their first class. Most are slower than a crippled snail—only the keen, the swots, and the bum-lickers move quickly. My class is on the top floor. I keep my eye out for Milky. If I see him, I could at least try to limit the damage he'll already be doing. But there's no sign. I think he has double Physics this morning, and that's in a different block.

Ten minutes later, Mr Cruickshank is letting me off with not doing my homework if I promise to double up on it for tomorrow. I agree, knowing there's no chance of that happening. I clock-watch my way through the lesson, picking up three warnings for not paying attention. When the bell rings, I'm off like a shot.

Skelp #3

I HIT THE ground floor at full pelt, only to find Mr McGary blocking the door.

'Is that you heading for my room, Robert?' he says.

Wonderful.

He clips my ear as he points back into the building.

I glance up and down the playground, but the masses hide any sign of Milky. I turn to trudge behind Mr McGary. Ahead lies a lecture on being late, the belt, then I'll be made to sit out the remainder of the break, contemplating my badness.

As I sit in the corridor, hands stinging from a good three belts, I fear that Milky will have, by now, rounded up a gang to visit the Woods at twelve.

After the break has finished, I head for double Geography. A subject I like. Foreign countries and faraway cities hold an eternal appeal. I'm confident on my knowledge of the capitals of the world. I can gush on the longest rivers. I'm smooth-tongued on seas, monumental on mountains—dead good on deserts. At Christmas, Geography was the only exam I passed, and I did so with aplomb. Top of the class. But today, I can't wait for it to be over. Milky's mouth has already had way too long to ruin my short-term future.

When the bell rings, I'm up to top speed in seconds. Milky goes home for dinner. Only in his house it's called lunch. Go figure!

Skelp #4

IN MY HASTE to track Milky down, I'm not as self-aware as I should be. I skip through the playground and plough headlong through a game of marbles, scattering the glass balls in the process. A hand reaches out, grabbing at my ankle. The injury from last night flares as Stephen Black pulls me to the ground. And that's not good. Blacky is a king loon. A member of the genuinely unhinged. Before I can react, he jumps on top of me and lands a fist on my jaw.

'Bannerman, you're getting a bursting.'

His favourite phrase.

'I was winning,' he informs me, while sitting on my chest.

I try to roll him off, but he has lard to spare around his waist. He is also well-practised in the art of 'bursting'.

'I'm late,' I say.

'For what?' he says, as he smacks my ear with his hand. A real stinger. I yelp.

'Bannerman, the only thing you're late for is a bursting.'

The rest of the kids close in, now that someone else is on the receiving end of Blacky's sadism. There's no help for me to be had from the gawkers. To intervene would be folly, you'd simply put yourself on Blacky's 'bursting' list. My only defence is to suck it up, take what's coming and hope that a teacher notices the tell-tale sign of a kid getting a doing.

I don't hold out much hope, even for that. Stephen Black is as feared amongst some of the teachers as he is amongst the kids. And he knows it. He's in fourth year. He'll leave school as soon as he can, if not before. And that makes him almost untouchable. Our school will be happy to see the back of Stephen Black. If a few first-year greenhorns need to suffer at his hands in the meantime, without interference, so be it.

Skelp #5

I LOOK UP as Blacky lifts his hand to strike me again. A trade mark clenched fist turned on its back. The knuckles readied to grind my skull. He smiles. A row of jagged black stumps poking out from his lips. A small spiral of soor-ploom flavoured saliva drips into my open mouth.

I close my eyes.

I wait.

Then something cracks off my head. But it's not Blacky's arse-to-tit fist. I open my eyes as the blur of a leg flashes across my vision. Blacky vanishes.

'Get your filthy hands off Ginger!' shouts a familiar voice.

I roll over to see Milky lying on top of Blacky, trying to punch him. He's onto a loser in the long run. Blacky has muscle and experience on his side, but Milky has surprise. I see my chance. I get up, my ankle hurting again, but adrenalin is in play. I'm moving as Milky leaps from Blacky, kicking him in the stomach as he rises.

'Come on, Ginger!' Milky shouts, glee in his voice. 'Let's get out of here!'

I need no second bidding.

'Milkwood, you're dead!' screams Blacky, but it's lost on Milky.

'Jesus, Milky!' I say as we fly through the school gates. 'He'll kill you later.'

'Only if he catches me. Anyway, forget him. I've got news about our man up in the den. And you'll not believe it.'

With this, he puts on a sprint, laughing.

I trail after him.

Wondering what it is I won't believe.

The Conversation

'WELL? WHAT WOULDN'T you believe?'

'Is it going to be like this the whole way through my story?'

'Like what?'

'Like a kid asking, 'are we there yet?' every five minutes.'

'Well, you could just skip the whole Jackanory thing and get to the meat of the story.'

'I could, but I won't and I'll tell you why.'

'Why?'

'Because I've never told this story to anyone before. I don't really know why that is. A lot of it made the papers at the time. It was the talk of the steamie for an age in our scheme. In fact, it was such a big thing that I got sick of answering questions. Kind of withdrew into myself a little when it came to talking about it all. But, as you'll find out, some of the people involved still have a connection to me. And they are why I'm here talking to you. Also, I'm not usually one for gossip.'

'Isn't this whole story gossip?'

'No. This is a secret.'

'And the difference is…?'

'A secret is when you tell only one person, gossip is when you tell one person at a time.'

'And why tell me?'

'I need to tell someone. But feel free to bugger off and do something else.'

'Funny man. And another funny thing—I knew a Stephen Black. He worked in the garage next to my work. Mad bastard. I mean certifiable. But he's long gone. I heard he got into a fight while out on a bender in

London a few years back. Someone stabbed him. Rumour was that it was planned. As I said, a nutter that just crossed the wrong people.'

'Might be the same guy. Last I heard, he had moved south.'

'Anyway, are you going to tell me what happened next?'

Chapter 3
'The Afternoon That Went Bang.'

MILKY PLAYS SILLY buggers with me all the way to the Woods. He sprints off into the distance, stops until I'm close enough to touch him before rushing off again. My ankle is slowing me down. Milky is desperate to get me up to the Woods, shouting 'Come on, you clown!' 'Move it ginger pubes!' 'My mum can run faster.' 'You're a bloody pudding.' And those are the clean cat calls. My predilections for wanking in the bath, wearing girl's clothing, rubbing chip fat on my balls and assorted other lies, half-truths and slander are also thrown in my direction.

The Woods lie at the top of the hill that my scheme is built on—once called the hill of Symes—hence Simshill. Climbing up is hard going with an ankle on fire, but no amount of pleading with Milky slows him down. Whatever it is he's discovered is renting a crack in his chest as he tries not to tell me. I resort to crude name calling as my weapon of defence, but Milky is bullet proof to that stuff. We've worn these tracks so often that they are as smooth as the soles of my sandshoes. The insults slide off him, Milky preferring to slap his hands together, waving at me to move quicker, rather than respond.

We reach the Woods and I'm down to a walk. Or, rather, a comical hirple. Favouring one foot over the other, creating a lop-sided gait that I think screams to the watching masses of a major injury—but probably doesn't. I limp up the lane that leads to the Woods. Milky grabs my hand, pulling at me.

'Jesus, Ginger!' he says. 'Can you go any slower?'

I drop my pace to a crawl and he howls.

'It'll be gone, Ginger. It'll be gone if we take any longer.'

'What'll be gone?'

'Move quicker. You'll see.'

With this, he tugs my hand then lets it go, springing off like a dog running in front of his master. Then he runs back to tug me again. Out, back, out, back. He repeats. It makes no difference to my pace. We start to cross the football pitch.

It wasn't really a football pitch. It just happened to be a patch of the wood where nature had planted two sets of natural goalposts—trees—forty yards apart, facing each other. The only downside to the pitch came in the shape of five other trees strung out across what was the halfway line. Not that the inconvenient trees stopped football being played. The arboreal midfield, as Miles Clachland—my brother's best friend—called it, played for neither team. They just stood there, eternally waiting on errant passes and kids who momentarily forgot about them. Their bark streaked with years of ball strikes and kids' blood.

We crest the top of the hill and follow the path towards our den. So far, we've seen no one else, but the air is alive with the shouts, yells and laughs of the kids playing at our old Primary School.

The Woods butted up to our old Primary School grounds a few yards from our den. Less than a year ago, Milky and me could have been seen climbing the chain-link fence at playtime, heading for our den where we would squat in the half dark to talk all things crap.

Habitually, we pass by the den before circling back, our way of checking that the coast is clear. When we are sure no one is around, we slide along a wooden fence to approach the den's entrance.

'Okay, Milky,' I say. 'Why are we here? Don't tell me the man is still around?'

I say this while still out of earshot of the den.

'No. He's gone.' Milky says. 'I came up this morning before school and…'

He does a small twirl with his hand, pointing one finger into the air and shouting bang, bang, bang.

'…I found something. He left something behind, Ginger!' He grins as he says this.

He grabs my hand again and drags me the last few yards to the mouth of the den.

'Inside,' he says.

We both duck down, slipping with practised ease into the dank, dark space. I sit in my usual spot. Milky takes up his.

'Behind you,' he says to me.

There are half a dozen wooden slats at the back of the den. Rammed into the earth to provide some support to stop the ground above falling on us. I look at them, but I can see nothing unusual.

'Pull out the bottom plank,' Milky says. 'It's loose.'

'Milky, what is it?'

'Just pull out the bottom one.'

I reach over, grabbing the wooden slat. It comes free with ease. Too much ease.

The summer before, when the roof had partly caved in, we had stolen wooden planks from the back garden of Jim Spence's house and jammed them home with our feet, pushing them deep into the earth at the rear of the den to support the roof. Every so often, when the roof began to rain dirt, we'd kick the planks deeper in for good measure. All of them should have been rock solid.

I place the loose slat to one side to examine the earth behind it.

'There,' says Milky in a triumphant tone. 'Right there.'

I reach in. I grab the object that Milky is talking about and lift it up. Dirt falls from it. I drop it right away.

'A gun!' I gasp.

'A gun, Ginger. A real gun!' Milky shouts.

I stare at the weapon lying next to my knees.

'The man must have hidden it there,' Milky barks.

'Milky, is it really real?'

Even in the gloom, I can see his face is alight. He's loving this.

'It's looks real alright,' he laughs. 'Bullets as well. I checked. It's full of them.'

I study the gun. It looks like the sort they have in Westerns. A thick wooden handle with a revolving part for the bullets. It's old and worn.

'We should fire it,' says Milky.

'What?' I exclaim. 'No way, Milky. No way on earth.'

'Of course we should. I've always wanted to. Just like Hoss in Bonanza. You know when he shoots bean cans off the fence. Only we could set up IRN-BRU bottles and blast them into smithereens.'

I stutter, unsure where to start telling Milky how bad an idea that is.

With Milky, it was always tough to get him to see the bleedin' obvious. I'd known him since before Primary School. His mum and my mum hitting it off not long after they both moved into the scheme. Us barely three years old. Since then, Milky had been the lead getting us into trouble. He had a gift for it. A real gift. I received more skelpings on the back of his misdemeanours than I care to remember. But a gun was a whole new level of disaster waiting to happen.

It dawns on me that, at this very moment, the man could be coming back. Coming back to catch the pair of us, his gun lying on the floor, red-handed. If the gun was his reason for telling us to get lost last night, what would he do to us when he discovers we know about it?

I can just batter your head in, stuff you in your den, bury you in the dirt and then piss on you for fun.

Isn't that what he had said? And what would he say now? Now that his gun is no longer a secret.

'Milky, we need to put the gun back and get the hell out of here.'

'But we could fire it,' he says. 'I mean really fire it.'

And as Milky speaks, I realise that we can't just put the gun back. What is the man planning to do with it? Who is he planning to shoot? After all, he's hardly likely to be thinking along Milky's lines. I don't think he has a gun for pot-shotting glass bottles. What if he shoots someone? What if they find out we knew about the gun after he does? Milky mouthing off to all and sundry. We'd be in so much trouble for not telling anyone we knew about the gun. And that raises yet another thought.

'Milky,' I say. 'Who else have you told about this? Who have you told about the gun?'

'No one,' he replies.

I didn't believe him. This was way too sweet for him. The only way to shut Milky up on something like that would be to sew his lips together. Even then, he'd have just written it all down for everyone to read.

'Who did you tell, Milky? Tell me!'

'No one. Honest.'

'You found a gun and didn't tell a soul. Milky, you couldn't find ten pence and not put it in the Daily Express.'

'This is different. I'm not stupid, Ginger.'

'So, Milky, no one else but you and I know about this?'

'No one. It's our secret. That's why we can fire it. No one will know.'

'Milky, everyone will know if we fire it. Everyone in Simshill Primary School and beyond will hear; the teachers, the kids, the janny, the people in the houses around us. Guns aren't silent. And what if you hit someone? A bullet won't stop for a bottle of IRN-BRU. It'll keep going. And what about when the man comes back and counts his bullets and finds some missing? Who do you think he's going to blame? He knows who we are.'

Milky looks crestfallen. I've just whipped the last sherbet fountain from his hands.

'We could fire one bullet, just one,' he says quietly.

'And when the police get involved and ask who fired the gun. What then? My dad would probably flay me alive if he knew I'd even been near a gun.'

Milky looks down on the weapon. 'Well, we can't leave it here either. What if the man is about to use it?'

'If he shoots someone, and they find out we knew about the gun,' I say. 'We'd be dead meat.'

'We need to get rid of it.'

'And do you not think the man will come after us?'

'He wouldn't know.'

'What, Milky? He wouldn't know what? That the gun he hid in *our* den has gone missing. That the two wee boys he noised up last night might have sneaked back to *their* den and found *his* gun?'

'But we can't put it back.'

This is no 'First-On-The-Ground' dilemma. This is a straight up genuine real—very real—life problem.

'Let's just take it down the Cart and sling it in,' suggests Milky. 'If we do it near the weir, no one will find it.'

The River Cart ran through the nearby Linn Park. At the weir, some kids said it was a thousand feet deep. Some kids thought monsters lived there. Some kids' imaginations were too vivid.

Milky reaches down and picks the gun up. Studying it. I can read him like an open book. I know exactly what he is thinking. *One bullet. Just one bullet.* He plays with the hammer.

'Milky, leave it alone!'

'I'm only looking.'

'We need to tell someone,' I say, reaching a conclusion. 'We tell my dad that we found a man in our den and that he threatened us. We tell him that you came back, found the gun and then you came and told me. That's what we say.'

'Your dad won't believe you.'

'It's the truth. He'll have to believe us will when he sees the gun. I bet that'll make him take us seriouser than serious.'

And I think, for a moment, that maybe it will work out that way. Dad will be home about three o'clock after he finishes early shift. I could tell him then.

'Ginger, won't the man just say it's not his?'

'It'll probably have his fingerprints on it.'

'And ours will be on it too,' says Milky, as he spins the gun around the trigger guard.

'Milky, stop that. It could go off!'

'It can't. I need to pull this bit back first.'

He plays with the hammer again.

'See?'

He pulls it back a little.

'I think you need to yank this all the way back and then pull the trigger,' he says. 'I was going to do it this morning, but I thought you'd want to be here.'

He holds the hammer back a little, pointing the gun at the den's entrance.

'See, just a little more pressure and then I can pull the trigger. Bang and off the bullet would go.'

Milky is pointing the gun in the direction of the back door of the house that sits behind the fence our den hides near.

'Milky, that's not a toy. Please put it down.'

'I've seen Hoss do it a million times. And he's good. I bet I'd be good. I bet I'm a crack shot.

'Milky, just put it down!'

'In fact, I bet I'm the best shot in the school. I mean, I can beat you hands down with my catty. Can't I?'

'Milky, that's not a catapult. Please just put it down.'

His voice had that lost quality that it took on when he was escaping this world for the one in his head. Milky adored westerns and war movies.

'I could be as good a shot as Kid Curry. Maybe better,' he says.

He levels the gun, peering along the barrel, his finger still on the hammer.

'Put it down, Milky. Please, just put it down!'

'Hands up there, stranger. No sudden moves,' he says in a faux-American accent. 'Make one wrong move and y'all is going for a ride in a pine box.' He drops the accent. 'They fan this bit, Ginger. That's what they call it when they have to fire more than one shot. Fanning. They use their palm to pull the hammer back and fire, pull it back and fire. Bang, bang, bang!'

He catches the hammer with his palm, silently mouthing the words bang, bang, bang. His face is framed in the light of the entrance. It catches his eyes. He's way out west.

'Milky...'

'What the fuck?'

The gravel voice of the man from last night thunders into our space as his shadow blocks out the light.

The gun goes off. A brilliant white flash fills the den. The sound punches my ear drums, stunning me. The man's shadow vanishes. There's a deep guttural howl. Milky crashes to the earth. My world is a head-wrenching mix of high-pitched squealing and smoke. And amongst it there is only one coherent thought.

Milky just shot someone.

Chapter 4
'The Afternoon That Became A Siege.'

AS THE SILENCE settled in our den, broken only by the quiet moaning of Milky, I was as scared as I'd ever been. Milky had just killed a man. Right then. Right there. My head had raced with what that meant. How bad it was. That a man was dead because of Milky. Because of me. Me. I should have pulled that gun from Milky. I shouldn't have let him keep playing with it. I should have just taken it from him. Thrown it away.

The gun is lying next to Milky, a few feet from me. I reach over and tug it towards me by the grip, dragging it over the dirt, away from Milky. I kick it into the corner and sit. Shivering.

'I never pulled the hammer back. I didn't. It just went off itself,' he pleads. 'Honest soldiers, it went off itself. And, and… my hand hurts.'

I know it is coming. I can feel it coming and there is nothing I can do to stop it. Nothing. I know the feeling well. Recognise the rising burble in my throat. My chest constricting. My mouth opening. The first snort riding down my nose.

And.

I laugh.

A low, blustery sound before a guffaw slips out. I try to stifle it. I may as well try to catch the wind in a net as I begin to howl like a clown on laughing gas. I fall onto my side, placing one hand on my mouth, trying to stop the unstoppable—a forlorn hope as I launch into a prime, gold-plated, super sweetie-flavoured, inappropriate and ill-timed gale of laughter.

The last time the inappropriate laughing happened was at my gran's funeral. Less than a year earlier. A black hole of a day that was full of steaming clothes, dripping hats and flooded shoes. Of strangers and old people. Wrinkles and grey hair. An ice-cold service held in an ice-cold room. Me at the front with Mum and Dad. Deke by my side, digging at my ribs when no one was looking. The minister droning on and me letting my thoughts fly—avoiding his words, avoiding looking at the coffin resting next to him, avoiding the truth of what was going down.

I'd looked to the ceiling, counting the rafters. I'd looked to the floor, counting the tiles. I'd looked at my shoes, counting the stitches. Behind me I could hear a tiny buzz of a noise. A bee caught in a jam-jar type of noise. I'd looked around to find a wizened old man in a dirty overcoat with one finger pressed to his ear. I'd traced a wire from his ear to his pocket and figured he had one of those new pocket transistor radios in there.

Gran's funeral was late on a Saturday afternoon. It didn't take much to work out the man was listening to the football. Dad had mentioned earlier that the Old Firm game was on. A lady next to the man had nudged him, pointing at his ear. He'd ignored her before giving a little fist pump. A goal for his team. He'd smiled at me and given me a thumbs up—and that's when the laugh started. Me trying to avoid any interaction with this terrible event, this man grinning like Tom the cat when he had Jerry cornered. Grinning during my gran's funeral. And somehow, instead of making me mad, that made me laugh. A deep belly laugh that burst into life like a submarine breaking the surface.

My dad had clipped me around the ear, but that did nothing to stem the flow. I knew I shouldn't be laughing. I knew the consequences. Yet something in the man's smile, the thumbs up, the earphone, the wire, even the manky coat triggered me. Triggered something that needed out. Where tears would have been acceptable, laughter could never be, but I'd rolled off the chair onto the floor, howling as my dad had given me a royal kick in the bum before hauling me up and dragging me from the funeral. Me laughing all the way.

And that wasn't the first time, nor would it be the last. I had no idea why I did it. I just did. The laughing when laughing was improper.

And now I'm on the ground, gasping for breath.

'My hand hurts.'

Milky's words spin through my head as I break into another gale. Milky who has just killed someone. Whose biggest worry is his hand. What's not funny about that? Why wouldn't you laugh? Why wouldn't you see the absurdity and vent?

His hand.

His hand.

Never mind the dead man outside or the coming shitstorm or the million questions that will fill our lives for ever more. Never mind the tag of killers. Of murderers. Never mind our futures vanishing on the single pull of a trigger. Of the pain that this will bring to our parents. The shame. The abuse. Never mind the impact on the dead man's family. Their sorrow. Their pain. Of all the lives ruined. Of the crime. There for all to see, for decades, for centuries, for ever. All of that and more will come to pass. Never mind it all—just think on how funny it is that Milky has hurt his hand. And I laugh some more. Almost gagging.

Milky rises.

'Ginger, stop that! What's funny about this?'

I haven't the capacity to speak. So, I point. Point at his hand. In the poor light, I can't see his confusion, but I know it's there. Written in felt tip across his forehead.

'Ginger, shut up! This isn't the time.'

'Your hand,' I gasp.

'It bloody hurts.'

And this sends in another wave of laughter to cripple me.

'Well, it does,' he moans.

He's not helping.

'Ginger, did I kill someone?'

The answer comes in the form of a barrage of swearing from outside

We are not murderers. At least not yet. The man lives. As to his injuries—there's no clue in his voice. He just sounds angry. And how can you blame the man? Someone has just tried to kill him, then they laughed about it.

'Get the fuck out of there!' he yells.

My laughter subsides, replaced with the sudden dread that reality brings to the table.

'Jesus, Ginger, what do we do?' asks Milky.

'I don't know. I told you to put that gun down, Milky. I told you.'

'What do we do?' he repeats.

'Get out of there, right fucking now!' the man screams.

'We sit tight, Milky. That's what we do. We sit tight.'

'He'll come in.'

'When he knows we have a gun? Would you come in?'

Milky thinks over what I've just said. Outside, the man continues to demand that we 'get the fuck out there'.

'Milky, think on it,' I say with a calmness that surprises me. 'He can't come in and we sure aren't going out. If he's injured, he'll need to go for treatment. If he's not, well, someone must have heard the shot. People will come.'

'Do you think?'

'Yes,' I'd said, but I wasn't so sure on the second part. The gun shot might have been loud in the den, but we were buried deep in the earth. When we

had dug this place out, we had tested it for sound. Me outside. Milky inside, shouting. No more than a few yards away from the entrance. Milky could hardly be heard. But a gun was a lot louder than Milky. Loud enough? Maybe. Maybe not. Even so, the man couldn't risk coming in and we couldn't risk going out.

'Milky, we stay here. No matter what he says. We stay here. Until he leaves or someone comes along.'

'And how long will that take?'

'As long as it takes, but we aren't going out.'

'I might not have shot him.'

'Okay, but what would you do to someone who *nearly* shot you?'

He says nothing.

'So, Milky, we sit and we wait.'

The man shouts for a few more minutes, then stops. Milky slides next to me, both of us facing the entrance of the den. Beyond, we can see the fence and nothing else.

'If you don't come out,' the man says. 'I'm going to start caving in that bloody hole of yours.'

I gather up some bravery and shout back, 'Come anywhere near us and we shoot again.'

'Don't be so dumb, son!'

I reach around, scrabbling for the gun. I lift it, point it at the earth floor a few feet in front of me, and pull the trigger. No need for me to pull back the hammer. Milky was wrong on that. Milky screams. The gun leaps from my hand as it goes off. The man shouts.

'See mister?' I say, scared to a core I never knew I had. 'I'll shoot again. Stay away!'

I can feel Milky shaking next to me.

'I had to do it, Milky. Dad is always saying that you need to let the bad guys know you are serious from minute one. Show them who's boss. If that man caves in the den, we'll be trapped.'

'Son?' comes a shout. 'No need for any more of that. Just leave the gun, crawl out and you can both walk away.'

'Sure, mister,' I shout back. 'Do you think we're daft or just stupid? I tell you what. You go first and we'll leave after you.'

'And the gun?' he says.'

'I take the gun.'

'I can't let that happen, son. So be sensible and throw it out, then crawl out.'

Milky grips my arm. 'We could try and run for it.'

We probably could. The man is huge and the gap between the fence and the den entrance is tight. We might be able to squeeze away in the opposite direction. But it's hard to tell where he is. To the right, the left, above us?

Above us?

'Mister, if I hear you above us I'm going to shoot through the roof of the den.'

'Son, don't do that!'

'Then don't come near.'

I listen hard. My ears are still ringing from the two gunshots, masking all but the loudest sounds. I want to know where he is. I want to know that he isn't waiting just outside to crawl in. To call my bluff. For there's no way I could shoot him. Firing into the ground was bad enough, but I couldn't shoot a person. And he must know that. *Has* to know that. But can he risk it?

'Milky,' I say as a loud as I can without shouting. 'If he comes in, I'll aim at his legs.'

Milky doesn't move. Doesn't speak. My words are for the man, not Milky.

'Son, don't fire that gun again,' the man shouts. 'Okay? I'm not coming in. I just want you to come out. There's no need for you or your friend to be involved in any of this.'

Adult speak. That's what that was. I know that now – and was learning quickly back then. The 'trust me, I'm older than you and I know better than you' speech. The 'I'm not the one with the issues and broken marriage and screwed up life and regrets the size of Ben Nevis' speech. Adults think their arguments and fights are invisible to kids. That, as kids, we didn't see them or hear them or experience them. Do what I say and just ignore what I do—isn't that the mantra when you become an adult? Your get out of jail for next to nothing card. Cajole, bribe and lie. That's the holy trinity of parenthood. And if all this fails, then there's violence. Only sometimes, it's violence first. And that's why Milky and I were not going to be moving soon.

Milky reaches out to touch me.

'Ginger, what do we do?'

'I've already told you. We sit tight. We wait it out. There's nothing more we can do. I kind of wish we'd built that escape tunnel we always talked about. It would be handy right now.'

'We still could,' says Milky, with a tiny sparkle in his voice. 'Pull out the slats and start digging.'

'No we can't, Milky. We just sit.'

'And if he comes in?'

I raise my voice again.

'We shoot him.' I say, shaking my head to let Milky know I'm lying.

'Jesus, Ginger! I didn't mean to fire the gun.'

I place my hand over Milky's mouth.

'I know,' I whisper.

Milky nods, spit coating my palm as he does so. I remove my hand.

'Ginger, how long do you think people will take to get here?'

I'd been hoping that someone would have been here by now.

'I need a pee,' says Milky.

A small ripple in my gut signals that my laugher monster might be on the way back.

'Empty the bucket and pee in it, Milky—then cover it.'

He shuffles away.

'And cover it quick. Your pee stinks!'

Milky tips the contents of the metal bucket onto the floor and squeezes into the corner. The rattle of fluid hitting tin reverberates around me, followed by the sour stink of urine floating in the air. He finishes off.

'What will I cover it with?'

'Use one of the magazines and be quick—that pure honks!'

I waft my hand uselessly in front of my face to try to move the smell on. It has no effect.

'Milky, you need to see someone about the food you eat. That smell can't be right.'

'It's the onions. Mum says onions are good for you.'

'Well, that doesn't smell good for you, or me. Do me a favour, tip some dirt in with it.'

He pulls up a few handfuls of earth and throws it in the bucket.

'Son,' says the man. 'We can't sit here all day. I've things I need to be doing but I can't leave you in there with a gun. If I have to, I'll call the police.'

Milky whispers, 'He won't do that. How would he explain the gun?'

'He's just trying to scare us out,' I say.

'Mister!' I shout out. 'Call the police if you want. In fact, it would be a good idea if you did. I'd like to tell them what happened.'

There's a pause and then, 'And who do you think they are going to believe when they get here? Eh? A kid or an adult?'

'Depends,' I reply.

'No, it doesn't. They'll believe me and that'll be the end of it.'

'Okay, call them, then.'

Another pause.

'Son, come out and I'll do just that. We can walk to the phone box and call them together.'

I let that one go. If I'd learned one thing about adults, it was that arguing with them never worked out in my favour.

I stretch out my legs and prop my back up against the wooden slats, laying the gun between my legs, the barrel pointing at the entrance. Milky settles down next to me. We'll both catch it for dogging school this afternoon. Half a dozen of the strap and detention will be the punishment.

'What if one of us makes a run for it?' Milky says.

'He'll catch us.'

'He might not. Especially if you fire the gun just before I run.'

'*You* run?'

'I'm the quickest.'

'And that leaves me here on my own.'

'I'll go. Get help. You can hold him off with the gun until I get back. What else can we do?'

'Wait.'

'What if no one comes, Ginger? Wouldn't they have been here by now if they'd heard the gun?'

'Maybe they are calling the police first. Would you come up to investigate a gun shot?'

'Of course.'

'Well, most people are not you.'

There's merit in Milky's suggestion that he makes a dash for it. But I place it as a back-up plan for the moment.

'Milky, let's just give it a wee while and then maybe we'll do what you say.'

'I think I should go now. He won't be expecting it. If I wait, who knows what he might do.'

'And who would you go to for help?'

'Dunno.'

'Well, it would help if we had a better plan than that. Knowing you, you'd go off to the Drake café and load up on Kola Kubes.'

'I would not.'

'Or up to RS McColl's to see if they've any copies of POPSWAP left.'

'No, I wouldn't'

'Well, who would you tell then? Your dad?'

'I'd tell Mum.'

'And would she believe you?'

'Yes.'

'Milky, she *never* believes you. You make so much shit up that she hardly listens sometimes.'

'She'd listen to this.'

'Why?'

'She just would.'

'And that fills me with confidence. She's just as likely to lock you in your room and where would that leave me?'

'Or,' he says. 'I'll tell *your* mum and dad.'

'They think you lie even more than your mum.'

'Do they?'

'Yes.'

'Why?'

'Milky, last week you told my mum you saw a monster in our back garden.'

'I did see one.'

'You said it was Bigfoot.'

'It was.'

'In Simshill? In our back garden?'

'I did see it.'

'Wearing a dress, Milky. You told my mum that Bigfoot was in our back garden and was wearing a dress.'

'A pink dress.'

'For crying out loud, why would Bigfoot be in Simshill, wearing a pink dress?'

'Dunno.'

'Mrs Calder, our next-door neighbour, wears a pink dress. The same one. All the time.'

'It wasn't her.'

'Mum talked to Mrs Calder. She saw you looking at her from my window. She was in our garden getting her dog. It runs in all the time. Sometimes she carries it by wrapping it around her shoulders. What you saw was Mrs Calder and her dog. That's what you saw, Milky. Not Bigfoot wearing a pink dress.'

'It was Bigfoot.'

'And that's exactly why, if you go to my mum, and tell her about the gun, she'll throw you out of the front door.'

'Well, who could I tell?'

'I don't know. So let's leave it alone for now.'

We sit for a few minutes. The ringing in my ear is still loud. It blocks a lot of the sounds from outside. I'd like to poke my head out of the entrance and see what's what. I wonder if I stick the gun out and fire it in the air, will that bring someone quicker? I park that idea. I don't want to fire that thing again. Not ever.

We wait.

I used to love that place. Our den. The escapism. The secrecy. The adventure. But it had soured a little by then. It seemed less like a place of mystery and more a place of sorrow. A dank hole that stank of damp and fading memories. It was more cramped than when we first excavated it. I knew that was because both of us were growing. Outgrowing the place.

Leaving Primary School behind and entering a new phase of life that I hadn't been able to quite figure out yet. The changes in my body more embarrassing than enlightening. Mrs Carol told me that it was our hormones kicking in. Milky said it's because we could get a stoner now. He thought that playing with your dick screwed up your brain. Although that never stopped him.

With nothing more from the man outside, we both lie back. I'm not for sleep. I'm too scared for that, but the feeling of blind panic has faded a little. I scuff the heels of my shoes into the dirt.

Waiting.

The Conversation

'DID YOU EVER *go back?'*

    'Back where?'

    'To those woods?'

    'A few years ago. For the first time since I was a kid. It hadn't changed much. I thought it might look smaller. You know the way everything back then seemed so large. But it just felt… familiar.'

    'Was your den still there?'

    'How do you know I looked for it?'

    'I would.'

    'You're right, I did, and it's gone. Caved in. The ground around is overgrown.'

    'But you wanted to dig a little, just to see if there might be something of it left. A bit of your childhood still buried down there. Am I right?'

    'Yes.'

    'Do you know that I only have a few photos from when I was young?'

    'Really?'

    'Yip.'

    'To be fair, I don't have many, either.'

    'And that makes going back to places important. Especially if they haven't changed. Pity your old school is gone.'

    'How do you know that?'

    'You said Simshill. I know someone who bought a new house where the school used to be. Or did I get that wrong?'

    'No, they knocked it down twenty years back. Who bought a house there?'

    'I can't remember. Anyway, you were in the den. How did you get out?'

Chapter 5
'The Scritching.'

MILKY NUDGES ME and my eyes open. Despite the fear, I must have fallen asleep. For how long, I've no idea.

'Ginger, listen!'

I rub my eyes and sit up. The ringing in my ears has faded a little. I hear nothing at first.

'To what?' I say.

'Just listen.'

'What for?'

'Can you hear scraping?'

And I can. Very faint. Like someone clawing on a door. An irritating scratching. A *scritching*. The noise is rapid, with breaks every few seconds. And maybe, just maybe, there's someone talking in the background.'

'Is it him?' I ask.

'I don't think so. Can you hear the voice? It's too high pitched.'

I listen.

'A girl, Milky?'

'Could be.'

The voice vanishes, but not the scritching.

'What time do you think it is?' I say.

Neither Milky nor I own a watch. Being late, early or on time is a constantly changing mix of judgement, luck and publicly accessible timepieces. The light beyond the entrance is darker, suggesting we are near tea time, if not past it. My stomach says the latter. The scritching is constant. I try to locate the exact source of the sound, where it is coming from. Twisting my head, I think it may be from behind and above. Back towards the path that leads up to the lane. The speed of the digging suggests real effort.

'Is he trying to dig in here, Ginger?'

'I'm not sure.'

'Fire the gun again!'

'No,' I say. 'I don't need to. He knows we have it.'

'So why is he digging?'

The scritching sounds stops for a minute. Then it starts up, if anything, a little louder. I want to shout out, to warn the man to stop, but at the same time I just want to get out of here. I don't want to be in this hole. I don't want to sit here with the smell of Milky's piss in the air, the night drawing in, with a knotted feeling in my gut that says the longer I wait, the worse it will get. No one is coming to rescue us. No one heard the gunshot. The man can just wait us out. Or he's coming in for us. Digging through the dirt.

'Milky, what if he's not trying to get in but is going to bury us in here?' I blurt.

'He wouldn't.'

'Maybe he's going to cave it in. He threatened to do that. You heard him. Get rid of us that way. Or he's trying to come in the through the back. He could be digging away all the weeds and plants,' I suggest. 'Looking for a way in.'

'You told him you'd fire if he tried anything.'

'I don't think a bullet would travel very far in the mud. And he probably knows that.'

We both look at the slats of wood, expecting a head to crash through and a hand to reach out to grab us both. We slide away a little to squat in the centre of the den. My eyes flick from the slats to Milky to the entrance and back. The scritching stops again, only to kick back in a minute later. It's still coming from up high, towards the rear.

'I think we need to run for it, Milky,' I say. 'No one is coming.'

'And the gun?'

'We take it with us. We bury it somewhere.'

'When do we go?'

'Soon.'

I move to the front of the den, dragging the gun along with one finger, unwilling to pick it up quite yet. Milky moves with me. If the man appears at the entrance right now, we'd both be goners. There's a thump. It sounds like it came from outside, to the left, where the man was, but noises in here are confusing. We both freeze. My gaze is rock solid on the entrance. Watching for the slightest movement. But it's just way too dark to see much of anything. I pull the gun towards me, lift it, holding the grip between my forefinger and my thumb. It slips and tumbles to the ground. I wince, expecting it to go off. I can't see Milky's reaction. He's all but invisible in the fading light, only his breathing gives him away.

I fumble around to locate the gun, this time picking it up properly, but keeping my finger away from the trigger.

Another thump from outside, this time from above, I think.

I make my mind up.

'Okay,' I whisper. 'I go first. Then you. We break right and stick hard to the fence. When we get to the football pitch, we cut straight across. Don't look back. Just run!'

'Ginger, I should go first.'

'Why?'

'I'm quicker than you.'

'Okay. You go first, but I'm still taking the gun.'

'The man had a torch last night. He'll be able to light us up if he still has it.'

'And?'

There's little to add to that.

'On three,' I say. 'Out, and to the right.'

Milky slides past me, feet first, the usual way we exit. I'd like to put the gun in my pocket to give me two free hands, but I'm scared it'll go off.

I count, 'Three, two, one, go, Milky, go!'

Milky slips from the den. I'm right after him. I grab the fence, push up and hear Milky move off. In the daylight, this would be easy. It's a well-worn route for us. In the dark, it's a different beast. Roots, branches, stones, holes, fence posts, tree trunks, discarded junk—all present an unwanted obstacle course. As I rise, I don't look back, don't look left or look right. Just straight on. I stumble along the fence. Near the top of the rise, I cut in towards the football pitch. For a fleeting second, I see Milky caught in the light of the new moon. He's already halfway to the lane. I pick up the pace to try to catch him.

I almost scream when something brushes my leg. A splinter of moonlight picks out a dark brown lump of fur. I recognise the dog. Lapper. A mutt that lives on Magnus Crescent, the road that the lane exits onto. Lapper jumps on me. We usually have a biscuit for him.

'I've nothing, Lapper,' I say as I push him away. He's covered in mud. Was it him digging at the den?

When I reach the lane, I sprint as hard as I can—flying out of the entrance onto the road. My ankle still nips, but it holds. As I exit, I spot Milky standing under a streetlight, looking in my direction. Lapper follows me out. Milky takes off. I also run.

Two street corners later and we are standing on my drive, Lapper still with us.

'I didn't see the man,' says Milky.

'Neither did I.'

'Shit, Milky. I think it was Lapper digging back there, not the man.'

'You think?'

'The gun,' says Milky.

I realise that I'm standing with a gun in my hand. I slam it behind my back, moving over to Mrs Reid's wall.

'Where are you going to bury it?' Milky asks.

'The Subby.'

There's an electrical sub-station opposite us. It has a razor-sharp fence, eight feet high surrounding it, but Milky and I have been in it so often that I can scale the fence with my eyes closed.

'Keep an eye out for the man!' I say as I head for the Subby.

I clamber around to the rear of the sub-station, checking no one is watching, before throwing the gun over the fence. I'm up and over after it, dropping to the gravel that surrounds the small brick built building. I pick up the gun, check the surroundings again. Milky gives me a thumbs up. Near the sub-station wall, I dig up the gravel. Before I bury the gun, I try to figure how to crack open the gun barrel. I succeed, tip the bullets out, put them in my pocket, drop the gun into the hole, shovelling gravel on top of it to hide it. I clamber back over the fence and re-join Milky.

'Okay,' I say. 'I need to see my dad.'

'What if he doesn't believe you?'

I pull the bullets from my pocket, checking that no-one can see me.

'I'll show him these. He'll have to believe me then.'

'If you say so.'

'And Milky, don't say a word about this to anyone. And I mean *really* don't say a word. This is a blood and guts thing.'

'Okay. Blood and guts.'

'A real blood and guts oath, Milky'

'Real blood and guts, Ginger. But Mum will want to know where I've been 'till now.'

'Tell her you went straight to the Woods to play with me after school.'

I don't hold out much hope that Milky will abide by his promise. He might have sworn our most sacred oath, but if his mum thinks there's something going on she has interrogation techniques that will mean he'll fold. I just have to tell Dad quickly, then let it all go from there.

'I'm off,' I say as I dash away, only stopping when I get to the bottom of the stairs to my home. The big light in the living room above me is on, curtains shut. Red and black flowered pattern things that are mum's attempt to add some colour to our planet.

That house was my first real home. I was in a few others when I was really young, but too young to have anything but a vague recollection of some half-forgotten moments. The windows were always steamed up, but that was the norm during the winter. Next door, the Dunnies had double glazing installed the year before. Their windows never steamed up and, according to Mum, the Dunnies had cut their heating bill by three quarters. All I know is that when I was playing in Kevin Dunnie's bedroom, it was as warm as toast. Without the fan heater on full blast, my room was so cold that you could see your breath. Even Milky wouldn't come around to play if the fan heater had been confiscated by Mum or Dad.

I slug up the stone steps, dreading what's coming next. Dad can be unpredictable. Even on a good day, it's hard to know which father I'll get. On a bad day, it's better to just walk away than talk to him. I sidle around the house to the back door. I pause before pushing into the kitchen. The smell of mince and potatoes hangs in the air. My stomach rumbles. Only now do I realise how hungry I am. The oven light is on. My tea will be in there. Crispy brown topping on everything. I'll need half a bottle of ketchup to stop it all drying up my mouth.

The Formica table is set with a knife and fork and a glass for some water. I cross the fading linoleum, dodging the large rip that extends out from the cooker. I can hear my dad's voice coming from the living room, followed by a muffled other. Not mum's voice. Too deep. One of dad's police friends in for a drink? That's good news. With his friends in the house, Dad is less aggressive.

I place my hand on the frosted glass door. I push it open, letting a cloud of cigarette smoke and whisky fumes escape the room. The electric fire is three bars bright, a rarity. The TV is on, but the sound is off. Reporting Scotland is just finishing.

Dad is sitting in his favourite chair, next to the fire, his back to our small round teak-effect dining table—the prime seat in the house to watch telly. He has a crystal glass of whisky in his hand. He's dressed in his casual trousers, white shirt and favourite navy-blue slippers. Next to him is an ashtray with half a dozen butts in it.

'What happened to Jimmy Russell?' he's saying, the cigarette removed just long enough for him to get the sentence out, a stream of smoke quickly chasing the words into the fug. He spots the door opening and turns to me, smiling. I stand there with the door half ajar. Whoever else is in the room is hidden behind the frosted glass, sitting on our couch.

I scuff the dirt brown carpet with my shoes, uncertain how to start,

'Hi,' puff, 'son,' he says. 'Been out playing? Your mum is over at Diane's. She left your tea in the oven. I'd get it quick before it's burnt to a crisp. Close the door when you go back in. You're letting the heat out.'

I turn the bullets over in my pocket with my left hand. Feeling the smoothness of the metal—the unfamiliarity of the strange shapes.

'Dad,' I reply. 'Can I tell you something?'

'I've company, son. Tell me later.'

Normally, I'd back off at this point. The word *company* is family code for me to get lost.

'Eat in the kitchen and then go up to your room,' he says. 'Do you have homework?'

'No,' I lie. 'Dad. I really need to talk to you!'

A steel glint crosses his eyes. In a second, they will darken. Hand to my backside will follow soon. I push the door open a little more and step in.

'I said to go eat in the kitchen,' he says. 'I won't ask again.'

I turn to see who else is in the room.

And the bullets in my hand turns to ice.

Sitting not two feet from me is the man from the Woods.

Chapter 6
'Early To Bed And No Food.'

'HI,' THE MAN says to me. 'You must be Bobby.'

I'm stunned. My head starts to reel like a top on a storm-tossed sea. How could the man be here? Is it really him? Really? Same thinning hair. Same growth. Same gravelly voice. So how did he get here? He has a drink in his hand. Dad is smiling at him. A smiling father means he knows the man. Knows him well enough to invite him in—an unusual event for a non-policeman. Knows him well enough to give him a drink. Even rarer.

The bottle of whisky is sitting on the floor next to Dad. I know what it is. It's called Dimple. Dad's good whisky. Dad's *best* whisky. The whisky that's kept for special occasions. How can this be a special occasion?

'Bobby, get your tea. Forget the kitchen. Go to your room.' Dad says.

I do the one thing that guarantees my dad's anger. I ignore him. My eyes, instead, fixed on the man on the couch. Him grinning at me. I finger the bullets in my pocket. Twisting them slowly.

The crack to the back of my leg from Dad's hand snaps me out of it.

'Bed, no tea. Now,' he says.

I'm too slow. I get a second skelp for my tardiness.

'Now!' he barks.

Even through the mire and confusion of the situation, I know I need to move. Any more delay will bring out the big guns from Dad, guest or no guest. I move forward, circling the man. I reach the only other door in the room. The one that leads to the small hall that sits at the bottom of the stairs leading to my bedroom.

I hesitate before leaving, taking one last look at the man. If he smiled any harder, his lips would fold in half.

I close the door behind me and, as I exit, the conversation starts up again.

The front door is to my left. I contemplate leaving. But to what end? Where would I go? And when I came back, I'd be a live target for Dad's right hand. Not to mention Mum's tongue. I start to climb the stairs.

When I was a little younger, I used to sit on the fourth step up on those stairs. The first three bent at ninety degrees to squeeze the staircase into the building—the fourth let me look out the small window that sat next to the front door.

Staring down from on high onto our street, I could watch life go by from the safety of my house. I'd wait there for the Alpine van to appear. When it did, I'd rush out, empties in hand to buy a bottle of limeade and a bottle of cola. A treat from Mum if money wasn't too tight.

Or, on a really good day, fifty pence in hand, I'd wait on the ice-cream man with his distorted jingle of 'Somewhere Over the Rainbow' playing over and over, me wanting a ninety-nine, Mum an oyster, Dad a double nougat. I'd sit on that step, the coin growing warm and sticky in my hand and, as soon as the jingle could be heard, I'd run out of the door like a nutter.

On Saturday mornings, the rag'n'bone man held my attention. Me with nothing to give him but a fascinated look, as his horse and the assortment of junk on his cart rumbled by. Junk that I sometimes envied.

The previous summer, I'd spotted a skateboard on his cart. A rare beast in our neighbourhood back then. A genuine skateboard. Not the plank of wood balanced on a roller skate that we called a skateboard. This was the real thing. And it didn't look broken. 'Why would someone throw away such a rare and beautiful object?' was my one and only thought. I'd trailed the horse and cart all the way down our hill, out of our scheme, thinking of ways to get my hands on that skateboard. Not that I was likely to get it without parting with cash. The rag'n'bone man was an evil old human; tight as a drum with cash, and happy to flick at children with his horsewhip if he thought you were eying something up. That day, I'd watched him turn onto the main road, stood at the corner until he was out of sight. When he returned the following week, I'd rushed out—but the skateboard was gone. Even to this day, I still think about that board.

Sometimes I'd sit on that fourth step just waiting for something to happen. When Milky was otherwise occupied, and no one else was around, I'd sit and watch the cars passing by. Cars were thin on the ground in Simshill. The posher five-room semis on our street had a driveway for a vehicle. We didn't. Only a few of the neighbours owned cars. My family was transported the public way—bus, train or leather sole.

I rise the first four steps and look up to the landing above before I turn to the window. *My* portal. A streetlight sits directly across from it. Beyond that is the window of Mrs Mark's living room. She never closes her curtains and Mum thinks that makes her an 'exhibitionist'. Not only can I see into her house, so can the world, as her window is level with the pavement.

She can be viewed, most nights, TV playing on her face. She prefers to have no lights on while she watches telly. Every so often she'll lift her eyes from the goggle box to look out at the world. Her lips mouthing words. Mum thinks she's not right in the head, but I think she's just repeating what's on the TV, something I do a lot. So if that makes Mrs Mark loopy doodles, then it makes me the same.

She's there, right now, her face flickering in the telly light, lips flapping, one hand resting under her chin. Her favourite pose. She likes to stroke under her chin, pinching at the loose skin on her neck every so often. She has a small bone china cup in her other hand. I'll bet you a penny she has a quarter bottle of whisky on the side table.

I've never seen her get up to make a cup of tea, but I've seen her polish off a thousand bottles of whisky. If that cup has ever held tea, it was a long time ago. Every drop of whisky she drinks is served in that china cup, as if drinking from a tea cup hides the fact she's slugging alcohol. She reveals the quarter bottle *(you owe me a penny)*, unscrews the latest bottle top and tips some whisky into her cup. If I sit, watching much longer, she'll fall asleep—through 'til morning, if she's on her second bottle.

My dad is still talking to the man downstairs. They both laugh. *Laugh!* The man that owns a gun is laughing with my dad, softening my dad up with some old friend's act.

Waiting to get his gun back.

Biding his time.

Why else would he be here? He can only be here for the weapon. Well, that's not going to happen. I need to tell dad all about it but if I go back in now he'll not listen to a single word I say. I could rush in screaming, *'I found a gun. A real gun!'* And all I would I get for my trouble is the back of his hand across my backside, and hauled upstairs to my room. I fondle the bullets. He couldn't ignore them. *Could he?* He'd have to pay attention then. *Wouldn't he?*

What if the man is here to kill Dad?

My heart picks up pace.

Is that what he's here to do? To kill my father?

Why?

I don't know, but he could be. *Couldn't he?* And if I rush in throwing bullets around, might that set him off? Dad's big, but this guy is bigger. There's a brass candle stick next to the electric fire. It's heavy. I've played with it often enough. It would make a fine cosh. Forget the gun. Go the Cluedo way. The big man with the candlestick in the living room. Dad dead.

I shiver at the thought. My imagination is working overtime. Why would the man be here to kill Dad?

More laughter rolls from the room. I decide to go to my bedroom, think about things, let my heart rest.

My room is cold and Deke is out. My Hardy Boys book is sitting on my pillow. I consider what they would do in this situation. A new, unwritten novel, *The Hardy Boys and The Case of the Missing Gun*. Frank and Joe Hardy would have a plan. They always have a plan. One where the baddy eventually, after the brothers have survived another wild adventure, gets caught.

But I have no plan and the baddy is currently drinking and laughing with my dad. I have no Joe to talk to and, for once, I'm hoping Milky doesn't do what I told him to do. That he lets his mouth run, tells his mum all about the man and the gun. That she picks up the phone and calls here. Only she won't believe Milky. Why would today be different to any other day?

My stomach rumbles, but all it is going to get tonight is water, straight from the bathroom tap. The next meal will be breakfast—unless Mum comes home and takes pity on me, slipping me a piece and sugar, making me promise not to tell Dad about it.

It's too early for sleep but it's also too cold to sit in the room. I slide under the bedcovers and lie my head on the pillow.

I think and think and think.

I slip from the covers for a second to push some of the bullets into my cubbyhole under the bed, then I slide back under the covers.

Half an hour later, there's a lull in the conversation downstairs. I hear the living room door open. Someone starts to climb the stairs. Not Dad. I know his steps well. It can only be the man. I close my eyes and roll over as I hear the man push into our bathroom. The sound of him peeing goes on for so long I wonder if he's emptying bottles of whisky straight down the pan. He flushes.

A second later, my door opens.

'I know you'll be awake, son,' he says. 'I'd be awake too.'

I say nothing, lying still.

'Let's make this easy!' His words are slurred. 'You have my gun and I want it back. You didn't have it on you when you came in and you didn't leave in it your wee den. So, while I take another dram with your father, you are going to sneak out and fetch it for me.'

I try to snore, but it comes out as a snort.

'I know you can hear me, son.'

He's right over me. His body odour and whisky breath dousing me in a cloud.

'Son, do what I say and everything will be alright. I'll give you half an hour. After that I'll tell your dad all about your den, your mags and the gun you stole from me.'

He punches my covers, catching me on the back. Not a soft punch. One that smarts.

'Half an hour. Got it?'

I stay stock still as he leaves. Not even breathing.

The door closes with a click. I roll back over. I yelp. The man is still in the room.

'I knew you were awake, son. I just wanted to make sure. You have half an hour.'

He clenches a fist, slamming it into his palm. He repeats the gesture three times, turns and leaves.

I hear him descend. He swears as his feet slip on one of the looser parts of the stair carpet. There's a pause before the living room door opens. A few seconds later, the conversation starts up again.

If my head was whirling earlier, it's now in full washing machine spin mode. My brains little more than clothes being thrashed around the drum. The Hardy Boys would be cool with this. Sitting back, assessing the situation, working on their *plan*. A glass of freshly made lemonade in hand. I'm the opposite of assessing. I'm the definition of *not assessing*. I can do little but run a repeating string of words through my head.

Gun. Bullets. Magazines. Killer.

I sit up, unsure what to do but knowing that I need to do something. But what? Run? Stay? Talk to Dad? I can feel the inappropriate laughter rising in my chest. I can also feel tears welling up. The tears are winning. I try to hold them back. Not wanting to give into them.

There's a rap on the window. I jump. I pull myself up over the bed's worn head board, wiping the first tears away, pushing the thin curtain to one side as a second rap cracks off the window. I wipe away the condensation, look down onto our garden. Milky is standing on our tiny patch of bare lawn, waving his hand. I unlatch the window handle and push it open.

'That man is in your house,' he whispers.

'I know.'

'I know who he is. Can you get out?'

'Who is he?'

'Get out first!'

It's possible to dreep from my bedroom window onto the ground below. I do it now and again when I've been confined to my room. But my room is above the rear window of the living room. The man on the couch could see me if he was looking that way when I drop. Our back curtains are never shut.

'Milky,' I say. 'Look in the window. Is the man looking this way?'

Milky drops onto the concrete path that surrounds our house, then leaps back onto the green.

'He's talking to your dad.'

'Keep an eye on him.'

I clamber out, push the window shut, sit on the windowsill.

'Tell me when he's not looking,' I whisper.

Milky vanishes below me as I turn onto my side and lay along the sill. I have to be careful. The ledge is narrow—just the smallest of slips and I'll take a header onto the concrete below.

'Now!' says Milky.

I let my legs fall over the edge and catch both hands on the sill. I'm hanging straight down. My feet will be visible from the living room.

'Milky, get out of the way!' I say.

I give him a second to get clear, then drop, bending my knees to catch the fall as I land. I crouch down and scuttle to one side. Milky is standing at my back door.

'We need to get out of here,' I say.

Milky leads the way. We dash down the front stairs and up the hill, back towards the Woods. We stop at the first corner.

'Milky, you said you know who the man is?'

'I met Greggy walking up the road.'

Greggy is David McGregor. Milky lives two doors up from him. Greggy is in the last year of Primary School and a friend of Milky's sister, June.

'And?' I say.'

'He told me that he'd just seen a man go into your house.'

'And he knows the man?'

Milky moves me off our street, up Mrs Reid's garden path. Out of sight of anyone that might leave our house.

'Greggy says that his big brother knows the man,' he says.

'Greggy's big brother knows him?'

'Greggy's big brother, Neil.'

'And Neil knows this man?' I ask.

'Greggy says the man gives him money for sweets when he wants to talk to Neil. Greggy gets sweets if he fetches Neil from his house. The man and Neil meet down at the shops at Croftfoot roundabout. On the lane behind.'

'Why?'

'Greggy says he knows, but he won't tell me unless I give him some cash.'

'Greggy's a wee swine. He's always grubbing for ginger bottles for the deposit or midge raking for junk. Why don't we just beat it out of him?'

'Because he'll clipe on us to Neil.'

Neil is a hard loon. Not to be crossed.

'That's true. Okay, how much money does he want?'

'He didn't say. How much do you have?'

I dig in my jacket and come up with eight pence.

'You?' I ask—showing him my money.

'Tuppence.'

'We'll offer him five pence.'

'He'll want more.'

'And if he we offer him ten pence and he wants more, what do we do?'

Milky agrees with that.

'Where is he, Milky?'

'He's waiting on us in his back garden. But not for long. His mum will be calling him in soon.'

We head off for Greggy's place, my head centred on the consequences of escaping my house. What with dogging school today, staying out late tonight, defying Dad and now escaping—I'm adding to my report card in a bad, bad way.

We reach Greggy's, sprint up his path and around the back as quick as we can, keeping low to avoid being seen. Greggy is sitting on a small wall beside a shed that looks like a good fart would blow it down.

'Greggy, tell Ginger what you told me!' says Milky.

'Money first!' replies Greggy.

Greggy is slight for his age—as thin as a liquorice stick. He has checked flared trousers on, a checked shirt and, like everyone at the moment, he's not wearing a vest. His hair is longer than mine. He's wearing a pair of the universally acceptable Greenlees' sandshoes.

'Greggy. I could batter it out of you!' I say.

'And do you have a twenty-six-year-old brother that goes to the boxing gym three times a week?' he replies.

'He'd have to catch me first,' I retort.

'Can you run the hundred yards in less than fifteen seconds?'

It's a dangerous game playing the 'big brother' card in our world. Sure, most brothers will be there for you if you really need them but, if you lay that one down too often, some brothers will let you sink—just to prove a point. My brother Deke is one of those. It also marks you out for a beating in the future. Your brother can't be there all the time.

'Okay,' I say. 'I've got 5p. That's it.'

'Ten.'

'Five.'

'Ten. Or nothing.'

Milky points to his wrist, as if he had a watch. I pull out all the coppers and drop them into Greggy's filthy mit.

'Right, this better be good,' I say.

'Sit down!' he orders.

We join him on the wall. Me on one side, Milky on the other.

'You can't tell Neil I told you this,' Greggy says. 'Okay? Promise?'

We both nod but neither of us swears blood and guts and that means, later, we can tell whoever we want. Greggy is still playing by Primary School rules. More fool him.

Greggy shuffles on the cold concrete. He checks the back door to his house, before he starts talking again, 'It was Neil that saw the man going into your house, Ginger. Not that long ago. I heard him talking to someone on the phone about it.'

'He called someone to tell them that a man was in my house?' I say. 'Why would he do that? Who did he call?'

'I'm not sure' he replies. 'But he called as soon as he came in.'

'What did he say?' Milky asks.

'I heard it all,' Greggy says.

You can tell he's enjoying this. Maybe a bit too much. Greggy can lie just as well as we can.

He continues, 'I've a hidey hole under the stairs. Right next to the phone in the hall. Neil never even knew I was there. He never does. It's my secret place. I've got some tape that I put around the door to stop the light inside getting out. That way, no one knows I'm in there. It's a great spot. I've got sweets, ginger and comics and all sorts in a box. Mum used to use the cupboard for the Hoover until she got a new one that one's too big for under the stairs. She keeps other stuff there, though. Cleaning stuff. You know, like Harpic, Brasso, Handy Andy, Oven Pads, Biotex, Ajax, Ibcol, Domestos, Bathbrite, Blue

Flush, Vim with Lemon, Mr Sheen, Radiant, Omo, Bold, Drive…'

'Jesus, Greggy,' interrupts Milky. 'Stop with the cleaning ad and get to what Neil said!'

Greggy's face falls a little. 'I was just saying Mum keeps a lot of the cleaning stuff in there, but once the washing is done at night, she never goes in. So I can.'

'Fab. And Neil?' I say.

'Well, he didn't say that much on the phone. He rang someone. They answered quickly. Neil asked to talk to some person called Heartbreak.'

'Heartbreak,' says Milky. 'Who is that?'

'I don't know, but I have heard the name before. Anyway, Neil had to hang on the phone for a long time. Maybe five minutes before he spoke again. He said that he'd seen Hornsby, that's what he called the man, Hornsby—and that Hornsby had not long gone into your house, Ginger. And then he stayed quiet, but I could hear that the person on the other line was talking. Eventually, Neil said he'd go and see what is happening. He hung up and left the house. As far as I know, he must still be up near your house right now, watching.'

'Milky, did you see Neil near my house?' I ask.

He shakes his head. 'No, but he could have been down the hill and we would have missed him.'

'Who is this guy Hornsby, Greggy?'

'Neil fetches things for him'

'Fetches what?'

'Parcels, from up in Castlemilk. He fetches parcels and gives them to this guy Hornsby. They meet at the back of the shops at the roundabout.'

'In the lane?' says Milky.

'Yes.'

'During the day?' I ask.

'At night. I've followed Neil a few times. But I don't go into the lane. I've seen Neil go in with a parcel and then come out with nothing. Then this guy Hornsby comes out holding the parcel.'

'The lane's not safe,' says Milky.

The shops that Greggy referred to were on the boundary between Castlemilk and Simshill. Castlemilk was a relatively new housing scheme then, huge, mainly council houses, and death to the likes of Milky and me if we entered it. Gangs roamed freely and didn't take well to strangers. The lane behind the shops was where some of the gang members hung out to smoke or drink. If you got caught there, you might as well have ordered up a slot in the Linn Crematorium.

'What's in these parcels, Greggy?' I ask.

'I don't know. All I know is that every so often Neil goes up to Castlemilk and comes back with one. I'm too fret to follow him there. Then later in the day, once it's dark, he'll take the parcel to Hornsby at the lane.'

'Sounds dodgy,' I say.

'He does other stuff too,' says Greggy. 'Mum is always on at him to get a job but he just lazes around or goes out to all hours. But he has money. He thinks I don't know, but he has a bank account with the Clydesdale Bank down in Shawlands. And he's always first to the post in the morning, always. And if there is a letter from the bank, he pockets it before Mum can see it. But I got to it once before him and opened it. He had over a thousand pounds in there.'

'A thousand pounds!' whistles Milky. 'Who has that sort of money?'

'And I think he has a stash of cash somewhere else, as well. He's always got money on him. More than Dad ever has.'

Greggy's dad, like many others in Simshill, was a policeman, and Greggy's mum worked on the till at the general store down at the roundabout. I'd often heard Dad moaning to Milky's dad that thirty pounds a week wasn't enough for the job they both did. Even with my poor maths, I knew that Neil nearly had as much money in his bank account as my dad earned in a year.

'And you don't know who Neil was talking to on the phone,' I say. 'Heartbreak? Is that what he said?'

'Yes.'

'And you've heard that name before?'

'Yes.'

'A stupid name,' says Milky.

'Not as bad as Tinker Bell,' says Greggy.

'Eh?' both of us say.

'Neil has a mate called Tinker Bell.'

'A girl,' I say.

'No. He's a boxer.'

'A boxer called Tinker Bell?' I laugh.

'He's huge. He comes here now and again. He can lift me up to the ceiling with one hand.'

Greggy's so light I reckon I could give that a good shot, so I'm not impressed.

'I also have an Aunt called Rumpelstiltskin,' Greggy adds.

'What?' exclaims Milky.

'It's true.'

'*You* have an aunt called Rumpelstiltskin?' I shake my head as I speak.

'It's true,' repeats Greggy.

'Who calls her that?' I'm still shaking my head.

'That's her real name,' Greggy insists.

'Rumpelstiltskin.' Milky stretches the word out. 'No one has an aunt called Rumpelstiltskin. What's her middle name? Rapunzel?'

'And her last name is what?' I add. 'Is it Ritley, Ritley, Ritley, Pun-Pun the Second.'

Milky laughs hard at that.

'Rumpelstiltskin, Rapunzel, Ritley, Ritley, Ritley, Pun-Pun the Second.' I sing the name.

Milky joins in. 'And her cousin: Ruger, Rustbucket, Roffy, Raffy, Ribbletide, Rot-Rot the Fourth.'

'She has a gran,' I say, giggling. 'Robot, Ringbot, Rakbot, Rebotty, Rif-Rif the Fifth.'

'Shut up!' shouts Greggy.

But we are on a roll. The man, the gun, the problems forgotten for a moment.

'What's your mum's real name, Greggy?' I ask. 'Mum, Mummy, Mammy, Mummikins, Ma-Ma the First.'

'Shut up!' he yells.

Greggy slides from the wall and places his hands on his hips glaring at us. 'Shut it. Shut it!'

More names tumble from Milky and me. Nonsense piled on nonsense. Greggy is starting to generate steam.

'Shut up, shut up,' he screams. 'You are both bastards!'

'David McGregor. What did you say?'

The back door to Greggy's home is wide open. His mother is standing there. Greggy freezes.

'Nothing,' he whimpers.

'Get in here right now. And I mean right now!'

Milky and I look at each other. Awkward being the most appropriate word for the moment.

'And what are you two doing?'
Neither of us has a reply that seems adequate.
'Get out of here!' she spits.

The Conversation

'*CAN I STOP you there?*'

'*What is it?*'

'*Why not just hand your old man the bullets? Why not walk in and get it done?*'

'*Sounds obvious, doesn't it? An easy out. Just go back, dump them in his palm. I've wondered a lot why I didn't do that. If I had, I'd probably not be sitting here. But kids don't think the same as adults. At least not in those situations. I was scared. And then there was Neil, the call to Heartbreak—the whole thing was screwing with my head. Who would act sensibly with that lot going on? And, anyway, who would you believe if I had gone to my father that night? Me, a twelve-year-old with a history of making up stories, or an adult like Hornsby?*'

'*Have you ever read William McIlvanney's book, Laidlaw?*'

'*No. What's this to do with anything?*'

'*You should. Brilliant. Laidlaw's a detective in the Glasgow polis.*'

'*Wonderful.*'

'*You're in the library a lot—go check it out.*'

'*I ask again, what has this to do with the price of bread?*'

'*Laidlaw lived in Simshill.*'

'*Really?*'

'*Yip. It seems McIlvanney heard about the number of polis there and decided that's where his main protagonist would live.*'

'*Who knew? And is that relevant?*'

'*Not really.*'

'*Do you want to hear the rest?*'

'*Of course.*'

Chapter 7
'A Night For A Plan.'

WE SLIP OFF the wall and slither from Greggy's garden, leaving the wee man to his fate. Out on the pavement, Milky swings on a nearby lamppost. Circling. One hand working its way round the concrete post. The other outstretched.

'What now?' I say.

'What would Frank and Joe do?'

'They would have a plan.'

'So, what's our plan?'

I slump onto the kerb, fingering a stank. I'm into playing marbles, and the small street stanks are an ideal playing board. The rectangular metal plate, full of holes, are at a premium come summer time. It's rare, when the sun shines, not to find one surrounded by kids gambling their marbles away.

'Milky, I've no idea. But that man, Hornsby, isn't going to let us keep his gun.'

'Maybe he'll just give up. If we stay out long enough.'

'No, he won't. He must have had a good reason to hide in our den. You don't do that unless things are bad. And I think he came around to my house just to get the gun.'

I tell him what Hornsby had said to me in my bedroom.

'He'll be well after you now,' Milky states.

'You don't say!'

'So how does he know your dad, Ginger?'

'I think he might be polis.'

'You think?'

As a policeman's son, you grew an unhealthy disdain for the police. A casual indifference to the uniform. It could get you into trouble, that attitude. Taking the police for granted wasn't a bright thing to do. It was easy to ignore their authority. As Mr Ricardo, our English teacher said, when our mouths get too smart for him—familiarity breeds contempt and contempt gets you a slap in the mouth. But that familiarity with the police was deeply engrained in me. It also meant I could sniff a warrant card at a million paces.

Up in the Woods, Hornsby hadn't struck me as polis. Hair too long, dress too dishevelled, but I was too scared to think straight. In my living room, I'd sniffed that recognisable air of superiority that comes with the job. I'd have bet my Hot Wheels on Hornsby being polis.

'I'm almost certain he's polis,' I say.

'And he's receiving parcels in the back lane of the shops from Greggy's brother.'

'And hiding out in our den,' I remind him.

'Why don't we spy on Neil? Let's see what he's up to!'

'Milky, these are Castlemilk people we are talking about here. You know? The sort that beat the shite out of you just because they breathe.'

'The gang stuff is getting worse around here, Ginger, right enough. Matty Thomson told me there was a big gang fight in Linn Park last night. The Tiki and the Valley going at it—Matty said there was axes, swords, everything up there.'

'There's always fights, Milky.'

'But axes and swords, Ginger? Axes and swords?'

Milky was spot on. Things weren't great then. The economy was in the toilet. My Dad let rip on it all, frequently. Three-day weeks, power cuts, a messed-

up Labour government, miners strikes, joining Europe, ten percent inflation and a whole bunch of stuff that I didn't understand.

Dad moaned about the oil crisis, electricity bills, that the speed limit on the motorway has been cut to 50 miles per hour. He talked of the way we had screwed up the Cod War. He said that the dustmen would soon be out on strike again, and ranted about the rats that ran wild, back in 1969, when they last stopped work. He yacked on about the trouble the polis were having with kids on the street carrying all sorts of weapons.

I thought the stories of axes and swords were nonsense, but Dad knew better. That he had caught a kid on Glasgow Green with a broad sword only a few inches shorter than he was. That made the papers.'

'If we go look for Neil and he sees us, he'll kill us.' I say, getting us back on track.

Milky puts on a bad American accent. 'Come on, Frank, this will be a piece of cake. They don't realize who they're up against. We're practically professionals.'

'Milky, he might not be watching our house.'

'And if he is?'

'And if he is?'

'Well, Greggy said that Neil told this Heartbreak person on the phone that he was going to see what was happening. Maybe he has to report back in person. You know, act as a lookout.'

'Or he could be off to the pub.'

'True, but what harm does it do to look? And do you really want to go home to that guy Hornsby?'

'No. But…'

'But what?'

'What if Hornsby wants the gun to kill my dad?'

Milky stops swinging. 'Your dad? Why would he want to kill your dad?'

'I don't know, but he might.'

'I don't think so,' he says.

'How can you be sure?'

'Do many killers sit in the front room of their intended victim sipping whisky, knowing they've been seen by the victim's kid and that the victim's wife is due back? And, if Hornsby is polis, he'd be a lot smarter than that if he wanted to kill your dad.'

And in a couple of sentences, Milky had done what he did best. Calmed me down. He was good at that. Wind me up high at times—at others he could cut through the nonsense in my head and put me back on the old straight and narrow with a few well-chosen words and a smile.

'So, let's go, Ginger!'

I can feel that deadly pull of Milky's trouble magnet working on me. I might not want to go home, but spying on Neil is an even worse idea on top of a bad idea.

But it's either:

a) Go home and take the punishment.

b) Stay out and think about going home to the punishment

c) Tag along with Milky, play spies on Neil McGregor and then go back to take my skelping.

The first option is too sore. The second option delays the pain, but it's too cold in my three-stripe college jumper to just hang around. Like Greggy, I'm not wearing a vest underneath— stupid if you want to stay warm. At least the Neil option would mean doing something—although it won't help when I get home. Other than a longer delay between now and a skelping.

'We'll need to be careful, Milky. Neil is a swine when he wants to be. He caught me a right one around my head just because I looked at him wrong.'

'Come on. Let's go and see what he's doing. You never know, it might be fun.'

Milky's idea of fun is often a new one on me, but I'm in for a pound on this.

What's to go wrong?

Chapter 8
'Late Night Games.'

IT DOESN'T TAKE us long to spot Neil. He's hardly trying hard to stay out of sight. Our house sits near the top of Simshill and, as Milky guessed, Neil is hanging around further down the road, looking up at our house, while leaning on a lamppost smoking. We are at the corner of the road leading towards the Woods, but we can't get any closer to Neil without being seen. Unless we take to the back gardens. And at that we are experts.

There wasn't a garden back then that we didn't know inside out, outside in, backways over and any other variation you'd care to think of. Every gate, fence, lawn, shed, patch of mud was mapped out in our heads. We were the kings of hedge-hopping. Running through back gardens of our scheme at full pelt, leaping to the next, and the next, and the next. There were records galore for it. I can still remember them. Top of our drive to the bottom of our drive—2 minutes 36 seconds. Round the crescent—3 minutes 18 seconds. The full run—top to bottom of our road and back up—5 minutes 16 seconds. All measured on Milky's dad's stopwatch, when he could borrow it without it being missed. There were a hundred more routes and times. Every one of them with the same simple rule. The only way from point A to point B was via back gardens. Never a foot would touch a front garden or a road or a pavement on the way.

I look down on my sannys. Not ideal footwear. I've a pair of segged-up Wayfinders back home, replete with animal footprints on the soles and a compass hidden in the left heel. My school shoes. Those are the ones for hedge-hopping. Sannys are too slippy, but I'm not going home to change.

'Subby to Old Castle Road?' I suggest.

'That's the one. We can stop at Ma Cummings' house. Neil's outside it. We can watch him from Ma Cummings' garage roof.'

'Ma Cummings is still after us for raiding her rhubarb, Milky. She'll skin us if she catches us.'

'She'll be on the vodka by now. When she's drinking, she couldn't catch a dead cat.'

We cross to the electricity sub-station. The gun lies there. Apart from us kids, and the odd South of Scotland Electricity man, no one goes in. And it's the other kids I'm worried about. Did I bury the gun deep enough? In the morning, will it be obvious where I hid it? The freshly disturbed gravel a giveaway? Even without the bullets, it's not something to be played with.

We both scramble to the back of the sub-station and crawl through a hole in Mr McNary's fence.

We were in no danger of being caught in McNary's garden. He was a tellyholic, spending his life in the front room watching the box. He had his entire garden, front and back, paved over in slabs years ago. There were no chairs or flower pots. No nothing. Just three-by-three slabs and weeds.

Some of the other gardens weren't quite as safe. The next, a case in point. In fact, it was up there as one of the most dangerous in the scheme. Occupied by an old lady called Mrs Telfer, or as we called her, Mrs Terror, it was a place that even the hardest of kids fear. Mrs Terror might have been old, but she had one hell of a throwing arm on her. She also had a ready supply of pool balls lying at her back door. Dad said she used to be a semi-professional tennis player. I don't know about that. All I do know is that if she saw someone in her garden, she let fly. A couple of months before, when I was trying to break the Subby to Old Castle Road record (2 minutes 49 seconds—a record that had stood for over a year), I'd misjudged Mrs Terror's hedge and landed face down in one of her prized flower beds. I'd enough presence of mind to get up quickly, but Mrs Terror was lightning fast. The first pool ball missed me by inches, but not the second. My shoulder blade took it full on. She was aiming for my head, the old cow. The third ball only missed because I tripped while running scared. She caught me twice more before I scrambled back over the hedge into McNary's garden and even then, she had leaned over the hedge and let loose with two more balls. One caught me on the thigh. I had four bruises the size of footballs for weeks. The one on the thigh so bad that it got me off PE at school. And that usually required a death certificate.

Milky pops his head over the hedge to check Mrs Terror's garden.

'Clear,' he says.

'Are you sure?'

'There's no sign of her.'

We launch ourselves at the hedge, hit the ground, bound up, and head for the far side of Mrs Terror's territory; all the while expecting an eight ball in the back of the skull. Our luck holds and it's on to old Snifty's place. A rubbish tip of a garden, laced with kid-killing debris—prams, metal tools, bicycle wheels, barbed wire, car bumpers—even the front end of a bulldozer. In one corner, rotting vegetables mix with wire shopping baskets. In another there is a mountain of glass, the returnable ginger bottles from it having been picked clean years ago. Only non-returnable bottles remain. Experience tells us to stick to the wall of the house, where a path has been cleared from the back door to the side of the building. We duck as we pass Snifty's rear window, and crawl, unscathed, under the hedge into Pete Hunter's garden.

Pete Hunter was in the same year as us, went to our Primary School. We had been friends until his mum and my mum fell out with each other at the army club dinner/dance two Christmases earlier. They had discovered, a month before, that they had bought the same dress from the Kay's catalogue and, even though there was time to reorder, neither was willing to change their dress. This festered right up to the dance, and turned into a cat fight, with mum ladling Pete's mum's head with a metal dustpan. Milky told me that his mum had also weighed in, and the dance had been abandoned when the police were called. My dad had been mad as hell at this. 'I'm a fucking laughing stock!' At least that's how he had phrased it for the next few months as he berated Mum for everything from the tea being too cold to the size of the electricity bill. As a result, I had been banned from playing with Pete.

Pete's garden is dominated by a neat square of lawn, wholly untouched by children—heaven protect anyone that stands on Pete's Dad's grass. We have no choice but to cross it, but the Hunters have French doors—their entire living room visible through the glass. To get by unseen means skirting the very rear of the garden and that means taking to the unsullied lawn. I trip on one of the three 'Keep of the Grass' signs and my left foot slices a line across the lawn, digging up the dirt beneath. A scar that will send Mr Hunter to the moon when he sees it. I scramble upright just as one of the French doors flies open.

'Stop!' comes Mr Hunter's voice. 'Stop. I know who you are!'

We launch ourselves into the next hedge.

But the hedge is huge, a real monster, and for good reason. The next garden is patrolled, night and day, by a vicious beast of a dog called Rotter. A gnarled old ex-police Alsatian with a taste for kid's flesh. We are barely five feet into the next garden when we both hear a way too familiar growl. I catch a glimpse of matted fur hurtling towards us. The hedge we are aiming for is the second to last before we reach our target. It's as massive as the one we just climbed over. Rotter's owner has the devil's own time keeping the dog in the garden. The hedges are designed to stop Rotter getting out.

We both leap. Milky slightly ahead of me. I feel the spray of Rotter's saliva as he throws himself into the air after us. I'm lower down the hedge than Milky, and Rotter is focussed on the easy meat. I slash out with my foot and catch the dog on the jaw. He spirals away, but is back with the sort of speed that should have left him many years back. I reach the top of the hedge. Thankfully, Milky is there with a hand to pull me up and out of reach of Rotter, who is now so angry he's trying to eat his way through the foliage.

We cross Mrs Marks's back green, safe in the knowledge she is on the whisky, lost in TV world.

The next garden is relatively safe. The owners are Mr and Mrs Latimer. Both are stone deaf. They can be seen most days, hand in hand, walking to the shops, oblivious to the kids shouting abuse at them—something that is a bit of a long-term hobby around here. Beyond this is Ma Cummings' house; the other half of the Latimer's semi-detached home. The garage we want to get to is on the far side of her garden. We've camped out on Ma Cummings' garage roof before. Many times. It looks down the hill towards our school, but also gives a near perfect view of Amanda Todd's bedroom window and that is a hell of a window to have a view of.

Amanda, for your information, was the big sister of Catriona—another Simshill Primary kid from our class. Amanda was seventeen and looked to me, and a fair few others, the spitting image of Suzi Quatro—leather trousers and all. Amanda was prone to leave the curtains open in her bedroom and, at times, there had been up to seven of us on Ma Cummings' garage roof. If we were lucky, we'd get a swatch of Amanda in her underwear. If we were really lucky, the underwear would be missing. Although, I was in the majority camp that had never seen this. Milky claimed to have seen her multiple times in the nude, but always when I wasn't there. Given his lying ways, I didn't believe him, but he said she has a fanny like a hairy warthog and massive tits. Not that I could verify this in any way. Nor could anyone else that had ever been on the roof, but Milky insisted it was true.

We'd been caught a few times. Once by Amanda herself who, one summer evening, when there was still enough light, spotted three of us on the garage roof, one holding a small pair of binoculars. I was one of the three. Milky wasn't. He had warned me, as we announced our imminent visit to the garage roof, that it was only safe after dark and, annoyingly, he'd turned out to be right. Amanda had told my mum, who'd sent me to my room. My dad, who I thought would lose the plot, simply popped his head round the bedroom door and threw me a square of Orkney Fudge—my favourite— with a smile and a wink.

We cross the Latimer's garden, leap the small fence and zip over Ma Cummings' grass before shinning up the garage drainpipe. Neither of us can help ourselves, and we have a quick look at Amanda's bedroom window first, but the curtains are closed. After that, we turn our attention to Neil.

We are about twenty yards from him. Us, at the rear of the house, him on the pavement at the front. The garage we are lying on is a decaying brick-built standalone with a torn felt roof. We are hidden in the dark and cut off from Neil by a broken-slabbed driveway hosting a rusting Wolseley that hasn't moved in a hundred years. Neil is clearly visible under the street lamppost and is still smoking. He's surrounded by half a dozen discarded butts. His hands are thrust deep in the pockets of his velvet sport-suit.

Neil is a glam rocker at heart. His platform shoes have small patches of glitter on them. It's not a good look, but he loves Brian Connolly of The Sweet, and has fashioned his hair in the same blonde feather cut. As he watches, he pushes his hands through the dyed locks, keeping his focus on my house.

'What now?' I ask Milky, as I gather my breath, checking my clothes for any rips or tears.

'We wait.'

'It's Baltic up here!' I point out.

We are lying face down on the gnarled felt just above the garage door.

I can almost smell the smoke that was around me. There were a lot of homes around there that ran on coal. The coal wagon tipping up every week. A mountain of black hessian sacks being offloaded by the gang of coalmen that hung off the back of the truck. A few hardy souls used heating oil. But, whether using oil or coal or just feeding off the grid—everyone was complaining like crazy about massive price rises. It was cold enough in our house at the best of times, but with the rolling power cuts, our house was just one of many icebergs waiting on the Spring thaw.

'Look,' Milky says. 'There's an old tarpaulin near Ma Cummings' door. We could bring that up. That would keep us warm.'

Even in the half light of the rear of the house, the thing looks manky.

'I think I'll suffer the cold,' I say.

Milky rolls onto his back. 'Look at the stars tonight!'

I look up, but don't roll over, keeping one eye on Neil.

'We were out at Strathaven with Dad a few weeks ago,' he says. 'Dad borrowed a car to pick up an old lawnmower that was going free. Out there you can see a million, million stars.'

I keep watching Neil as Milky talks.

'We'll soon be living on the moon, Ginger. That's what Tomorrow's World said on telly. That's what the Apollo missions are for. To prepare for a moon base. That would be so good. Imagine living on the moon!'

'Milky, what would you do on the moon? You get bored if you have to sit still for thirty seconds.'

'Aye, but being an astronaut is never boring. And I'd be famous. And I'd be rich. And I'd not have to go to our school. It's well known that astronauts don't go to normal schools when they are kids.'

'Where do they go?'

'They go to space school in America or Russia. I'm thinking of applying.'

'Milky, you failed all your exams at Christmas.'

'So, what? I told you astronauts don't go to a normal school. They don't bother with sums and words and all that stuff. They teach you things like how to spacewalk and how to drive a spaceship and other cool things.'

Neil pushes off the lamppost. I think he's about to move. Instead, he just shuffles to his left a little and leans the other shoulder on the post, taking out another cigarette from the packet and lighting it up. As he blows out the smoke, I'm shivering. Milky is still star-gazing.

'I could even go next year,' he says. 'I'd be good at steering a rocket.'

'Milky, you need to have gone to university to be an astronaut. Science and engineering stuff. Really smart stuff.'

'That's rubbish!'

'It *is* not. I saw it on telly. What's his name said it.'

'Who?'

'The baldy guy that does the science programmes. Burke. That's him, James Burke.'

'What would he know?'

I can feel my anger rising.

'Milky, we're not doing this.'

'What?'

'You know fine what? I'm not arguing with you.'

'That's because you know I'm right.'

'No, you're not.'

'I am.'

I take a breath. I can feel a fight coming on. Milky won't back down on this. I could fly James Burke in by helicopter to explain how astronauts are trained, and Milky would still stick with his story.

'You know I'm right,' he adds.

Salt. Wound. Poured.

'Milky, you're the one that's wrong.'

'Am not.'

I try another deep breath, but I'm not for backing down either. I kneel up.

'Don't be such a spaz, Milky!'

'You're such a doofus.'

'Spaz!'

'Doofus!'

Milky rolls over and readies to attack, just as a car roars up. It stops next to Neil. Milky drops back to the roof. We both roll onto our stomachs to watch, fight forgotten. The car is a red Vauxhall Victor. Neil approaches the driver's window as it's wound down. Parked right under the lamppost, the shadows don't allow us to see the driver. Neil talks through the window, although all we can hear is a low murmur. A few seconds later, the car moves off. Neil stubs out his cigarette on the lamppost, flicks it into the gutter and walks out of sight, up the hill.

'Quick!' I say.

We both dreep from the garage and a few seconds later emerge onto the road. Neil is fifty yards ahead. The Victor has parked at my house, but no one has got out. Neil walks past the car.

'Do we follow Neil or watch the car?' asks Milky.

'The car,' I say. 'I think they must be here for Hornsby.'

Neil keeps walking and vanishes over the brow of the hill. The car sits, exhaust dribbling into the night. Milky and I cross the street, slipping into Kevin Watt's garden, using a dividing wall as cover. I hear voices and look out. My dad and Hornsby are standing at the front door of my house. The rear and back doors of the car fly open. Two men leap out. Hornsby shouts and vanishes around our house. The men sprint up our stairs, ignoring my dad, and dash towards our back garden. My dad shouts to stop, before setting off after them.

'Come on,' I say to Milky.

We both run up the hill until we reach the stairs to my house.

'Up!' I say.

We run up the stairs. The front door is open.

'In!' I order.

We dash inside. I lead Milky up to my bedroom. Thankfully, my brother is still out. I shut the door after Milky is in, before looking out of the window onto our rear garden.

My dad is standing on the garden green, but there's no sign of either Hornsby or the pursuing men. Dad is looking at the back wall. Milky joins me. We both watch as Dad slowly walks to the rear. He steps over the wall, into our neighbour's garden.

'What do you think that was all about?' Milky asks.

'Whoever was in the car was after Hornsby. When they pulled up outside Ma Cummings' place, Neil must have told them he was still in our house.'

Then I have a thought. 'Milky, was there anyone else in the car?'

'What do you mean?'

'Other than the two that chased Hornsby, was there anyone in the car when we ran by?'

'I didn't look.'

'If there was, they must have seen us. We need to check. Stay here. Don't make any noise! If Dad catches you in here, we are both on for a hiding.'

I creep out of the bedroom and push open the door to the only other room up here, other than the toilet, Mum and Dad's bedroom. Once a very familiar place to me when I was younger—me snuggled in between the two of them when I had nightmares—it's now forbidden ground. If I'm caught in here, I'll get my arse well skelped.

Dominated by a huge double bed, the room mixes Dad's ciggie and booze smell with Mum's favourite perfume, Charlie. I scramble onto their bed, pulling the curtain to one side, ears open for the sound of creaking stairs.

The car is below me. The engine still running. I can't see into it from this high up. The two men that chased Hornsby appear at the top of the hill, walking quickly down towards the vehicle. One is an older man, maybe Dad's age, with crewcut hair and wearing a snorkel parka. The other man is younger, long hair trailing on his shoulder—he's sporting a denim jacket and flared jeans. The man in the parka hesitates briefly to look up at our house. I duck down and, seconds later, I hear the car drive off. I'm still none the wiser if there was a third person in the car. I return to my room and tell Milky what I've seen. But, before I can finish, Dad come in the front door. I hear him start to climb the stairs.

'Under the bed Milky!' I whisper, and he dives under. I slip my shoes off and leap into bed, pulling the covers up and rolling over to face the wall, just as Dad comes in. I lie stock still, praying that Milky has the sense to do the same. I can smell the stale stench of cigarette smoke and whisky from Dad. An ever-present smell in the house. He doesn't come fully in to the room and eventually closes the door. He descends the stairs. When I hear the door to the living room click shut, Milky emerges.

'Milky, you need to go home.'

'What do we do next?'

'I'm not sure, but there's nothing to be done tonight. I'll pick you up on the way to school and we can talk then.'

'Those men really wanted Hornsby.'

'They did that.'

'I wonder why?'

'I've no idea, now get going. Out the window and don't let Dad see you!'

He opens the window and eases himself onto the ledge. He drops off. I get up to look out the window, but he's already gone. I wait a few seconds to see if Dad has spotted him, before I strip, fearing tomorrow.

Chapter 9
'A Day For A Run.'

MILKY IS DRESSED and waiting at his front door when I arrive at his house the next morning. He skips out before I can get to the door and shouts 'bye' to his mum. I push him onto the pavement and urge him to move—I've no intention of being late for school today. It'll be bad enough taking the heat for dogging yesterday afternoon, without giving the school even more reason to leather my hands.

I've got my PE stuff in a poly bag in one hand, my books in another poly bag in the other. PE is first up. We were told last week that we are going for a run. Some of the kids have trainers for outdoor running. I have my sannys. Jim Brass has a pair of Adidas Gazelles, but then again, his dad is loaded.

It's cold and that means if we go for a run in the park, the ground will be hard—and sore on my feet. Sandshoes have soles as thin as tracing paper. For gym, I have an old cheesecloth top my brother used to wear, and shorts that are getting too small for me. I'll freeze. Our PE teacher is a lazy swine. He'll take us over to King's Park, making us run circuits while he sneaks back to school for a cup of tea and a fag. That will let the loons in our class have their freedom. And that means that they might fancy picking on a few of us for the hell of it. The only way to avoid that is to run as fast as you can from the start, find somewhere to hide, hope you don't get found until it's time to get back to school for break.

'Okay, Milky, what do we do next?' I say, as we start walking to school.

The gun is still uppermost in my mind. I'm certain that someone will find it and, if not, I'm sure that Hornsby will hunt me down for it.

'I can't go to Dad now with the gun,' I say as we walk. 'He knows Hornsby and there will be hell to pay if he thinks I stole it.'

'What do you think Hornsby did that those guys in the car wanted him so much?'

'It has to be bad. Why would you have a gun, hide out in the woods, if it wasn't something bad? Why would you run?'

'Maybe he killed someone in Simshill.'

'You think? Who?'

'I've no idea. I haven't heard of anything. Have you?'

I don't read the papers or watch the news, but if someone had been killed around here, it would be on everyone's lips.

'I've heard nothing,' says Milky, as we trip down the stairs between Shetland Drive and Seil Drive.

'Milky, did you spot Neil again when you went home last night?'

'No.'

We walk on in silence. A few other school kids are making their way along the road with us. I check that none are loons. Loon spotting is a never-ending task. We start to talk over last night again, but get no further on what might be going on. When we arrive at school, I slap Milky on the back as the bell goes, and we split up to go to registration.

I'm in my seat before Mrs Carol comes in. An unusual occurrence. She notes it with a nod. I wait on the inevitable call out to explain where I was yesterday afternoon, but it doesn't come. Once registration is taken, Mark Anderson leans over from his desk.

'Did you dog off yesterday afternoon?'

'A bit,' I reply. 'Did anyone notice?'

'You're lucky Mr Badder was off sick, and so was old Jetter.'

Mr Badder takes physics and Jetter history. The two classes I'd missed yesterday afternoon.

'They both have London flu,' says Mark.

London flu had been a real fear the year before. Despite my aversion to newspapers, I had read Dad's Daily Express about the outbreak in America and how it had killed people. There was a rumour it was now in Glasgow. At that moment in time, anyone that was struck down with any lurgy at all, was suspected of having London flu.

'London flu?' I say.

'That's what I hear. It's a horrible way to die.'

'Badder and Jetter died?'

'Good as. You can't be cured when you have London flu. And that's a fact you can take to the bank.'

'I saw Badder go into the science block this morning.'

'I know. That's why London flu is so deadly. One day you have it. The next you feel fine and then you die.'

Mrs Carol shouts at us to stop talking and I'm left wondering who'll take physics or history if Badder or Jetter are dead.

When the bell goes, I wander to the gym. Getting ready for PE is the usual assault on the senses. Thirty boys trying to strip in a space made for twenty—none wanting to show more than they have to for fear of ridicule or, worse still, the flicked towel—of which the maestro is one Simon Amers.

Simon's not one of the loons. In fact, he's one of the smartest people I know. He just happens to be the devil's own wonder at towel flicking. A veritable superhero at it. He can flick a polo mint off the tip of your willy at five paces. And, if he is in the mood, can inflict pain on the remotest parts of your body. Being naked is just too much of a temptation for him.

Sometimes you're lucky and sometimes you're not.

Today I'm not.

Simon catches me in my Y-fronts and neatly cracks the tip of his towel off the bottom of my right bum cheek. I scream and jump at the same time. Everyone nearby laughs and I'm left hopping around. I put my hand on my bum to discover a wet trickle of blood. Simon doesn't even bother to watch the aftermath of his actions. He's already looking for a new victim. I finish changing with one eye on Simon. He loves seconds.

When Mr Masters comes in, he saves me from a second flick as Simon is gearing up for another go.

'All of you, out,' Mr Masters says. 'Across to the park!'

We troop out. A bedraggled bunch that looks like a prison gang heading for a day in the fields. The wind has picked up and, in our cheap PE outfits, shivering, chittering and trembling replaces any conversation. We reach the park gates. Mr Masters, dressed in a track suit, heavyweight Swedish army style coat, fur-lined gloves and a trapper hat with ear flaps, orders us to stop.

'Right, it's bloody freezing, so get running. Five of the usual laps. No slacking. No bunking off. No kidding around. Got it? Now go!'

A few kids start to move. Others mill around.

'Move. Now!' Masters shouts.

We all set off.

As we all head through the park gates, I put plan A into operation and make like Valeriy Borzov at the Olympics. I get to the front of the crowd and, when Mr Masters is out of sight, immediately swing left, into some bushes. I push through laurel until I'm tucked in deep enough in to be hidden from the path. I hunker down. I need to be careful where I tread in here. The laurel bushes are a well-known place for the kids, and the desperate, to take a quick crap.

Buried in the foliage, cut off from the wind, it's not as cold as standing at the park gates—but it's still colder than an ice cube on your nipple. I could try and stay here for the duration. Tough it out, wait for Mr Masters to return. That's over an hour away and there is somewhere warmer and safer to hang out—back at the school. If I can cross the main road without being seen, I can reach the gym block and bury myself in the toilets. Normally the least safe place on the planet, but it will be loon-free at the moment.

I give it ten minutes, until my shivering is a constant companion, and crawl back out. If I've timed it right, the keen runners will be at the far side of the park, the loons will be housed up somewhere warm and I'll get a free run at the school. I stand on the park path, checking for any signs of life. An old man appears, out walking his scabby dog. He gives me the once over as he passes by. He's wrapped from head to foot in cloth and leather. In contrast, my exposed skin is taking on a deep blue tint. I walk to the main gates and look out.

Clear.

I'm just about to cross the road when there's a roar of a misfiring engine and the squeal of badly maintained brakes. The red Victor that Milky and I saw last night slams to a halt right in front of me. The older man with the crewcut, still wearing his snorkel parka, jumps out and, before I can take off, he grabs me by the arm.

'In the car!' he growls.

He throws me into the back of the vehicle. I tumble across the vinyl bench seat as the man with the crewcut jumps in.

'Move it, Streak!'

The driver is the long-haired man with a thing for denim. He moves us away with purpose. I tumble forward into the seat-well as the car accelerates. The man with the crewcut reaches down to haul me back up. I have no idea what is going on.

'Mister...' I say.

Crewcut clips me over the back of my head with his hand.

'Shut it!' he says.

So, I shut it.

The car rises up the hill that my school sits on, before sliding down the other side towards the roundabout and the shops that separate Simshill from Castlemilk. We pick up speed as we pass the Coopers Fine Fare supermarket. I have a Saturday afternoon job in there, stacking shelves. I spot Mr Marshall, the manager, standing next to the fire door, smoking a cigarette. I reach for the window winder. Maybe I could shout out.

Crewcut slaps me again. 'Leave it!'

I leave it.

'Streak,' Crewcut says. 'I'm out of fags. Stop in at the Drake café for two minutes. You can get me twenty Embassy Tipped.'

Streak looks over his shoulder. It's clear he's not happy at being ordered about, but he whirls the car around the roundabout and onto the small road that fronts the shops.

'And you'll sit still,' Crewcut says to me. 'Don't move a muscle. Don't say a word, or I'll crush one of your balls!'

Streak gets out of the car. I desperately search the thin straggle of shoppers to see if there is anyone that I recognise. A woman pushing a pram with a busted wheel passes us, but she's too focussed on trying to get the pram to steer in the right direction to notice me. Mrs Paul, a woman who works with my mum, is chatting to the postman not five yards away. I look at

Crewcut, who is looking the other way. I raise my hand to knock on the window. I get another slap for my trouble.

'Do you like the idea of only having one testicle?' Crewcut says.

I slump back in the chair.

Streak emerges from the café. He throws a cigarette packet into the back seat as he gets in.

'Next time get them yourself, Smiff.'

'Don't mouth off to me, Streak.'

'I'm just saying, you know.' he whines.

Streak gets us out of there. He circles back to the roundabout before taking us in the one direction that makes my bad situation worse, up the hill to Castlemilk. I slump further down into the chair, thinking the only good thing about this whole escapade is that the car is warm. But that hardly makes up for the real fear coursing through me. Streak surprises me and doesn't turn into the scheme, choosing to stay on the dual carriageway that cuts up the hill between the Valley and the main estate. We pass a number 31 corporation bus, entering the road that leads up to the village of Carmunnock. Countryside springs up either side. Suddenly Streak pulls us in and parks next to a farm gate.

'Okay, son,' says Smiff, lighting up a cigarette. 'Listen good!'

I listen.

'Last night never happened. You never saw no one in your dad's house. You never saw us outside your house. You never saw this car and neither did your little runt of a friend. Do you understand?'

I don't move.

'Do you understand?' he repeats.

This time I nod.

'Talk to anyone and your dad gets it. Polis or not.'

Again I nod.

'But if you see that Neil McGregor, tell him he's a marked man. We know what he's up to. And he needs to know we know. Your job is to tell him, got it?"

I've no idea what that means.

'I asked if you got it?'

The smack to my face is hard enough to rock me sideways.

'We're serious here. No kid's games. Got it?'

I try not to cry, but this is too much for me. My eyes fill up.

'Mister...' I say.

'Cry all you want. This is a man thing. Now get your wee scrawny bum out of the car now!'

I'm frozen to the chair, tears tumbling down my cheeks—scared I'm going to pee myself.

'Out of the car,' says Smiff.

He reaches over and opens the car door. An ice-cold blast of air rushes in.

'Out now before we all freeze,' Smiff says. He pushes me hard. I slide across the seat, flying out of the open door, landing in the frozen mud of the farm entrance.

'Remember what I said!' Smiff shouts as the car roars away.

I sit on the ground and watch the car leave. A few seconds later, it reappears, heading back where we just came from. Streak flicks me two fingers as he drives by. Smiff is looking at me, cigarette in his mouth, smiling.

I cry for a few more moments. I don't think I've ever been this scared. Eventually, I get up. The road is squeezed between farm hedges at this point. There is no pavement. I've not much choice but to walk back to school.

Ten minutes later, I emerge from the countryside at the top of the dual carriageway that leads back to my scheme. Glasgow is laid out in front of me. A dirty grey landscape of smoking chimneys and high-rise flats. Dark clouds loom above and the wind, coming from the north, ignores my thin top—chilling my blood. I start to move, and move quickly. It's downhill all the way back to the roundabout, and this is *definitely* not a place I want to be caught in. I decide to run. Not only will it keep me warm, but if I'm quick, I might just make it back to the park entrance before Mr Masters returns.

My sandshoes provide little protection for my feet as I pick up speed. Every step stings my soles, but I'm not for stopping. I hear a diesel growl coming up behind me. I turn to see the green and yellow colours of a bus. It's a tuppence fare one-way, but I gave Greggy the last of my money last night and even if I hadn't, I've no pockets in my shorts to carry change in. I could put my hand out and pray that the conductor will take pity on me, but the nearest bus stop is a few hundred yards away. I watch the bus roll away. Something triggers more tears.

I keep running, my eyes full of water. A boy sitting on the grass beside the road sees me and calls me a fanny. I keep running, using the slope to help me run as fast as I can. Half way down the hill I slow it down, begin to think a little straighter. I don't want to be seen at the shops at the roundabout. Someone is bound to know me. That would mean explaining what I was doing there when school was in. I cross the first two lanes of the road to the central reservation, letting a lone Ford Capri climb past me on the far lanes before crossing them as well.

A TSB bank lies ahead and, parked outside, is Victor's fish and chip van. Beyond that, there are another four lanes of road and then I can nip into Thorncroft Drive. King's Park lies that way. I can easily jump the park fence at the end of the road and work my way back to the main gate.

The bank sits on its own corner, facing the roundabout. I could sneak around the back to keep myself out of sight, but I know that the rear of the bank is another hideout for the local neds. I risk passing in front of the building, conscious that just about everyone that Mum and Dad know has a bank account in there. I put my head down and sprint, bundling past the bank, keeping close to the fish and chip van, smelling the all-pervading odour of fat and grease from the vehicle. I leave the shelter of the van, sprint across the road and onto Ashcroft. I calm it down a little as I slip onto the avenue. I check behind to see if anyone is following. It's clear.

Thorncroft Drive is lined with grey and red pebble dashed two-up-two downs. I don't know anyone around here. This is the catchment area for Croftfoot Primary School, not my old school. I slow to a walk, feeling a little safer now that I'm away from the prying eyes of shoppers.

The fear from the car subsides a little; my head clearing. The fact that I've just been lifted proves that there had been someone else in the car outside my house last night. Milky and I *had* been seen. My gut had told me that someone else had been in the car. And I was right, but how Smiff and Streak knew I'd be at the park gates this morning is a mystery. They must have been watching me.

I walk on, unsure of what to do next, other than a desire to get back to the park gates in time.

A bin lorry is sitting at the end of the avenue. Two dustmen are heaving bins out from a house, the metal cans slung over their shoulders. They tip the contents into the lorry with ease. Humping bins in all weathers is not something I'd like to do. It's hard work. When our bin is full I can't rock it, never mind lift it. Yet, these men heft them up and onto their shoulders as if they weigh less than a packet of Golden Wonder. The men jump onto the back of the lorry and it moves away.

I reach the fence to the park, scale it, dropping into the bushes beyond. I exit onto a path to find myself in the midst of my running class mates. A few give me a glance as I emerge from the foliage. I simply point to my groin.

'Piss,' I say and join in the run.

'How many laps have we done, Jimmy?' I say, running up to a boy wearing a string vest and shorts the size of a Zeppelin.

Jimmy Balfon looks at me.

'We? I've done five, I'm not sure about you, Ginger.'

I drop back to join the tail of the group, my head still thinking about Streak, Smiff, and their threats. We reach the main gate a few minutes later to find Mr Masters waiting for us. Some of the faster runners are lying on the ground panting. A group of loons are standing next to the gate, no sign of exertion on their faces, traces of ciggy smoke on their breath.

'Hurry up you lot, I'm Baltic here!' shouts Mr Masters.

We all run up to the gate. He counts us off.

'Okay, over the road and get changed.'

As we cross the main road, I can't help but look out for the red Victor. I don't see it.

Back in the gym block there are showers waiting for us, but I, like many, am not going to risk getting naked with the loons and towel-master Amers lurking. The changing room soon fills with a cloud generated by steaming boys. The bell goes for the break just as I pull on my shoes. I run up the stairs to the playground to look for Milky—to tell him what happened. I find him playing Pitch'n'Toss.

'Jesus, Ginger!' he says once I've finished my tale.

We are sitting on the wall that lines the far end of the playground—a concrete expanse of nothingness filled with kids. Behind me, I can look down on the school blaes. Around us, kids are playing, fighting, talking, running—plus more or less any other ing you can think of.

'And I've some news as well,' Milky says.

'What?'

'I saw Hornsby outside the school gates this morning.'

'When?'

'About ten. I was looking out the window during Maths. I saw him standing there, looking up. I thought he was looking right at me. And then, just before the bell, I saw him again, same place. I think he's waiting for us.'

'This is getting scary, Milky. And I've no idea what's going on.'

'We need some help,' he says. 'We can't deal with all of this. Can we?'

'I don't think so. But what kind of help? We can't talk to anyone. The men that grabbed me told me they would squash one of my balls, *and* do in Dad if I did.'

'Why, Ginger?'

'Why what?'

'Why threaten you?'

'Because we saw them.'

He shakes his head, 'But so did your dad. What difference does it make that we saw them as well?'

I think on that. 'You have a point, Milky. I'm not sure what kind of point, but you have a point. Anyway, that's all the more reason to get help.'

'From?'

'Dunno.'

'Perfect!'

Milky watches as two older boys get into a fight. One pins the other to the ground, sitting on him. It's over a few seconds later when Mr Chambers, the assistant head, stops it.

Milky jumps up. 'Got it!'

'Got what?'

'Help.'

'Help, meaning?'

'Why don't we talk to Ivan, Ginger?'

'Ivan?'

'He'll listen.'

'And he might make us tell our parents about what is going on.'

'No, he won't. He's not like that.'

Ivan, full title Mr Ivan Peters, was the janitor from our Primary School. For the first four years of our time at Primary School he was a figure of fear. Called Ivan the Terrible, he was the school's protector and someone we avoided at all costs until, back in P5, our teacher had asked Milky and I to help Ivan clear up the dining hall. We'd dawdled along the corridor to the hall, glad to be out of class, taking an age, only to discover Ivan wasn't there. We'd headed to the small office he called home. Ivan had no idea he was being sent help and when we entered his space, without knocking, we found him, bottle of Smirnoff in hand, pouring a large one. He'd hid it quickly, but we'd seen it. We told him why we were there. He'd pushed us into the dining hall and told us to start stacking the chairs.

When we'd finished, he'd slipped us each a greaseproof paper wrapped bar of tablet, with the clearly unspoken promise that we kept the little vodka bottle incident to ourselves. After that Ivan became our 'friend' for want of a better word. We'd run the odd errand for him, earning the even odder bar of tablet. We'd even fetch him booze now and again from a friend of his who lived down on Simshill Road.

Up until the vodka incident, Ivan had been a man to avoid. After that, he'd become someone we could talk to. He knew all the gossip in the school. Who was winching who. Which teachers were up to no good. Which parents were up to no good. To us, he was a revelation. He enjoyed our company. At least that's what I thought. We often sat in his office at playtime listening to the latest goings on as he sipped at his vodka and coke. An odd trio, but one that worked for us all.

'I was told to talk to nobody,' I say to Milky. 'Nobody. And Ivan isn't no one.'

'Ginger, where will that get you? Or get us?'

I shrug. 'And Ivan will help, Milky?'

'Look,' says Milky, pointing down at the main road, beyond the blaes pitch. The red Victor is sitting at the bottom gate. 'And there,' he says, pointing up the hill towards my home. Hornsby is heading away from the school. At that moment, he turns and looks back. He points his finger at me, forms his hand into a gun shape, places it to his head and pretends to pull the trigger.

Milky looks to the sky, maybe for inspiration, 'Ginger, all I know is that we need help. We really need help!'

I lean back on the wall. Milky has a serious point. We can't handle this and I can't go to Mum or Dad. Milky's mum and dad aren't options either. Ivan is a good call in some ways. We might be kids, but he's never talked down to us. He plays fair. And we did a lot of running around for him for little more than a few lumps of boiled sugar. He's been the one adult in my life that I felt was listening when I spoke. Was *really* listening. And, importantly, *would* still listen. And, even more importantly, will say nothing about it to anyone else.

I hope.

Hornsby repeats the gun gesture, before turning away—and that seals the deal.

We need help.

The Conversation.

*'*THE JANITOR. *With all the shit that was going down, you thought it was a good idea to talk to the janny?'*

'We needed some advice?'

'But a janny?'

'Who else? A teacher? Maybe our grandparents? What about the local MP? The Daily Record? Would that have been better? Dear Deidre, as a twelve-year-old boy I have recently discovered a man on the run, found a gun, have a friend who nearly shot a man, been kidnapped by a couple of neds who are threatening to beat up my father. By the way, I'm also behind on my homework. Any advice? Plus, I've told you, what kid thinks straight in these situations? How many times, even now, have you woken up the day after being an arse and thought, shite what did I say or do?'

'Okay, I'll give you that.'

'He's dead.'

'Who is?'

'Ivan. The janny.'

'We all go at some point.'

'He only passed last week.'

'Last week? How old was he?'

'Must have been a fair age. I'd say he was in his late forties back then.'

'God, he must have been Glasgow's Methuselah, given how old you are.'

'Funny bastard.'

'How did you hear about his death?'

'Come on, how do you hear about anything around here?'

'Fair call. Gossip is king and all that.'

'I was kind of sad when I was told. I mean, he was a good man. Well, maybe not that good, but…'

'But what?'

'Nothing.'

'So, did you go see the janny that day?'

'We did.'

Chapter 10
'Going Back.'

I ARRANGE TO meet Milky behind the gym at dinner time. If Hornsby is waiting for us, we need to sneak out the back way. Ivan will be in his room up at our old Primary School for most of the dinner break. If anyone catches us there, we'll just say we are back to pay him a visit.

I have Maths the last two periods this morning. I catch it big time for not having done the extra homework. I'm subjected to three of the belt, have to agree to do the outstanding homework, take detention at the end of school.

I spend the rest of the lesson looking out of the window. Twice, I spot Hornsby in the distance, and once the red Victor. The bell goes for dinner. I'm first out of the class. Milky is waiting for me behind the gym block.

'Okay let's go!' I say.

We sprint across the blaes pitch, down a grass verge before clambering over the chain-link fence that borders the rear of the school. We skip through a garden, and, when we hit the pavement, we start to head towards the Primary School. We hug the edge of Linn Park to avoid passing through our scheme. The last thing we need is to be seen if we can avoid it. We approach the back gate to the school, eyes wide open for Hornsby and the red Victor.

The Primary School playground is in full swing and there's a real sense of the familiar as we pass through it. A care free innocence that I envy. Something in the transition from Primary School to Secondary burst that bubble. We don't run into any teachers, reaching Ivan's office without incident. I push open his door and there he is, sipping at a cup of tea, the familiar faint stench of booze floating in the air.

'My boys!' he says.

Ivan is a rotund man who lost most of his hair in the time we were at school. He has a purple, cratered nose that's erupting from his face. His eyes are half-closed, ever-watery.

'And what brings you back here?' he asks.

Milky and I had discussed the approach we should take with him on the way here. We landed on the simple idea of telling the truth.

'We'd like your advice, Mr Peters,' I say.

'Take a seat then and here...' He pulls open a drawer in his desk and hands us two greaseproof paper-wrapped pieces of his wife's home-made tablet. 'And close the door!'

I shut the door. We unwrap the tablet as we both sit down.

'Okay boys, what is it you want to tell me?'

I take the lead and the words flow from my mouth in a torrent once I get going. Tumbling into the air. As if they wanted to come out. *Needed* to come out. My story is jumbled, often out of order. Milky frequently corrects me. Ivan intervenes now and again to clarify some points. As I talk, I study his face. If I expected him to be surprised, I'm disappointed. He sits back when I'm finished.

'Ginger, that's some story. And you say it's all true?'

'Blood and guts, Mr Peters,' I say.

'It's true, Mr Peters,' adds Milky. 'Blood and guts true. All of it.'

'And this man, Hornsby, and the men in the car—they were all hanging around your school this morning.'

'*All* morning!' I say. 'What do you think we should do, Mr Peters?'

He picks up his tea, sliding open the bottom drawer. The drink drawer.

'A wee nip will help here.' He pours a slug of vodka into his tea.

Why Peters had never been dismissed for drinking was something that Milky and I had never figured out. It's not as if he was subtle with it or waited until the school day was over. Once, when we were helping him set the dining room up for parent's night, he'd asked us to come in half an hour before school to dig out the extra chairs that were kept in the basement. He'd been hungover from a session the night before, and was more than happy to tell us how he, and a few friends, had vanished into a bottle and half of Whyte & Mackay.

Before we moved any chairs, he had tipped an entire quarter bottle of vodka into a mug. Drank it all as he watched us work. When we'd gone to visit him at playtime, he'd been fast asleep in his room, door wide open for the world and his auntie to see. And that wasn't the only time he'd taken a mid-morning or mid-afternoon kip. Mum and Dad knew about his drinking. So, did the whole scheme, it would seem. Yet no-one seemed to do anything about it. I'd nicknamed him Ivan the Bullet-Proof, and Milky's dad, hearing what I'd called him, laughed and said it should have been Ivan the Hundred Percent Proof instead. I'd had to look that one up in the dictionary.

'What do you think, Mr Peters?' I ask, once he has his drink sorted.

'What I think,' he begins. 'is that you have got into something of a guddle. A right guddle.'

'We need help,' says Milky.

'Aye, you do.'

He sips at his drink. Saying nothing. Which isn't like him at all. Normally, it would take a shopping bag taped around his head to stop him talking. Milky and I look at each other. Maybe Ivan has finally had one too many playtime alcohol breaks and is losing it. Advice was his middle name when we were here. Advice even if you didn't want it. Advice like Charley the cat.

'Well?' Milky grunts.

'Well, boys,' he replies. 'Leave this one with me. It needs a bit of thought.'

Definitely not the words we were looking for. We need the instant Smash potatoes kind of advice. Or at least a starter for ten, as my dad always says.

'What do we do just now?' I say.

'Sit tight, Ginger,' he says. 'Say nothing to anyone. And I mean say absolutely nothing! Let me have time to put the old grey matter to work.'

'But Hornsby and the men in the Victor are out there right now,' Milky says, pointing to the window. 'Waiting on us.'

'Just stay out of their way for the moment. You can do that. I know you can.'

We both look at each other.

'It's the best I can do for now,' he adds. 'Now I need to get on. It's been good seeing you, lads. Run along, or you'll be late back to school.'

He ignores the disappointment on our faces and stands up to open the door for us. We both troop out in silence, trudging through the sea of kids playing. We exit by the back gate, barely checking for Hornsby or the men.

'Well, that was rubbish,' I say. 'What was the point in that?'

Milky looks hurt; after all, it was his idea.

'He's gone looney tunes,' says Milky. 'I thought he'd help. Even just a little. All that vodka has stewed his brain.'

We trail back to school, making it just in time for the bell. We part without saying anything to each other.

None of my classes are facing the outside of the main block in the afternoon, so I can't see if Hornsby or the Victor are still around. And, with me confined to detention after school, it's gone five o'clock before I leave the premises.

It's dark. The cold of last night, if anything, is deepening. I stand at the school gate for a few moments, unsure what to do. Milky is long gone and I'm on my own. There are plenty of spots for Hornsby to corner me on the way home and, in the dark, taking the back ways or the park ways is asking to run into trouble of a different sort.

A few stragglers and teachers are dribbling from the school grounds but, soon, I'll be on my own. I can't stay here, so I move. Eyes on stalks that have stalks. Ears pinned so far back, they are touching each other behind me. Head swivelling like a Thunderbird puppet.

I'm one street away from safety, beginning to relax a little, when a shadow from within a shadow emerges in front of me. Hidden in the dark of a fence, the figure grabs my arm and pulls me out of sight.

'You're a hard little bugger to keep track of,' says Hornsby.

His breath would stun a Rhino.

'I'm not giving you the gun,' I blurt.

'No need to, son,' he says, patting his pocket. He opens his jacket to show me the barrel.

'I found your little hidey hole. You're not as smart as you think you are.'

I look up and down the road, but there's no one in sight.

'Right, Ginger! Isn't that what they call you? Ginger. I've got a job for you and that little friend of yours.'

I say nothing, my head trying to figure if I can make a run for it, but he's got a tight grip on my upper arm.

'I need you to meet me later tonight,' he whispers into my ear, alcohol fumes flooding my world. 'Then I'll tell you what to do. Don't think of running away in the meantime. I'm not afraid to use this gun. Your old man and me go back a long way but, even so, I might have need of a little target practise. Do you know what I'm saying, son?'

I nod.

'Eight o'clock at the lane behind the shops. That's where you need to be and bring your mate with you. If you're late...'

He makes the gun shape with his hand and fingers and points it at me.

'Bang, bang!'

He lets me go.

'Eight o'clock,' he says. 'Not a minute after.'

With this, he shoves me away. I hesitate for just a second before I start to run, trailing my two school bags behind me like parachutes.

Bang. Bang.

I don't stop running until I reach my house, barging in through the back door. Mum is at the cooker. She turns as I rush in.

'Get washed Bobby, tea is in five minutes,' she says, returning to stirring a pot.

Dad is in the living room reading the Express. Deke is lying face down on the floor, head in his hands, watching Ivor the Engine. I almost miss the change in TV—it's that big.

'A new telly?' I say.

'Twenty-six inches,' says Deke. 'And a new record player.'

Sitting on the shelf above the TV is an Alba record player. Large wooden-cased speakers either side.

'Stereo.' Deke smiles.

As I pass him to examine the TV and record player, Deke tries to kick me. Dad growls for me to get upstairs now. I reluctantly leave, climb the stairs and dump my bags before slumping on my bed. I look at the window, already hard with frost, and wonder if I could just leap out and run and run and run.

Bang. Bang.

Tell Dad?

No.

Tell Mum?

No.

Tell anyone?

No.

Bang. Bang.

Even without Hornsby's threat, there's still the threat from Smiff and Streak if I blab.

'Talk to anyone and your dad gets it. Polis or not.'

Any way you look at this, I'm going to get my dad hurt if I don't meet Hornsby.

Mum calls out for me to come down for tea.

I dive into the bathroom, throw some cold water on my hands and descend the stairs. The dining table is set for four. Mince and tatties sit on four plates. Dad's favourite, and a meal we have three or four times a week.

'I've Arctic Roll for pudding,' says Mum.

Normally that's a treat and half. Pudding is usually instant custard. If there's pudding at all. But I don't even acknowledge the words. Mum scowls at this.

'Well, if you don't want it,' she says to me. 'That's all the more for the rest of us.'

I try to smile, but it comes out all wrong. It looks like I'm taking the piss. Dad slaps me across the back of the head. I rub the spot and start to eat. I'm starving. If I don't eat quickly, Dad might just decide my response to Mum's pudding news means I've to go to my room with no food again. I wolf the lot in less than two minutes, not looking up from the plate. When I'm finished, I sit back as the others eat, waiting.

Not talking at tea is an unspoken rule unless Dad chooses to break it. Otherwise, it's a time for filling your bellies. I could easily eat more as I'd skipped dinner because we'd visited Ivan. But skipping meals is the norm in my world. If Mum and Dad are out when I get back at dinner time, there's often little more than a piece and sugar—sometimes not even that.

When Dad has finished his plate, mum clears the dishes and brings out the Arctic Roll. I'm given a slice, but it's half the size of Deke's. My punishment for not welcoming it with more open arms.

'Tea?' says Dad, as he polishes off the last scrape of ice cream. He looks at me as he says this and I rise. My turn to make it.

I scrabble around the kitchen for Dad's mug, Mum's cup, and Deke's Superman mug. The metal teapot is hiding in the cupboard under the sink. I fill the kettle, stick it on the cooker ring. I lean on the sink, waiting for the water to boil, trying to banish thoughts of Hornsby—but I can't.

How did he find the gun? He couldn't have seen me bury it. He was in the house talking to Dad when I'd jumped the fence to the Subby. Did he happen to be looking out our window? Did someone else see me? If so, why would they tell Hornsby? Or did Milky blab to his parents, they to mine and onto Hornsby? But that makes no sense. If Dad knew about the gun, I'd be black and blue.

The water boils. I tip a little into the teapot and swirl it around to warm the pot, before draining the cooling water down the sink. I fetch the Typhoo, tip in four teaspoon's worth and one for luck. I fill the pot from the kettle. I grab a bottle of milk from the fridge, take the teapot and milk through to the living room and return to fetch the cups, mugs and a bowl of sugar, finish it all off by digging out the tea strainer. With everything on the table, we all sit in silence as the tea infuses.

After a few minutes, I stir the teapot. I put milk in everyone's cups and two sugars in everyone's but Dads. He takes three. I give the teapot another quick stir, place the tea strainer over Dad's mug and pour. Once all four cups are done, I sit back down.

'Any biscuits?' says Dad.

I rise to check the kitchen food cupboard. It's surprisingly full. *Amazingly full.* There's a packet of Bourbons to hand. I take them through. I hand Dad the packet. He takes two. I take one and pass the packet to Deke, who takes three. Mum takes one. She says nothing about Deke's greed. If I'd taken that many, I'd have been sent upstairs in a flash. There's times when I really hate my brother.

'Homework?' says Dad in between mouthfuls.

'None,' says Deke.

That has to be a lie.

'I'll do mine upstairs,' I say.

'You'll do it down here. I'm going to check it,' says Dad. 'Go fetch it!'

I do as I'm told, Mum helping by clearing the table to let me set up. I lay out the Maths I was given. Staring at the undecipherable, looking for divine inspiration. The Maths book is open at the right page, but I'm none the wiser. I play with my pencil and start by writing down the question number in my jotter. And then stop. Mum comes over.

'Hard?'

I shrug.

'Let me look.'

She studies the question, then asks me for the pencil. She fetches a bit of scrap paper from the sideboard before sitting down next to me.

'Here,' she says, the sweet scent of Charlie enveloping me. 'Look, it's not that hard.'

She scribbles a string of numbers and a few letters.

'Just follow this,' she says.

I read what she has written.

'Do you see how it works?' she asks.

I don't. Or, hang on, maybe I do see something. Mum writes again. Something akin to a very small lightbulb goes on in my head. She writes out the sequence of numbers and letters one more time. This time I follow the pencil as it moves, taking in each number, each letter in the equation and the progression as required.

'Try the next question!' she says. Her tone light and encouraging.

I pick up the pencil. I look at what Mum has just written. I study the next question and write a few numbers in my jotter.

'Nearly,' says Mum and rubs one number out. 'Try again!'

I inspect Mum's workings again. I follow the logic, underlining the answer after I've written it.

'Very good,' Mum says. 'Now try the other questions!'

I work through each question in turn. By the last one, I don't need any help from Mum. This could be something of a moment in my life. It's the first time I've completed any Maths homework since I got to secondary school. And, bonus, I've even done the extra questions I got for failing to do the original stuff.

'Have my biscuit!' says mum handing me the Bourbon that she's kept by her mug of tea.

Despite the impending doom of meeting Hornsby, I look down on my jotter and smile. Dad comes over, stares over my shoulder and pats me on the head. My smile widens. I pack away the jotter, ignoring the fact that I've some Geography to do. I feel like bathing in this tiny moment of triumph first. Dad bursts that bubble.

'Any other homework?'

I dig the Geography work out. It's easy and I'm repacking five minutes later, glancing at the clock. I've a couple of hours to kill before I'm supposed to meet Hornsby. I decide to lie on the floor, let the news on the new telly wash over me. I get lost in the colour picture. It's so real.

'Can I go see Milky?' I ask as Reporting Scotland comes on.

'Be back by half eight!' says Mum.

I climb the stairs and change into my college jumper, but leave my school shoes on. I root under my bed, digging out my pen knife. The blade is barely three inches long and has never been used for anything other than whittling wood for a cattie. I put it in my pocket. Somehow it helps a little at the thought of the meeting with Hornsby.

Outside, the promise of a colder night is taking shape. I should have worn my jacket but, at the moment, it's not the cool thing to do. Kids around here are freezing for the sake of fashion. Jackets don't show off your jumper. So jackets stay on their hooks.

I keep my eyes open for the red Victor as I make my way to Milky's. When I reach his house, I circle to the back door and walk in. There's no standing on ceremony at Milky's place. I've been walking in his back door since I was five. The kitchen is a dead space. No heat. No sign of recent cooking.

'Milky?' I shout. 'It's me!'

Nothing. I open the door to the living room. It has the same layout as my house, only the furniture is a little newer. Cloth instead of vinyl covering the sofa and chairs. In the corner, a G Plan dining table. Mum would *kill* for one of those. I've heard her say that a thousand times. With the big light out, the only illumination is coming from outside, through the geometric orange circles of the curtains.

'Milky?' I shout again.

Still nothing. The house is silent. Milky has an older brother, Tom, along with his sister, June. But the place is a cemetery.

'Milky?'

I open the door to the stairs and shout again.

Nothing.

Milky didn't mention that he was going out with the family. The fact the back door was unlocked means little. Few people around here lock up unless they are going away for a holiday. I leave by the back door, walk to the front door and stand.

The single thought that I'd be hanging onto was that at least Milky would be there when I met Hornsby. The fact that the entire family is out doesn't bode well. Milky has a gran, his mum's mum, in a care home down near the River Clyde. If they've gone to visit her, they won't be home 'til the back of nine. His dad likes to load up on five penny bags of chips from Mario's in town when he gets the chance. Then, if he has a mind, he'll make the whole family walk the four miles back to the house to save on the bus fare.

With over an hour to kill, I go for a walk. At Rodil Avenue, I jump the corner garden and make my way to the rear. The house is up for sale, the previous owner having died a few weeks ago. Milky had discovered that the shed at the back was open and there was a Calor gas heater that still worked inside. We've been here a few times since, the last time the gas was still holding out. I'm in need of heat. I slip into the shed.

It's as we left it, all the tools pushed to one side to give us somewhere to sit. I turn on the gas and press the ignition switch on the heater. It sparks a few times, then, with a whoosh, the three grates flood with flame and quickly turn red. I crouch down, absorbing the heat. After a minute, I slump to the floor.

The first time Milky and I were in here, we'd nailed some old cloths to the window in case anyone saw the light from the fire. With the shed door shut and the fire hissing away, I lean on a wooden work bench.

I don't remember the name of the previous owner, but I do know he worked as a maintenance man somewhere in Rutherglen. He had come to our house one day to try to fix the lone storage heater that sits in our hall. He had failed, and Dad had never called on him again.

The shed is bursting with tools. I touch my pen knife, wondering if I need something more substantial for the upcoming meeting. I stand up and rifle the workbench. I pick up a chisel and weigh it in my hand. It would neatly fit in my trousers' pocket. I try it for size. It slips in easily. But I can feel the blade nipping at my leg through the worn material. There's a roll of insulation tape sitting in a box. I take it out and wrap the end of the chisel in it. I put the chisel back in my pocket. It doesn't nip anymore.

Why I'm doing this is a little beyond me. The neds carry real knifes around here, but not me. I'd be skelped into next week if I was caught with one. Dad hates knifes.

In those days, two doors down from us, lived a guy called Drew Lachlan. He was stabbed a year earlier. David was nineteen and worked in a factory on Drakemire Drive in the Valley. He was working late one night and instead of waiting on the bus, he'd cut across the Linn Park golf course. A bad idea. He ran smack into a gang of loons. He'd managed to escape, but not before one of them had slashed his face. The scar it left was horrible, running from his nose to his left ear. It never went away. My dad also had a scar on his back from his time in the army. Seventeen years old, it still looked fresh when he took his top off. He never told us how he got it, but he hated knives with a passion that bordered on obsessional. If ever there was a reason to avoid knives in my world, it's what happened to David Lachlan and Dad. But Hornsby and the men in the car had me spooked out of common sense.

I wrap my fingers around the chisel grip. A small metal guard at the end of the handle stops my fingers reaching the blade of the chisel itself. The handle is smooth. It once had finger grips, but these are almost all worn away. I yank the tool from my pocket, holding it out in front of me. Quick-Draw Bannerman in action. I repeat the process a few times, then look for an alternate weapon. There are no end of choices, but something draws me back to the chisel, and I sit down, still playing with the handle.

With no watch or clock to guide me, I wait a little while longer, soaking up as much heat as possible before leaving. Once I've killed the fire, I head down the road to the shops, stopping short of them.

A Mark 1 Ford Escort crawls up the hill. It's the first car I've seen this evening. It belongs to our next-door neighbour. I turn my head away from the car, but Mr Elder is as nosy as they come. I know he saw me. That'll get reported back. When the car is gone, I risk a look along the lane behind the shops. I see no one.

The lane is shaped like a backward L, with one leg running along the rear of the shops that face Castlemilk before turning ninety degrees, thirty yards later, to run behind the shops facing Croftfoot. The end I'm at opens on to my road but the other end faces onto back gardens. Getting caught in that far leg of the L means you are out of view of the passing world. And that is very, *very* bad news.

There's no sign of Hornsby, so I back off to wait.

Ten minutes later, he appears around the corner. He has Neil McGregor, Greggy's brother, in tow. That throws me.

I remember Smiff's words in the Victor.

'But if you see that Neil McGregor tell him he's a marked man. We know what he's up to. And he needs to know we know.'

Hornsby spots me and waves to join him. I consider running. Taking off. Never coming back. Making my way to London. Or Paris. Or Outer Mongolia. Anywhere but here. Instead, I walk towards the lane, before slipping into the dark where I find Hornsby and Neil smoking. Hornsby is leaning on the rear door of the Drake café. Neil is standing in the middle of the lane.

'Okay, son,' says Hornsby, who is looking rougher by the hour. 'Where's your wee friend?'

'He's out with his family.'

'I said I wanted you both.'

'He wasn't in. He might be in later.'

He drags at his cigarette. 'This can't wait. I need you to fetch something for me.'

He draws on the fag again.

'There's a house up in Castlemilk. I need you to get something from it.'

'What?' I ask, my voice trembling.

'A cassette. That's all. A cassette tape.'

'A tape?'

'A *cassette* tape.'

'What's on it?'

'None of your business. You'll go with Neil here and get the tape—and once you've got it, you'll hand it to him and that's the end of it. Then you walk away, your dad stays healthy, and so do you. Get it? Tape or the Victoria Infirmary. Okay?'

'Why can't Neil go and get it?' I stammer.

'Because,' is all the answer he offers.

'Because what?'

'Just because. Neil will show you the house. You go in and get the tape. It's that simple.'

'I don't understand,' I say, looking back along the lane. 'Why do you need me?'

'Because the people with the tape know Neil and they don't know you.'

I'm getting more confused by the minute.

'But if the people don't know me, why will they give me the tape?'

'They won't.'

More confusion.

'If they won't give me the tape,' I say. 'Why am I going?'

'They won't give you the tape. You'll need to take it from them.'

'Take it?'

'Steal it.'

'Steal it?'

'From the house. You are going with Neil to break into the house and steal the tape for me. It's that simple.'

Chapter 11
'Late-Night Thief.'

WITH THOSE WORDS, Hornsby stubs out the cigarette on the wall and throws the butt to the ground.

'Okay, both of you get going!'

He walks away, deeper into the lane, vanishing around the corner, leaving me with Neil. Neil lights up a second cigarette from the tip of the one he is smoking.

'Neil,' I say.

He steps towards me, lifts his hand in the air. I wince, expecting to be hit.

'We need to go,' he says, pointing to the lane's exit with the raised hand.

'Neil, can I ask a question?'

'No.'

'But…'

This time he does clip me across the back of the head.

'I said no, you can't ask any questions. Now move!'

We exit the lane and Neil drops in behind me. 'If you try to run, I'll find you and put you in intensive care, understand?'

It seems I've become the south side of Glasgow's most threatened person.

We walk along the shop fronts past the general grocer, past Greenlees shoe shop, the optician and the Drake café, before Neil pushes me over the service road, towards the roundabout.

I look up on Castlemilk, and the fear of God grips me. I freeze. Neil walks into the back of me.

'What the hell?' he spits.

'Neil, I can't go in… there.'

Another smack to my head.

'Move!'

'We'll get killed if we go in there,' I say, pointing at the scheme.

'Don't be stupid. No, we won't. Just stay with me.'

'Jesus, Neil, even you can't protect us from some of the nutters in there!'

'Just walk.'

He kicks my ankle and pushes my shoulders.

'Just move!'

I stumble forward and across the road. Neil shoving me in the back every few steps. We cross the dual carriageway I ran down earlier, walking past the bank, now closed tight. Victor's, on the other hand, is up and running; a small queue standing in the cold to load up on fish and chips. I don't recognise anyone in the line.

'Up the hill!' says Neil.

We climb until we are level with Castlemilk's West Paris church; an odd-looking beast that, to me, resembles a spaceship that's landed on its side. Mum thinks it looks like a theatre from the thirties.

'That way!' says Neil. He pushes me onto the grass in front of the church.

There's fifty yards or so of wet grass to cross and my shoes are soon soaking the water up like a sponge. I stare at the tenement blocks as they creep towards me—ugly, late fifties buildings.

Do you know they built some nine thousand homes in that place, then dumped near on forty-five thousand souls on the edge of Glasgow? Most were decanted from the tenements that the council trashed, such as the Gorbals. Okay, so things were bad in those areas and promises of a wonderful new life were attractive to many—but it was a shit storm of lies and incompetence. Castlemilk was built with next to fuck all facilities. Chronic transport links. In their infinite wisdom, the council built the whole scheme and then declared it a dry area. No pubs. Who thought that was a good idea? And it would have been bad enough if this was the only disaster of a housing idea—but given our Glaswegian leaders repeated the exercise in Easterhouse and Drumchapel and elsewhere—they obviously thought they were onto a winner. Then they ran out of cash and did what they should have done in the first place, refurbed the old tenements. Just dumb, the whole thing. My Dad would tell you how dumb ten times a day, if you got him started on the whole thing. And boy, did he like to rant on about anything that made a policeman's life harder. He firmly believed that the many good people in those schemes were being fatally poisoned by the few that saw the council's stupidity as fertile ground for badness. Talk about breeding gang culture—it's hard to find a better lesson.

Rant over.

The streetlights around us all go out. As do the houselights.

'What the hell?' I say, stopping dead.

'Power cut,' says Neil. 'It was due. That's why we are doing this right now. Keep walking, it'll help us.'

The rolling power cuts were a pain in the tonsils. Two or three hours of enforced cold and darkness. The government's way of saving energy with the miner's strike, and when the price of oil went up and up. They even cut the TV off at half-past ten some nights. Milky used to say that the world was now officially turning back to black and white. And I agreed with him. I'd avoid most of the adult chat on stuff like the economy, but things had never seemed so drab. Save the music. Glam rock was ruling the record players. And that was anything but drab. Glitter was king. A small sprinkle of sparkle in a dark time.

'Get moving!' says Neil.

Flickering lights start to appear in the rows of tenement windows as we walk. People lighting up candles and paraffin lamps, many huddling into a single room to maintain the heat. Early to bed for others. The sky is loaded with cloud. But then again, the Glaswegian sky is always thick with the threat of rain.

With no moonlight to see by, we have to walk slowly. If we bump into any of the neds in this light, we'll be lucky to escape alive. In the dark, they can maim without worrying about being caught. A dark playground for them to frolic in for as long as they fancy.

Neil instructs me to go left into another canyon of tenements—a world that I've avoided all of my life. I only live a few hundred yards from here, but have never been on these streets. Around me, the spooky, quivering light coming from the homes throws a myriad of shadows, sometimes giving brief glimpses of the lives behind drawn curtains. Neil is right about using the power cut as cover—no one will be outside now.

Except the loons.

'How far?' I ask.

Smack is the reply.

I rub my head.

We dig our way deeper into the scheme. We see no one, save a lone car that passes—weak headlights a strange intrusion in the dark.

'Okay,' says Neil. 'Stop!'

He stands beside me. 'In here.'

He shoves me up a path, into the lee of a close.

'Now here is where you earn your money. You want the close three up from here. The flat the tape is in is on the top floor. Right-hand door at the top. Remember that. Right-hand door.'

'And I just walk in. Will it not be locked?'

'Take this.'

He hands me a key.

'It should be empty.'

'Should be?'

'Everyone is out. At a do in town.'

'Is this something to do with Heartbreak?' I ask, and instantly regret the slip of information.

'Who told you about her?' he says, grabbing my jumper collar.

'No one,' I say.

'Shite!' he says. 'Who told you that name?'

'I'm not sure,' I whimper. He has me up close, fag breath in my face.

'Tell me or I'll kick your head in!' he grunts.

'Milky,' I lie. 'Milky said the name. That's all I know.'

'And who told him?'

'I don't know.'

'My little dickhead brother did. Didn't he?' he guesses. 'Snooping little shit. Sitting in that bloody cupboard under the stairs.'

He pulls me even closer. 'You're going to forget that name. Do you get it? Forget it.'

'Okay, okay. I'll forget it.'

'And I'm going to cream David for this.'

I should have kept my mouth shut. Neil is seriously pissed off. I reckon the only reason I'm not facing a broken arm or leg is because he needs me to fetch the tape.

'Right, get going!' he grunts.

'Where is the tape in the house?'

'How would I know? It won't take long, there's next to sod all in the flat. But there is a black and silver Panasonic cassette recorder somewhere. Probably under the couch. Make sure you check it. If it has a tape in it, make damn sure you grab it. And don't miss any other tapes in the house. Take them all!'

'Neil, why don't you go? You know what you're looking for.'

He pulls me back out along the path a few feet. 'Look!' He points along the road.

At first, I can see nothing, then I spot a small red glow hovering in mid-air. A face briefly appears, lit by a fag.

'There's always two of them. One at the front of the close, and one at the back green. They know me. I can't be seen here.'

'How do I get past them?'

'That's for you to figure out. Now get going and don't come back empty handed!'

'What's so important about this tape?'

'Just fetch, like a good boy.'

With that, he gives me another shove and I'm out on the pavement on my own.

I stand, trying to work out what to do. The greatest urge is to run.

'Get going,' Neil hisses. 'The others will be back soon. Get a move on!'

I begin to walk. A couple of closes along, I stop. I can still see the glow of the cigarette and the man's face lit when he inhales. There's no way past him to get in to the flat. Maybe the rear is less well-guarded. I finger the chisel in my pocket. It provides no comfort. I shuffle through the close next to me, out of the back door onto the back green.

Walled in on all four sides by the rear of four high tenements, the green is the size of half a football pitch. It's dark as deep sin.

I look to my left as I sneak out of the back close. There's no obvious sign of anyone. I cling to the nearest wall, beginning to work my way along.

I hear, before I see, the rear guard. A quiet moan. He's not standing in the close. I can see a squat dark shape that's probably the midden. It's just visible in the dancing light from the rear windows of the surrounding homes. The sound came from behind that. I edge forward. The man moans again. I hear the word 'bloody freezing'. And he's spot on. The temperature is dropping like a shot cow. I cross to the back of the midden, tiptoeing along. I need to know if he can see the rear entrance to the close from where he's hidden.

I reach the brickwork, the smell of rotting rubbish strong, even in the cold. I hear another moan. It sounds like the guard is lying against the wall just beyond me. And that's not great news. Even in the dark there's no way I can get into the close without being seen. There's just enough light filtering to silhouette me if I try to enter. I carefully back track.

What to do? I could try to make a dash for the close, but even if I get in, I'll be trapped. One guard at the back and one at the front. No way out. There's no other way in.

So why go in at all, if that's the case? I could argue with Neil that it was impossible to do. Would that save me, save Dad? Probably not. But does Dad need saved at all? He's Polis after all. Hornsby might have a gun, but would he really try to shoot a copper? A *fellow* copper, if I have him right. Over what? A cassette tape?

The guard near me lights up a cigarette. I hear the first suck in the still of the night.

I could back off, try to find Smiff and Streak. I could tell them that I know where Hornsby is hanging out, trade him for me and Dad getting out of this. Except I don't know where

Hornsby is right now—and I'd guess that Hornsby has probably told Neil to grab the tapes and leave me stranded. I can't see him taking me back with him. But I know where Neil is right now; I know where he lives and that he's the one running around after Hornsby. Given what Smiff said to me, I'm guessing that Neil is playing both sides—Hornsby and Heartbreak—off each other and has been found out. So, if I grass up Neil to Smiff and Streak, they could use Neil to get to Hornsby and that's it all over. That could work.

Couldn't it?

I chew on that thought and slide to the ground. But the more I think on it, the more I'm living in Banana Splits land. Would any of that work? Would Smiff and Streak listen to me? Would Neil lead them to Hornsby? What if Neil warned Hornsby first? Would Hornsby act before he was caught? He has the gun.

I have no choice. I need to try to get into the flat. I *have* to get that tape. And for good reason. Whatever is on it, Hornsby is desperate to get his hands on it. With the tape, maybe I have a little bargaining power. I don't trust Hornsby, and there is nothing to say that he won't still harm my family if he gets what he wants. If I get the tape and find out what is on it, I can trade it. Hornsby obviously thinks that, as a kid, I'll not consider that. That I'm shit-scared, will do what he wants.

I look up to where the flat must be, but in the dark, there's little to see. It's four floors up. Unlike the other tenement blocks, there are no lights on at all.

I check that I still have the flat key in my pocket. I've the start of a plan in my head. Rush to the close, climb up the stairs and get into the house. Next, find any tapes I can and grab them. Next, throw them from a window into the back green—then the hard part—pray I can get past the guards. In the dark, there might be a chance I can do that. The stairwell inside must be close to pitch black. If neither guard has a torch, it might work.

In.

Up the stairs.

Find the tapes.

Grab them.

Out the window.

Back down the stairs.

It's that simple.

And if I say it a few times more, maybe I'll believe it.

But I don't.

This is a suicide mission.

But one that I need to take.

Okay, Ginger. Get it done!

Deep breath.

Ready.

The tap on the shoulder makes me jump and I yelp.

The sound alerts the guard.

'Who the fuck is there? If you don't fuck off, I'll chib you!'

Milky speaks, quietly, 'Shhh, Ginger. Jesus!'

'I nearly pissed myself,' I whisper. 'Where did you come from?'

'I followed you from the shops.'

'You were out when I called.'

'We were at my gran's. When I was getting off the bus at the roundabout, after visiting her, I saw you cross the road with Neil. I told Mum and Dad I was going to get a sweet at the café and trailed you. When the power cut hit, I nearly lost you. What's going on?'

'I haven't time to explain, Milky,' I say. 'But you can help.'

'How?'

I keep my voice so low that I need to talk right into Milky's ear.

'There's a guy over there, Milky. Near the midden. I need him out of the way. Just for a few minutes until I can get into that close.'

'For what?'

'I'll tell you later. Can you get him to move away?'

'Sure.'

'But you need to be quiet. There's another guard at the front close. You can't let him hear you.'

'Okay.'

'Once you get the man at the midden to move, come back to this wall. Wait on me. Be right here. In this dark, I'll miss you if you wait elsewhere.'

'What's going on?'

I'm conscious that Neil talked about the house owners returning soon.

'Milky, just get the man to the other side of the bin house. Even for a few seconds. I'll be as quick as I can.'

'But…'

'Milky, just do this! Okay?'

'Okay!'

He moves away from me, his shadow vanishing at speed. I slide along the tenement wall, hands rubbing the pebbledash. The close entrance is ten paces away.

'Hoi. Mister,' comes a low voice from the other side of the bin house. 'You're a right wanker!'

'Who the fuck is that?' says the guard.

'Wanker!' repeats Milky.

'I'll fucking gut you, whoever you are!' spits the guard.

I move. I can't tell if the guard has taken the bait, but even if he hasn't moved, he must be looking in Milky's direction. I slip into the close, bum cheeks clenched, waiting on a shout. My first step inside clicks and I look down. My Wayfinders have segs in the heels—the metal slugs will click with every step. Ahead of me, the other guard is framed in the dim light from the surrounding homes. I reach down and pull both shoes off. I feel the cold concrete through the multiple holes in my socks. I hug the wall and grab the stair banister with one hand, while holding my shoes in the other. I pull myself up the first step, eyes fixed on where the front guard should be. I climb, and, as I reach the second floor, I hear voices from below.

'Did you see anyone?'

It's the guard from the back green.

'Nah. Why?'

That has to be the other guard.

'Some wee tit was calling me names out back.'

I keep rising, the voices getting fainter.

'What kind of names?'

'It disnae matter as long as you didn't see anyone.'

'I didn't. Now get back to your spot. Heartbreak will stab out our eyeballs with a fork if she finds us talking.'

I keep climbing.

The stairwell is so dark that I can't see my hands, even if I place them up against my face. I reach the top stair and stop, listening. I thought recent events had topped my fear meter, but this is a new level. I'm trying to concentrate on what I'm doing and, all the while, my head is telling me is to get the hell out of here. I take out the key, feeling my way towards the door. I've no idea how I'm going to find anything in the house without light.

I place my ear against the door and listen. With no sound from inside, I fumble the key around until I find the lock and, despite my shaking hand, manage to insert it. I turn it, wincing at the noise. I push. The door opens.

The rank smell of BO, drink and stale fag smoke rushes out on a tidal wave of heat. I push in, nerves singing. I'm alive for sounds. I yelp as I stand on something sharp, reaching down to discover bare floorboards. I pull out a splinter from my toe, decide, noise or no noise from my segs, that I need my shoes on. Not least if I have to make any sort of run for it.

Shoes on, door closed behind me, I move forward, my segs singing out my presence. I find a door and push it. It squeals as it opens, and I freeze. No one comes. I move into the room. The curtains are pulled back and what light there is confirms that the room is a bare shell. I retreat. I check out the next room, finding it stripped bare as well. The subsequent door is the bathroom. It stinks to high heaven of pish and shite. So strong that I gag. I'm not searching in there regardless of any threats. The next door leads to the kitchen. It has a cooker, a single wall cupboard. A small table next to a wall is all the furniture. I can see the outline of a kettle, a bottle and a few cups on the table. I open the cupboard, feel around, but there is zip.

I'm wondering if I'm in the right place. Whatever tape Hornsby was talking about, there's not many places it could be hidden. The house looks abandoned. The final door takes me into the living room. With the curtains open, the half-light reveals two couches at right angles to each other, a dining table, a sideboard—underfoot is carpet. The smell of bodies, booze and ash is far stronger in here. If Hornsby's tape is going to be anywhere, it's going to be in here.

I check the couches first, pushing my hands down the cracks. but I can't feel anything. I walk around the room, peering in the gloom. There's little in here other than the sparse furniture, certainly no stack of cassette tapes. I circle the room twice, running my hand along the couches again, opening the sideboard (empty), and looking under the dining table (nothing). There's no sign of any tapes. This whole thing's beginning to stink worse than the bathroom. I'm out of here.

As a last throw of the penny, I remember the tape recorder. I run my feet under the couches and hit something on the one nearest the window. At the same time, I hear voices from outside. I run to the window and look down. The red Victor has pulled up outside the close. I can just see Smiff and Streak getting out. I dive back to the couch and pull out the object that my foot hit. It's the tape recorder. I fumble with it to eject the tape, but the mechanism is either broken or stuck. I can't tell if there is a tape in it in this light.

I go back to the window. My heart racks up another twenty extra beats per minute when I see that the car doors are closed. Everyone has already entered the close. I scramble to the hall, tape recorder in hand, and hear voices rising up the stairs. There's no way I'll get down without bumping into them. I try to find some form of calm in my head. What to do? The best I can come up with is to hide in the first room I'd searched, hoping no one comes into it.

I slip into the room, the door squealing as it opens and closes. I sit down, praying to the God of SSEB that the power doesn't return to Castlemilk anytime soon.

The front door opens. I hear Smiff talking, then a higher voice, one that I don't recognise. Sounds like a woman. Maybe Heartbreak? The woman's voice tells Smiff to fuck off and find a drink. There's a faint light under the door that suggests someone has a torch. Another door opens and closes. Then another. I sit, hugging my knees, shivering despite the warmth. A few more doors open and close. The sound of someone pissing echoes. A few minutes pass, the toilet is flushed, more doors open and close. I'd guess that everyone is now in the living room. Time to get out of here.

I have to force my legs to work. To rise. I'd rather stay seated, but that would be madness. I need to leave.

I know the door to this room is going to squeal. That it will ring loud and be heard in the living room. The walls are paper thin. I can hear the chat in the living room, almost clear enough to make out exactly what they are saying.

I stand up. I try to open the door as slowly as I can. It still squeals. Caution to the wind, I just go for it, throwing the door open. I dive at the front door, heaving it wide as a voice shouts out from behind me to stop. Torch light dances around. Tape recorder in one hand, I slide across the landing, find the top stair and throw myself down.

Above me, a voice—Smiff's—screams for me to *stop right fucking there*! I keep going.

'Gobby, Richie,' Smiff shouts. 'There's someone coming down the stairs. Stop them!'

From beneath, I hear muffled shouts. Gobby and Richie must be the two guards.

I keep heading down, each step an opportunity to trip and take a header. The torch light above provides some illumination – it'll also light me up like a neon sign if it's played on me. I reach the first-floor landing and stop. I can hear the two guards working their way up towards me. I hunker down against the wall and wait.

'Do you see him?' shouts Smiff. The torch shines down the stair well.

Smiff's voice is close. A floor up. He has been following me down. I'm now the fish paste in a nutter sandwich. I can't go up and I can't go down. I try to melt into the wall.

'No,' says one of the guards. 'Not yet.'

'Are you both coming up?' Smiff shouts.

The two say yes.

'Don't be so stupid,' Smiff yells. 'One of you stay at the bottom. It's fucking pitch black! He could be anywhere.'

I see my chance. I slide on my backside across the landing towards the last flights of stairs. I slam into one of the guards as he mounts the top stair.

'What the...?' he hollers.

A hand slaps me on the face. I roll forward.

'He's here!' shouts the voice.

I roll away, flipping down the first stair. Without rising, I push myself down, tumbling a few steps before I hit the next guard in the back. He grunts.

'Fucking get him!' yells Smiff. Now even closer.

I pull myself up by the banister. I feel someone grab for me. A hand wraps itself around my sleeve. I nearly lose the tape recorder.

'Got you,' the voice says.

I lift my arm up, seek out the gripping hand with my mouth, open wide, and bite hard. There's a scream, and the hand lets go.

'I'll fucking kill you!' he screams.

His hand brushes my hair, I duck and stagger down the last few stairs, moving too fast for the dark but too scared to move slower. Torch light from above lights up the close. The tape recorder bangs off the wall. I reach the ground floor. Smiff and the two guards are flying down the stairs. I look up. Smiff is one floor up. The first of the guards is only two steps from me, the other is just behind him.

'You!' shouts Smiff as he sees me. 'Bannerman's little shite.'

I rush out of the back close and immediately turn right.

'Milky!' I shout into the gloom. 'Run!'

I hear him move off. I follow.

'This way,' says Milky.

As he crosses the back green, there's just enough light to see him in front of me.

I hear Smiff and the guards exit the close behind me, shouting threats. The torch light is being thrown wildly around. Milky swerves to his left. I follow. We cut straight across the back green. The noise behind is confusing. The walls of the homes around us mean our pursuers cries are bouncing around like a Superball. Making it hard to tell where anyone is.

There's a crunch, and the torchlight goes out. Smiff shouts, 'Fuck!'

Milky and I reach the far side of the green.

'In here,' says Milky and vanishes into a close.

I follow him. We are back to total dark. I slide my hand along the tiled wall. A few seconds later we are in the open at the front of the building. Milky points to his right and we set off.

'Milky,' I say as I run. 'Smiff saw me.'

'Later!' he shouts and keeps running.

We soon emerge from the scheme, back near the West Parish church. We aim for the roundabout.

'Stop!' I say.

Milky slows down but doesn't stop.

'We can't stop Ginger. They'll be looking for us.'

'Where are we going? I told you one of the guys from the car saw me. They know where I live. They probably know where you live.'

'Keep moving. We'll go to the abandoned shed. We can talk there.'

The dual carriageway in front of us is empty. We run across it and, as we approach the shops, we keep moving to our left, past the foot of my street and onto the next one, Rockall Drive, and re-enter Simshill.

We climb the hill, aiming for the corner house where the shed I'd hidden in lies. I hear the noise of a car behind us. We dive over a hedge of the nearest garden, falling onto wet grass. Under the hedgerow I can clearly see the red Victor as it crawls by.

'Ginger,' says Milky. 'They must have seen us enter Simshill.'

He's right. The logical start point for them would have been to drive up our street first. Not this one. The car slows and stops. The doors open. The two guards and Smiff get out.

'Show yourself!' shouts Smiff. 'We know you're here. We fucking saw you. And we know where you live so just fucking show yourselves!'

He's about fifty yards down the hill. He's turning his head, looking up and down the road. They may have seen us enter the scheme, but I don't think they saw us jump the hedge.

'Milky, let's go,' I whisper and begin to crawl across the grass, heading in the direction of the house with the shed.

Milky trails behind me.

'Anyone see them?' Smiff's voice is coming from the other side of the hedge we are next to.

We both stop, falling on our faces.

'I saw them running into this street. They can't have got far,' says one of the guards.

'I'll go check the ginger shite's house,' says Smiff. 'You two look around here.'

As soon as he moves away, Milky and I start crawling again. We reach the road we need to cross to get to our destination. I pop my head up. The two guards are further up the hill looking the wrong way. There's no sign of Smiff. I signal Milky to run. Head down we sprint. We make it across the road, into the deep shadow cast by the corner house. We reach the shed and, once inside, we both slump against the wooden work bench. I listen for the sound of our pursuers but can hear nothing.

'Oh my God!' I say. 'They'll kill us when they find us.'

'What is going on, Ginger?'

I tell him, in fits and starts, about Hornsby catching me in on the way back from school, about the meet at the shops and the stupid tape that he wants.

'But there weren't any tapes,' I finish. 'Just this.'

I lift up the tape recorder.

'Ginger, put on the fire!' he says as he examines the tape recorder.

He clicks the fire button. Light and heat join us.

I don't really need the warmth from the fire. It's ice cold in here but the running and the fear have heated me up to something just short of lava. However, the glow is friendlier than the dark, and friendly is good at the moment. I back away a little from the warming grills.

'I couldn't get it to open,' I say to Milky.

Milky fiddles with the tape recorder and, with a soft click, the cassette door pops open. Milky extracts a tape and holds it up. It's a blank C 90 Phillips tape. My brother has a recorder. He uses the same tapes to record the charts from Radio 1 on a Sunday night, squatting over the pause button to try and cut out the DJ's chat, microphone pointed at his small tranny, me under threat of dismemberment if I make any noise while he is recording a song.

'Is this what Hornsby wanted?' Milky asks.

'Who knows, Milky.'

'Why would he want a blank tape?'

'Maybe it's not blank.'

'We should play it.'

'We should. Does the recorder work?'

Milky points to a small red light near the function keys.

'Looks like the battery is good.'

'Make sure the volume is way down,' I say.

Milky puts the tape back in, turns down the volume and presses the play button. It immediately clicks back up. He presses it again and it pops back up again.

'Flip it over,' I say. 'It's at the end of the tape.'

He ejects it, re-inserts it and presses play. After a few seconds music comes out. It sounds like someone practising the recorder, badly. We both stare at the tape as the 'musician' tries to eke out Do-Re-Mi—and fails. We listen to failed attempt after failed attempt.

'Why would anyone want that?' says Milky.

'Try the other side again!'

He flips it over and presses play. The sound of men talking rises from the tiny speaker. It's hard to make out what they are saying and, before we can figure any of it, the tape stops again.

I yank the tape recorder towards me and pull the tape out. I locate the small tab at one end that prevents recording if you break it off, and snap it with my thumb, flicking the tiny piece of plastic under the workbench.

'I'm just making sure we don't record over this by accident,' I say to Milky. 'If this is the tape that Hornsby wants, then it has to be important.'

I rewind the tape to the beginning and press play. More recorder music, still just as bad. I hit fast forward with play pressed and the tape screeches. The recorder now playing at ten times the speed. Suddenly, the recorder playing stops, and the speeded-up sound of voices takes over. I stop the tape and rewind it to where the conversation begins.

'The Tape.'

Man 1: '...and the girl at the bar told me that she wasn't Julie's sister. I'd have sworn she was. Now, Hornsby fuck off outside and wait 'til we call you back!'

Sound of a door opening and closing

Man 2: 'Thanks for the update on the family life of the Beechwood's bar staff.'

Man 1: 'Fuck you! I was just talking piss until that idiot was out of the way.'

Woman: 'Look. Let's decide what the fuck we are doing here. I need to give Hornsby the Christmas cash to dole out. Do we need him to do anything else? If not, I'll just pay him and kick him out.'

Man 2: 'No we're good.'

Man 1: 'How much is he getting in his Santa bag to hand out?'

Woman: 'Three grand.'

Man 2: 'Whit?'

Woman: 'That's what it takes to sew up a police station nowadays.'

Man 1: 'And that means the Dougrie Road station will be all done and dusted?'

Woman: 'Sweet as a nut. It only takes a couple of bent coppers to let us run free up here at the moment, but I think it's time we thought bigger.'

Man 1: 'Like what?'

Woman: 'I think we should expand.'

Man 1: 'Where to?'

Woman: 'The city centre.'

Man 2: 'Spanner's territory?'

Woman: *'Yes.'*

Man 1: *'Spanner's got a huge crew. He runs Glasgow city centre. Are you nuts?'*

Woman: *'I hear that he's just lost half of his gang to a raid. Most will be in for a stretch at BarL by next month.'*

Man 1: *'Heartbreak, we haven't the men to take on Spanner. Even if he has lost half his team.'*

Woman: *'We don't need men.'*

Man 1: *'How does that work?'*

Woman: *'Same as here. We get the right pigs on the take at Turnbull Street station in town and let them take care of Spanner.'*

Man 2: *'Christ, Heartbreak! Spanner Johnston is a complete psycho. Do you not think he'll have already stitched up Turnbull Street?'*

Woman: *'Maybe, but he's never been weaker. If we don't move in, someone else will. And quickly. You can be sure that any pigs on the take will just as easily open their hand to a rival as to Spanner.'*

Man 1: *'We don't know enough coppers in Turnbull Street that we can go after.'*

Woman: *'We don't need many.'*

Man 2: *'Why not?'*

Woman: *'It's simple. We do what we did at Dougrie. Just find the right beat cop first. Turn him and then use him to find out who else we can go after further up the food chain. You don't need that many on the take to run the show. Just the right ones. And I know just the man to start with.'*

Man 1 and Man 2: *'Who?'*

Woman: *Ronnie Bannerman.'*

Man 1: *'Who?'*

Woman: *'He used to work on the same beat as Hornsby.'*

Man 1: *'How do you know he'll take the money?'*

Woman: *'I hear he is right in the shite financially.'*

Man 2: *'Fuck, Heartbreak! Spanner. Really?'*

Woman: *'We're doing this and if you question me again, I'll chib you!'*

Man 2: *'Okay, Heartbreak. I'm sorry.'*

Woman: *'Now go get that ex pig, Hornsby back in here. I'm…'*

Chapter 12
'Thursday Night Blues.'

THE TAPE STOPS. A few seconds later, the play button pops up as the cassette runs out. We both sit in silence for a moment.

'Jeez, Ginger, they were talking about your old man,' whispers Milky, his eyes wide.

I stare at the tape recorder. 'It could be another Ronnie Bannerman.'

'The woman on the tape said he was polis at Turnbull Street. That's where your dad works?'

I slide down the workbench I'm lying against. My dad's full name is Ronnie Robert Bannerman. The voices on the tape were muffled, but they sounded like the two from the Victor; Smiff and Streak, and the woman that had come with them to the flat in Castlemilk. Smiff, Streak and Heartbreak and, if I'm right, they are after my dad.

'It has to be your dad they were talking about,' Milky says.

I don't want it to *has to be* anything.

'Will your dad take the money?'

I stared at that bloody tape recorder for an age. Things in the house had always been tight on the money front. Two months earlier, my brother and I had lain upstairs while Mum and Dad had a blazing row that resulted in Mum storming from the house. Dad had been at the pub and came home late. Mum had flown off the handle, saying that he spent more money in the pub than he spent on his family. The screaming row had ranged across every aspect of our lives. How they met (and Mum saying she wished she had just fucking walked away). Getting married (and Dad saying he had been told by everyone not to rush into the bastard thing). Having kids (Mum saying it was Dad that wanted them, and she was too bloody young). Buying the house (too bloody expensive). Running the house (too sodding expensive). The fucking food bills. The fucking clothes bills. The lack of any decent furniture (all fucking second hand). Drinking. Gambling. Dad's leeches that he called friends. Mum's friends that drank wine in the middle of the fucking day.

The argument had built and built, not going anywhere new, but when Mum stormed out, it left Dad with no one to vent his anger on. So, he came upstairs and shouted at my brother and I, saying that we had to get out our fucking fingers out and earn more fucking money.

I was the one that worked at the supermarket. Deke did nothing. Not even a paper round. But that was usually forgotten or ignored, but not that night. Dad went after Deke like a Polaris missile. Nearly fucking sixteen. Lazy bastard. Quit school when you can and get a fucking job. No, getting a fucking job now. Clean fucking toilets. Any fucking job. Stop eating so much. Why do you wear out your clothes so fucking quickly?

Deke had cowered under the bedclothes at the verbal assault. Then it was my turn. Fucking too many sweeties. Too many bottles of ginger. No more fucking ice cream in the future. No Christmas this year. And I fucking mean it!

Dad had slammed the bedroom door so hard that the loose handle had flown off on our side. Deke had waited a full ten minutes before he'd got up to put it back, only to find that the handle on the other side had also fallen off, taking the connecting rod with it. We were locked in. I'd thought about jumping out of the window and I'm sure Deke did, but we could hear Dad stomping around downstairs before the TV began to blare, the volume up to maximum. Getting caught dreeping out of the window would have probably got us both killed.

It was the next morning before Dad let us out, Mum still in the wind.

So, when Heartbreak had said, 'I hear he is right in the shite financially,' she was right.

'Milky,' I say, leaving the money thing to one side. 'If we hand this tape to the right person, those three on the tape would be in real trouble.'

'And they would come after us and chop off our willies,' Milky points out.

'They wouldn't know it was us that handed it in. They don't know I have this tape. The recorder was rammed under a couch. Hidden. We could just post the tape through the letter box down at Craigie Street station with a note and run.'

'And that would make all this go away, Ginger?'

'Not all of it—but surely they'd all be too worried about what's on the tape to bother with us.'

'Do you know who Spanner Johnston is?' Milky asks.

'Dad's talked about him sometimes.'

'They say he's the hardest man in Glasgow. A real nutter. A grown-up loon. That everyone is scared of him.'

'Dad's said that as well.'

'And here is this woman, Heartbreak, saying she's going to try and muscle in on his patch. Muscle in on Spanner's patch!'

'I heard.'

'Ginger, if she's willing to do that, how hard do you think it will be for her to kill us, our families, and anyone else we know?'

'She's not going to do that.'

'Why not?'

And that's the killer question. Why not indeed?

'Because,' I say. 'We have this tape. That's why.'

'Ginger, it's that tape that will get us killed. They just admitted that they are bribing some police up at Dougrie Road. They can't possibly let that get out in the open.'

'That's why this tape is so valuable. Think on it! Hornsby knows about it, but the three in the flat don't. If they did, it wouldn't exist. They would have scrubbed it clean by now.'

'And.'

'I think Hornsby recorded this but, for some reason, had to leave it in the flat.'

'Why?'

'Who knows? The last person to use it before Hornsby was playing the recorder into it. There would be no reason to think that any conversation was on there. The sound is muffled. It was probably recording under the couch. Hornsby thinks this is a secret. That he has one over on Heartbreak.'

'And where does that leave us?'

'Not sure.'

'Okay, what do you think we should do, Ginger?'

'Dunno. You?'

'Dunno.'

Milky pulls the tape recorder over and pops the tape out. He lifts into the air to study it in the light of the fire.

'Why not give it to your dad?' he says. 'I mean he must be able to use it.'

It's an idea.

Then it's a bad idea.

A really bad idea.

An idea that sends a chill right down my spine.

'Jesus, Milky, we can't do that!'

'Why not?'

'Because we have a new telly and a new record player.'

'What has that got to do with the world?'

I rub my hair, scratching at a pluke that's growing on the side of my neck. An unwelcome side effect of puberty.

'We just got a new telly and a new record player,' I say again.

'Good for you.'

'You don't get it, Milky. The TV doesn't have a rental sticker on it. It's bought. So is the record player.'

'I still don't understand.'

'Where did the money come from for them both? Mum and Dad are always arguing about money. So where did the money come from for a twenty-six-inch colour TV and a stereo record player, all of a sudden?'

'Dunno.'

Then his eyes widen.

'Jesus, Ginger! From that woman, Heartbreak.'

'That cassette tape recording could be a week or two old, Milky. Maybe Dad's already been approached and taken the money. That would explain the new telly and Hi-Fi.'

'If that's true, there's no way you can hand that tape to your dad. And we can't give it to anyone else. Your dad would get arrested and sent to jail.'

The fire splutters and begins to fade. The gas has just run out. We sit in the residual glow, the light slowly fading.

'Ginger?'

'What?'

'You know you got told not to talk by the two men in the car?'

'Yes.'

'And that doesn't make sense as your dad saw them at your house. So why threaten you?'

'Yes.'

'Well…'

'Well what?'

'Maybe this Hearbreak has got to your dad right enough. Knows he won't talk. If you see what I mean?'

The complexity and scale of all of this is overwhelming. Thoughts trip through my head like stones skipping over the River Cart. Hornsby and his threats to me and Dad. Hornsby and the packages brought to him by Neil McGregor. Smiff and Streak's threats to me. The tape. Bribes. The gun. Hornsby maybe killing someone in the future and us knowing about the gun. Hornsby shooting my dad. Dad taking bribes.

I push myself over to lie on the dusty floor, curling up, wrapping my arms around my legs, rocking from side to side. Milky is staring at the ceiling.

'We could just tell someone that we think Heartbreak is bribing policemen,' suggests Milky.

I could see Milky's thinking. Clear as day. What was the downside to Milky if he told what we knew? He wasn't the one with the dad on the take. He wasn't the one with the threats against his family. He wasn't the one who stole the tape. He wasn't the one spotted running from a gangster's flat. For the first time in my young life, I wondered if Milky would really be on my side when I needed him. But I managed to burst that bubble with speed.

'And what if your dad is also taking money, Milky? He works at Turnbull Street as well. You heard how they make it work. Find one policeman that will take a bribe, then they work their way up.'

'My dad's a constable, too. They said work their way up.'

'They also said that they had a *few* beat cops on the take at Dougrie Road. Not one. A few.'

There's a small flicker in Milky's eyes. Just visible in the dying light.

Bubble definitely burst.

'If we tell anyone about this, then both your dad and mine could be in real trouble,' I say.

'You think my dad is taking cash?'

'What do you think?'

He scratches at his mop of hair.

'Mum and Dad haven't been talking about money lately,' he says. 'And that's usually what they talk about most.'

'And what does that mean?'

The implication sinks in.

'Jesus, Ginger! What in the heck do we do?'

And the truth is, I don't know. I just don't know. I think on asking Milky what the Hardy Boys would do, but that seems wrong. Too childlike. Not adult enough and this is all too adult for me.

'We can't stay here all night,' I say.

'Why not?'

'We need to go home.'

'To do what, Ginger?'

'Dunno, but I'm going to get leathered as it is.'

'You and me both, but so what? We'll still wake up in the morning and this won't be gone.'

'Maybe Ivan has come up with an answer, Milky.'

'Like what?'

'Dunno. But he was going to think on it.'

'He's probably forgotten about it all. Drunk it away.'

'We have to do something, Milky!'

A car crawls past outside. I tighten up my arms further, pulling my legs in to my body.

I felt physically sick right then. A feeling that I'd first encountered when I was nine and I'd stolen a Freddo Bar from the general store at the roundabout. I hadn't set out to steal it. The shop had been busy, and I'd been sent for a loaf. While waiting to get served, I'd stood next to the rows and rows of sweets that ranged along to the till. There had only been one shop keeper serving and the place was full of factory workers just finished for the day. I was lost in a sea of giants while I waited my turn. I'd scanned the sweets but knew I didn't have the money to buy any. A plain loaf was fifteen pence and that was exactly what I had in my hand. No one was paying any attention to me. Everyone was hustling and bustling. My hand sort of reached out and grabbed a Freddo Bar. No problem there. I was still in the queue. To anyone watching, I was just waiting to pay. Except I stuffed that bar into my trouser pocket and, when it came my turn, I had asked for a loaf, paid and left.

It was the first thing I'd ever stolen. You could say it was the start of it all. And far from being afraid, I'd been amazed at how easy it had been. No one had even looked in my direction as I left. No chasing shopkeeper. No flashing blue light of a panda car hunting me down as I walked home. I'd dropped the loaf off at home before sneaking up to the Woods to eat my stolen chocolate.

When I'd returned, I'd nearly pissed myself. There, standing at our door, was the shopkeeper from the general store. Chatting to my mum. I was too slow. Mum spotted me, waving for me to come over. I didn't. I panicked and ran away. I hid out in the Woods, climbed my favourite tree and, hours later, listened to my mum and dad shouting for me as they searched the darkening trees below, torches in hands.

There was no den back then. It would be built, in part, as a response to getting caught halfway up that tree. Me deciding that in the future I needed somewhere safer to hide. When Dad had spotted me, he had yanked my leg, yelling at me to get down.

I'd been dragged back to the house, leathered and put to bed. No mention of the Freddo Bar. No explanation as to why the shopkeeper had been at our door. I never found out why, either. If it was to do with me stealing, it was never mentioned, and I doubted my parents would have let that lie.

Which lead me to believe that if I had just gone in when Mum had seen me, I'd have missed out on a serious skelping and three days confined to my room.

I can still remember sitting up that tree. Scared. And the longer I sat, the worse it got. Me imagining I was going to be sent to jail. Solitary confinement. Key thrown away. Crying myself dry. The worst feeling of my life. No laughing then. That came later. After the Freddo Bar incident.

I say, 'Milky, I'm going home.'

'The gang might be waiting for you.'

'I'm still going home. Sitting here is not going to help.'

'But what if they are waiting?'

'I don't know, Milky. I don't know what I'm going to do about any of this, but I'm going home.'

I stand up, pocketing the cassette tape.

'I'm gone, man.'

Milky hauls himself up as well.

'Well, I'm not staying here either,' he says. 'What will I say to my parents?'

'Say you were out playing with me.'

I push open the door. Milky follows. I skirt the wall of the house, looking out on the street. There's no sign of Smiff, the car or the other guys. I jump the hedge, starting up the hill. I don't look left nor look right nor look back. I just walk. I just want home. Into my bed. Sort it all out tomorrow. Or not. Either way, it's for tomorrow.

I wave bye to Milky at my street corner. There's no red Victor outside my house. No sign of Smiff, or the guards, or Hornsby, or anyone. I shove through my back door and find Mum and Dad talking in the living room, Deke watching the new TV.

'G Plan, Ronnie?' Mum is saying. 'Really? A G Plan dining table. Should we not hold off?'

'You deserve it, Kerry. And don't forget the leather chairs,' he replies.

'Oh, that's wonderful. Isn't it Bobby?' she says to me.

'G Plan,' I say.

'I've always wanted a G Plan dining set,' she beams. 'I hate our dining table. Your Dad thinks we should get a new one. Do you want to see the picture?'

She reaches down beside her and pulls up a glossy brochure.

'This one she says,' pointing at a large wooden dining table surrounded by brown leather seats. A price has been scribbled next to it. Two hundred and fifty pounds.

'Isn't it just *wonderful?*' she smiles as she says it.

I smile as well. Enough of a one to convince Mum I'm happy. But I'm not. A new telly. New record player. Now a new G Plan dining table and chairs. And Dad on thirty pounds a week.

I hear he is right in the shite financially.

'Your tea is in the oven,' says Mum.

No telling off for being late. No harsh words. No threat of violence. I troop back into the kitchen, extract my mince and tatties with oven gloves, plonk them on the table and dig out a knife and fork. I slosh on ketchup and eat, the burnt taste familiar. When I'm finished, I put the plate in the sink and take out a can of Creamola Foam, tip four teaspoons of the powder into a glass, fill with water and stir. I drink it all down in one go before I go back to the living room.

'A hotel, Ronnie,' Mum is saying to Dad. 'Oh my God! A wee break in a hotel.'

'We both deserve it,' says Dad. 'Mary over the road will watch the kids.'

'That would be sensational, Ronnie,' Mum says. 'Just sensational.'

I cross the living room to the sound of my mum quizzing Dad on where and when they are going away. I exit the room, climb the stairs, and throw myself under my covers. Wanting sleep. Wanting out of this. Away from this. Deal with it all later.

I heard Mum laughing downstairs that night. Such a rare sound. Not unwelcome, but unsettling. A sound from somewhere in my past. Like a ghost was calling. My dad laughed too, and he was sober. Laughter and sober did not sit well with him.

They were happy. Sounding happier than I remembered for a long while. When my brother joined in with his stupid girly giggle, I felt like they all knew that I was in a bad place, that they were laughing at me. That somehow my own happiness had been stolen by them. All three roared and I'd pulled the pillow over my head.

I wanted out of it all.

Right out.

The Conversation

'CAN I ASK *why you haven't told anyone about all of this before now?'*

'I didn't feel like it.'

'And you do now? Why? Because of where you are?'

'It's not my first time here, but it'll be my last. Maybe that's why.'

'You can't know this is your last time.'

'I know.'

'Can I tell you a story?'

'Don't you want to hear how mine panned out first?'

'Yes, but mine's short. It won't take long.'

'I can't stop you. It's not as if I have anywhere else I need to be.'

I got a phone call at home a wee while ago. The caller said 'Bet you never thought you'd hear from me again.'

'Who was it?'

It was my brother. I hadn't talked to him in a long, long time. He told me he was ill. Cancer of the throat. His voice was all but gone. He was calling to tell me he only had weeks to live. I was devastated. I arranged to meet him. I had stuff that meant I couldn't do that for a week. Stuff that I should have dumped, but I didn't because of the way me and my brother split all these years back. A dumb fight over a dumb person. A really dumb person. Someone that wasn't worth it.

But the way my brother and I fell out was bad. It hurt me. I thought it was all my brother's fault. Had done for years. It wasn't, but I didn't find that out 'til later. And some of that still burned in me when I got that call from him. Even though my brother was dying, I was still angry. And, heaven help me, I didn't just drop everything and go and see him. I waited. Only a week. But a week mattered. He died the day before I was due to see him. He was rushed to hospital, unconscious. No one knew I existed. He had no one. He died on his own. No friend. No family. A nurse told me she sat with him for his last minutes. She was a real angel, but it was still a stranger's hand in his at the end.'

'I'm sorry. That must have been hellish, but is there a reason you are telling me this now?'

'Sometimes it's too late to say what needs to be said.'

'And?'

'And that's my story. Now you tell me the rest of yours.'

'Because it's not too late?'

'Maybe. We'll see. So, what happened the next day, after you stole the tape?'

Chapter 13
'TGI Friday.'

I'M UP WELL before Mum shouts for me. I'm up before she's even out of bed. I wash, get changed, slip downstairs and switch on the fire. I pull back the curtain on a dark and rainy morning. No red Victor. No Hornsby. Just West of Scotland weather in all its glory. I make myself some toast, open the front door, and lift the two pints of milk from the doorstep. I grab a cup from the kitchen to pour out a glass of milk. I return upstairs, pack my poly bag with the stuff I need today for school. I have double English first thing.

We were asked to pick a favourite book and bring it in with us. We've to tell the class why we like it so much. I have the first edition of the Guinness Book of World Records in my bag. A large, plain green bound book with the title picked out in gold leaf, a harp below. I'd found it at a jumble sale last year. It had cost me 5p. At Christmas, I'd received the latest one for 1974, but there was something about the first edition that I liked. Reading about records that might or might not still stand. I loved the opening few lines in the foreword:

Wherever people congregate to talk, they will argue, and sometimes the joy lies in arguing and would be lost if there were any definitive answer. But more often, the argument takes place on the dispute of a fact, and it can be very exasperating if there is no immediate means of settling the argument.

Written by the Rt. Hon. The Earl of Iveagh KG., C.B., C.M.G of Arthur Guinness Son & Co Ltd, Park Royal Brewery,

London in August 1955—the words were made for Milky and me, my mum and dad—for my life. I wrap the old book in a second poly bag for protection and look at the clock. Milky won't be ready, but I leave anyway, shouting up to Mum that I'm going.

Instead of heading my usual way, I cut to the left at the bottom of my stairs and down the hill. I keep my eyes peeled for the red Victor or Hornsby before breaking into a run for a few minutes. I dive into the park, stopping near the playground, waiting to see if I'm being followed. No one appears and I wander down to the river.

It's swollen with rain. During the summer, you can almost walk across it at this point without getting your feet wet. Now it's a torrent that would sweep you away. I take the path that leads under the old castle sitting high above the river. It's a long way around to get to school, but I need to think. And I need to avoid my pursuers. But most of all, I need to put some perspective on the storm that I seem to be sitting in the middle of. As I exit the park near the old mill, I'm none the clearer on what to do next.

I have the cassette tape in my pocket. I want a copy. I can do that in the language lab in the school. They have a tape-to-tape recorder, and, if I can sneak in at break, I'll be able to make a couple of copies.

I see a dog scrabbling in the wet earth of the mill's garden. Digging it up. Looking for something. That forces my mind to think about the gun that I'd buried, and how Hornsby had known where it was. Someone had to have seen me in the Subby. But who? There was only Milky and I there. I'm sure there was no one else. Sure, somebody could have looked out of their window and seen me. But then, how would they know to tell Hornsby? Or did they tell my dad and he told Hornsby? That

makes *no* sense. If a person saw me in the Subby and told, I'd
have been skelped by Dad. It's a no-go area. And even if they
did see me in the Subby and told Dad, how would Hornsby have
found out? And even if he had, how would he know I was
burying a gun? Or did he just guess?

I stop my thoughts.

This is all way too hard on my head.

Another dog comes along and growls at the first one. I stop
to watch them both. They could be about to fight. The dog that's
digging rolls back his upper lip and snarls at the other. Both are
Heinz 57s. Scabby mutts with no way of telling what kind of
dogs they originally descended from. The digging dog drops
onto his front legs, lowers his head, stretches out his back and
deepens the growl. The other dog circles at a safe distance before
walking away, looking back just once. It runs into some bushes.

Ivan.

The name flashes into my head. We told *Ivan* about the gun.
Ivan Peters knew exactly where I had buried the gun and why.
Ivan knows the whole story. Well, everything except the trip to
Castlemilk for the tape. This is a Hardy Boys moment for me in
every way. A moment of revelation. The key to the mystery.
Hornsby and Ivan know each other? Is that it? It would explain
how Hornsby knew where the gun was.

I pull my hood a little tighter as the rain starts to belt down,
wrapping my hands around the plastic handles of the bags to
keep the rain from getting in through the tops. I need to tell
Milky my suspicions, but I've been wandering too long. He'll
have left home by now. I'm not sure what it means if Ivan and
Hornsby talked, but it must mean something.

With the rain in full flow, shelter is already at a premium
when I arrive at school. Luckily, there's some space near the gym
block where I cower with another twenty odd fellow

schoolmates. Thankfully, none are loons. The loons preferring to brave it out in the rain to prove how macho they are. I scan for Milky but can't see him.

The school bell goes. We all steam our way through the first lesson. I'm second up to talk about my book. I quote the opening few lines, before describing what lies inside. The reaction of my classmates is a little underwhelming, but at least I don't make the mistake of choosing books from Primary School and getting laughed at for picking a kid's book.

At break there is still no sign of Milky. At dinnertime he's still missing. I decide to skip on going home for dinner. The chances of getting caught without taking the long walk back are too high and by the time I walk the long way, there'll be no point in going home.

My stomach grumbles as I stand in the playground. It's crying out for food, but I have nothing to offer it. I'm used to skipping out on meals. It's part of life. Our cupboards bare. But when I'd gone into the kitchen this morning, the food cupboard had been full of tins and packets, a fresh loaf next to the sink, the fridge with way less empty space than usual. So much food was a sure sign that there was some spare cash around.

TV. Record Player. G Plan Dining Set. Hotel. Food.
I hear he is right in the shite financially.

I'm cold and hungry when the school bell goes for the afternoon lessons. I crawl to double Physics: a subject that is a mystery to me but always entertaining. We are working on force and mass at the moment. This means pushing blocks on wheels around and being told why one moves the other when they collide. Thomas Bell provides the light entertainment for the afternoon when he is sent to the headmaster's office for bouncing a block off Stuart Acker's head. Stuart is sent to the first aid room.

Milky is still missing at afternoon break and is nowhere to be seen when the mad rush that follows Friday's bell is unleashed.

I'm usually in a great mood at this point. A whole weekend free of school ahead, but my frame of mind matches the weather—dark, miserable, and promising more of the same.

To make matters worse, I'd been unable to sneak into the language lab to make a copy of the tape. I take the long way home: thoroughly drookit by the time I get to my house. Mum comes home and gets going on the cooking. Dad is upstairs trying to get some sleep. He's on night shift, I think. Mum pulls out the wooden clothes-horse. I strip, draping all my wet clothes over it. Mum shoves it in front of the electric fire and I'm given a towel to wrap around myself. I stand for a few moments next to the clothes-horse, taking in the heat.

When I feel ready, I carefully climb the stairs as quietly as I can, slip into my room and dress. But, before I head back down, I pull out Deke's tape recorder. It's a double cassette player. Deke uses it to make copies of his Top 40 tapes. He sells them to the younger kids. I locate the chat on the tape from Heartbreak's flat. I make a copy. I stash the original back in my cubby hole. I keep the copy in my pocket.

When I get back downstairs, I ask if I can switch on the telly. Mum nods. I sit down to watch Crackerjack. Not my favourite programme, but with the new TV and an unexpected square of Orkney Fudge thrust into my hand by Mum, I'm happy enough to chew and view.

I wonder where Milky got to today. He could have just been avoiding me, although I doubt it. Last night was way too scary for him not to want to talk about it.

Mum lets me eat my tea on my knee while watching the telly. Something that's never allowed when Dad is in the room. The plate of mince and tatties is huge and, worryingly, it's followed by ice cream and jelly. A treat that appears once in a blue moon. Deke plonks himself next to me on the couch. Mum sings in the kitchen as she scoops Deke's tea onto the plate.

I watch the TV, still amazed at the size and clarity of the picture. Deke watches with me. Mum makes three cups of tea and sits on the couch in between the two of us to drink it.

'My boys!' she says, rubbing both our heads.

Her smile is wonderful to see. It lights up my heart. She has been so down of late, but now she is positively radiant.

'Is that a new dress?' asks Deke.

'Came this morning from the catalogue. I bought two. It's so soft. Feel it.'

Deke touches the material and nods. I'm expected to do the same, so I do.

Add dresses to the list of new stuff that's accumulating in our house.

'I also got a new pair of shoes,' she says. 'And tomorrow we'll go into town and get you two some new clothes. You're growing so fast!'

That was true. My trousers are flying at half-mast and my Wayfinders are pinching at the toes.

'The Barras?' I ask.

'Oh no, dear,' replies Mum. 'Goldbergs for us. And then fish and chips.'

Shopping at Goldbergs, the department store, just screamed 'cash is flowing'. Most of my clothes were second hand from the Barras; Glasgow's market of choice for those on a budget, or those looking for the less than legal. Goldbergs was Mum's go-to store for posh stuff. And that wasn't somewhere she went very often.

The mention of new clothes, a trip to town, and fish and chips should have made me feel good. It didn't. It just makes me think that my dad was definitely on the take. I remember looking to the ceiling and imagining him

curled up in bed above me. Happy we had money, but maybe more than a
little afraid at how he'd got it.

'Mum, can I have fifty pence? I'm going to the BB tonight,' says
Deke.

'Of course,' she replies.

And that seals the deal. A whole fifty pence, just like that. No
fuss. No questions asked.

'Mum,' I say. 'Could I have some money for sweets?'

I wait to see if this gets the usual negative.

'Of course, dear,' she says, handing me some coins.

That makes me feel even worse. All my sweetie money comes
from the pay I get for working at Coopers Fine Fare.

'Mum, if we are going shopping, I'm on at Coopers Fine Fare
at one o'clock tomorrow,' I say.

'Don't worry,' she replies. 'We'll be back from town by then.
I have an appointment at the hairdresser at 12:30.'

Another rarity.

'Can I phone Milky?' I ask.

'Sure,' she says.

I'm normally not allowed to use the phone.

Do you know how much it costs to use that thing?

A Dad phrase.

'Just keep it quiet, your dad is trying to sleep. He's on night
shift from tonight.'

The phone sits in the hall on a small table with an address
book next to it. I dial Milky's number and his mum answers.

'Is James there?' I ask.

'He's in bed, Bobby,' she replies.

'Was he at school today?'

'You don't know?'

'Don't know what?'

'He said he was with you last night when it happened.'

An alarm bell rings in my head like a klaxon. Does she know about the flat? The tape?

'Well, Bobby,' she says. 'Was James with you last night? He's in a bad way.'

'Eh,' I say. 'I need to go. Mum wants me. I'll pop down and see him soon.'

'Bobby, what happened last night?'

'I need to go, Mrs Milkwood.'

'Bobby...'

I hang up.

I really need to talk to Milky.

'Mum, I'm going down to see Milky,' I say, leaning my head into the living room.

'Don't be late' she says.

'I won't.'

I grab my anorak from the clothes-horse. It's still soaking wet, but it'll do. Outside it's stopped raining, but a cutting wind is blowing hard. I scan the road for Hornsby et al. Nothing.

Milky's bedroom is at the back of his house. Like me, he shares it with his brother. I sneak around his home and lob up some gravel at his window. I wait and then repeat the process. The third time produces a result. The curtains are pulled back. Milky's brother looks out. He opens the window.

'Hi, Tom,' I say. 'Is Milky in?'

'Why don't you use the back door?'

I don't have an answer for that.

'Is he there?'

'He's not well. What happened last night?'

'Tom. Is he there?'

'He said he fell,' he says. 'But it must have been a big fall.'

Milky appears next to him.

'Get lost!' he says to Tom.

Tom slaps him on the head. 'I'll tell Mum that you have ginger-pubes in the house if he climbs up.'

When he's gone, Milky says, 'Climb up anyway.'

There's a metal downpipe that runs from the roof gutter down past Milky's window. I grab the first stanchion and pull myself up. When I reach his window, I slip in.

Milky is sitting on his bed, bent over a little. Tom is nowhere to be seen.

'Close the window and, if you hear Mum or Tom coming, get in the cupboard,' he says. 'Mum's mad at me.'

'What for? Why weren't you at school? Did you tell her about the flat in Castlemilk and the tapes?'

Milky looks up. I notice the shiner on his left eye for the first time. A real beauty.

'Jesus, Milky! Did Tom do that?'

Instead of replying, he lifts his pyjama top. A massive bruise stretches across his stomach. He turns around and lifts the back of his top. There's another bruise running down his spine.

'And he kicked me,' he says, lifting his right trouser leg, showing off another bruise.

'Tom?'

'No.'

'Who?'

'Neil McGregor.'

'When?'

'He caught me last night, coming home. After I left you. He was waiting on me.'

'What did you tell your mum?'

'That we were playing up the trees and I fell.'

I sit down next to him.

'Does it hurt?'

'Like crazy. Mum's got me on Askit powders, but it isn't helping.'

I study the shiner. It's big, spreading down onto his cheek and up to his forehead. Neil must have really lamped him one.

'What did he want?'

'The tapes. He knew I was there with you. Up at Heartbreak's place.'

'He saw you?'

'You shouted my name up in Castlemilk. He heard you.'

I think back and he's right. In the nonsense, I'd forgotten Neil was waiting on me coming back with the tape.

'Sorry Milky. And you told your mum you fell?'

'What else was I going to say? If I told her it was Neil, she'd have been round to his house in a flash.'

'You should still tell your mum what really happened.'

'Neil will just deny it and I'll just get double from Mum for my trouble.'

'Milky, this is all out of hand.'

'It's also really sore. Neil wanted the tapes badly. When I said I didn't know what he was talking about he went bananas. I thought he was going to kill me.'

'Why didn't he wait on me? Why you? I was in the flat looking for them.'

'Dunno.'

'You didn't tell him about the tape recorder, did you?'

'No.'

Milky had taken one hell of a beating and said nothing.

'Jesus, Milky. That should have been me!'

He tries to smile, but winces instead.

'God, Milky, this needs fixed! We need to tell someone.'

'We tried that. We told Ivan and he was useless.'

'Worse than that,' I say.

'Why?'

'I think Ivan might be the one that told Hornsby where the gun was buried.'

'Ivan?'

'How else would Hornsby know? We told Ivan, he told Hornsby.'

Milky lies back against the wall. He has to shuffle three or four times before he finds a spot that doesn't pressure his bruises.

'We did tell Ivan, didn't we?' he says.

'We did that, and I can only think of one thing to do now.' I say.

'What?'

'We need to find out if my dad and your dad are taking money from Heartbreak.'

'I thought you thought they were?'

'I need to be sure. If they aren't, then I can tell him all about it.'

'And if they are?'

'I've no idea.'

'How can you find out?'

'At Dad's station?'

'Turnbull Street? What would you be able to find out there?'

'I have an idea.'

'James,' comes a cry from below. 'Have you someone in your room?'

'Jesus, Ginger hide!' Milky whispers and then shouts back, 'No Mum. Just me.'

'Tom says that Bobby was out back talking to you,' his mum yells.

'He was, but he's gone.'

I hear her start to climb the stairs.

I push the toys in the nearby cupboard to one side and crawl in. I pull a few boxes over me.

'How are you feeling?' Milky's mum says, walking into the room.

'Better, Mum.'

'Do you need anything?'

'No.'

'I'll be up again shortly with another Askit.'

With this, I hear the door click shut. I push out of the cupboard.

'What's your idea?' Milky asks.

I ignore the question. 'Can you come up town tomorrow after I'm finished with Coopers Fine Fare?'

'What's your idea?' he repeats.

'Can you just meet me at the back entrance to Coopers Fine Fare at five o'clock?'

'Okay.'

With that, I rise and clamber out of the window to wing my way back home.

Chapter 14
'Saturday Mornings Are Not For Lying In.'

MUM HAS DEKE and I up and dressed before nine o'clock. We are down at the bus stop near the shops not long after. While we are waiting on the bus, Hornsby appears at the entrance to the lane where I met him two nights ago. He looks more of a mess every time. His stubble is now a beard, his clothes look manky. I pretend not to spot him, but he clearly sees me. The bus arrives and he watches us leave.

When we get into town, Mum marches us directly to Goldbergs, where she kits us both out in trousers, shirts and shoes. She then takes us to the store's restaurant for an early dinner of fish and chips. We are back on the bus home in time for Mum to make her hairdresser appointment. When the bus pulls in, Hornsby is still in the lane, watching. I'm early for my shift at the supermarket, but I decide it's safer to clock in than hang around.

Mr Marshall, the manager, raises his eyes when he sees me.

'Wonders will never cease,' he says. 'Bobby Bannerman is here early. I need to call the Daily Express and let them know.'

Mr Marshall likes to think he is a comedian. He isn't.

'Well, now you are here, go stack the tinned veg,' he says. 'It needs refilled.'

I wander through to the back-store, pulling on the white jacket that we all wear. It's too small, but it is the only one to be had. I head back out to the shop floor to check the tinned veg aisle. I mark how many cases I need of each product on a scrap of paper and make for the back-store again to load up a trolley. Once loaded, I push the trolley out, grabbing a pricing gun on the way. I reach the aisle and, as I strip each case with a Stanley knife, I check the pricing on the shelf for reference, adjusting the gun. I sticker all the new cans. As I load up the shelves, Mr Marshall appears.

'Pull the old ones forward first, you lazy git,' he says. 'Redo everything you've done!'

I don't argue. There's little point. I just pull all the cans off the shelf and start the laborious task of placing the new cans at the back and the old at the front. It's a pointless pain given the sell-by dates on all the cans are months away. I work along the shelves, stripping, pricing, placing and facing up. Mr Marshall passes by on a regular basis. This forces me to take some pride in doing the job right. Although I always make a point of doing the job right—why do a bad job?

The store is quiet, the early Saturday morning shoppers now gone. An old lady approaches me and asks where the tea is. I give her directions. She returns a few minutes later, having not found it. I'd take her to it, but the store has a rule about that. We aren't supposed to leave what we are doing to show customers where stuff is, unless we are asked by them to accompany them. I read the rules once and I couldn't find that one, but Mr Marshall is a stickler for it. The old lady doesn't ask to be shown, but I lead her to the aisle anyway. On the way back, Mr Marshal stops me.

'Did that lady ask to be shown to an aisle?'

'Yes,' I lie.

'Are you sure?'

'Yes.'

I get back to my shelf stacking. The old lady returns. This time, she wants to know where the apples are. I tell her, but she heads off the wrong way and I know she'll be back. When she returns, I explain again where the fruit and veg is. I notice that Mr Marshall is hovering in the next aisle, listening. I watch the old lady leave once more. She is back before I can face up a single row of cans. I try to explain again, wanting her to ask to be shown, but she doesn't and takes off again. When she comes back for the third time, I put my pricing gun down and lead her to the fruit and veg. She thanks me. Almost immediately Mr Marshall pounces.

'That lady never asked to be shown where the apples were,' he says.

'She came back three times, Mr Marshall. It saved time to show her.'

'You know the rule. Unless they ask you, just direct them.'

'But she would have just kept coming back.'

'Rules are rules. And that's an end to it. Do it again and I'll dock your wages!'

I look at him and something inside snaps. The last few days piling up like a car crash.

'So, Mr Marshall, rules are rules?' I say.

'Yes, and don't you forget it!'

'And is it right that I'm supposed to be fourteen to work here?' I say.

That stops him in his tracks.

'Sorry?'

'I am supposed to be fourteen years of age to work here. Isn't that correct? That's a rule?'

'Are you saying you're not?'

I stamp my foot. 'You know I'm not. You also know that at least five others in here aren't fourteen. But you're short on cheap staff. We keep your costs down. Hiring adults is too dear. Or am I wrong on that?'

I realise that I'm in the process of talking myself out of a job but, at this precise moment, I don't care.

'Don't you talk to me like that, son!' he says.

He expects me to back down. But I'm not for doing that. He might be scary when he's mad and he might be the manager—but compared to what I've been through in the last few days, he's suddenly a lot less scary than he was. A *lot* less scary.

'Isn't Mr Carmichael due to come here on Monday?' I say.

Mr Carmichael is the area manager, Mr Marshall's boss. When he visits the store, Mr Marshall is like a nervous kitten on the subway's third rail.

'What has that to do with anything?' he asks, as he steps in close.

'Mr Gant told me that Mr Carmichael isn't happy with you at the moment. He'll be even unhappier when he finds you're employing underage workers.'

Mr Gant is the assistant manager. He has a big mouth. I've just dropped him in it but, again, I don't care.

'Are you threatening me?' Mr Marshall growls.

I ignore that.

'That's why none of the others who are under fourteen are down to work on the Monday evening shift,' I point out. 'Because Mr Carmichael is here, and you can't risk him asking how old we are. Well, I'm free on Monday night. I might just pop down and say hello. Been a while since I've seen Mr Carmichael. We had a nice little chat last time. He'll remember me. I made him laugh. Maybe I'll tell him it's my birthday soon. Maybe tell him that turning a teenager is exciting.'

'I don't like your tone,' Mr Marshall says.

'And I don't like being told off when all I'm trying to do is help customers.'

A few customers have stopped shopping and are watching us. Mr Marshall looks around, clearly regretting having this conversation here and now. He hadn't expected me to push back. It's the first time I've ever done so.

'Get back to your job, Robert!' he orders.

I turn, deliberately squealing my shoes on the linoleum, leaving a black mark. I'll pay for that, but maybe not in the way I would have a few days back. I'd just seen Mr Marshall back off for the first time. A small shift in the power balance between me and him. And I like it. Like it a lot.

I return to my shelves to finish the stacking. After which I head to the back-store where Mr Marshall points to the cardboard bins and tells me to empty them outside. I gather up the loose cardboard, feed it into the press before filling a trolley with bales. I push the full trolley into the car park. As I tip the cardboard into the bin, I hear a voice, right on my shoulder.

'Where is the fucking tape?'

I turn to find Neil McGregor standing between me and the back-store entrance.

My feel-good feeling from fronting up to Mr Marshall dies instantly.

'I know you went into the flat,' Neil says. 'So where is the fucking tape?'

I'm about to make up a story when he punches me in the stomach. Hard. I double up, falling down next to the bin.

'Tape,' he hisses. 'No shite, just tell me where the tape is! Your wee crap of a mate claimed to know nothing—but I know that's shite.'

He kicks me in the thigh. 'Fucking tape!'

I howl.

He kicks me in the ribs. 'Fucking tape!'

I scream again, curling up as he pulls his foot back for another kick.

'What's going on here?'

I've never been so glad to hear Mr Marshall's voice. He's standing at the door.

'And you can fuck off, Marshall,' Neil says. 'Turn around and walk back in. This has fuck all to do with you!'

I try to crawl away. Neil spots me moving and stamps down hard on my chest. 'Stay there!'

I look up at Mr Marshall. I can see fear in his eyes. A scared adult. His star has fallen so far from my sky in no time at all. From boss, to weakling, to coward in ten minutes. He looks at me on the ground.

'Fucking leave!' Neil says to Mr Marshall. 'Unless you want a bit of this.'

Neil brushes at his Connolly haircut, then sweeps his hand down his sport suit. He's confident. His face hard. Eyes dark.

'Mr Marshall, please,' I plead. 'He'll kill me.'

My confrontation with Mr Marshall in the store now feels like a big mistake. But he wouldn't leave me out here with Neil? Would he?

'If you don't fuck off in five seconds, Marshall, I'm going to chib you,' Neil says.

He whips out a flick knife, snapping it open. Lifting it high, he leaves Mr Marshall in no doubt that he'll use it.

Mr Marshall's face drains of colour. He looks at me again, back at the knife.

'Mr Marshall, don't go!' I shout. 'Please.'

He turns away. I reach up, hand outstretched.

'Oh God, please Mr Marshall. Please!' I'm crying.

He doesn't look back, reaches for the door handle, pulls it open.

'Please don't go!' I yell.

'That's a good boy,' says Neil to the retreating figure. 'Now piss off and have an attack of amnesia.'

With the door open, Mr Marshall hesitates. Neil steps forward, knife high. Hidden by the industrial sized bin and with no cars in the car park, anyone in the street will only see the heads of Neil and Mr Marshall. I'm invisible. I try to push up as Neil releases me to step towards Mr Marshall. With the knife in plain sight, Mr Marshall backs into the shop. He lets the door close behind him and I scream.

Neil turns and looks down.

'Now, where is that fucking tape?'

'And fuck you!' screams another voice. A familiar voice.

Neil whirls around to meet a half brick square in the face. He yells and falls to one side, clutching his head. Milky appears above the bin.

'Run, Ginger. Run!'

I don't need to be told twice. I ignore the pain and rise. Milky is already sprinting out of the car park, towards the main road. I follow him. Neil doesn't move. Milky really brained him with that brick. A full-fat, in the face blow. As I run, I spot a bus heading our way on the opposite side of the road.

'Milky,' I shout. 'The bus. Catch it!'

He hurtles across the tarmac, throwing out his hand, almost head-butting the vehicle's radiator. The bus slams to a stop. He leaps through the doors. I follow. We head upstairs as the bus prepares to move off.

We enter a cloud of fag smoke—half a dozen people smoking away on the top deck. The front seats are free. We take up a pair of seats each, giving us a grandstand view to the front and either side.

As the driver drops the bus into gear, I look back across to the supermarket car park. From up here, Neil is obvious. He's half upright, blood clear on his face even at this distance. He staggers forward and looks up, but is too dazed to notice us. The bus moves away from the kerb. Neil clings to the wall before he falls down again, slumping against the back-store door.

Milky all but knocked him out. Milky could have just signed his own one-way trip to the knacker's yard.

The bus accelerates down a small incline before climbing back up towards our school. The conductor rises up the stairs. I have enough for two single tickets to town. We crest the rise and leave Neil behind.

Chapter 15
'Bus Talk.'

'JESUS, MILKY!' I splutter as I sit back on the seat, eyes still looking back. 'I thought he was going to kill me.'

'Just as well I turned up early.'

'You've got that right.'

I touch at my various wounds and examine the damage.

'The pain will get worse,' says Milky helpfully.

'It already is.'

'Here.'

He digs into his pocket to pull out a packet of Askit powders. He removes one and gives it to me.

'You'll need to swallow it dry.'

I unwrap the paper square to reveal the white powder within. I shuffle it into the centre, fold of the paper, tip it up to my mouth and pour the powder in. With no liquid, it makes me gag. It has a sour, bitter taste that reminds me of aspirin tablets when they are crushed up. I work the powder into a paste in my mouth, managing to swallow most of it. I rub at the rest with my tongue while Milky talks.

'Neil isn't involved in all this just because he's a mule for Hornsby,' he states.

I wave my hand for him to go on as the bus swings ninety degrees to negotiate a corner. From up here, it feels like the whole vehicle is about to keel over, but it doesn't, and we head for a trio of railway bridges.

'He's way too angry and violent to be just doing what Hornsby is telling him to do,' Milky says. 'It has to be personal.'

I nod.

'He's a bad person, but I've never heard of him being *this* bad before.

Neither had I. There was no restraint in what he had just done to me. He hadn't really given me a chance to talk in between kicks and blows. And threatening Mr Marshall with a flick knife was up there in the desperate stakes. I couldn't blame Mr Marshall for backing off in the face of the knife, but he still left me to God knows what fate. He hadn't even tried to talk Neil out of it. He'd just backed away when the knife came out.

I manage to dislodge the last of the Askit powder from under my gums, rubbing away the last traces by poking my finger around them.

'Smiff told me, when I got lifted in the car, that Neil was a marked man.'

'But he was their lookout.'

'Maybe he was playing both sides. And they just found out that Hornsby and him are working together.'

'Why act as the lookout?'

'Maybe he had no choice, anyway up I'm figuring that the reason Hornsby was hiding out in the Woods is because he stole that money mentioned on the tape. The bribe money for the police up on Dougrie Drive.'

'The three thousand pounds?' says Milky, too loud.

'Shhh!' I spit, looking around.

He shrugs.

'You think?' he says.

'Yip, and Neil is in on it.'

'That's why he wants the tape.'

'If Hornsby has taken Heartbreak's cash, it would explain why he is so desperate for that tape,' I say. 'And,' I add, 'if Neil has hitched himself to Hornsby, then he will be right in the firing line with Heartbreak. And the way he went after you and me suggests that tape is their only way out of this.'

Milky sits back, chewing over what I'm saying.

'But how did Hornsby know there was a tape in the first place?' he asks.

I look out the window as we swing towards a string of shops that range along Battlefield Road. The bus rocks every so often as a blast of wind hits it.

'Do you want my best guess?' I say.

'Yes.'

I rub at my chest, screwing my face up. I'm not sure what a broken rib feels like, but it can't be far off what I'm feeling.

'Okay,' I say. 'So, the tape recorder was hidden under the couch in the flat. Out of sight. The flat was near empty. Only one room used, and it was stripped bare, bar a few pieces of furniture. No one lives there. I'd guess it's for meetings only. We know from the tape that Hornsby was sent out of the room just when the tape starts. We also know that the tape runs out before they get him back in the room.'

'And?'

'Well, what if Hornsby pressed record on the tape recorder before he left?'

'He brought a tape recorder to the meeting, Ginger. They'd not let him do that.'

'True, but what if it was there already? Maybe to tape the person playing the music.'

Milky nods, 'That would work. Hornsby sees the recorder, presses record, shoves it under the couch and Bob's your uncle.'

'It would explain why the tape runs out so quickly. He wouldn't know how much was left. Anyway, he hits record but can't retrieve it. He couldn't get to it while everyone was in the room. So he sends me in later to retrieve it.'

'Ginger, you heard Heartbreak on the tape. If she's mad enough to take on this guy Spanner, then she might kill someone who took cash from her.'

He looks out the window as we swing past the Victoria Infirmary, a grim grey building that I'm over familiar with.

'Where is the tape now, Ginger?' he adds.

'I made a copy. I have one and I hid the other.'

'How did you make a copy?'

'I used Deke's tape recorder.'

The bus pulls up to a stop as the conductress comes up the stairs. I ask for two four penny returns to town. She punches in the buttons on her machine. I pay with the sweetie money Mum gave me. The conductress hands me two tickets.

'I owe you four pence,' Milky says.

'I'll add it to the bill.'

A man hauls himself up the stairs, already removing a cigarette from a pack, ready to light up. He studies the two of us. I'm thinking that maybe we are in his preferred seats. He pauses for a second at the top of the staircase. He looks at me and then at Milky and it's not hard to figure what he's thinking. If Milky moves to my chair or me to his, the man could use the other chair. But, as is usual if the bus is quiet, Milky and I are sprawled out. Two seats each.

The bus heaves on as the man lurches towards the back of the bus. When he sits down, he casts us both a dirty look.

'Milky,' I say.'

'What?'

'Let's say we are right. That Hornsby took the cash. That he somehow pressed record and got a little bit of the conversation. And now he wants it.'

'Go on.'

'Well, he can't know what is on the tape. Can he? I mean, he's never heard it. Has he? For all he knows, they talked about the weather, or the tape never picked up what they were saying or ran out or, or, or…'

Milky has another moment to himself before he says, 'He could have heard what was being said when he was waiting outside the room.'

'Now there's a thought. He can't be sure the recorder captured it all, but you're right. When I was hiding in the other room, I could hear the voices in the living room. I'd guess if Hornsby was in the hall, he could have heard the whole conversation.'

'And what does that all mean?'

'He must have been desperate to steal the money.'

'So, did he plan it?'

'No idea. Maybe he did or maybe he didn't. Maybe he's never known how much cash was involved. He gets the packages delivered by Neil. Takes them to the police station. That's his job. But in the hall, he hears the figure of three thousand pounds and thinks to himself…'

'…that's a lot of lolly,' finishes Milky.

I nod. 'So, he heard what was said in the room,' I add. 'Knew the recorder might have captured it and that's why he took brave pills and stole the cash. It would explain why he wants the tape so badly. With that tape, he figures he has Heartbreak over a barrel.'

'It's a big risk, Ginger. If there is nothing on the tape, he'd have nothing. Worse, Heartbreak could have found the tape recorder.'

'If he heard what was being said, Milky, it would be a hell of a thing to have that recording in his possession. I mean, think on it. If Hornsby gives the tape to the police, Heartbreak is screwed. Even worse if Hornsby gets it to that guy Spanner. What then? That tape makes him bullet proof.'

'Man, Spanner would kill Heartbreak if he found out.'

'And I have another thought.' I add.

'What?'

'If Hornsby has cut Neil in, then Heartbreak will be after him as well.'

'True.'

'That would explain why he nearly kicked me to death.'

'But does Heartbreak know about the tape?' Milky says.

'I doubt it. The recorder was well hidden.'

'Hornsby could blag it, Ginger. If he heard what went down in the living room, he could pretend he has a tape.'

'And if Heartbreak calls his bluff? What proof does he have? Without the tape, she'd probably just do him in. With a tape, he can blackmail her.'

'So where does this take us?'

'Dunno.'

'And what are we going to do when we get up town? You said you had a plan.'

'I have a *sort* of plan.'

'What kind of plan?'

'I'm still working on it, but I'm thinking it's the only plan I have that might work.'

The bus rumbles on, filling up stop by stop and, as we trundle down Victoria Road, Milky is forced to give up his seat to a lady with a young kid. The kid has a pair of clackers in his hand. As soon as he sits down, he starts clicking them, smacking the small plastic balls, hanging from string, off each other faster and faster until they are hitting at the top and the bottom of the swing.

We'd just had clackers banned in our school. A few of the kids with parents that had cash had been on holiday in Spain where they were all the rage the summer before. The kids had gleefully brought them back and showed them off in school. But if you played with them long enough, sometimes the balls shattered. There were stories of kids losing an eye. But then again, there were always stories of kids losing an eye, or a leg, or an arm or a combination of all three and more.

'The plan, Ginger?'

I shoosh him. I wave my hand. The bus is full. It's too dangerous to talk anymore. We take to looking through the misted-up windows.

We pass the Odeon at Eglinton Toll. Live and Let Die is on. I so want to see it. It was released last summer, but I didn't have the money to go then. It appeared back on at Christmas and, with Mum now flush with cash, maybe I'll get to go next week.

The thought of the extra cash makes me realise again how much of a mess this all is and how much of a longshot I'm embarking on.

The bus hits the Larkfield terminus. We stop as they swap drivers. Outside, the wind has brought rain and Glasgow is vanishing into its familiar washed-out coat of grey. When we reach St Enoch Square, everyone gets off. Milky and I run up to Arnott's department store to shelter from the rain under the canopy that wraps the store. Dad's police station lies about half a mile from here in the less posh end of town. He won't be on duty. Mum said he was on nightshift tonight. As I watch the rain bounce from the pavement, my plan now seems weaker than the water running in the gutter.

'Okay,' says Milky, as if reading my thoughts. 'Come on, what's the plan?'

'There's a man at Dad's station called Sergeant Calder,' I say. 'He's the duty bar sergeant. He's been at our house loads of times. He's also been around for ever. He also used to be the duty sergeant up in Castlemilk. If anyone knows anything about Heartbreak, then it will be him.'

'What are you going to do? Just walk up to him and say, 'Hi. Can you tell me about this Heartbreak woman?''

'Kind of.'

Milky's face takes on an incredulous look. One that he uses on me a lot.

'Okay. Not quite that way,' I say. 'But he likes to talk and talk a lot. You can't shut him up when he's up at ours. He seems to like me. Dad has left me with him in the station a few times while he was supposed to be looking after me but fancied the pub instead. Sergeant Calder also loves chocolate. You should see him. He's huge.'

'I know him. He's been to our house as well.'

'He could help us.'

'How?'

'We need to talk to someone.'

'That worked well with Ivan.'

'This is polis.'

'And how is that better?'

'It's the best I have. Have you anything up your sleeve, Milky?'

He shakes his head.

The rain is being swept across the pavement, picking up crisp and sweet packets, blowing them into a swirling mass in front of the subway entrance across from us. It's nearly five o'clock and shops are beginning to close up. People are heading for home, heads down, most are hoodless or without umbrellas. It's the Glasgow way. Get wet, moan about it, get dry and repeat.

'We'll get soaked between here and the police station,' says Milky.

'Not if we door hop, Milky, and we can also run through Lewis's if it's still open. Come on let's go!'

I wait until there is small drop in the wind and run, Milky in tow. Every two or three shop doorways we stop and huddle. We reach Lewis's, Glasgow's multi-floored department store of choice, to find it's still open. We climb to the first floor of the giant building, navigating the perfume counters, before dropping to the ground floor at the far end of the building- back to rain and wind. By the time we reach Marks and Spencer's at the corner of Glassford Street, despite our best efforts, we are drowned rats. We run along to the Trongate and, at the cross, head right and down the Saltmarket. We zip left, past the Tontine Hotel to arrive at our destination, Turnbull Street.

The police station sits opposite St Andrew's Square. Dominated by a huge church with a soaring clock tower, Dad once told me that it was inspired by St Martin's in the Field in London.

I had no idea what he was talking about.

I dive into the small courtyard that protects the police station. Around me four canyon walls of red brick rise. To my right is the reception area. Not only is this the Central police station headquarters, but it's also the District Court. There are rows and rows of cells buried nearby. Dad took me in there once. It's a horrible place. I think he was trying to scare me—and he succeeded.

As Milky and I push through the swing doors of the reception, my luck is in when I spot the giant of a man that is one Sergeant Calder, wolfing down on a Bar Six, an oversized mug of tea lying on the wooden reception in front of him.

'Bobby Bannerman and James Milkwood,' his voice booms out as we enter.

Sergeant Calder acts as if he owns the place. Dad says even the high heid-yins are scared of him.

'Hello, Sergeant,' I say.

'Have you been swimming?' he asks and laughs.

The tiled floor beneath us is pooling with water as Milky and I stand there dripping.

'Get around here, go into the toilet and dry off. Someone will go their kite on the puddle you're making.'

He lifts the hefty wooden top that protects the front from the back of the reception area, and we both slip in. As we enter the toilet, he has already lifted a mop and bucket and is seeing to the water on the floor.

The toilet is as cold as it is outside, but we both take off some clothes, wringing them into the sinks.

'Here,' says the Sergeant appearing behind us.

He throws us two police overcoats.

'Give me as much as you want to take off,' he says. 'And I'll sling it all on the radiator for a bit.'

I hand him my anorak and jumper. Milky does the same. We pull on the giant coats and are swamped by them. They must have been hanging over the radiator, as mine is as warm as toast. The Sergeant hands us a couple of towels for our hair.

Once we are a little drier, we head back to the reception.

'So why are you here?' the Sergeant asks.

He is, if anything, larger than the last time I saw him. His black Crimplene trousers are held up by a belt on its last hole. A hole that looks hand-made. As he talks, he constantly pushes his white police shirt back into his trousers. His tunic strains at the double sewn seams in all the wrong places. He's Big Daddy from the wrestling world to me. And could probably give the guys on ITV's World of Sport a run for their money.

'Me and Milky were up town and we thought we'd pop in and see my dad,' I say.

'Your dad's on night shift, Bobby,' he says. 'He won't be in for a few hours yet. Don't you know your dad's shifts yet?'

'I forgot.'

'So why are you really here?' he asks.

Sergeant Calder is nobody's fool. He can spot a smart arse at a hundred paces, and a liar on the other side of the Clyde.

'I wanted to ask you a question,' I say.

'And your dad can't answer it?'

'Eh…'

'Oh, I get it,' he laughs. 'A little personal, is it? Girls?'

I see where he's going with this.

'Jesus, no, Sergeant Calder! It's not that, I just…'

I'm not sure what I just… I should have thought this through a bit more.

'Well, whatever it is, you better be quick,' he says. 'Celtic were playing Ayr away today and won 5-1. The fans will be on the train back up to Glasgow now and that'll mean we'll be bursting with the drunks soon. Those bastards in Ayrshire polis will be packing them on the trains like sardines. Getting them off their patch. Not wanting to deal with any trouble. Half my bloody force is up at Central Station to meet the trains when they come in.'

'Eh, Sergeant Calder, can I ask you a question that won't reach my dad?' I say.

'That all depends, son. I can't make promises I can't keep. Is it about your dad?'

'No,' I lie.

'Well?'

I leap in, feet first.

'Do you remember a woman called Heartbreak from your time up in Castlemilk?'

He stands up, tucking in his shirt, reaching over for the remainder of the Bar Six.

'Why would you ask that? That's not someone you want to be mixing with. Are you in trouble with her?'

'No. It's just…'

Lost for words again.

'It's just,' says Milky. 'That we kind of scratched her car and she saw us.'

'Is that where you got the shiner from, James?'

'Not from her.'

'One of her gang?' he asks.

'A brother of a friend.'

'And does this 'brother of a friend' know Heartbreak?'

'We're not sure.'

'You need to go to your dad on this one,' he says, the remnants of the Bar Six floating down from his lips.

'Sergeant Calder, you know my dad,' I say, following Milky's lead. 'If he finds out what we did, he'll skelp my arse red.'

'And what do you want me to do about it?'

'Can you tell us about Heartbreak?'

He washes down the last of the chocolate with a healthy slug of tea.

'She's a nasty piece of work,' he starts. 'Born and bred in Castlemilk. Her real name is Paula Hart. In her day, a bit of a looker. Liked to play the field a lot and left a lot of men crying into their beer. Hence her nickname. She also used to run with a few local gangs when she was a kid. One of the few girls to do so. Her father, Michael, was the kingpin back then, but he died in a suspicious fire. He had no sons and Paula saw herself as the heir-apparent to the scheme. She had to fight hard. A woman wasn't the natural successor. The gangs are used to men running things. But Paula was harder than a brick wall. She fought the others to a standstill. She got to the top. Un-bloody-touchable by the time I left Castlemilk. We could never hang a thing on her. She was always a step ahead. Smart as hell, and I'm sure she had a few of the polis up there on her payroll.'

He says this with such casualness that I'm taken aback a little. I pull my coat a little tighter around me and ask, 'Do you mean she was bribing policemen?'

Calder laughs. 'You'd like to think we're all above that, wouldn't you, son? But pay being what it is—a few hundred quid every so often can look like a no-lose bet on the nags to some. You learn to live with it.'

'Did you know who was taking cash?'

'I could have guessed, but I'm not about to tell you.'

'And that'll be the same here? In this station?' asks Milky too quickly.

'Where is this really going?' the Sergeant asks.

'We're just asking,' I say.

'Son, I've been in this job a long, long time. I can smell crap if it's doused in a gallon of Chanel Number 5. Last time I heard, Heartbreak was driving a battered old Vauxhall Victor with more scrapes and scratches than a stray cat, and the way you two were wincing when you got changed, you've both taken a good kicking. Heartbreak might be a grade one nutter but I can't see her beating the living daylights out of two twelve-year-olds for a scratch on an ancient motor. So, as I said, where is this going?'

I lean against the radiator, a giant cast iron monstrosity that's spitting hot to the touch.

'Look Sergeant Calder,' I say, lifting myself clear off the radiator double quick as it starts to burn me. 'We've got caught up in something that I can't talk to Dad about. Nor Mum. Nor anyone.'

'And you came to me to do what? Tell me a bunch of lies?'

'No,' I say. 'It's not easy to talk about. Really. But I don't know what else to do.'

The door to the reception area barrels open, and two police constables roll in with a young man between them. He's wearing a bright red, two button, double-breasted blazer and high-waister trousers. He's small, even with his burgundy three-inch platform shoes. His hair is a swept back copy of Jason King from Department S.

He's swearing as if it's going out of fashion.

'I'll fucking kill every one of you! Every single pig and your fucking families!'

The sergeant rolls his eyes. 'Tony, what are you doing here so early?'

'These bastards,' says the young man. 'Lifted me for nowt!'

The police constable on the left shakes his head. 'He was pissing on the window of Krazy House, sarge.'

'Is that so, Tony?' says the sergeant.

'A man needs a piss—so he has a piss.'

'On the window of Krazy House, Tony?'

Do you remember Krazy House? It was a clothes shop at the Trongate. A wild place stuffed with 'What the Butler Saw' machines and pinball tables. A toy train ran around the ceiling, from which two cages were hanging, Go-Go dancers inside. Bouncers on the door stopped kids getting in without parents.

'Tony, you only got out of here this morning,' says the Sergeant.

'Fucking discrimination!' Tony says.

'Correct, Tony,' replies the Sergeant. 'We make it a policy to discriminate against those that piss in public and threaten to kill us.'

Milky and I watch as Tony is booked. A process that would be a lot quicker if Tony felt that he should co-operate. But he doesn't. When he's led away to the cells, the Sergeant turns to us.

'Are you going to tell me what is really going on now?'

'You're going to tell Dad about this, aren't you?' I say.

'About what? You've told me nothing.'

We both stand there.

He approaches us and bends down. 'Look, if you are in trouble, then it's your dads you need to talk to.'

'And if we can't?' says Milky.

'Why can't you?'

We say nothing and the Sergeant closes in a bit more.

'Are your dads involved in whatever it is?'

Our silence says more than we want to.

'Bobby/James you need to tell me what's going on?'

'I really can't,' I say.

'Because you both think that your dads will be in trouble? Is that it?'

Again, our silence says too much.

'Bobby, James,' he says. 'I've known both your dads for years. Both are good cops. Both are fair men. And that's not something you can say for everyone in here. Okay, Bobby, your dad might be a bit sharp and quick to temper, but that's just his way. And James, your dad can be quite distant. But both of you need to go talk to them, tell them whatever it is that you need to say, and I'll tell you why.'

He leans in a bit more. 'Because, and I choose my words wisely, Paula Hart is a real cunt.'

We both gasp.

'And she hangs out with more of the same. There's no way on God's green earth that the two of you can get involved with someone like that and come off well. You're kids.'

'Dad could get hurt,' I blurt out.

'Bobby, your old man can take care of himself. He deals with people like Hart every day.'

'But...'

'But what, Bobby? But what?'

The Sergeant's eyes are dark brown and unwavering. Years of listening to bullshit lie behind those eyes—so do years of sifting out the truth.

'So, tell me, do you think your Dads are involved with Hart?' says the Sergeant.

Nothing from us.

'Bobby?'

Nothing.

'James?'

Nothing.

'Is he?'

'Sergeant, I don't know,' I say.

'But you think he is?'

'I really don't know.'

'What, like taking cash? Is that it?'

Milky was way too quick to ask about police taking money here. I didn't mean to let things get this far, but the Sergeant is a past master at extracting information.

'Sergeant, we don't know anything,' Milky says. 'Not really.'

'A bit late for walking down that innocent road now, James. You know enough that you came to see me and not your dads. Not many kids would do that. Not unless they had good reason. Look, tell me what is going on and I promise I'll help if I can.'

The doors open again. A woman pushing a pram comes in. She shoves the pram to one side and approaches the desk.

'Hiv you seen ma man? I saw him get lifted.'

'Hello Mrs Yoker,' the Sergeant says. 'Your man Tony is in the cells.'

'Whit fur?'

'Urinating in public.'

'That's pish.'

'It is that, Mrs Yoker. He's also as a drunk as a skunk.'

'I hiv a wane that needs feedin'.'

'He'll be home in the morning, Mrs Yoker.'

'He's a lazy drunk. Can I talk to him?'

'Not just now. Maybe later.'

'I need money!'

'I can't help.'

'Hiv you goat a tenner y' can lend me?'

'No.'

'Whit am I supposed tae dae?'

'Tell your man to lay off the sauce for a while. That would help.'

'Y'r a lazy bastard,' she suddenly screams at the rear door. 'Tony Yoker yir a waste of fuckin' space!'

The Sergeant lets her shout for a little while before saying, 'Okay Mrs Yoker, that's enough. Time to go home.'

'There's nae food in the hoose.'

'I can't help you.'

'No fur me but fur the wee wan. He's starvin'.'

The Sergeant looks at the pram and says, 'Give us a minute.'

He disappears through a door and comes back a couple of minutes later. He has a plastic bag in his hand.

'Some milk, some bread and a pot of jam. It's the best I can do.'

'Thanks. But I dinnae ken why I meyret the bastard,' she says, taking the bag of food.

'As I said, he'll be out in the morning.'

She bundles the bag under the pram.

'Tony ses yir wan oh the good pigs,' she says.

'I try, Mrs Yoker.'

'Nae many good pigs in here, right enough. Bit yir wan.'

'On your way, Mrs Yoker. This is no place for a baby.'

'Yir the biggest arse in Glasgae, Tony Yoker,' she shouts.

She pushes out of the door and the Sergeant turns to us.

'Look sons, this place will be heaving soon. I can't help if you won't talk to me.'

'I can't, Sergeant,' I say.

'Okay,' he says. 'Here's what we are going to do. Bobby, your dad is on tonight at eleven. James your dad's not on 'till seven tomorrow morning. I'll be tied up with stuff 'till your dad gets in, Bobby, and then I'm off duty. I'll not say anything to anyone 'til then, but I'll tell him you were in when I do see him.'

My face clearly drops.

'I'm not trying to get in you trouble, Bobby. But I think you've got yourself into something bad. Hart and bad are the same thing. If your dad finds out you were in and I say nothing, there will be hell to pay for me. It's up to you, but if I were in your shoes, I'd go home and tell your dad what is going on. You too James.'

This isn't what I was expecting, although I'm not sure what I was expecting. There's no way I can talk to Dad on this. Not if he's on the take. What would he do to me?

'And,' says the Sergeant, 'I'll tell you both something that you should listen to. Both your fathers have fifteen years on the beat. Neither have ever wanted promotion. They like it on the street. Some men do. Some don't want the responsibility that comes with stripes. They want to put their shift in, help people, give the bad guys a kicking and get on with the rest of their life. There's nothing wrong with that. God alone knows, I could do with a dozen more of your dads and then some. Things aren't easy around here at the moment. The pay is crap and there are a lot of disgruntled police officers that feel they don't get the reward they should for dealing with the pish that Glasgow's scum have to offer. And that makes them easy meat for the criminals with money. Bastards like Hart. But I'll tell you now, Bobby Bannerman and James Milkwood, that's not the way either of your fathers work. It's not their way. Both are good men.'

I think about the new telly, the other stuff in our house and I'm not sure.

'And I know both of your mothers,' he adds. 'And they would die if they thought your dads were up to no good. Especially your mum, Bobby. Given what she went through as a young woman, she knows better than most what kind of life you live when you get in tow with shite like Hart. So, go home and think on it. Talk to your Dads! That's all I can say.'

I'm about to ask what he means about my mother when the door slams open. Two men, wrapped in green and white scarves are pushed in ahead of two constables. Both Celtic fans are singing to high heaven.

'The start,' says the Sergeant to both of us. 'Now go get your clothes. Go home!'

He turns to the first police constable behind the two football fans and says, 'What do we have here?'

Milky and I go back to the toilet. A few seconds later the Sergeant appears and hands us our still wet stuff. We pull it on, the material clinging to our skins like a bogie sticking to an upper lip on a cold day. We both step back into the reception. For a moment we hover near the radiator watching the two Celtic fans being processed—trying to absorb as much heat as possible before returning to the wind and rain.

The main door opens again and in rushes Ivan Peters.

Milky and I do a classic double take.

The Conversation.

'I KNEW EDDIE Calder.'

    'The Sergeant?'

    'Yip.'

    'You did?'

    'Well, not me, exactly. My grandpa did. Most anyone that lived in that neck of the woods knew Eddie Calder back then. As that Mrs Yoker said, he was one of the good ones. My old grandpa used to talk about Eddie now and again. Said he was someone you could trust to give you a bit of straight advice. Regardless of who you were. I can see why you went to him.'

    'In hindsight, my conversation with him back then was so bloody stupid. I was too rash—just way too young. I rushed in. Didn't think it through. But you don't, do you? Not as a kid. How did you grandpa know Calder?'

    'You could say they he was in the same game.'

    'For or against?'

    'Mostly for. Occasionally against. Anyway, it's getting early—get on with the story. Ivan Peters has just rushed in.'

Chapter 16
'An Evening Of Change.'

IVAN LOOKS AT us before approaching the reception desk, nodding at Sergeant Calder as he waits behind the two arresting officers. He doesn't seem in the slightest surprised that we are there. The Sergeant waves back at Ivan, indicating for him to sit on the bench near the door. Ivan turns, sits down, staring at us as the Sergeant finishes processing the football fans. Ivan's usual smile of welcome is patently missing, replaced by a deep scowl that suggests all is not well with us being here. I expect him to come over and say hello, but he just sits there, glaring.

The Celtic fans are duly put through their paces and hustled off to the cells, leaving Milky, me, Ivan and Sergeant Calder looking at each other.

'Ivan,' says the Sergeant. 'Long time, no see!'

'Trouble,' Ivan says, pointing to the fans.

'No, good guys that just overdid it.'

Ivan looks at us as the Sergeant speaks.

'So, Ivan, what brings you back to this neck of the woods?' the Sergeant asks.

The word woods makes me jump a little.

Ivan stands up and walks across the reception area, eyes on us, not the Sergeant. I feel about as welcome as a dog turd in school custard.

'Eddie,' Ivan says, reaching out to shake the Sergeant's hand. He turns to us 'And what brings you two here?' he asks.

'We were in to see Dad,' I say.

'Is he not on night shift?' replies Ivan.

Now, how would he know that?

'Eh,' I reply. 'He is. I got his shifts mixed up.'

'Why are you here?' says Milky.

'Ivan used to work here lads,' says the Sergeant.

'Work? Here?' I say.

'Also did my job back in the bad old days up at Dougrie Road as well,' he adds.

'Mr Peters,' I exclaim. 'You were a policeman?'

'A sergeant,' he replies. 'Just like Eddie here.'

Clearly, my ability to spot polis is not as good as I thought it was. In the years I've known Ivan he had never hinted at, nor had I even vaguely guessed at, him being polis.

'I had a life before being a janny,' is his next reply.

'And you worked in Castlemilk?' Milky asks.

'I can give you lads a lift home,' Ivan says. 'Just give me a minute with Eddie here.'

The alarm bell ringing in my head is so loud that I fear someone else must hear it. I already think that Ivan is the one that told Hornsby about where I'd planked the gun. But now I'm wondering who else he knows and who else he has talked to. Heartbreak had police on the take up on Dougrie Road. Was Ivan one of those on the take? And if he told Hornsby about the gun, then maybe he will know everything that Hornsby knows. Tape included.

I walk over to the desk.

'Mr Peters,' I say, staring up at him. 'You must know some of the bad guys in Castlemilk.'

He tries to blank me, but my implication is as subtle as Noddy Holder's voice.

'And even the ones in Simshill,' adds Milky.

'And the ones up town,' I add.

'Wait outside,' he says. Voice ice cold. 'I said I'd give you a lift.'

Sergeant Calder lifts the wooden panel. We traipse out into the reception area, eyes on Ivan.

'And, lads,' Ivan says. 'If I were you, I'd think about giving up what doesn't belong to you.'

'Sorry, Mr Peters,' I say. 'What do you mean?'

'You asked me for a little advice the other day—and I'm giving you it. It's not a good thing to hang onto something that isn't yours.'

'What sort of thing?' says Milky. 'What is it that we are hanging onto?'

'You know,' he replies.

Sergeant Calder watches the exchange with a creased face. One that he probably uses fifty times a day when some low life is piling on the crap in an attempt to talk themselves out of jail.

'I'm sure I don't know what you're talking about,' I say.

Ivan leans off the desk. His face hasn't a hint of the warmth that I'd grown accustomed to in his office.

'Being funny, son,' he says, 'is not good for your health. Now wait on me outside!'

He turns to Sergeant Calder, showing us his back, and asks after the Sergeant's wife. Milky and I wait a moment before deciding that leaving is our only choice.

Outside, the rain is still falling hard. The courtyard protects us from the wind, but not the heavens. Through the entrance, I can see wave after wave of water been blown along the road as successive gusts blast through the city.

'Well, that seals the deal,' I say.

'How did we not spot that Ivan was ex-polis?' Milky asks. 'You'd think someone would have said.'

'He must have told Hornsby about the gun. Polis stick together.'

'And he's probably going to tell Sergeant Calder about it all.'

'And he knows about the tape.'

'He does?'

'Of course, Milky. He just told us to give back what isn't ours.'

'He means the gun.'

'No, he doesn't. If he's talking to Hornsby, then he'll know he already got the gun back. He can only be talking about the tape.'

'I don't think we should take any lift from him.'

'I totally agree.'

'Maybe Ivan was one of Heartbreak's policemen that took cash up in Castlemilk.'

'That would be dangerous for him, Milky. Heartbreak wouldn't take well to Ivan helping Hornsby, if he took that cash. He couldn't afford Heartbreak to find out that's he's helping Hornsby. Could he?'

'You know he'll ask the Sergeant why we were here.'

'He will that, Ginger.'

'And then the Sergeant will tell my dad and he will talk to your dad and by tomorrow morning we'll both be up to our necks in brown stuff.'

'Unless we tell them both first.'

'Even if we tell first, Milky. *Even* if we tell first.'

Milky doesn't like that answer, so he moves on. 'Ginger, the Sergeant didn't think your dad or mine were on the take. At least, that's what it sounded like to me.'

'I know, but that doesn't explain where all the money in our house has come from.'

'No. So what do we do now?'

'That, James Alexander Milkwood, is one big question.'

We should get out of here, but I need another plan of sorts first. Ivan might want us to ride with him, but he can't force us to get in his car. Not here at a police station.

Can he?

'Milky, we have maybe five or six hours to straighten this out before Sergeant Calder tells my dad we were here. We have the tape. We know what is on it. We know about the missing cash. We know about Heartbreak and her plans. We know a lot. That will protect us and our dads. Heartbreak won't want the tape getting out. I think we just do as Sergeant Calder says, confess all, and take what is coming.'

Milky huddles next to the wall, trying to avoid the rain. 'And if our dads *are* on the take?'

'Okay, Milky, think on it. If our dads are taking cash, the last thing they need is for that tape to get out.'

'And Heartbreak would probably thank them for getting the tape.'

'True.'

'And they can't afford for Hornsby to talk. Not if they are part of it all. So, they would silence him.'

'And hand him over to Heartbreak.'

'Would they really?'

'If they are taking cash, probably.'

'And the same goes for Neil McGregor.'

'They'd hand him over, again, if they are on the take.'

'And Ivan.'

'Well…'

'Okay, Ginger, stop with that!'

'But if our dads are clean,' I say. 'Then they will go after the bent police at Dougrie, and warn Turnbull Street. Then they'll probably still leave Hornsby and Neil to Heartbreak. And maybe even go after Heartbreak, if they can pin anything on her. The only thing I really know is that, one way or another, our dads need to know the tape exists. Then let them sort it all out.'

'And that will end it?'

'I don't know, Milky, but I don't want beaten up again. I don't want to be looking over my shoulder for Neil or Hornsby or even Heartbreak, especially if she finds out about the tape. I want this over.'

'We will get real hell from our Dads for this.'

'Better that than the alternative.'

The door to the reception bursts open. Ivan flies out. He starts across the courtyard. Spotting us, he slams to a halt, wheels around. I look at Milky. We both move away from the wall, aiming for the way out, but Ivan cuts us off, forcing us back to the wall.

'Right!' he says. 'I don't know what the two of you are up to, but it ends now. Eddie told me that you've been asking some dumb questions.'

'Dumb?' I say.

'Why were you talking to him at all?' he asks me.

'I told you I was here to see Dad.'

'Fucking shite!' he growls loudly. 'Look, I know all about that fucking tape and I want it.'

In the years that I've known Ivan, I've never heard him raise his voice or swear at me. He's just done both.

'Look!' he says, checking that the courtyard is empty. 'You may think you have some nicey, nicey relationship with me. That all those bars of tablets and moments in my office were something special. Well, let me disabuse you of that notion right now. The job at the school is for pish. But it's what I have, and getting the likes of you to do me errands made it all a bit easier. And that was it. End of. No more to it.'

It's as if an evil twin has appeared before me.

'I hear that you have a tape,' he continues. 'Something that some guy called Hornsby wants. And I want it before him. Got it? And you're both going to go fetch it when we get home.'

There's no reply to that from either of us. We are stunned by the change of person before us.

'Now both of you get in my car! I want that tape as soon as possible. Do you understand?'

The wind howls outside the courtyard entrance, the sound of rain battering off the cobbles filling the silence.

Ivan stands to one side. 'Get moving!'

Neither of us shift an inch.

'Do you know what, Mr Peters?' I eventually say.

'I haven't time for your kid shite,' he says. 'We are going to get that tape and we are going to do it fast.'

'Do you know what, Mr Peters?' I repeat.

'Just move!'

'Do you know what, Mr Peters?' I say again. 'Milky and I are not bad kids.'

'Look, I don't care. Just get your skinny arses in my car!'

'We're really not bad kids,' I say, looking up at him. 'We're really not.'

'I…'

'We didn't mean to get into any of this, Mr Peters. And I think I made the mistake of thinking I could fix it all without help from my mum or dad. But I can't. I can't fix this. I'm not sure anyone can fix this. It all seemed like a game at the start.'

'I'm not in the mood for your chat. Get your arse on the move!' he snaps.

I ignore him 'But when I think on it, I *knew* it was never a game. I was just being stupid. After all, I'm a kid. And a dumb one. One that thought you were a nice man. Someone we could trust.'

'You're making me cry, son.'

He turns away.

'But I can't trust you. Or anyone. I'm not coming with you, Mr Peters. And if you want to try and force me, I'll scream and scream. And in here they know my dad. That will stand for something. I'm not getting in your car, Mr Peters. But I am going home. I'm going home and I'm going to tell my father everything. About it all. Every little thing and then I'm going to take whatever punishment is coming. And I'll tell him about you. That's what I'm going to do, Mr Peters. That's exactly what I'm going to do. I don't want to be part of this anymore. As Mum often says when I get out of hand: *No more games, Bobby*. So that is exactly what I am going to do. Go home. Tell all. Including about you, Mr Peters, including about you.'

Ivan wipes water from his head.

'You are getting in my fucking car!'

'No, I'm not,' I say, trying to keep my voice strong.

He looks around.

'Okay, do what you want, son,' he says. 'But first you'll bring that tape to my house tonight. You've no idea what or who you are fucking with here.'

'No, Mr Peters,' I reply. 'I'm not fetching anything for you or anyone else. Are we Milky?'

'That's right,' Milky says, backing me up. 'No more games is just about right.'

'You think?' Ivan says. 'You think it's that easy? You tell your dad, and this all goes away?'

'Don't bother with the threats, Mr Peters,' I say. 'I've had enough of them.'

'And your dad? Will he take well to threats?'

'My dad,' I say, 'is Glasgow polis. He'll know what to do. I should have gone to him long ago.'

'And your mother?'

That stops me.

'What about Mum?'

'How will she take to threats?'

'You wouldn't hurt my mum? You're ex-polis.'

'There are things about your mother that you don't know. Things that would hurt you and your family if they got out.'

'Like what?' I say.

'Do you know what your mum did before she met your dad?'

'I don't care.'

'I think you will care, because unless I get what I want, I'll broadcast it on the BBC. So, get that tape!'

I decide to walk. He lets me past but doesn't stop talking.

'You really don't want me to talk,' he says, as Milky also slides past him.

We both keep walking.

'Do you know your dad met your mum not far from here?' he shouts after us.

I head for the exit.

'Up near the Barras,' he says, raising his voice. 'In a tenement flat.'

I reach the arch that protects the entrance to the station.

He shouts his last words across the space. 'In a brothel, Bobby Bannerman! He met your mother in a brothel. Now wouldn't that fuck up life if that news got around Simshill?'

Chapter 17
'A Saturday Night On The Town.'

I DON'T TURN back when I hear those words from Ivan. I just keep walking. I turn left. Milky runs to catch up with me. We walk away. I expect Ivan to chase us down. A few minutes later, he crawls past us in his car, window down.

'Tape. Mine. Tonight,' he shouts. 'Bring it!'

I watch the car turn the corner.

'Is what Ivan just said true?' Milky says.

I'm still processing what Ivan just told me.

Brothel?

Mum?

As far as I knew, my mum has been working on factory floors since she left school.

Brothel?

'That can't be true,' says Milky.

Until a year earlier, I'd not a clue what a brothel was. Then there was a police raid on a house not far from our school. Multiple panda cars and a lot of fuss. I got the story second-hand from a number of sources. How the police cars had piled in, all at once, and how the door of the house had been kicked in. Of how a bunch of women were marched from the house and put in police vans. Of how two men, one of them the dad of a girl in our year in school, were marched out in handcuffs. Of how the police removed bags full of stuff from the house. Of the headline in the Evening Times that night:

'Brothel Uncovered in Southside Suburbs.'

Our Primary School was alive with stories about the house, and exactly what a brothel was. Something of a revelation to many. A source of misinformation for most. Parents were disgusted, or pretended to be so. They refused to talk about it to the kids, deep-seated embarrassment that Simshill had become a focus of attention for something so dirty. But amongst themselves, it was the gossip to end all gossip.

My mum, usually one to try and answer even my most stupid questions, refused to discuss the subject. Dad skelped me a couple of times for bringing it up.

And now Ivan was telling me that Mum had been in a brothel when she had met my dad. And that couldn't be right! Mum had told me that she met Dad on a bus. Him getting on the bus to go to work. Her with shopping bag in hand, trying to get off. A shopping bag whose handle chose that moment to break and spill her messages over the bus floor. Dad had helped her pick up the shopping. Stepped back off the bus to make sure Mum was okay. According to Mum, they chatted for a while. Dad missed the next two buses, before asking her if she would like to go to the dance on Friday night at the Plaza. She had agreed. That was the story I knew. The story I grew up with. Only now Ivan was telling me there was no bus, no broken handle on a shopping bag, no chat at the bus stop. Now there was a brothel up near the Barras.

'Is it true?' says Milky.

'No!' I spit.

'Why would he say it then?'

'Why do you think, Milky? Why do adults say anything? Eh? I'll tell you why. To get what they want. That's why they say what they say. To get what they *want*. And Ivan wants that bloody tape. And that's why he's lying about mum.'

'You think?'

'Yes. That's what I think. That's exactly what I think.'

But it's not what I think at all. I'm not thinking he's lying. I'm thinking that he *might* have been lying. 'Might' being the word I dislike.

'But what if he's right?' says Milky as we turn onto the Saltmarket.

'He's not.'

'Okay. But...'

'He's not,' I snarl. 'He's bloody not!'

I'm not looking at Milky. Instead, I'm storming up the street, trailing him in my wake.

'Okay, Ginger. I believe you,' he says. 'But if he says that to anyone else, they might believe him.'

'No one will believe that rubbish.'

But that's not true. Not where we live. Where we live, they could easily believe him.

'Dad would kill him if he said anything,' I say.

'But it would still be out there.'

'Forget that. It's time to end this, Milky. I'm going home to do that right now.'

Milky walks by my side. Neither of us is trying to avoid the rain by sheltering. We are both ploughing a furrow down the middle of the pavement. Hoods down. Taking the weather full in the face. A tramp stumbles from a doorway in front of us. He tumbles to the pavement, vomiting a thin stream of yellow as he lands on the ground. He splashes my shoes in spew and I leap into the air. Milky has to jump over his body. On any other day that would have grossed me out, and Milky and I would have been laughing about it five minutes later. There's no laughter today. Not even my inappropriate version. As the drunk rises, he tries to clean himself. I step off the kerb and slosh the spew from my shoes in the running water of the gutter.

Home. I just want home.

'Ginger,' says Milky, as we reach St Enoch's Square.

'I don't want to talk.'

'I know you don't, but I need to tell you something.'

We reach the bus shelter, but it's full and the end of the queue is out in the rain. We join it, hoods still down.

'Please, Ginger. I just need to tell you one thing, then I'll shut up.'

'It won't make any difference, Milky. I'm going home to tell everything and that's that.'

'Okay. I get that, but please let me tell you one thing.'

'It's a free world, Milky.'

He pulls me slightly out of the queue, getting himself between me and the others.

'Don't get mad with me on this,' he says, quietly.

'About what?'

'Please, Ginger, just don't get mad.'

'What is it?'

'It's about what Ivan said about your mum.'

'I don't want to hear it.'

'You need to, Ginger. You do!'

'No, I don't.'

He stops talking and stares at his shoes.

'Okay, what, Milky, what?'

'Look, I'm not saying that Ivan is telling the truth, okay?'

'Bloody right. It's a bag o' shite!'

'It is. But...' He kicks at the ground.

'Just talk, Milky!' I half shout.

He talks, 'Look, a while back your dad and mine were in our front room drinking whisky. I was in the kitchen, doing homework, and I heard them talking. Dad can be loud when he's had a drink. Most of the stuff they were saying was boring. In fact, until Ivan said what he just said, I thought all their chat that night was just the usual rubbish. Mostly about work. But something they said now sounds a little less rubbish.'

'What?'

'Well, my dad said one thing. It sounded odd, but I never thought about until back there.'

He stops talking again. I feel like kicking him.

'What? Milky. What? Just tell me!'

'They were talking about the brothel on Elmore Avenue. You know, the one that made the papers. Well, they knew most of the coppers that took part in the raid. I wasn't listening too hard to the chat. More dipping in and out. But when they talked about the brothel, my ears pricked up. You know? In case they had new information. And that's when your dad said that you never know where the girls come from in brothels. He said they come from all walks of life. Then they talked about what became of the women from Elmore Avenue. And my dad said that most would go back to working somewhere else. And your dad said that maybe one would go onto marry one of the coppers that raided the place. And they both laughed. But not a nasty laugh. Do you know what I mean?'

'Milky, what the hell does that have to do with this?'

'I'm just saying.'

'Just saying what? That my dad and your dad were laughing about mum coming from a brothel?'

'No.'

'Of all the conversations you've heard, you happen to remember that one?'

'I heard what I heard.'

'Aye, and you lie what you lie.'

'What does that mean? I'm trying to help.'

I step in, close. 'Milky, how are you trying to help? How can remembering some half-baked conversation between two drunks help me? Milky, how are you *ever* trying to help me? Ever? That stupid den was your idea. If we hadn't built the den, then there would be no Hornsby or gun or tape or any of this.'

'That's not fair. You can't blame me for all of this.'

'I can. I should have just talked to Dad up front. But you talked me out of it.'

'It was *you* that decided not to tell him. Not me. You saw Hornsby in your house and bottled it.'

'I did not bottle it!'

'You bloody did!' he shouts. 'Okay, go home, Ginger. Tell all and if Ivan is telling the truth about your mum, then what? Do you think that'll go down well with the neighbours or your dad or... your mum, Ginger? Do you?'

I throw my arms up and look him straight in the eye.

'My mum,' I scream. 'Is not a prostitute!'

Every single person in the queue turns and looks at me.

I know a few.

Shit...

A red mist descends. I slap Milky hard across the face before storming off. I skirt St Enoch Square and, with no destination in mind, end up by the side of the River Clyde. I cling to a barrier that's so low it wouldn't stop idiots like me jumping in. I begin to cry. Tears flowing. No inappropriate laughter. Just plain old-fashioned tears. Gallons of old-fashioned tears. My head hangs out over the flowing river water. A dark ribbon of filth that's being splattered by rain drops. The tide has pushed the water high up the stone bank. Close enough to touch if I climbed over the barrier and leaned down a bit.

'Son, are you okay?'

I don't look up.

'Do you need help?'

The voice from behind me is female.

'It's dangerous hanging out over there, son. You could slip.'

'Go away,' I say.

'Happily, if you'll just step away from the edge of the river.'

In a stupid act of defiance, I slide myself a little further out over the barrier.

'Oh, don't be so daft,' says the voice.

'I'm not daft!'

'Well, you could have fooled me. You fall in there, son, and it'll be the Riverman that'll fish you out from the King George V dock with his pole. He'll dump your dead body in his rowboat. Is that how you want your family to remember you? Drowned in a river of shit?'

'Go away.'

'I tell you what, let me push you in and I'll go away.'

I'm not sure I heard that right.

'Well,' the voice continues, 'if you are determined to hang out over there, I'll give you a hand. I'm late as it is. But one way or other, I'm not leaving 'til you're in the river or safe on the pavement. I've a train to catch, so make your mind up. I'll give you ten seconds and, if you haven't decided, I'll just give you a wee shove, then I can be on my way.'

I try to push back a little, conscious that I'm close to over-balancing, but my hand slips on the wet metal fence. I lurch forward and, for an instant, I'm heading for the river. My head suddenly snaps back, the collar on my anorak grabbed from behind. I fly back, landing on my backside on the pavement.

'Son, you nearly took a header.'

I look up. The voice belongs to a woman dressed in a dark grey overcoat, a Rainmate wrapped tight around her head. She's tiny. Smaller than Milky. She still has my hood grasped in her hand.

'I didn't want to,' I say. 'I wasn't going to…'

'Most people don't, son. Most people don't. Now get yourself home!'

She shuffles away and I watch her as she heads up Dixon Street towards the bus terminus.

I think she might just have saved my life. I shout after her. 'Thank you!'

She doesn't turn back and, at this distance, I'm not sure if she heard me or not.

I squat on the pavement, my trousers soaking up water where liquid hasn't yet invaded. A delivery van rumbles past me. It catches a puddle in the gutter, sluicing a wave of dirty rainwater over me. I don't move an inch as the fluid flows over my face, through my collar and down my chest. A car approaches. I brace for another wave, but it misses the puddle.

The rain is turning to sleet. My feet are turning to blocks of ice. My head is empty of thoughts. My eyes full of pavement. My heart packed with lead. My world darker than anytime I can remember. I see nothing in front of me. Just a wall of misery.

A train rumbles over the Central Station bridge nearby. Maybe bringing some early evening revellers in for the night before taking away the last of the shoppers. I glance at the road as the reflective flicker of the train carriage lights ripple on the wet road below the bridge. Another car approaches the puddle. I take a second drenching, swallowing some of the mucky water. I cough it out, lie back. Staring at the sky. Clouds invisible against the streetlight. I close my eyes.

'What the heck are you doing, Ginger?'

I open my eyes to find Milky standing over me.

'Get up, Ginger!'

I close my eyes again. Milky kicks me, gently.

'Come on,' he says. 'This isn't helping.'

'Nothing will help,' I say, my eyes still closed.

'What are you going to do? Lie here all night?'

'Maybe.'

'Stop being a baby. Get up!'

'And do what?'

'I don't know. What would the Hardy Boys do?'

'This isn't a kid's book, Milky. This is serious.'

'Do you think I don't know that? But lying in the street isn't going to do anything that will help make it less serious.'

Another car rolls by. Milky leaps out of the way of the wave. I take it full on. I still keep my eyes tight shut.

'Look, Ginger. If you don't get up,' says Milky, 'I'm going home and telling all. It's up to you.'

'My mum isn't a prostitute,' I say.

'I never said she was.'

'You said you heard it.'

'I heard what I heard. It might be nothing, but I'm only giving you ten seconds to get up and then I'm off for the bus. There's one waiting at the terminus right now. If I run, I'll make it.'

He doesn't count out loud, but I know he'll be doing it in his head. I do likewise and, with three to go, I open my eyes.

'Okay, Milky. Have it your way. I'll get up, but I don't know why.'

'Let's get under the rail bridge, out of the rain.'

'Why? I can't get any wetter.'

'I can.'

I push up and shake off some of the water. If I had gone for a swim, I'd be drier.

Milky rushes along to the shelter of the bridge and, a few seconds later, I join him. I lean on one of the giant stone pillars that supports the metal structure above. Another train rumbles by above us.

'Okay, Milky. You got me up. So, what do we do now?'

'Dunno.'

'Well, that's really useful.'

My red mist is thinning fast. The cold taking over my soul.

'I didn't say I had an answer, Ginger. It's over to you.'

'Me? You think I know what to do? I've been wrong on everything so far. You've been beaten up. I've been beaten up. I've got my family threatened. I've got your family threatened. I don't see any way out. And what if Ivan is right about Mum? And what if Dad is on the take? Where would that go, Milky? Dad in jail? Mum trying to look after me and my brother? How could she afford that? Would she go back to the brothel? Is that it?'

'Come on, Ginger. That's not going to happen.'

'How do you know, Milky? What if she gets fired from the job in the factory when they find out what she did? What then? Will she invite men back to our house? The walls are like paper in our place. Would I have to listen to her in the next room? Would I?'

'Jesus, I don't know, Ginger! I really don't know what will happen and what won't. And I don't know what to do, but I'll go with what you say, Ginger. That's all I can do. If you want to tell all, then do it. If you have another idea, then that's what we do. But talking like this isn't helping you, me or anyone.'

I slide down the pillar, feeling the large rough blocks rubbing through my soaking clothes. I'm starting to shiver. I shuffle around the pillar to put it between me and the wind.

'But the one thing I do know,' Milky says, following me round the pillar. 'Is that if you do nothing, then the Sergeant will talk to your dad tonight. He won't get the full story. But enough of a story to have to act.'

'So what?'

'So what, Ginger? *So what?*' I'll tell you what! We have a tape that sinks all of them. Hornsby, Neil, Heartbreak. We have the way to end it, one way or the other.'

'Milky, that tape isn't the answer.'

'Okay, so what is? We have a few hours, at best, to come up with an alternative plan. Now you can lie on the ground. You can lie in the rain. You can lie anywhere you want. You can guess what might or might not happen in the future. You can do all that, and what's going to happen will happen anyway. Unless you can think of something else we can do to change it.'

I wrap my arms tight about my anorak. I'm freezing, and that's not helping my thinking.

'Where can we go that's warm?' I ask.

Milky looks back.

'There.'

He's pointing at the public toilets that sit at the end of the road bridge next to us.

'The bogs?' I exclaim.

'It's out of the rain.'

I stand, plod back through the rain and enter the toilets. There is no one using them. The smell from the giant porcelain urinals is intense. But Milky is right. At least it's dry. I sit on the edge of one of the sinks and start to run the hot water. When it's warm, I put my hands under the tap and after a few minutes I strip off my socks and shoes. I put one foot after the other under the stream until my toes lose their white tinge. I rinse out my socks, strip my anorak and jumper, wringing out as much water as I can. A man comes in for a pee. He looks at us. We both shrug. As I keep squeezing water out of my clothes, he takes a piss. He doesn't wash his hands before he leaves.

I pull my wet clothes back on and sit back on the sink, occasionally dipping my hands in the hot water, now filling the sink.

Hot water.

Hot water.

That's what I'm in.

But...

'Hot water, Milky!' I say.

'Yes, it is,' he replies, looking at the sink.

'No. Not the water in the sink. Us. We're in hot water.'

'Never.'

'But why just us?'

'What?'

'Why are we the only ones in hot water?'

I can feel things in my head clear, a little,

'Because we are kids and everyone else is an adult, Milky. That's why. People believe adults. They don't believe us. So, when the shite lands, they jump over it, and we are planted in it.'

Milky lets me fly.

'Look, Milky! Everyone else is in hot water and yet we are the ones taking all the heat. Hornsby is probably wanted by Heartbreak for taking cash. Neil is in this up to his neck and both are desperate for that tape. Heartbreak is in a bad place if word gets out about her plans. Especially to Spanner. He might just decide that he needs to nip the threat in the bud. And Heartbreak is also in the shit if they catch her bribing the police. Even Ivan must be in this deep or he wouldn't want that tape. And yet we are the ones shitting ourselves about it all.'

'Go on.'

'I don't understand the half of it all, but why should we be the ones taking all this on the chin? Why don't we make them take it away from us? They have much more to lose than us.'

'Keep going!'

'What if…'

I stop, trying to let my head get ahead of my mouth for a second.

'What if,' I say. 'We put Hornsby, Neil, Heartbreak and Heartbreak's gang all in the same place?'

'What?'

'Well, we think Heartbreak wants Hornsby for stealing the cash. Right?'

'Yes.'

'And Neil is involved with the money as well.'

'Yes.'

'Well, what if we tell Hornsby and Neil we'll give them the tape, and at the same time we tell Heartbreak that we'll give her Hornsby and Neil. And then put them in the same place, at the same time?'

Another man comes into the toilets. We wait while he does his business.

'And how would that help us?' Milky asks when the man exits.

'If Heartbreak is half the nutter we think she is, then it won't go well for Hornsby and Neil.'

'And the tape?'

'Insurance. We keep it.'

'And Ivan?'

'One step at a time!'

Milky slides down the wall, thinking. I let him. I need to think this through as well. A few minutes pass. A few more men take a slash.

Milky speaks, 'Do you know that might just work?'

'It might, mightn't it?'

'Heartbreak must be desperate to get Hornsby.'

'Probably.'

'And if they all get together, we'd be history.'

'Exactly!'

'Although it doesn't fix things about our dads, if they are on the take.'

'No, but we might have that wrong.'

'How do we do get them all together?'

'I'm open to ideas, but we would need to do it tonight and quick.'

'And when they all get together? Won't they come after us?'

'Milky, they won't be bothering about us, will they? I mean, can you imagine what it will be like when they meet?'

'But anything could happen!'

'It could, but can you think of a better set of people for it to happen to?'

The permutations of such a meeting are endless.

'Jesus, Ginger! How do we get them together?'

'I'll bet you a penny chew to a bottle of ginger that Hornsby and Neil will be waiting for us when we get off the bus.'

'And Heartbreak?'

'Want to also bet a red Vauxhall Victor will be somewhere nearby?'

'What. Looking for us?'

'No. More likely looking for Hornsby. Heartbreak will still have her men hunting him.'

Two more men come into the toilet. One goes to use the cubicle while the other favours the urinal. The man in the cubicle passes an industrial fart. A few seconds later, Milky holds his nose and points to the door.

'That bloody stinks, mister,' he says as he leaves. 'You should go and see a doctor.'

The man in the toilet tells Milky to fuck off.

Milky runs out of the door. I follow him once I've put my shoes on. We head back to the rail bridge. Milky wanders to the river's edge. He picks a few loose stones from the path and begins to lob them into the water. I slide back down the pillar watching him—then sit bolt upright.

'You're a genius, Milky!' I shout watching him heave stones into the river.

'I'm a what?'

'That's how we get them together.'

'How?'

'Easy. We write a note, wrap it in a big stone and chuck it at them. That way we don't get caught.'

'We do what?'

'We write a note. One for Neil and Hornsby and a different one for Heartbreak, and her men. We throw and run.'

'Eh?'

'On one note we tell Heartbreak's men that Hornsby wants to meet up. On the other we tell Hornsby that we want to hand over the tape. Same place, same time. Get it?'

'And ask them to meet where?'

'The lane? Behind the shops. Where else.'

'Will that work?'

'Dunno. I'm open to other ideas.'

Milky returns to lobbing rocks into the Clyde.

'We'd need paper, pencil and rubber bands,' he says, as he heaves one rock in with two hands, the splash lost to the noise of a train passing above.

'I've got that back home,' I say

'And if you go home like that, you'll be given a right grilling. You'll not get back out.'

'You're right.'

'Don't we need to get Ivan at that meet?'

'Why?'

'He wants the tape as well.'

'Let's deal with him later. One thing at a time.'

'How did Ivan know where we were, Ginger?'

'He could have followed us.'

'Maybe he saw us jump the bus.'

'Maybe. Or he found out another way.'

'All a bit 'The Ghost at Skelton Rock'.'

'The race against time to find the atomic bomb?' says Milky.

'That's the book. That's us. Look I'm sorry I hit you, Milky.'

'You call that a hit?'

I smile, a little.

I loved that Hardy Boys book, but, right there, right then, the whole Hardy Boys thing was wrong, so wrong. We didn't have even half a plan. We hadn't thought through a quarter of what we needed to. We had no solution to our dads, if they were on the take. To Ivan wanting the tape. To him spreading stories about my mum. We were kids trying to deal with adults, and adults that wouldn't think twice about tossing us both in the river with a brick in each pocket. But we were trying to do our best.

'We need to get going,' I say.

'Where do we get paper, etc.?'

'RS McColl's.'

'I'm skint.'

'I have a few pence left,' I say. 'If it's not enough, a little bit of shoplifting will be nothing in the scheme of things.'

'There's an RS McColl's on St Enoch Square.'

I stare out at the sleet beyond the bridge. The cold is seeping back into my bones. My clothes clinging to me like wet newspaper to a clatty cat. The thought of what we've just agreed to do is monumental, pushing me down. Making me want to sit where I am. To do nothing. But I rise and join Milky at the riverbank.

'Milky, this is as serious as it gets. It's not child's play. These guys aren't going to hold back if they catch us.'

'I know.'

'And I've no idea what will happen if we manage to get them altogether in the one place.'

'I know.'

'And if we have to tell my dad, I'm not sure what will happen, either.'

'I know.'

'And Ivan…'

'I know.'

'And Mum.'

I know.'

'Anything you don't know?'

'Everything, Ginger. I don't know a single thing. Now are we going to get this done?'

Milky shapes his hands into an air guitar and starts singing, interspersing each line with guitar noises:

'Don't Get Yourself in Trouble,

Don't Get Yourself in Trouble,

Don't Get Yourself in Trouble,

Don't Get Yourself in Trouble.'

He stops.

'Bachman Turner Overdrive?' I guess.

'Dad thinks I should adopt it as my theme song.'

That manages to force another smile from me.

'Saturday.

Saturday.

Saturday.

Saturday Night's Alright for Fighting,' I sing, badly. 'My tune.'

Milky smiles this time.

'Let's go break the law!' I say.

The Conversation.

'THINGS SOUNDED BAD?'

'They were. I still remember that woman grabbing my hood. I really think I would have been a goner had she not stepped in.'

'Milky sounds like a real friend.'

'He was. He's probably the person I've been closest to in my entire life. Always there when I needed him. He was the spark that set every day alight.'

'School friends like that are rare.'

'Very rare.'

'Do you miss him?'

'I do. For a long time, I pushed my childhood to the back of my mind. But of late it's up front and centre. I don't think I really knew what I had in Milky.'

'Do you think he felt the same?'

'Yes. In his way.'

'Did you ever discuss the future back then?'

'Not seriously, not that I can remember. Maybe some wild ideas. Him wanting to be an astronaut. Me, a guitarist in a rock band. We did talk of adventures a lot. The whole Hardy Boy thing obsessed us for years.'

'And of growing up, having families, that sort of thing?'

'No. Why?'

'No reason. Just curious. Now you have me hooked on your story. Carry on.'

Chapter 18
'Saturday Night's Alright For Fighting.'

THE NEWSAGENT IS quiet. Too quiet. After a quick scan of the shop, I realise I don't have enough money and that stealing paper, pencils and rubber bands is not going to be easy. All three items we need lie in plain sight of the man standing behind the counter. He's already watching us as we pretend to choose sweets from a shelf.

I'm just about to call it quits when the door opens and a gaggle of teenagers roll in, laughing and pushing each other. They're a lot older than Milky and I, maybe fifteen or sixteen. They all trawl the shelves, lifting a whole bunch of sweets. One by one, they dump them all on the counter and wait as the shopkeeper starts to add up the cost. Two of them circle back towards the newspaper and magazine rack, looking up at the top shelf—it's not hard to see what's on their mind. Escort, Mayfair, Playboy and the rest. Height wise, out of reach for Milky and I, but not for the lads hovering in front of the rack.

The shopkeeper totals the sweets. The kids go into the usual comedy routine on who will pay for what. We wait, biding our time, as I think we might be about to be presented with the opportunity we need. The kids pile money on the counter, a small mountain of pennies and tuppences. The shopkeeper counts it all out. The kids grab the sweets, stuffing them in their pockets and, as they turn to leave, the two at the rack reach up and grab a handful of dirty mags each. Then they are out the door, their mates trailing behind. The shopkeeper shouts out, slams up the countertop and dashes past Milky and me.

As he runs out of the door in pursuit, I stuff a small notepad in one pocket, a clutch of pencils in the other. Milky grabs a bag of rubber bands and we make for the front door.

We exit as the shop keeper runs across the square. I spot our bus at the bus stop, engine revving, just about to leave, door closed. We sprint to the bus door. I batter my fists on it. The driver reluctantly opens up, and Milky and I dive upstairs. Our favourite seats are free, but we chose to huddle together on the front left-hand one only. The periscope that lets the driver look upstairs sits above the right-hand seat. The left-hand front seat is the only blind spot up here. The driver can see every other seat from his position down below—bar the one we are in. A common piece of knowledge to any kid in Glasgow.

Outside the window, through the sleet-soaked glass, we can see the shopkeeper standing near the subway entrance. If the kids have gone down there, he would have to leave the shop unattended to follow. He shakes his head and walks back to the newsagent as our bus moves off. For an instant he looks up at the top deck, straight at where we are sitting. His step wavers. For a moment he looks like he's about to change direction. Has he seen us? But he's only avoiding a puddle, and, we must be a blur to him through the misted window. He makes his way slowly back to the shop.

'Okay,' I say as the bus whirls around the square. 'I'll write the notes.'

I pull out the notepad. A small rectangular pad with a wire loop at the top holding the punched paper in place. I pull out the pencils and curse. All of them are flat ended. We need a sharpener. Milky pulls his pen knife out and gets to work. A minute later, shavings scattering the floor, he has sharpened two pencils.

It takes me a few goes to get the wording correct. I'm conscious of time. The bus will take about twenty-five minutes to reach the bus stop at our shops. But we need to get off before then and walk up. The stop at the shops would put us right in the firing line if Hornsby or the red Victor are already there. That means we have less than twenty minutes to write the notes and agree what we are going to do.

I finally scribble.

Note 1

If you want the tape, be at the lane behind the Drake Café at 8 o'clock tonight. If you don't appear, we will give the tape to Heartbreak and tell her where we got it.

Note 2

If you want Hornsby and Neil McGregor, be at the lane behind the Drake Café at 8:15 tonight.

I write two copies of each. Milky reads them and nods.

'We need big chuckies to wrap these in,' I say. 'If we get off at the stop near our school, we can nip into the park and find a few.'

'What for?'

'We wrap the notes in the chuckies and tie them on with the rubber bands. Then lob them at Hornsby and the Victor.'

'Will they go for it?'

'I think so. As long as they read the notes. I mean, it's what they want.'

'How do we find them all?' Milky asks.

'I'm betting that they find us first, and then we see what's what.'

'We could get caught if we're not careful.'

'Aye, and we could meet aliens that want to probe our bums with a cattle prod! Milky, I know we could be caught, but this is the plan. Are you in?'

He nods.

I pocket the notes, slipping them in between the pages of the notepad to keep them dry—my pocket is a miniature swimming pool.

The bus rumbles on, providing us with an age-old condensation, rock'n'roll view of Glasgow's southside. We pass pubs that are already full, shops that are closed and streets that are busy despite the weather. As we approach Battlefield, I turn to Milky.

'Ready?'

'As I'll ever be.'

We turn along King's Park Road and hang a right onto Carmunnock Road. A few moments later we are climbing the hill towards our school. As we pass the gate to King's Park, where my PE running lesson had started, we both nip down the stairs and stand, waiting for the driver to halt. He pulls in at the stop. The doors open. We are about to step off when the conductor grabs me.

I nearly yell in fright.

'Where's your ticket?' he asks.

My heart thuds so loud I'm sure he can hear it. I swear I thought it was Ivan or Hornsby or who knows who. I root in my pocket and extract a sodden ticket, barely legible because of the water. Milky does likewise. The conductor studies both tickets as if they were coated in cat's piss.

'I can't read these,' he says.

'Not my fault, mister,' I say as I jump from the bus, Milky on my heels. We sprint towards the park gates.

We head for the shelter provided by the park's overhanging trees to look for rocks, and, ten minutes later, we have five decent-sized chuckies. In the shelter of the trees, I wrap the notes around four rocks and fix them with elastic bands.

'Why two of each note?' he asks.

'In case we miss with the first ones.'

'Good idea.'

'Milky, if I put these chuckies in my pocket, the notes will get soaked. I can't carry them either. If they get wet, the notes will be unreadable.'

Milky doesn't say anything but, instead, crawls into the bushes and emerges a few seconds later with a clutch of used crisp packets.

'Will these do?'

I place a rock in each packet, tying the ends with another rubber band. I hand them over. Milky pockets them all.

'That'll work,' I say.

I move towards the gate. Milky grabs my shoulder.

'We'd be better off cutting through the park, Ginger. There's nowhere to hide between here and the top of the hill. And if we are caught out on the road...'

He doesn't need to say any more.

I'd normally avoid going through the park in the dark in the same way I'd avoid eating Milky's ear wax, but in this case Milky is right.

'Let's hope the loons are tucked up tight,' I say.

'In this weather, you'd need to be a right loon to be out.'

'They are the worst sort, Milky.'

Even with the rain falling from the heavens in bathtub lumps, I'm not sure there still won't be a few loons buried in the park waiting on a victim. After all, parks are simply hunting grounds at night. We, the prey.

There are two ways to get to the park gate nearest the shops from here. Follow the path that runs into the park before it circles back to the gate, or cut up the side of the bushes and skirt the fence that lines the road. The former is easier as, even without moonlight, there's enough light to see the path. But it's also the best way to get caught, if any loons are lying in wait. The latter route is fraught with trip hazards; we'd be almost blind. It'll also take far longer, and time is not our friend.

'We need to risk the path,' I say. 'We walk side by side and at any sign of loons you go left, and I go right.'

You can tell we've been here before—the side by side and left/right plan is our best chance of escape.

We walk in to the dark. The sleet is gone, light rain now falling, but the wind has picked up, whipping away any warmth from our bodies. The gusts rushing through the trees block any chance of hearing anything. I can only just see the outline of Milky beside me. Every so often, one of us wanders off the tarmac onto the grass.

We reach the point furthest from both gates, the point of no return. If anyone is going to attack, it will be here. I turn my head side on to the wind to try to catch any sounds.

There's an irony in the fact that if we get caught here, and get a doing, that it won't be half as bad as the one we could get from Hornsby or Heartbreak. Almost a light-relief kicking, in fact. The loons in here just want your money and to have a bit of fun. The irony and the word fun make me want to laugh. My inappropriate laugh. I can feel it building. I know that bursting out in laughter will be a dead giveaway if anyone is waiting in the dark. I bite on my tongue and pinch my wrist. But it doesn't help.

A snort comes out. I clamp my hand to my mouth. Another grunt explodes through my fingers, and I start to laugh.

'Shut up!' says Milky. 'Please, not now.'

I can't stop. I know I should, but I can't. I stop walking as unfounded glee takes over. I laugh hard and Milky slaps me on the back.

'Shut up, Ginger. For heaven's sake, shut up!'

I wish I could, but I'm bent double, hands on my knees, laughter pouring from me in waves. Milky rabbit punches me on the back of the head, only half connecting in the darkness. Something about that makes everything even funnier.

'Jesus, Ginger! Please, *please* stop.'

I hold my stomach; my throat is starting to hurt. Gales of laughter wash over me. I find it hard not to fall to the ground. I'm howling like a crazy person while everything inside tells me I need to stop.

Slowly the lunacy passes, and I stand up, a last splutter escaping my lips.

'Finished?' says Milky.

'I'm sorry.'

'Well, at least we know we're alone,' says Milky. 'They could have heard that in the back seats of the Toledo.'

'I'm sorry. Let's get going again.'

We move off, cursed by a wind that, if anything, has put on its serious shoes. The spray in my face stings. I tug my hood tighter, but it does nothing to help.

We reach the gate. I can still feel the distant, laughing monster lurking. We take to the welcome shelter of the trees that guard the park entrance. We can't see the shops from here. They lie over the small rise that my Cooper Fine Fare sits on, but if we can cross the main road, there's a tiny ribbon of trees that separates the main road from the road into our scheme. They run up the hill to finish at the top of the rise, just where the shops start. They'll provide cover to that point. After that, we will be out in the open.

I wait until the main road is clear, then signal for both of us to run. My shoes are full of water, my clothes sodden, and my legs are tired. I want to sprint but can manage little more than a watered-down jog. Even so, we both make the strip of trees undetected. After a few seconds, and after Milky has checked the chuckies are still in his pocket, we begin to work our way up to the shops.

Across the road from us, the Coopers Fine Fare is closed. The small car park deserted. The bin that Neil ambushed me behind is piled high with cardboard, and I wonder how much damage Milky did to Neil with the brick. After all, Neil collapsed back to the ground after his first attempt to stand up. I doubt he would know when to stop kicking Milky, if he catches him.

The first shop at this end is a hardware store—a dusty maze of shelving loaded with greying cardboard boxes. Next to the hardware store is the entrance to the back lane. Hornsby had watched us get on the bus from there earlier this morning. I look for any sign of him in the shadows, but the lane is too dark to reveal anyone. There are a few people walking on the pavement next to the shops. A lone car is parked nearby. The only shop open at this time of night will be the café, and it's around the corner from where we are standing.

Milky squeals, 'The Victor!'

I turn. Just exiting the roundabout, and about to come our way, is the red Victor.

'Give me a note!' I say.

Milky dips his pocket and takes out a chuckie.

'This is the right one,' he says, handing it to me. He'd put the Heartbreak rocks in his right pocket, Hornsby's in his left. I slip the rock from the crisp packet and crouch.

'I tell you what. Give me it,' says Milky. 'I can throw better than you.'

He's right. Not that I'd usually admit it, but I hand the rock to Milky. The Victor labours up the road. We will be within six feet of it when it passes by, barely hidden by the small trees around us. In the driving rain all the windows are up but Milky winds up to throw anyway.

As the car draws level, he lets fly. The rock smashes through the passenger side window, glass shattering. Immediately, the car slews to a stop. The passenger door flies open.

'Hit them with another rock,' I shout.

Milky fumbles one from his pocket. Smiff is out of the car, Milky dumps the crisp packet from the rock.

'If you want Hornsby read this,' he shouts, giving the rock his best right arm.

The rock catches Smiff square in the chest. Before he can react, we leg it into the nearest garden. We run to the rear of the house, jump the fence into the next garden. Milky edges up the driveway to look back on the main road. He comes back a few seconds later.

'Winner,' he says.

'What?'

'They are reading the note. We were too fast for them. One is reading and the other is looking around.'

'One down, one to go,' I say.

We scamper over a hedge, through the garden behind, emerging onto our drive.

'Where do you think Hornsby will be?' I say.

'If he was waiting on us coming back, he has to be in the lane or up at my house.'

'In this weather?'

'He's desperate. Let's check the lane first.'

There is a strip of garages behind the shops that sit to the rear of the lane. If we can get to them, it would be possible to look down on the lane and see if anyone is there.

'Milky! The garages. We can go there and look.'

'Okay.'

We back up into the garden and clamber along to a fence, stopping dead when we hear a cough. I poke my head up over a fence. There's enough light from the streetlights to see a couple of shapes outlined against the nearest garage door. Two glows appear, one after the other. Both figures are smoking.

'I think they are both just there,' I whisper, ducking back down.

'They must be as wet as we are.'

'I'm not sure anyone is as wet as I am, Milky.'

I hear some more chat. I pop my head back up. One of the shapes is on the move. I watch as the figure walks down the small incline from the garages to the lane. It's Neil. He rests himself on the wall at the end of the lane and looks out.

I duck back down again.

'Neil is watching the bus stop,' I say. 'They must be taking it in turns. Milky have a look. Could you hit Neil from here with a chuckie?'

Milky shoves me aside and rises. He studies the scene for a moment.

'Easy!' he says, as he drops beside me.

He pulls out a rock out of my left pocket and removes the crisp packet.

'Make it good, Milky!'

He stands up. He lets fly, screaming. 'Read this McGregor.'

'Run!' Milky says, as soon as he stopped shouting at Neil. 'I caught him on the head.'

We scramble across the garden and hedge-hop three times before lying flat.

'Do you think he read it, Milky?'

There's no sound of anyone giving chase.

'Dunno. But I certainly hit him.'

'A half brick and a rock,' I say. 'Milky, he will kill us if he catches us.'

'More me than you.'

'We need to be sure he read the note,' I say. 'I'm going to see what's what. You stay here.'

I rise up, looking back towards the garages. I can see two figures again. Neil is back with Hornsby, assuming the other is Hornsby. It's too dark to make out faces. I clamber over the hedge, catching my anorak on a branch. I hear a rip. I keep going. I stop a garden short of where Milky had thrown the rock. I can hear the faintest of voices. I'll need to get closer to make out anything meaningful.

I check that both figures are still together, crawl over the next hedge and work my way to the far end of the garden.

The voices are clearer now, but I'm still struggling to hear what they are saying. My only choice is to climb over the last fence and hope they don't see me. I need to know that they have read the note.

I raise myself slowly, working my feet up the wooden fence. It creaks, but the noise is lost in the sound of the wind. I flop over the top, falling onto the concrete near the garages, and lie still. A stream of water courses around me, but I'm beyond caring.

'The wee fucker hit me on the head!' says Neil. 'I'll kill the wee bastard. He already fucked up my nose with a brick and now I've lost a tooth!'

There is no mention of the note.

I climb back over the fence, shouting out. 'Hey dimwits, read the note on the rock!'

I dash back to Milky.

We wait.

When it's clear they are not coming after me, I make a return trip to the last fence, once more lying in the temporary river, listening.

'Eight?' says Hornsby.

'That's what the dumb note says. We get the tape ate eight. In the lane. We should go after the wee bastard,' says Neil.

'You think? They know this scheme like the back of their hand. Do you want to go chasing through gardens in this weather? Let's see if they turn up at eight. If not, I'm going up to the wee ginger haired prick's home, wait for him there. Beat it out of him.'

'All for a bloody tape.'

'It's the only way out of this, McGregor. I can't stand much more. I'm starving, freezing and out of options. That tape is my ticket to a better life.'

'They're not just going to hand it over to you. The note is stupid.'

'What choice do we have at the moment? If they turn up, I'll make sure they give me that tape. Don't worry about that.'

'And where's my money in all this? Heartbreak knows I'm working with you now. I'm dead meat.'

'You'll get your money. How many times have I told you that you'll get it?'

'Three grand,' Neil says. 'Three grand? You stole three grand from Heartbreak.'

'You think I don't know?'

'So, give me my share now. You deal with the tape. I want out.'

'Well, I can't give you it.'

'Why the hell not?'

'It's gone. I owed it.'

'All three grand is gone? You told me I'd get half!'

'You will.'

'How? If it's gone, where are you going to get fifteen hundred quid from?'

'Fucking don't keep on! You'll get your money. Once we have that tape, you can have all the money you want. I'll have Heartbreak's fanny over an open fire.'

'I fucking hope so. I'm so in the shite because of you.'

'Eight o'clock,' says Hornsby. 'The lane at eight.'

'That's what the note says. They said they'd give us the tape then.'

'I tell you if the wee bastard doesn't turn up, I'm going back to trash his house proper this time—to find that tape and then burn the whole fucking thing down.'

Back?

My heart picks up. Hornsby's anger is as clear as the water cascading around my head. I reach up to grab the wooden fence to climb back over. With a snap, the plank I'm holding breaks and I fall back.

'There's someone there!' shouts Neil.

I jump up, clambering over the broken fence.

'It's the wee ginger shite. Stop!' Neil shouts.

I collapse on the far side of the fence. I pull myself back up. But I feel like I'm wading through thick mud. I've no energy and, despite my fear, I can't summon any. I'm hardly upright when Neil appears above me.

'You are a dead man!' he screams.

His face is one large bruise, his nose crooked. Milky certainly caught him square in the face with the brick, the stone or both.

I hirple across the slick grass as Neil throws himself over the fence. There's no way I'm going to outrun him. I slip and fall to the ground. As I roll over, I feel the chisel, still sitting in my pocket, digging into my hip. I reach in and drag it out. The insulation tape protecting the blade falls to the ground, a wet lump. Neil is on me, pinning me to the grass before I can raise it.

'I am going to break every fucking bone in your body,' he shouts in my face. 'You wee shite!'

My arms are trapped at my side by his knees as he throws his first blow, skelping me on the head. I scream. A second blow rocks my chin and my head snaps to the right. I try and roll him off me, but he's too heavy. He catches me on the chest with a fist. Air flies from my lungs.

'Where is the fucking tape?' he shouts.

Behind him, I see movement and Hornsby looms.

A new voice booms out.

'What's going on here?'

The new voice is accompanied by a swathe of light from the back door of the house we are next to. Neil looks towards the source of the sound and his knee lifts off my right hand. The one with the chisel in it. I swing it up. The chisel finds something soft and buries itself in Neil. His scream is psychedelic. He rolls from me, clutching his side. Energy or no energy, I move, throwing myself over the next hedge. I scramble, tumbling towards the next one—and I'm over. Milky is waiting.

'Oh Jesus,' I say. 'I think I just killed Neil?'

'What?'

'I think I just killed Neil!'

'How?'

'With…'

The chisel is back in the garden. Still in Neil.

'Oh my God, Milky. I think I killed Neil!'

Milky stands up and looks back the way I just came. He studies the scene and drops back to my side.

'I've no idea what is going on, Ginger. There's a lot of shouting, but I can't tell what is what.'

'Milky. I really think I've killed Neil.'

'Stop saying that.'

'But I have. I stabbed him.'

'What with?'

'A chisel.'

'Why did you have a chisel?'

I don't answer.

'Okay,' Milky says. 'You head a few more gardens up. Up to Jimmy Anderson's place. He's in hospital. Hide in his greenhouse. I'll go check. See what I can see. Then join you.'

He leaps away and I'm left on the ground. If I thought I was scared before, I'm now in a new world of fear that I never imagined existed. I've killed a man. The thought pins me to the grass like a giant iron nail through my heart. I've stabbed a man. A man. A human being. I've just taken the life of another human being. I don't move. I can't move. Even if Hornsby, Heartbreak, Ivan and every mad loon I know appeared right now, I couldn't move. I couldn't even raise a finger.

I lie. Rain falling on my face.

Staring into the sky.

For an age.

I just killed a man.

Milky comes back a few minutes later.

'Jesus, Ginger! We need to move. Why are you still here?'

'Is Neil dead?'

'Jamie Lawrence's dad is in the garden, but there's no sign of Neil or Hornsby.'

'But I stabbed him.'

'Well, he's not in the garden.'

'That doesn't mean he isn't dead.'

'Do the dead walk away?'

'But I stabbed him.'

'Okay, okay. I get it. You stabbed him. But he's not there. We are here, and we need to get away.'

'Why?'

'Because we do.'

'It's all over, Milky. My life is all over. I'll go to jail.'

'I told you, there is no body in the garden. Neil isn't there.'

'Hornsby could have taken the body.'

'Jesus! Just stop talking Ginger, and move.'

He grabs my arm, but I'm dead weight. He pulls and I don't help.

'Ginger,' he says. 'This is now past stupid. I've had enough.'

He stands up and, in the gloom, crosses his arms in front of his chest.

'Ginger, if you want to lie there, feel free, but that's it for me. I'm through. Enough is enough. I don't want to leave you here, but I can't go on with this. It was crazy enough, but now it's bat-shit crazy and unless you get up right now—I'm going home.'

He drops my arm.

I lie, and, after a few seconds, he simply turns and walks away.

More rain falls on my face and I'm clueless as to what to do next.

Chapter 19
'Late One Saturday Night.'

HALF AN HOUR later, and I'm still flat on my back. The rain has eased off a little, but I've no feeling in my hands or feet, and I can't stop shivering. My only thoughts are circling back to me stabbing Neil. Eventually, something deeper down tells me I need to get up and move. I roll over, and, with almost superhuman effort, I stand. I trudge to the road and begin to walk up the hill to my home. As I draw level with Milky's house, I stop to look at his front window, but the curtains are shut tight.

I'm about to start walking again when a shape moves near Milky's front door.

'So, you can walk?' says Milky's voice from the shadow of his house.

'I'm going home, Milky.'

'I wouldn't. Not just yet,' he says. 'Come in. There's no one in my house.'

'I just want to go home, Milky.'

'Just come here, idiot! Just for a moment.'

I sigh and traipse down his path. He opens the front door; the warmth that flows out is a living thing on my face. I stand in his hall dripping.

'Go upstairs and get out of all that wet stuff!'

'I don't want to.'

'I'm not trying to be nice,' he says. 'Mum will lynch me if you drip water over her new living room carpet.'

Like a robot, I mount the stairs, enter the bathroom and strip. Milky knocks on the door, throwing me in a huge bath towel.

'It's all I have,' he says as he leaves.

I drop all my clothes in the bath and follow him back downstairs. The living room is a haven of heat. The three-bar electric fire is full on. I huddle around it, desperate for warmth.

'Why have I not to go home?' I ask.

'You're not going to like this!' Milky says. 'It's not good news.'

'What? How can things possibly get worse?'

'I met Greggy when I got back here,' he informs me. 'He was almost beside himself, wanting to tell me a story.'

'What story?'

'About your house.'

'Jesus. What about my house?'

'It was broken into.'

'Say that again!'

'He said the police were all over your place.'

I'm going back to trash his house proper this time. Hornsby's words. *Back.*

I just sigh.

'I checked it out. There were two police cars outside, and your dad was talking to one of the policemen. I got close enough to hear them say that someone broke in while your dad was asleep. He woke up and nearly caught them.'

'This isn't happening, Milky. This really isn't happening.'

'Greggy says that he saw your dad chasing the robbers.'

'All my fault,' I say. 'All of it. My fault. It's that bloody tape they were after.'

'You don't know that.'

'Yes, I do. I heard Hornsby saying he was going back to my house. Back, Milky.'

I still can't feel my hands or feet, but at least I've stopped shivering.

'It's still only seven o'clock,' says Milky.

'So what?'

'We still have an hour before they all start to turn up at the lane.'

'Hornsby and Neil won't turn up now. Not after I stabbed Neil.'

'Ginger. Neil isn't dead.'

I turn from the heat. 'I stabbed him!'

'Well, unless he's now a zombie, I saw him ten minutes ago walk right past here. He didn't look happy, but he looked very alive to me.'

'Are you sure?'

'Positive!'

The relief is overwhelming.

'I think you might have nicked him,' Milky says. 'He was clutching his side, but walking well enough. He didn't look fatally wounded to me.'

'You sure?'

'He's walking. There you go. You're not going to jail for murder.'

'I could go for assault.'

'I don't think so. I can't see Neil going to the police and telling them about how a twelve-year-old stabbed him with a chisel.'

'He could. My fingerprints are on it.'

'Get away with yourself! Neil's not going to admit you got the better of him. How would that work out amongst his mates? Chibbed by a kid! Anyway, given the trouble he's in, he'll avoid the police like the plague.'

Milky's right. The relief is even greater.

'But Neil didn't go home,' Milky says. 'He walked right past his house and up the hill.'

'I wonder where he was going?' I ask.

'To your house?'

'I doubt he'll get close with the police around.'

'You think?'

'Maybe?'

'What do we do between now and eight?' Milky asks.

'I'm not going to the lane tonight, Milky.'

'Jesus, Ginger! Get your right head on. You're supposed to be the smart one. How the hell will we know what happens if we don't go and see? Or are you just going to go home and wait and see who turns up at the door?'

'I thought you'd had enough of all this?'

'I found my sensible head when I got back here. We need this to end. Both of us need it to end.'

'I've no clothes.'

'Have you any in your house?'

'In my room.'

'Is your bedroom window open?'

'Yes.'

'I'll be back!'

Before I can stop him, he's out of the door and gone. I push my hands closer to the fire and the relief from the news on Neil and the heat is calming me down a little.

Fifteen minutes later, Milky's back, a bundle of clothes under his arms.

'I couldn't get any shoes.'

'My shoes in your bathroom will do. Did you see anyone at my house?'

'Your dad was still talking to a policeman, but there was only one panda car outside, not two. They were so busy chatting it was easy to shin up the drainpipe.'

'Was Deke in?'

'No.'

'Did you see if anyone had been in my room?'

'Given the mess of your room, how would I have known?'

He hands me my clothes and I pull them on. As I pull on my socks, I throw him the towel. The feeling is returning to my extremities.

'I'm hungry,' I say.

Milky vanishes and reappears with two pieces and sugar, and two glasses of Creamola Foam. We eat and drink it all in seconds.

'I've also no coat,' I say.

'Are you now saying that you are going to the lane?'

'I've no coat,' I repeat.

'Your anorak is upstairs.'

'And sodden.'

'It'll have to do. I'll wring out the best I can.'

Again, he vanishes, and I realise that Milky is more than keen to make the meeting. I doubt that Hornsby will appear, but what else can I do? Heartbreak's men will be there, and if Hornsby does appear, then maybe...

Milky comes back with a wooden clothes horse and my anorak. He lays down newspaper in front of the fire and places the clothes-horse on it, before draping my anorak over the top. He disappears again; this time he comes back with my shoes, which he stuffs with newspaper and places right next to the fire.

'Thanks Mum!' I say.

With food in my stomach, sugar coursing my veins, heat in my body, clothes on my back and Neil not dead—I'm thinking in a very different way to less than thirty minutes ago.

I spend most of the next half an hour turning my anorak over, stuffing and restuffing my shoes with newspaper, trying to dry them both out.

'Where are we going to watch from?' Milky asks.

'I have a thought on that,' I say. 'Some of the flats above the shops have roof gardens at the back that look down on the lane. If we shin up to there, we can find a hiding place to watch from.'

'Well, we need to go soon,' he says. 'We want to be in place before anyone gets there.'

The thought of the cold and the rain is a drag. The thought of everything else is a blur. Milky checks the window and ducks back quickly.

'Jesus, Neil McGregor!' he cries.

'Coming here?'

'No. Walking down the hill towards the shops.'

'So, he really isn't dead *and* he's heading for the lane.'

'See, Ginger. This might still work.'

We give it a few minutes before I pull on my anorak. Warm but still wet. As are my shoes.

Once back on the street, I point across the road.

'We need to hedge-hop.'

'The whole way?'

'From the bend at the bottom of the road, at least. We can't risk meeting anyone on the road.'

The two of us pull up our hoods against the rain, now more of a heavy smirr than the full-on nonsense of earlier. Our eyes are open for red Victors or any of the other myriad of people that seem to be after us.

'Ivan will probably be looking for us as well,' Milky says.

'And if he's in tow with Hornsby, I'm thinking he'll appear at the shops.'

'How would he know about that?'

'You said that Neil didn't go into his house when you saw him?'

'He didn't. He walked up the road.'

'Maybe to tell Ivan what was going on?'

'Maybe.'

We reach the bend in the road. We nip up the driveway of Jimmy Anderson's house.

'Over to the gardens on the other side!' I say as we reach the greenhouse. 'We'll work our way down the houses across from here. Jamie Lawrence's dad will be out checking every so often after the stuff that went down between Neil and me. We can't risk getting seen if we go that way.'

The gardens on the far side are not ones we are familiar with. I know one person on this road, but they live further down, right across from the park gate. We start to work our way back to the lane.

'How do we get up to the roof gardens?' asks Milky.

The flats above the shops are one storey up.

'At this end of the lane, just where the road to the garages is, there's a drainpipe. I've not climbed it, but I've heard a few people have been up and you can hop from one garden to the next, right to the last one that sits above the bend in the lane.'

'Neil and Hornsby might be hanging out at the garages again.'

'Maybe,' is all the answer I have.

When we reach the last garden, I hear voices again. Milky was right, Hornsby and Neil are back at the same spot they were at earlier.

'Okay, Milky,' I say. 'Can you see the drainpipe right across from the hedge? That's the one we climb. You go first and I'll keep an eye on those two.'

Milky is up and over the hedge in an instant. He scales the drainpipe like a spider with a hot coal up its arse. I follow suit and join him on the first roof garden. I count four more gardens between here and the bend in the lane. Each separated by a low wall. The last garden ends in a brick wall. The flats on the other leg of the lane don't have gardens. We head for the end, and, when we arrive, I look down into the lane. It's dark, but there's enough light to make out some detail. If someone walks past, I could almost reach down and touch them on the head.

'We wait here,' I say.

The garden is only about four yards by four yards square. The flat behind us has two windows and a door; all look out on where we are squatting. One window has flickering light coming from it. The other window and the door are dark. Saturday night TV. Maybe they're watching the tail end of Dixon of Dock Green, or is Cilla on yet?

There's a battered old picnic table next to the wall that looks down onto the lane—we can squeeze under it to get out of the rain. Thoughtfully, the owner has left an old tarpaulin over it. We might not be warm, but we'll be dry and, importantly, out of sight of anyone from the flat if they look out. I lift the tarpaulin and we both squeeze under. I prop the tarpaulin up a little to let me pop out and look into the lane if needed.

There's nothing to be done now, but to wait.

I'm aware that this whole plan has more holes in it than my underpants. I don't even bother going through the list of problems with Milky. Either everyone turns up or they don't. If they don't, then I'm going to find my dad and tell all. If they do arrive—well, that's where the fun could start.

Milky reaches into his pocket and pulls out a squashed Curly Wurly.

'We can go halfers on it,' he says.

He strips the Curly Wurly from its packet and splits it in two, handing me the smallest piece. Today has been an okay food day, but the Curly Wurly just makes me hungrier.

'Can you see Hornsby or Neil from here?' says Milky.

I slip forward, slipping out from under the tarpaulin. I stare over the wall, looking up towards the garages. Two red glows tell me that Hornsby and Neil are still in place. I'm just about to duck back when I spot the red Victor cruise past the end of the lane at the bottom of my drive. It looks like there are three people inside. I wait and watch. The car returns, slowing almost to a halt at the lane entrance. The passenger side window winds down; Smiff looks out. He spends a few seconds looking in my direction—but I'll be hidden in the darkness. He pulls his head back into the car. It moves off again. I swivel my head to ensure that Hornsby and Neil are still in place. They are lost in chat.

I keep watching and, seconds later, Smiff appears on foot at the end of the lane where the car had been. He's on his own and doesn't enter the lane, but hangs back, leaning on the wall. He flicks a fag out of a packet, lights up and starts smoking.

'Wait here!' I say to Milky, and slide from the picnic table. I run back along the gardens to the other end of the lane. I sneak up to the point where we climbed up and look over. At the entrance to the lane is Streak, he too is smoking. Hornsby and Neil are hidden from him by the garages. The red Victor is parked across from the lane entrance. I can see a figure in the back seat. If Hornsby or Neil move to look down the lane, they'll see Streak. But even with the car where it is, Hornsby and Neil could get by Streak and scarper. I need to get Smiff into the lane as soon as possible to stop that.

I run back to the picnic table and look over. There's a metal grill on a window below. I tell Milky to wait and climb over the wall, working my way down the grill to drop into the lane. I'm at the junction of the L, and I walk quickly towards Smiff. I'll be all but invisible in here until I get close. I'm within five yards of him when he sees me.

'You!' he shouts. 'You little shite!'

I take off back down the lane and throw myself up at a grilled window, grabbing the metalwork. I pull myself up and over the wall. I peek back over. Smiff runs past below me and up to where Streak is standing. I hurtle back along the gardens to reach the end just as Smiff turns the corner to find Streak.

'Did you see him?' he says.

'Who, Hornsby?' says Streak.

'No, the wee Bannerman kid.'

'No.'

'He must have come up here. I just saw him.'

I look up to the garages. The glow of a cigarette moves. Neil pokes his head out. Smiff and Streak are still talking and don't see him. There's a flowerpot at my side. I pick it up and sling it as hard as I can in the direction of Neil. The pot shatters on the upslope to the garages. Smiff and Streak turn to the noise. They see Neil.

'Fuck!' shouts Smiff. 'It's McGregor.'

Smiff and Streak run at Neil, who vanishes behind the garages. I hear a car door open and close. A figure passes beneath me—a small, compact woman in a large, dark coat. She rushes to join the others behind the garages. Shouts go up and, a few seconds later, Neil comes hurtling down the slope. I pick up another flowerpot, and, as he passes beneath me, drop it. My aim is world-class, and he goes down like a sack of tatties. Smiff barrels down the slope and lands on Neil, pinning him to the ground. I hear more scuffling from up behind the garage as Milky appears by my side.

'What's happening, Ginger?'

'Smiff has got Neil pinned on the ground just down there,' I whisper, pointing down to the lane.

'Who's Smiff?'

'One of the guys from the Victor that lifted me. I think Heartbreak and the other guy from the car, Streak, are fighting with Hornsby up at the garages.'

I look up as Hornsby appears. He face-plants the ground. The small woman steps into view, holding what looks like a gun. Streak appears and kicks Hornsby in the ribs. The wee woman and Streak lift Hornsby up. They drag him to where Smiff is holding Neil against the wall. In a few seconds, all five are below us. Milky and I look over. We are so close that we can hear them breathing.

'Get them both in the car!' says the wee woman.

Smiff walks to the edge of the lane and looks out. A few seconds later, he's back.

'Pigs!' he says. 'It's the pigs, Heartbreak. We need to get out of sight.'

Heartbreak forces Hornsby around the corner into the lane. Smiff does likewise with Neil. Milky and I shuffle to the back wall of the garden we are in and look over. All five are now hidden in the lane below us. They can't be seen from the road.

'The pigs are parked just around the corner, Heartbreak,' says Smiff. 'They have their lights out. They could just be taking a break. They were chatting. I think one of them was eating something.'

'Can they see our car from where they are?' says Heartbreak.

'It's right across from them,' Smiff replies. 'And they'll see us as soon as we leave the lane.'

'I'll get your money, Heartbreak,' says Hornsby suddenly. 'I promise.'

Heartbreak punches Hornsby in the gut and points the gun at him. 'You're the one that brought this gun with you,' she says to the doubled-up Hornsby. 'I should just blow your brains out and leave you here. You're such a fucked-up moron, they'll probably think you committed suicide.'

'It was his idea,' says Neil.

He gets a punch for his trouble.

'And you can shut it as well,' says Heartbreak. 'I trusted you, McGregor, and this is what you do in return? I always knew this ex-pig prick would roll me at some point. But you? I thought you were solid.'

Heartbreak leans down, prodding Hornsby with the gun.

'Bent coppers can't be trusted. Now get up!'

Hornsby stands up, slowly.

'Three lousy grand!' Heartbreak says to Hornsby. 'What were you going to do with three lousy grand? A year in Spain and then what? Fuck, I always thought if I gave you serious cash you'd run, but not three lousy grand.'

'I owed big time, Heartbreak,' Hornsby says.

At that moment, Neil springs up and tries to run. Smiff is too fast for him. He brings him down with a kick to the leg and spits on him. 'Try that one more time, and I'll carve up your face into a map of the Gorbals.'

Neil lies there.

'Okay,' says Heartbreak. 'Smiff, go see if the pigs are still there!'

He leaves and is back in less than a minute. 'Still there, and both are eating. We could walk out the other way, Heartbreak.'

'And do what?' she says. 'Will they see us get in our car?'

'Probably.'

'Well, I'm not walking all the way back to the flat. No, we'll wait it out. I can as easily say here what I was going to say in the flat. Then we'll see what's what.'

The rain is all but gone, but the wind has wound up in its place. Milky and I are sheltered if we hunker down behind the garden wall, but the lane is a wind tunnel. The only one dressed in anything vaguely windproof is Heartbreak. The others will be feeling it.

'Get him against the wall!' says Heartbreak, pointing to Hornsby. 'And tie up McGregor!'

Smiff takes Neil's wrists and threads a wire through a metal downpipe, tying Neil's wrists either side, ensuring he can't run. Then Streak and Smiff grab Hornsby, pinning him to the wall. He struggles, but he's weak. He's been out on the street for at least four days and is spent.

'Okay,' says Heartbreak, stretching out her arms. She looks up. Milky and I duck back quickly.

'Right, let's get this done!' Heartbreak says from below.

I can hear her clearly enough. I decide to lie and listen rather than risk being seen.

'Milky,' I whisper. 'Keep your head down!'

He nods.

'I want my money back,' says Heartbreak. 'All of it, plus interest. Five percent per day and an extra 25% per week. Smiff here will work out the payment plan.'

'I'll get it,' says Hornsby.

'I haven't finished.'

There's a click and then a muffled scream. I risk looking over. Smiff has his hand over Hornsby's mouth only a few feet below me. Heartbreak is folding up a flick knife and Hornsby is squirming. I dive out of view.

'And you'll lose another finger every time you miss a payment,' she says.

Milky gags next to me.

'Another?' he whispers.

'I think Heartbreak just cut one of Hornsby's fingers off,' I whisper back.

'Wrap that in something, will you?' says Heartbreak. 'I don't want blood on this coat. Bloody good camel-hair coat, this is. Nearly five hundred quid's worth.'

Hornsby is moaning.

'And stuff something in his mouth 'til he stops whining!' Heartbreak adds.

The moaning drops off in volume.

I hear Neil plead, 'Not my fingers, please. We'll get the tape back for you.'

'Tape?' Heartbreak says. 'What tape?'

'Hornsby recorded you up in the flat, talking.'

'He did what?'

'When you gave him the three grand. He recorded you, then he sent Bannerman's kid in for it.'

'Is that why the wee shite was in my flat? After some tape.'

'Yes,' Neil moans

'Hornsby? Talk!' says Heartbreak. 'Smiff, take the gag out!'

Hornsby also moans.

'What's with this tape?' Heartbreak asks. 'What's on it?'

'We don't know,' says Neil.

There's a slap and Neil yelps.

'Keep him quiet!' says Heartbreak. 'Do you want the pigs round here?'

'Sorry Heartbreak,' says Smiff. 'I was just trying to get him to tell us the truth.'

'I am,' says Neil. 'I really am. We don't know what's on the tape.'

'And you,' Heartbreak says.

'I don't know either,' whimpers Hornsby. 'I just saw the tape recorder sticking out from under the couch. When you asked me to leave the room, I pressed record. That's it. I never got to sit back down again. I don't even know if it recorded anything. You called me in and gave me the money at the door. I never got the chance to get the tape.'

He starts moaning again.

'Tape recorder?' says Heartbreak.

'A black and silver thing,' says Hornsby.

'Wee Pauly's recorder. I wondered where that had gone. Last I saw, it was up in the flat when he was practising his chanter. He records the bloody noise on it. He must have pushed it under the couch. We lost that thing two weeks ago. That was the last time I was in that shithole. Very convenient for you.'

There's a muffled sound and Hornsby moans again.

'What's on the tape?' Heartbreak asks again.

'I don't know,' says Hornsby.

'And I don't believe you,' replies Heartbreak. 'You were just outside the room, waiting, and you can hear every bleeding burp in that place. What did you hear?'

'Nothing.'

Another moan.

'God, please stop!' says Hornsby. 'I only heard a little bit of talk.'

'About what?' says Heartbreak.

'About you and the bribe money for Dougrie.'

'And?' says Heartbreak.

'And something about taking on Spanner Johnston.'

'Fuck!' Heartbreak says. 'And you think that's on this tape?'

'I don't know,' replies Hornsby. 'I've not heard it. There might be nothing on it, Heartbreak, nothing.'

'So, you send in Bannerman's kid to get the thing,' Heartbreak says. 'And then what were you going to do? Blackmail me?'

Silence.

'The kid ran off with it,' he whines.

There's a thump and Hornsby moans again.

'So, you thought the Bannerman kid was coming here tonight to do what? Hand it over? Is that why you are here?'

'We told him that we'd do in his dad and grass up his mother if he didn't,' says Hornby.

'His mother. What's to grass up about her?' says Heartbreak. 'Kerry Dunlop, isn't it?'

Dunlop is Mum's maiden name.

'Ah,' says Heartbreak. 'You were going to tell about her time up at the Barras, weren't you? She was a good bloody worker was Kerry, before she got eyes for that pig, Bannerman. A right looker. Punters paid well for her.'

Milky squeezes my hand.

Jesus it's true. Mum worked in a brothel!

'Well, the wee shite chucked a rock with a note on it and said he'd be here tonight,' says Hornsby.

'And then stabbed me,' adds Neil.

'Clever little fucker!' says Heartbreak. 'Did the same trick with the rock to us. Told us you would be here and here you are. He's trying to get rid of his problems by putting us together. Put us all in the one place and see what happens. Smart shite! And he probably knows exactly what's on that tape. And I can't have that thing out on the street. Not if it has on it what you say it has on it.'

She pauses.

'And that clever wee swine is probably earwigging this whole conversation right now—if he's half as smart as I think he is,' she half shouts.

Milky and I do the stone statue thing. Not a muscle moves.

'Well, son,' she continues, voice loud. 'If you are listening, I want that tape back and any copies you might have made. If you're smart enough to dream up this little meeting, son, you'll be smart enough to be around here to see what happens. You've got something about you son, something about you—but the games are over. I need that tape.'

There's a flash of light from behind. I look back. The small window on the door to the flat has lit up. The door opens and an old man, wrapped in a ragged dressing gown peers out.

'Who's out there?' he yells.

The old man steps out. He's wearing battered slippers. His straggly beard is bright yellow at his mouth from who knows how many years of smoking. Milky and I duck behind the table but another few steps and he won't fail to see us.

'I said who is out there?'

From below us there is silence.

The old man takes another couple of steps.

'Who are you?' he says.

We've been spotted. Both of us jump up. Milky heads for the wall above the exit to the lane, and I follow. Milky vanishes from view and I leap over the wall after him, grabbing the drainpipe. I drop to the lane. Smiff appears around the corner. He's less than three feet from me. I dive away and tumble out of the lane. Smiff doesn't follow. The police car has to be on his mind. I look towards the car and both policemen are looking right at me. I turn away, walking towards my school, expecting a shout or the sound of a car engine firing up. Neither happens. As soon as the police are out of sight, I dive up the driveway of the nearest house. I wonder what has happened to Milky. I cross back to Jamie Anderson's house and out onto my street. Milky almost flattens me as he flies by.

'Run, Ginger!'

Behind him Streak is piling up the street.

Chapter 20
'Confession Time.'

I FOLLOW MILKY'S lead and start running, but as I round the bend in our road, I can see that Streak is way faster than even Milky.

'Split up!' I shout.

Milky flies up the path to the next house. I run across the road. Streak doesn't hesitate, he follows me. He knows who I am from the flat up in Castlemilk, but more likely he's chasing me because he can tell I'm the slower one. As I hit the far pavement, he is less than three steps behind. I leap into the garden in front of me, run up to the front window and batter it hard. Streak is on me, but I manage to duck under his arms and skittle into the garden next door. I bang on that window as well. Streak snatches at my anorak. With a rip, the tear that I got earlier widens and the arm all but comes loose. I yank hard and the sleeve comes away. Streak stumbles back, sleeve in hand, just as the door next to the first window opens. A burly woman in a bright yellow and orange dress appears. Streak ignores her and grabs me. The door next to me also opens and Mr Sinclair, a police Inspector that works with Dad, steps out. Mr Sinclair sizes up what is going on.

'Let the lad go!' he says.

Streak tries to pull me towards him. Mr Sinclair, a bear of a man with a gut like a pregnant pig, snatches my other arm.

'I said, let the lad go! I know who you are, Streak,' he says. 'What in the hell are you doing?'

Streak has one of my arms, Mr Sinclair has my other. I'm the rope in a tug-o-war.

'Let him go!' says Mr Sinclair.

'What's going on, George?' says the woman in the yellow and orange dress. She's standing right behind Streak.

Streak looks back, looks forward, and lets me go.

'The wee bastard chucked a rock at me,' spits Streak.

'Did you?' Mr Sinclair asks me.

'No, Mr Sinclair,' I say.

'Why would he throw a rock at you, Streak?' he asks.

'I don't know, but the wee shite is lying. I was down by the café, and he lobbed a half brick at me.'

'That's not true!' I say.

'I'll take care of this,' says Mr Sinclair. 'Leave the lad with me!'

Streak clips me around the back of the head. 'I'll find you.'

'Stop that now,' says Mr Sinclair. 'Now get moving or I'll lift you!'

Streak clips me again and I yelp, but he walks away.

'What was that about?' Mr Sinclair asks me.

'I never threw anything at him. He just started chasing me when I was coming by the shops.'

'Why chase you, if you did nothing?'

'Dunno, Mr Sinclair.'

'Well, get yourself home!' he says. 'I'll see your dad at work and tell him about this.'

Joy.

'We need to do something about all this nonsense,' says the woman. 'We need more policemen around here. There aren't enough on the beat. That's what I say.'

'Mrs Wilson,' Mr Sinclair says. 'Simshill has more policemen per square yard than anywhere else in Christendom.'

'Aye, but we still get trouble.'

'What trouble, Mrs Wilson?'

This sounds like a well-worn argument.

'Like this,' she says, pointing at me and then at the retreating Streak.

'Ginger, go home!' says Mr Sinclair.

I don't need to be told twice. I walk down the path as Mrs Wilson launches into a story about how she was sure someone was looking in her back window last night, and that the police took ages to arrive.

I walk onto the pavement. Streak is standing further down the street. As I head up the hill towards my house, he crosses to the far side of the road, and, with one eye on the on-going discussion between Inspector Sinclair and Mrs Wilson, he starts to follow me. Inspector Sinclair isn't a policeman to be messed with, but it's clear that Streak would rather cross him than go back to Heartbreak empty-handed.

Mr Sinclair spots him walking past. I break into a run. So does Streak.

'Streak, stop!' shouts Inspector Sinclair, but the words have no effect on him.

There's no way I can outrun Streak. My only option is to take the gardens and hedge-hop. I'm just about to get back to the Simshill world of gardens when Milky rushes out from a path and charges Streak in the side. Streak goes flying, landing on the road. Milky runs past him and joins me. We both belt up the nearest path and take to the realm that we know best.

We stop running when we are deep in the garden of the most dangerous woman in the world. Old Ma Carol's. If Mrs Terror is to be feared—Old Ma Carol is her more evil twin. No kid would dare enter her garden for fear of the wrath—and that makes it a great place to hide—if you can get away with it. She has a small shed that backs onto Links Road. There's enough space between it and a fence to squeeze in.

'What now?' says Milky, once we are settled.

'Who knows?' I reply. 'I'm assuming that Hornsby and Neil are going to have enough to worry about, what with owing Heartbreak money and the threat of more missing fingers.'

'Aye, that was gross,' says Milky.

'Jesus, she really cut it off, I think! What will happen to Hornsby and Neil?'

'I hate to think.'

'Heartbreak will want the tape, though.'

'I'm sure of it.'

'And what will Heartbreak do to get it from you?'

'Who knows? She could break into my house.'

Milky grimaces. 'So what do we do now?'

'Tell all,' I say. 'Tell all and see what happens.'

A voice intervenes.

'That sounds like a good idea.'

Both of us jump. The voice that just spoke comes from over the fence.

'Get the hell out of there!' the voice orders.

I look at Milky and he looks at me and we both say, 'Ivan?'

'Get the hell out of there or I'm coming in!'

A hand latches onto the top of a fence, then another, and Ivan's head looms over the top.

'Get out!' he orders.

We both rise.

'Now!' he says and drops from view.

'Run?' I suggest.

'Again?' says Milky.

'And don't think of running,' Ivan says. 'I'll just go straight to your house and wait for you.'

I'm suddenly too tired to run, or argue, or cry, or laugh, or do anything other than comply. I shuffle out from behind the shed and Milky follows. We both climb the fence and drop to the pavement.

Ivan stares us down.

'Okay, first things first. Where is this bloody tape?'

'In my house,' I say.

'Heartbreak and his idiots have just driven up to your house.'

'Will they wreck it?'

'Probably.'

'I've got to stop them.'

'And how would you do that?'

I have no idea.

'Will they find the tape?' he says.

'Not unless they know where to look.'

'Are you sure?'

'They would have to know where to look.'

'Like under your bed.'

'How do you know that?'

'I don't, but it seems a bloody obvious place to me.'

'Okay, but it's under the carpet and in a hidey hole beneath a floorboard.'

'They'll find it. We need to get it first. Can you sneak in and retrieve it?'

'Maybe, but what if Heartbreak is already in my house?'

'Wait here,' he says. 'Don't bloody move a muscle!'

He walks to the corner of the road and looks down. When he comes back, he says, 'They're still in the car. Can you get in the house quick—without them seeing you?'

'Yes. But why should I?'

'Do the maths, Bobby! You either deal with me or Heartbreak. Your choice.'

I'm at a loss.

'Give me the tape and I can sort all of this out for you!'

The Ivan of school is back. Friendly.

'How?' I ask.

'I'm telling you I can. I can get Heartbreak out of your life. And your dad will never know.'

'I don't believe you.'

'I don't care what you believe, I just want that tape.'

'No. I'm going to tell Dad.'

'You think he can solve all of this? Stop Heartbreak? Save you? Do you?'

'Yes.'

'Okay, try it. See where that goes. But I'm telling you now, give me the tape and I can make this all vanish.'

'You're in it with Hornsby,' says Milky.

He surprises us by laughing. 'Hornsby? Not a chance. I don't back losers.'

'You talked to Neil.'

'I talked to both of them. They told me everything. Idiots. I used to work with Hornsby up in Dougrie Road. He's a fool! A bent fool. How do you think I found out about that tape? But, as I say, I don't back losers. Did Heartbreak catch them at the lane?'

'How do you know that?'

'McGregor told me you were delivering the tape there. Didn't take a genius to figure what the two of you might be up to. Smart. I wouldn't give a rat's arse for Hornsby or McGregor—I doubt you'll see them again.'

'So, you work for Heartbreak then,' I say.

'Still a loser. I only back winners. That's why I can make this all vanish. Now go get that tape!'

'No.'

He grabs Milky and forces his arm up his back. Milky screams.

'I *will* break it,' Ivan says. 'Get me the tape, or I'll break his arm!'

The evil Ivan is back in full view.

He shoves harder and Milky yells.

'Okay, okay,' I cry.

'Now! We all go together.'

'We need to go through the gardens.'

'Just go!'

We all cross the road, climb into the first garden and cut through to ours.

'That's my window,' I say, pointing up. 'I can climb up the pipe and get in.'

'Go, now!' orders Ivan, Milky still in hand.

Before I can move, I spot someone climbing our front stairs.

'Shite, Heartbreak is coming,' says Ivan. 'In the house. Is anyone in?'

'Dad should be. We just got broken into, remember?'

He pushes Milky and me forward, through the back door.

'Lock it!' he says.

I twist the large dead bolt. Ivan has to give me a hand—it hasn't been locked in a while.

Dad appears at the kitchen door.

'Ivan?' he says.

'Ronnie,' he replies.

'What the hell is going on?'

'All you need to know is that Paula Hart is just about to try and break into your house.'

'Heartbreak?'

'Yes, and right now!'

The backdoor handle rattles. Dad walks past me.

'Whoever is out there can just fuck off,' he says.

'Hi, Ronnie,' comes Heartbreak's reply through the door. 'Long time since we last talked.'

'Paula, I've no idea what this is all about, but I'm not opening the door. So just get lost!'

'Sorry, Ronnie,' she replies. 'No can do. Your son has something of mine and I need it back.'

Dad turns to me, but Ivan intervenes.

'Ronnie,' he says to Dad. 'There is nothing in here that we should give to that woman, okay?'

Dad stares at me. 'What in the hell have you done?'

Before I can reply, Heartbreak is rattling the door again.

'Look,' she says. 'Just let us in! Once we get what we are looking for we will be gone.'

Ivan shakes his head.

'Paula!' Dad says. 'I've no idea what's going on. Give me five minutes to figure what is what. Okay?'

'Fair enough, but don't think on phoning for help. We can sort this out without more of your friends here. If you get what I mean…'

'Just give me five minutes,' Dad says. 'And get out of my garden!'

'Not going to happen, Ronnie,' she shouts back. 'I'm staying right here. Five minutes to hand over what's mine.'

Dad ushers us all into the living room. The place is a mess. Drawers lie on the table, ornaments smashed on the floor, plastic bin bags are open, waiting on debris—it looks like Dad has been trying to tidy up.

'Right,' says Dad. 'I don't give a flying eff about anything other than why Paula Hart is at my door. We've just been broken into and I'm due on shift soon, so, Ivan, start talking!'

He shakes his head. 'Not me Ronnie. I don't know the half of it. It's your son here you need to ask.'

'You must know something?'

'Dad,' I interrupt. 'Look, I'd have said something sooner but…'

'I'm talking to Ivan,' he says.

'Dad…'

'Shut it!'

'Honestly, Ronnie,' says Ivan. 'Your son knows much more than me.'

Dad tilts his head to one side. He lets out a small sigh.

'Okay, Bobby. Tell me!'

Where to start? I haven't said more than four sentences in a row to my dad in my entire life. Talking to him is so difficult. He's polis. Hard wired to believe nothing he hears. To trust no-one. To expect the worst.

'Hurry up!' he says.

And so, I do the only thing I can think of and let rip. And if the session we had with Ivan was a rambling road of a story; this is far worse. Dad stands. Halfway through Heartbreak shouts, 'Time's up!'

'I need ten minutes more or we all do this the hard way, Paula.'

'I'll not be stalled.'

'I'm not stalling.'

'Ten minutes and then we come in, ready or not.'

'Get on with it!' Dad says to me.

I fly through the rest. When I get to the end, he doesn't launch into a bunch of questions. He simply stands back and stares at the ceiling.

'Okay, Bobby,' he says. 'I'm not even going to start with what's going to happen to you. I also don't have time to rip this crap apart and try and get at the truth.'

'But it is the truth!' I say.

'To be fair, Ronnie,' says Ivan. 'I'd say it probably is, from what I know.'

'So, if we give Hart this tape she'll go?' asks Dad.

'Sorry, Ronnie but that isn't going to happen,' says Ivan. 'I need that tape. You'll just need to tell Heartbreak to piss off.'

'You need it. Why?'

I'm about to mention the copy I made of the tape, but something tells me to hold on to that piece of information.

'Just give it to me!' says Ivan.

'And what will happen then, Ivan? Hart will try to break in anyway.'

'She isn't going to do that,' says Ivan. 'There's three of them and two of us. And the two idiots she's in tow with are pricks. Heartbreak I'd worry about, but not the others. If she has to come in here, I'd put money on her sending for back up first.'

'What in the hell is exactly on this tape, Bobby?'

'I'll get it,' I say.

I run upstairs and extract the tape. I bring it down, along with Deke's recorder. I hand them both to Dad. He inserts the tape and is about to play it when Heartbreak shouts out that she is coming in. Dad goes to the back door and opens it.

'Look, Hart. Take one step in here and I'll make sure all of Dougrie Drive, Craigie Street and Central Division go through your whole fucking life with a flea comb. Stop with the threats and give me time to think!'

'I need that tape, Ronnie. And I need it now!'

'Well, you're not getting anything.'

'Just give me the tape and be done with this!'

'No.'

'How's Kerry doing, Ronnie?'

'She's nothing to do with this.'

'She doesn't have to be.'

'Leave her out of this!'

'Give me the tape and I'll be glad to. After all she was one of my best workers back in the day. I probably owe her.'

I've wandered into the kitchen and I'm standing behind Dad.

'You must be young Bobby,' says Heartbreak. 'Do me a favour and get the tape you stole!'

'Stay there Bobby,' says Dad. 'Do nothing.'

He slams the door in Heartbreak's face and locks it.

'I don't give a flying eff what you've done, Bobby, but I'm not having your mother threatened.'

He goes back to the living room and then to the hall.

'Bastard,' he shouts and comes back in. 'She's cut the bloody phone line!'

He picks up the recorder, presses play.

Nothing happens.

'What's up with this thing?'

The small red light that signals there's power is not lit.

'The batteries look dead,' I say.

'We don't have any in the house,' says Dad. 'Son, just tell me exactly what is on it.'

Then the lights go out.

'Power cut,' says Milky.

'You have to be bloody joking,' says Dad. 'Bobby, get the candles, quick!'

I dig them out of the sideboard. A car engine fire up. Ivan moves to the window and pulls back the curtain. As I light up the candles Ivan announces, 'The Victor is gone, but Heartbreak and the long thin wanker are still there.'

'Reinforcements,' says Dad. 'Paula is sending for more people. Okay, Ivan, I've had enough. Two of them and two of us. We can handle this.'

'No, we can't,' says Ivan. 'Look!'

Dad goes to the window.

'A gun?' he says. 'She has a gun. She didn't have it at the back door.'

'She got the gun from Hornsby,' I say. 'Maybe someone in the car gave it to her before they drove off.'

'Why doesn't she just come in now?' asks Milky. 'I mean, if she has a gun.'

It's a good question.

'Tell me what's on the tape, Bobby!' says Dad.

As best I can, I tell him what I remember, and Milky helps out.

'Let me get this straight,' Dad says, still looking out of the window. 'Hart gave Hornsby three thousand pounds in money to bribe some police in Dougrie Road. Hornsby did a runner, and he no longer has the cash because he owed someone the money. And Hart is planning to try the same bribery nonsense at Turnbull Street and I'm the target for the money? Is that it?'

'Yes,' I say.

'So, it's true? Heartbreak is going to move in on Spanner?' says Ivan. 'Interesting, Bobby. Is that right?'

'I think so,' I say.

'Then I don't need that tape anymore' he says.

Dad has the recorder but doesn't let it go.

'Let me get this straight, Bobby,' Dad says. 'You didn't mention this tape or any of the rest of this to me earlier because you thought I was already taking money from Hart.'

I lower my head.

'Is that it, Bobby?'

'Well, we got the new telly, Dad, and the new Hi-Fi. New dining table. G Plan. You were talking about taking Mum to the hotel and, and… you and Mum were laughing, and you never laugh. Also, Mum gave Deke money when he asked for it and…'

'And you thought I was on the take? Me?'

I look even further down.

'Because we bought some things,' he says. 'Because of that, you believed some arsehole of a wannabee gangster rather than talk to your father.'

'There's no point in talking to you,' I say, quietly.

'Say that again, Bobby!' Dad says, dropping the curtain, walking over to me.

'You never listen to anything I say, Dad. You just hit me if I speak out of turn.'

'Don't you talk to me like that!' he growls and lifts his hand.

'See,' I say. 'You're going to hit me.'

He's left hanging, hand in the air, mouth open.

'That's why I didn't say anything, Dad. You'd have just accused me of lying and leathered me. Hornsby would have called me a liar if I'd told you that night. And you would have sided with him.'

I lift my eyes a little. Milky and Ivan are watching the exchange side by side, Ivan leaning on the sideboard, Milky sitting on the arm of the couch.

'Given what you've just told me, I should leather you for a bloody month!' he says.

Silence descends.

'Maybe the lad's got a point, Ronnie.' Ivan states. 'Hard to tell your dad something if he never listens.'

'Are you trying to tell me how to deal with my own son?'

He shakes his head. 'Just saying.'

'Deke doesn't get any grief,' I add.

'What?' says Dad.

'You've never given Deke any grief. He gets away with murder.'

'He's fifteen.'

'He was staying out late when he was ten. Came home drunk one night when he was twelve, and all you did was put a basin next to his bed and a tea towel. He didn't even get grounded. You would have half-killed me.'

'I'm not having this conversation here.'

'You never want to have a conversation with me anywhere!'

'We will talk later.'

'You mean you'll talk, and I'll listen, then you'll hit me.'

'I should give you a hiding now!'

'Ginger's not the bad person here, Mr Bannerman,' says Milky.

'What has this to do with you?' Dad says.

'I'm his friend. He wanted to come to you about all of this a number of times but was scared what would happen if you were taking money. And also, if the story he heard from him about his mum is true,' he points at Ivan when he says the word 'him'.

'Ivan told you about Kerry?' Dad says. 'What did he tell you?'

Milky nods. 'He told us at your police station that he would tell everyone what Mrs Bannerman did up at the Barras.'

'Which was what?'

Milky drops his head.

'Which was what?' says Dad. He looks at Ivan. 'What did you tell them?'

'Only what's going to come out if we don't deal with Heartbreak,' says Ivan.

'About Kerry.'

'About the tenement up at the Barras.'

'Don't you fucking dare talk about Kerry like that!' Dad shouts.

Ivan doesn't blink an eye.

'Don't you say one more word about her!' he spits. 'Not one more fucking word!'

Ivan moves over. 'Calm it down, Ronnie.'

'I'm not having any bastard talk about my wife in that way.'

'Dad?' I say.

'Not a fucking single word.'

'Dad?'

'I'll fucking skin anyone that says anything!'

'Dad?'

'What? Fucking what?'

'Milky is right. I was scared, Dad,' I say. 'Scared of them, scared of you, and scared of the stories. Of what would happen if the stories were all true.'

'Well, they are not true. Not a single bit of it is true.'

Ivan shakes his head. 'Ronnie, the boy needs to know at some point.'

'Does he hell?' Dad says.

'It's up to you, but I think I'd rather hear the real story from my Dad than the gossip from the likes of me, Heartbreak or others.'

'Dad, tell me the story about Mum isn't true!' I say.

My dad visibly slumps. His shoulders sag. His knees bend. His usual bolt upright stance, *the polis stance*, is gone. As if sucked from him by a Hoover. He leans on the mantlepiece.

'Son…,' he says and stops. He shakes his head. Then he stands up again and the polis stance returns.

He's back in police mode.

'Son,' he says, 'I'll talk to you about what you need to know once this is fixed. But let's get a few things straight. I'm not on the take. Never have been, never will be. Some do,' He looks at Ivan. Ivan smiles. 'And some don't. I don't.'

'My dad?' asks Milky.

'Not your dad either, son.'

'So, can we talk about your mother later,' he says to me. 'Is that okay?'

I don't think my dad has ever asked me if something is okay. I never get any say in anything.

'Eh?'

'I promise I'll tell you everything you need to know but just not now. Is that okay?'

I nod.

'Good,' he says. 'Now, Ivan, what is Hart doing now?'

Ivan pulls back the curtain.

'Sitting on the wall with the other guy, smoking.'

'And there is no one else?'

'No.'

'But she's sent for more people?'

'Probably.'

'Okay, we don't want to be here when they arrive.'

'I agree,' says Ivan. 'But with a gun, why has she not come in?'

'Maybe she thinks we're armed.'

'Unlikely.'

I have a thought.

'Mr Peters. Did you tell Hornsby where the gun was?'

'Did I hell!'

'So, who knew it was in the Subby?'

'Son' says Dad, 'what has this to do with anything?'

'Milky, you didn't see anyone when I was burying the gun? Did you?'

'No. Except I couldn't see the whole street.'

'But what if Neil saw me? It would explain how Hornsby got it back. He was watching our house from down the hill. He could have seen me bury it, if he walked up a little.'

'And the bullets?'

'What about them?'

'You didn't bury them with the gun, did you?'

'No. They are upstairs. I emptied the gun before I buried it.'

'And that means?' Milky smiles as he pauses for my answer.

I smile. 'Maybe the gun is still empty.'

Milky nods. 'That would explain why Heartbreak is still outside. An empty gun isn't much use.'

Chapter 21
'Saturday Night Blast.'

'ARE YOU SAYING the gun is empty?' asks Dad.

'I can't be sure,' I say. 'Hornsby could have been carrying spare bullets.'

'But if he wasn't, it would explain why Hart is sitting on my wall with a shit-eating grin waiting on her pals,' Dad says. 'But even if the gun is empty, we still need help before her gang gets here.' He looks at Milky. 'James?'

Milky jumps off the couch arm as if it was electrified.

'Yes, Mr Bannerman,' he says.

'I need you to go up to Mrs Reid's house on the corner. Ask to use her phone. I want you to call Craigie Street police station and ask for Sergeant McAndrews. Tell him it's urgent. Use my name. Tell him that we are in real trouble. We need a couple of cars up here as soon as possible. Tell him about Hart and the gun! Have you got that?'

'Yes, Mr Bannerman.'

Dad pulls out a small black notepad from his back pocket. It's his police note pad. He carries it everywhere with him, whether he's on duty or not. He extracts the chewed black pencil that is secreted in the binding and scribbles on a sheet of paper. He rips the piece of paper free and hands it to Milky.

'Use that number. It'll get you straight through.'

'Mr Bannerman, what if he doesn't believe me?'

'If he doesn't listen, just say what's written below the telephone number!'

Milky studies the paper and reads out loud. 'Bobby Shearer once played 165 consecutive games for Rangers.' He looks up. 'What does that mean?'

'It means he'll know the message came from me and that you're not making it all up. That's what it means—now get out the back and move quickly! Jean Reid is in, I saw her watching us earlier. And tell her not to come down here. Tell her I'll come up and explain it all later. And for God's sake, don't get spotted by Hart!'

'I…'

'Now James, go now—no questions. Out the back right now before Hart's cronies arrive!'

Milky hesitates but, with a gentle shove from Dad, he leaves.

'Ronnie,' Ivan says, when Dad comes back into the room. 'Before Craigie Street's finest come here, what are you going to do with that tape?'

Dad pops the tape from the recorder, slings the recorder on his chair and pockets the cassette.

'It might come in handy. In case you've forgotten—that woman out there has dodged two, think on that, two murder charges and countless other shit over the years. You were up in Castlemilk. You know exactly what she is capable of. If she wants this tape, then I'm hanging onto to it until help gets here. From what Bobby has told me, Hart wants this thing. And that makes it our bargaining chip, if we need it.'

'Ronnie, it's worthless. If you release it, Paula will just say she was bragging. That there's nothing to what she said. And even if there are a few bent coppers up the hill, we'd need to know who they were, catch them red-handed and even after all that, they'd probably not grass on Hart. Hart will have gen on whoever she's backhanding. Enough to shut them up for good. So, this tape is all but worthless.'

'True,' says Dad. 'But it would cause a stir. She wants it, and because of that, *I* want it!'

We wait in silence until Milky comes back. He's taken less than five minutes.

'Did you get a hold of McAndrews?' says Dad.

'Yes,' says Milky.

'And?'

'And he'll send someone when he can.'

'When he can? Did you not tell him it was important?'

'Yes, but he says there's a pitched battled down at Toryglen between gangs. Every policeman he has is down there, and the same is true for Dougrie Road and Rutherglen stations. He says even Central have sent up everyone they can spare.'

'He must have someone free. Did you mention the gun?'

'I did. He said he would get someone here as soon as he can.'

'Looks like the cavalry won't be here any time soon,' says Ivan. 'Maybe we should consider getting the hell out of here. Heartbreak might employ some right idiots, but she employs some right *vicious* idiots. Ronnie, send the kids away first, then you and me can get the hell out of here and let it all settle down.'

'And Hart will trash my home looking for the tape?' points out Dad. 'Or what happens when Kerry comes back, and Paula is still here? I'm not for bailing. The kids? Well, that's a different game. Maybe they need to get out. I need to figure another way to deal with this until help gets here.'

A car roars up outside. Dad pulls back the curtain.

'Heartbreak's men?' says Ivan.

'Could be,' says Dad. 'It's a Black Ford Granada.'

'A black one?'

'Yes.'

Ivan joins my dad and looks out. 'Well, it seems I was wrong; the cavalry *has* arrived.'

'Who is it?'

'Heartbreak's worst nightmare.'

'Who?'

'You'll see.'

I go over for a look, and I'm surprised my dad doesn't tell me to get back.

The black Granada has stopped a couple of doors down. The exhaust is belching out a cloud of fumes, but no one has got out. Heartbreak is standing looking down at the car. As is Streak. A second car pulls up behind the Granada. A shiny new looking Austin Allegro. No one gets out of that either.

'Who are they?' says Dad to Ivan.

'Some guys that don't like the sound of what they are hearing from this part of the world,' Ivan replies. 'That's who.'

At the top of the hill, the Red Victor appears. It stops a few doors up. Behind it a Blue Cortina, with more scrapes and bashes than our rubbish bin, parks up.

'Heartbreak's men?' says Dad, pointing to the new cars.

Ivan nods. 'Looks like it.'

'And the Granada and Allegro. Who are they?' Dad asks.

'Looks like we are about to have a showdown,' says Ivan.

'Spanner's men?' says Dad.

Ivan says nothing.

All four cars look full to me.

'All this over a tape!' says Dad.

Ivan studies the cars. 'It's not the tape. This has all been coming for a while.'

'I heard that Johnston was struggling,' Dad says. 'We put a shed load of his men down recently.'

'And everyone and his auntie is lining up to step into his shoes. But Spanner didn't get where he is by rolling over. He knows he needs to take the fight to those that want his patch. It's the only way he can shore up his own kingdom. Heartbreak isn't the only one with ambition in this city.'

'And how would a school janitor know so much about these things?' asks Dad.

'You'd be amazed at what a school janny hears, Ronnie. Kids talking in the playground. Parents at parent's nights. Teachers at break. Jannies are invisible in schools—unless they are needed. A kid vomits on the floor? I'm there with sawdust and a bucket. A broken window? Me with wood and nails to board it up. A snapped climbing rope in the gym? I'm on hand to replace it. The rest of the time, I'm a ghost, and a ghost in a school that is dominated by police kids. Nearly every child in Simshill Primary has a dad or an aunt or an uncle or a grandpa in the force. And I'm ex-polis. To be trusted. Stories fly around the school like confetti.'

'And you and Spanner have history?'

'We knew each other when I worked Central.'

'And now he has you as a nice spy in the nest of police that settled around here?'

'He likes to keep his ear to the ground.'

'And did he have you in his pocket up town, Ivan?'

'We had an arrangement.'

'One that meant you phoned him earlier.'

'Ronnie, you need to back the winning team in any game. I guessed what was on that tape from the conversation with Hornsby, but I wanted to be sure. Now it doesn't matter. Spanner suspects Heartbreak is planning to move in. This should be fun!'

We all look out again.

Heartbreak is looking nervous. Her smile is gone as she looks up at the cars at the top of the hill and back to those further down.

'I'm thinking,' said Dad. 'That even if I go out and hand this tape over that it's not going to stop what's about to happen.'

Ivan nods. 'Not a chance. That tape is old news now.'

The door to the Granada opens. A man as thin as a ten-year-old toothbrush gets out. He's wearing a knee length leather coat. His hair is army regulation short. He walks to the front of the car, stands in the road, and looks up in our direction.

'Hart!' he shouts, the words crystal clear through the thin, single pane of our windows. 'I'm here to sort you out.'

Heartbreak, standing at the top of our stairs, looks down on the man in the leather coat. Her face is stone.

'You figure, Spanner?'

The man in the leather coat pulls up his collar. 'Stephen to you. No one calls me Spanner to my face unless they know me well. I don't like it and I sure as hell don't like you.'

'Well, *Spanner*,' Heartbreak shouts back. 'I don't like you and I certainly don't like people on my patch.'

Both voices are loud. A few curtains start to twitch in the surrounding windows.

'I'll make this simple, Hart,' Spanner shouts. 'Just you and me. Right here. Right now. Winner takes all, as they say. Nae chibs. Nae nothing. Just you and me.'

'Sounds like the rumours are true then,' Heartbreak shouts back. 'All your good muscle is in BarL. You're out doing your own dirty work, Spanner. Taking on a woman? Is that your style now? Takes a big brave man to do that. Is that wee boys you have in the cars?'

Heartbreak's smile is back.

Spanner walks up the hill. 'I don't care if you're a lassie, a lad or a fucking dog—we are going to sort this out.'

Heartbreak lifts the gun and points it at Spanner, but if she expects him to stop walking, she's disappointed. Spanner is wearing shiny spats, the hard leather soles clicking on the wet road as he walks.

Heartbreak waves the gun. 'I'd stop there.'

Spanner keeps walking until he's level with next door's stairs.

'I said stop!' Heartbreak barks, stepping forward to lean over the wall. Spanner keeps up his march. His arms swinging freely—head high. Full of confidence. When he reaches the foot of our stairs, Heartbreak has to stand on the wall to see him.

Across the road, a door opens, and a man looks out.

'We have an audience,' says Ivan.

'Colin Pettigrew,' says Dad. 'A DI at our station.'

'He was a beat cop when I was there.'

Another door opens three down from us. A woman steps out.

'Helen White,' Ivan announces, before Dad can speak. 'I know her. Has a kid in P3. She's a police liaison officer. Dealt with my retirement.'

Spanner has now vanished from view, hidden by the wall at the foot of the steps.

Yet another door cracks two down. An older man steps out.

'Angus McFarlane,' says Dad. 'Retired Chief Inspector.'

'I never knew him, but this is a hell of an audience,' says Ivan.

'Come on down here, Hart, you little coward. Put that gun away!' shouts Spanner.

'Fuck you, Spanner!'

Spanner's head appears, rising up our stairs, slowly, deliberately, eyes locked on Heartbreak. No hesitation. No apparent concern for the gun.

My dad turns and pushes me back.

'Bobby back, all of us back! The gun. It could be loaded!'

It dawns on me that all of us are watching the scene unfold as if we were chomping down on popcorn at the pictures.

Angus McFarlane shouts out, 'Stop this now. Put that gun down!'

I can't see now. But I can hear.

Heartbreak: 'Spanner that's far enough.'

Angus: 'Gun down!'

Dad moves to the hallway door.

Heartbreak: 'One more step and I'll shoot.'

Dad is into the hall.

Heartbreak: 'Last warning.'

Dad opens the front door.

Dad: 'Hart, put the gun down!'

Heartbreak: 'Get back in the house, Bannerman!'

Dad: 'Just…'

The gun goes off.

And we all fall into silence.

Dead silence.

Chapter 22
'Too Late?'

NO ONE MOVES. Milky is on the couch, hand covering his mouth. Ivan is standing in the middle of the room, eyes on the hallway door. I'm next to him. Through frosted glass, I can see that the front door is wide open. And there's no shadow. No outline. No Dad. I totter forward. Ivan puts his hand on my shoulder. 'I'll go. Stay here!'

From outside, noises start to creep in. Car doors slamming. Voices. An engine revs. A woman screams. Ivan reaches the hallway door, and it slams open in his face as Dad barrels in.

'Down!' he shouts, but no one reacts.

Behind him Heartbreak runs in, gun high. She looks at us one by one, her eyes flicking around like Christmas lights. She reaches over and yanks Milky by the collar. She pulls him close.

'Close that front door. Lock it!' she screams into Milky's face and pushes him into the hallway. Milky does as he is told. Heartbreak reaches into the hall once the door is shut and yanks Milky back in.

'Everyone sit down!' she shouts.

Dad steps forward and Heartbreak points the gun at the ceiling. She pulls the trigger. The gun shot is as loud as the one in the den.

'Down!' Heartbreak screams. 'I'm not fucking around here!'

We all get down, Dad last.

'Okay Paula,' says Dad, quietly. 'Take it easy. We'll do what you say. Just put the gun down!'

'Aye, right!' she says.

'At least point it at the floor, Paula,' Dad says. 'You don't want to shoot anyone else.'

Anyone else, I think. *Did she shoot Spanner?*

'Nice and easy, Paula,' says Dad.

Dad's voice is ice calm and I realise that this is my father doing what he does every day of his life. Talking to people. Talking to people who don't want to be talked to. Talking to the violent. To the insane. To those on their own personal edge. To the unpredictable. To the horrors.

'Just stay calm, Paula,' he says.

'Fuck you!' Heartbreak growls.

'Paula, there's children in here. You don't want to hurt kids. Do you, Paula?'

The deliberate, repeated use of Heartbreak's first name is Dad's way of calmly trying to connect with a woman who is scaring me stupid.

'Close that curtain,' says Heartbreak. 'You!' She points at me.

'On you go, son,' says Dad.

I get up and pull the curtain closed, but not before looking out. Spanner is lying on our top step. There are men running towards our house from the Granada and Allegro. Up, at the top of the road, men are out of the Victor and the Cortina, but they are not coming our way. They are just standing.

'Away from the window!' shouts Heartbreak. I let the curtain drop.

'Okay, Paula,' says Dad. 'Let the kids go. There's no need for them to be here. Just let them go!'

'No,' she says.

'Paula, you don't want to involve them.'

'They involved themselves in this. They know what is on that fucking tape.'

'Okay, Paula, but that's no reason to put them in danger. Just let them go to the kitchen at least—and we can talk.'

'Sure. And they will run.'

'Paula, you have kids. A daughter and a son. Same age as Bobby and James, aren't they? What's their names? Pauly and Wendy? Isn't it? Would you want them here, like this?'

Heartbreak swings the gun back and forth about her hip. Dad's words are getting through and, despite the danger and the fear, I'm seeing Dad in a new light. He's so assured. *So effective.*

'Just send the kids to the kitchen, Paula, and we can talk about this.'

'What's to talk about, Bannerman?' she says. She pulls back a corner of the curtain, and quickly peeks out, her eyes off us for less than a second.

'Shite!' she says. 'Who called the pigs?'

'Is there a police car?' asks Ivan.

'Just pulled up,' Hart says. 'Who the fuck called them?'

Dad offers a suggestion, 'Could have been anyone of the hundred policemen and women who were watching you out there.'

'What's happened to Spanner?' asks Ivan.

Heartbreak ignores the question. She has another look out the window.

'Bannerman,' she says to Dad, once she's closed the curtain again 'Tell your pig friends to stay where they are!'

'Move the kids first!' he replies.

'Just lean out of the window. Tell them to stay on the street. Tell them not to come up here.'

She backs off to allow Dad to get to the window.

Dad doesn't move.

'Fuck, Bannerman!' Heartbreak says. 'I can as easily shoot you in the leg, let you bleed, push you out the door and tell them to back off myself.'

Dad rises and makes for the window. He pulls the curtain to one side. He surveys the scene.

'Spanner looks like he needs medical help,' says Dad. 'Someone will need to come up the stairs.'

'Just do what I told you!' Heartbreak says.

Dad unlatches the window and leans out.

'Stay down there,' he shouts out. 'Martin, can you tell the others to stay there? We have a woman up here with a gun!'

'Is anyone hurt?' comes the reply.

'Spanner Johnston might have been shot. He's at the top of our steps.'

'Anyone else?'

'No.'

'Who is the woman with the gun?'

Heartbreak pulls Dad's arm.

'In. Shut the window! Enough chat.'

Dad moves back into the room.

'You're on your own, Paula,' he says. 'Your team have gone.'

'Don't talk shite!'

'Have a look yourself. They've gone.'

'What about Spanner's men?' asks Ivan, as Hart pulls back the curtains again.

'They are gone as well,' says Dad.

'Shit!' says Heartbreak when she looks out. 'Fucking cowards. They've all gone. I'll chib every one of my lot, when I get to them.'

'Some takeover this is turning out to be, Heartbreak,' says Ivan. 'First sign of the police and your lot run for the hills.'

Heartbreak growls, 'Shut the fuck up!'

'Look, Paula,' my dad points out. 'This isn't going to end well for you. Give me the gun and hand yourself in.'

'Oh, sure,' says Heartbreak. 'And then what? A date at the High Court? I don't think so.'

'At least let the kids go, Paula,' Dad repeats. 'You know the guys down there will have called the firearm officers by now. You don't want a shoot-out with kids in the house.'

'I'm happy to go with that. They shoot. I shoot back,' says Heartbreak. 'Only I'll be shooting from in here. They won't shoot with kids in here.'

'Look,' Dad says. 'Just let the kids go and let someone up to treat Johnston!'

'Fuck off!'

'If Johnston is still alive, you should let them treat him, Paula.' says Ivan. 'Murder carries a long sentence.'

'That fucker came at me,' says Heartbreak. 'Self-defence. That's what it was.'

She's now standing with her back against the wall, next to our new telly. Every so often, she brings the gun up and waves it at one of us. Each time she does this, the person involved recoils a little. All save Dad, who is inching closer to Heartbreak each time she looks away.

'He just kept coming. I had to shoot,' she mutters.

'Paula, you need to act now,' says Dad, and then he turns to me. 'Bobby, get up! You too, James.'

We begin to rise.

'Fucking sit down!' shouts Heartbreak.

'Paula, you don't need them,' Dad says. 'Us, yes. But not them. Just let them go. I'll do what you want if you let them go.'

Heartbreak moves to the window and looks out again.

'Shite, more pig cars!'

There are spinning blue lights pulsing our curtain. Enough to suggest there's more than a couple of vehicles down there. In the distance, we can hear the nee-naw of an ambulance approaching. Heartbreak takes in what is happening outside the window. Dad slides forward. A few more feet and he'll be close enough to try to get the gun. He takes a small step to his left, behind Heartbreak. He leans forward, one more step, he's up on his toes and...

Heartbreak swings around. The gun up and ready. Pointing right at my dad's chest.

'No!' I shout.

'Don't move another fucking inch,' grunts Heartbreak to Dad. 'Not one more fucking inch!'

Dad wavers, almost vibrates. His muscles taking him towards Heartbreak and the gun telling him to back down. Heartbreak raises the gun up, swings it hard and connects with my dad's head. He collapses onto the telly and falls to the floor.

I leap up and run at Heartbreak. 'Leave my dad alone!' I scream.

'Bobby, no!' shouts Ivan.

Heartbreak sees me coming. She raises the gun. Ivan shouts again. I put my head down, ignoring the weapon. All my attention is on hitting Heartbreak. I throw myself at her. She flicks at me with her free arm, and I barrel towards the windowsill, hitting it with my shoulder. I go down as Ivan shouts 'No' again.

'No one else moves,' shouts Heartbreak. 'No one!'

I roll over. Heartbreak above me. She reaches down and lifts me up as if I were a two-pound bag of sugar. She drags me across the living room floor to the kitchen door.

'I'm going out the back to see what is what,' she says, her fingers locked on my upper arm. 'If anyone follows me, I'll shoot the boy.'

Heartbreak drags me through the kitchen door and, just before the room vanishes from view, I see my dad, lying on the floor, looking up at me—starting to get up. Then I'm in the kitchen. Heartbreak stares at the back door. She lets me go for a second to open it. It's a chance to run, but she grabs my arm before I can act. She looks out into the garden and pushes me out. She closes the door behind us.

'Where does that lead to?' she says, pointing to our back wall.

'To Mrs Robertson's garden.'

'Move!'

She shoves me onto our back green, towards the rear wall.

'Go,' she orders, following me into the Robertson's garden.

'That way,' she says, shoving me towards the driveway that runs up the side of Mrs Robertson's house. She takes the lead and, when we reach the far edge of the house, she looks out onto the road.

'Keep moving!' she says and drags me onto the street.

There's a noise behind. Heartbreak turns and so do I. It's dark back there, but it looks like someone else is climbing over the wall. A siren goes up as a panda car appears at the bottom of the street we are on.

Heartbreak pulls at my arm, yanking me across the road. The entrance to the Woods is in front of us.

'Where does that go?' she says.

'Into the Woods,' I say.

She forces me up the lane.

'Do you know this place?'

'Yes.'

'I want back to Castlemilk, and no fucking funny business!'

I think on leading her the wrong way. She slaps me across the back of the head, hard.

'Castlemilk!' she repeats.

I point towards the football pitch. 'That's the way—but you'll need to jump the school fence at the bottom.'

She looks back down the lane. A figure appears. She levels the gun and fires. The sound is a living thing. The gun only a few inches from my head.

'Stay out there!' she shouts.

I was so wrong on the bullets. I wonder if Dad is following me. Has Heartbreak hit my dad? She pulls me away.

'Show me the way!' she snarls.

I stumble up the path and over the brow of the hill towards our den. I pass it and make for the bottom corner of the Woods.

'There,' I say. 'Climb there, the fence is broken! That's my old school.'

'Simshill Primary?'

'Yes.'

'Good. You first.'

'Let me go, Mrs Hart!'

'Get the fuck over!'

She almost throws me into the school grounds. As I land, she shows a surprising twist of nimbleness, and follows me over. We cut along the back of the new annexe that was Milky's and my home for the last year of Primary School. We head down through the Primary One playground. We take the stairs that lead down to Simshill Road, passing Ivan Peter's bungalow on the way. When we reach the bottom of the school driveway, there's a double gate. It's locked tight. Heartbreak doesn't hesitate. She can see her goal, Castlemilk, from here. She pushes me up onto the gate, constantly checking the road in front and the drive behind us. With the power still out, the world is one giant shadow. When I'm over the gate, she climbs over after me, grabs my arm and points to the other side of the road.

'We'll cut through the golf course,' she says.

Linn Park golf course is a public course. Milky and I have hit many golf balls on it. An eighteen-hole affair, it separates Simshill from the area we call the Valley. It's where our neighbour, David Lachlan, was slashed. We push through a fence onto the eighteenth fairway.

'Please, Mrs Hart. Let me go! I'll not say where you went.'

'Just fucking move!'

She slaps her hand into the small of my back. I stumble on. She yanks me left. We track the fairway back to the eighteenth tee. We have to keep to the fairways; in the dark, it would be near impossible to cross any of the rough without falling. We move until we hit the green on the 12h hole.

This is the only par 5 on the course, and runs parallel to the Valley. Through a small line of trees lies Drakemire Drive and, beyond that, an industrial estate.

The distant sound of a siren focuses Heartbreak. She pushes me into the trees. We climb another fence onto the road. To our left is the fire station. I look for any sign of life, but there is nothing. I'm tired, but Heartbreak keeps up the pace. Every so often pushing me. We skirt the industrial units until she reaches a gate. I'm manhandled over and into a small car park. She jumps over. The spinning lights of a police car appear. We hide behind a wall as a panda car zips by. She keeps me moving. We slide between two buildings.

'Don't stop!' she urges as I slow down.

We emerge into an area that acts as a warehouse delivery point; large metal shuttered doors sitting behind a raised concrete platform to allow lorries to back up and offload straight into the factory. Heartbreak leaps onto the platform and pulls me up. We walk past half a dozen doors, reaching a small wall separating this factory from the next.

'I'm tired,' I say.

'Move!'

Once over the wall, Heartbreak looks up at the trees behind the factory and points. We scramble over yet another fence and my anorak, already a sleeve down, rips near a pocket. I almost want to break into my inappropriate laugh as I think on what Mum will say when she sees the damage.

Heartbreak seems to know this bit of woodland well. We emerge on the drive that leads down to the crematorium. Ahead is a stretch of grass that leads up to Carmunnock Road and beyond that is Castlemilk. If we cross here, we will be out in the open. The panda car that passed us earlier has to have come up this road unless it went to the crematorium. If they are looking for us, hopefully they will come back this way.

We hide in the shadow of a tree. Heartbreak looks out.

'We are going to run,' she says. 'Straight up there.' She points to the grass-covered hill. 'As fast as you can. Do you get it?'

'I can't run, Mrs Hart. 'Really, I can't. My legs are beat.'

'I don't care if you've lost the use of both legs. We are running.'

She waits for a bus to lumber up the main road at the top of the hill. Through the mist of the windows, there are a few bodies visible.

'Now!' she says.

She takes off with me in front. I've no idea how old she is. Older than my dad. And, quick as she has been over the fences, she's soon huffing and puffing up the hill. To be fair, I'm not doing much better. Halfway to the main road, she slows to a walk. I follow suit. She curses as she stands in a fresh dog turd.

The smell rises like a bad fart in a tent. She's really cracked the shell off a stinker.

We reach the pavement, and she uses the kerb edge to scrape the worst of the turd from her shoe. She returns to the grass to rub away the remainder. But, by the smell she brings with her when she re-joins me, she's not been that successful.

'Let's get out of here!' she says.

She drags me across the dual carriageway I ran down a lifetime ago. There's no sign of any panda cars. There's more grass before the tenement's start. By the time we reach concrete again, she's puffing as if it's her last day with lung cancer. She drops to her haunches but doesn't take her eyes off me.

'Mrs Hart, why do you need me here?'

'Insurance,' she huffs. 'Now let's get to the bloody flat!'

I look back the way we came and, for a second, I think I see a figure halfway up the grass hill we've just climbed. Heartbreak turns to see what I'm looking at and the figure drops out of sight.

'Is someone following us?' she wheezes.

'No,' I say.

'I hope for your sake that's not a lie.'

I glance back down the hill, but there's no movement.

'This way,' she says and, once more, I'm back in the one scheme I've spent my life avoiding.

The few cars that litter the road are frosting up across their windows. The wind has dropped, the cold deepened. A Glasgow cold. One that seeps into your bones, your core. Glasgow likes to soak you, blow on you, then deep freeze you in a well-worn sequence that's designed to defeat even Arctic clothing. A couple of puddles we pass are already sheet ice. If it wasn't for the exertion in getting up here, I'd be an ice lolly by now—my body is a small furnace after the climb.

I expect to see to police when we turn onto to the road that Heartbreak's flat sits on, but it's deserted.

'Bastards,' says Heartbreak. 'They just ran out on me. Probably down the Beechwood pub at this moment telling themselves they had no other choice.'

I realise that she was hoping the red Victor or the Cortina would be here.

'Why are we here?' I ask.

'None of your business. Just get in the close!'

With no power, the close is as dark as last time I was here. Heartbreak takes out a match box and strikes it. We make it up half a landing before she has to extinguish the match to strike another. It takes four more matches to guide us to the top floor. All the way up, we meet no one. When she opens the flat door, the wall of heat and the same stale smell of sweat, booze, fags, shit and pee rolls out to meet us.

'This place stinks,' she says, forcing me in. 'Into the living room.'

As we enter the room, she lights another match, pushing me onto one of the couches, pulls out a couple of candles and lights them. She places them around the room, ensuring that the curtain is shut.

'I need a drink,' she says.

She vanishes. I hear a clink from the direction of the kitchen. She comes back with a cut crystal tumbler of what looks like whisky in one hand, holding a lit candle in the other. She slugs half the whisky before placing the glass on the dining table.

'I hate this place,' she says. 'But it's got its uses. The whole block is mine and there's not a soul living in the other flats, so if you fancy screaming for help, feel free!'

'What are you going to do?'

'Do, son?' she replies. 'Well, as they used to say in the old westerns, I think it's time to get out of Dodge for a while.'

'Where will you go?'

'Why the hell would I tell you that?'

She polishes off the rest of the whisky. She takes out a small packet of Hamlet cigars, extracts one and lights up. I'm trying to figure why she's come back here. There's nothing in this place.

She leaves the room again. This time, I hear scraping and grunting. When she returns, she has a leather holdall in one hand. It looks dusty and heavy.

'So, Bobby Bannerman, this is where we say our goodbyes.'

There's a knock at the door. Heartbreak spins on the spot. 'Who the fuck is that?'

She rushes to the window.

'No one down there I can see,' she says. 'Stay here!'

She leaves the living room and comes back a minute later. 'It's too dark to see anything through the peephole.'

My first thought was that the police were at the door, but I doubt they would have only knocked once.

'I need to go,' she says. 'But I need to know who is out there. Stand up!'

I push myself up.

'Okay, I'm going to open the door. You are going to look out. Take that candle,' she says, pointing at the one she had placed on the dining table. 'And I have the gun. Just remember that.'

With one hand on the gun and the other on the leather bag's handles, she kicks me in the back of the leg to move forward.

'What if it's Spanner's gang?' I say.

'How would they know about here?'

'I don't know, but you shot Spanner. They'll be looking for you.'

'Just go!'

She reaches the front door, unlocking it, gun high. She steps back. The candlelight in my hand catches her face. She looks tired. She pulls the door open. I wait to see if we are going to be invaded. Heartbreak kicks me on the back of the leg again.

I totter forward, candle in front.

The landing is clear. I walk to the banister and shine the candle over. I look down. At first, I can see nothing. Then, just as Heartbreak whispers, 'Is there anyone?', I see movement. Milky sticks his head out from the landing below. He waves at me and mouths something. I shrug. He repeats the action, and, on the third attempt, I think I know what he is trying to say.

The polis are coming.'

'Is it clear?' whispers Heartbreak.

I back up. Head trying to work out what to do next. If the police are on their way, I can't let Heartbreak leave. Especially with the bag. If I was to guess, I'd say there will be a cash in there. And that bag could hold a lot of cash.

'Well?' she says.

I could run. Snuff the candle and dive down the stairs. There's no way she could catch me. But she has the gun. Would she shoot after me? It's one thing shooting a thug like Spanner when he's bearing down on you. It's another to shoot a kid when he's running away.

Or is it?

But I know I can't run. Heartbreak might get away and, at some point, she could come back—and go after Dad or Mum. I fight the urge to flee. If my dad was here, he would be screaming at me to get out of there.

I don't.

I back up and re-enter the hallway.

'What is it?' Heartbreak asks.

'I think there's men at the foot of the stairs.'

'Who?'

'I'm not sure, but it could be the same ones that were with Spanner back at my house.'

'There's no cars outside.'

'I don't know about that and I'm not sure, but I think there are men down there.'

'Fuck. Get back in!'

She closes the door and my chance to escape vanishes. If I misread what Milky was trying to tell me, then I've just sealed myself in with a desperate woman. I don't think Heartbreak is one to go down without a fight and I'll be right in the crossfire. What if Milky was saying something else? It was dark out there. I was reading his lips in the light of a single candle a floor down. He could have been saying 'Get out of there!' Same number of words. Or 'Heartbreak's gang is coming.' Or. 'There is no-one coming.' Or…

Heartbreak stands in the hall, thinking.

'Okay, you need to draw them away,' she says. 'Give me a chance to get clear.'

'How would I do that? They are at the foot of the stairwell. They'll be on me as soon as I reach the bottom.'

'Get back in the living room, give me that candle!'

She drops the leather bag to the floor and takes the candle from me. 'Go on, get in the other room!'

I shuffle off to stand in the room, waiting.

Heartbreak comes in a few minutes later. 'Take these!'

She hands me a set of keys.

'That one,' she says, pointing at a Yale key, 'is the key for the first flat on the right as you come up. You're going to go in and head to the bathroom. Open the bathroom window, drop down from there to the back green, then make sure the men see you and follow you.'

'It's pitch dark.'

'There's a drainpipe next to the bathroom window. It's been used before.'

'Why don't you use it?'

'I'm way too old to keep running if they see me. Anyway, the pipe is knackered. You should be okay, but I doubt it'll take my weight.'

I listen for the tell-tale sign of a police siren approaching but hear nothing. I wish I'd spent a little longer making sure that I'd understood correctly what Milky had mouthed.

'They'll kill me if they catch me,' I say.

'They don't know who the hell you are. Just shin down the pipe and make a noise out back. I only need a couple of minutes. Get them into the back green. And don't think of running off without taking them with you!'

I shuffle my feet a little, showing no signs of moving.

'Just go!' she says, slapping me across the back of the head.

I'm just a punchbag for adults at the moment, as if it's the only language I understand. Ginger, do this. Slap. Ginger, do that. Slap. Ginger, do whatever I say. Slap!

'Stop hitting me!' I shout.

I get an unexpected reaction from Heartbreak, who actually recoils, albeit only a fraction.

'Why does everyone think it's okay to hit a kid?' I say. 'Why?'

'Don't get mouthy. Just get a shift on!'

'I'll tell you why kids get hit,' I say. 'Because there's no danger of getting hit back. I'm not stupid, Mrs Hart. I know what you want me to do. I don't need hit to do it. But I'm scared. I've been scared for days Mrs Hart. Days and days—and hitting me isn't helping.'

'I'll smack you black and blue if you don't get down those fucking stairs!'

'No.'

'What did you say?'

I need to stall this in the hope the police arrive.

'You can't make me, Mrs Hart.'

'I fucking can and I fucking will!'

'No, you can't. Even if I do go down the stairs, I can just run away. Or I'll tell them downstairs that you are up here. It's not me they want, is it?'

'If you do...'

I stop her. 'You'll do what, Mrs Hart? Kill me, kill my dad, kill my mum, kill the world?'

'All fucking four!'

And I was scared. Down and dirty shit-scared—but I was also seeing things in a new light. A light that showed me adults in a slightly different hue. My dad as the confident policeman. My dad asking me if it was okay for him to tell me about Mum later. Hornsby's scream, scared, when he lost a finger. Streak's need to catch me, regardless of what Inspector Sinclair said, because he couldn't go back to Heartbreak empty-handed. Heartbreak shooting Spanner because she was scared. My lessons in adulthood were piling up. Seeing adults for what they really were. People with as many conflicting emotions as me. Just older versions of me. Not some alien race. Me, but with the thought that they could better control their emotions and control their worlds. And back then, that's what I thought they were good at. That being an adult gave you control. But that night I learned it didn't. Seeing how quickly Heartbreak's world was falling apart was a lesson. And Dad had shown me a way to take advantage of that. He must have been scared when Heartbreak came into the house, gun in hand, but he didn't show it. He put on a face and fronted her up. And that's when I realised what the real difference between kids and adults was. Some adults could take a raw emotion and use it. Kids can't. They just react. And I could see that. For the first time I could see that—and needed to use it.

'I tell you what, Mrs Hart,' I say, sitting down on the couch, trying to hide my fear. 'If you tell me about my mum, I'll do what you want me to.'

'This isn't the playground, son. There's no games of make believe here. You just do what I say!'

Then, I utter words that are just plain insane. 'Well, shoot me then! Because I'm not going downstairs until you tell me about Mum.'

'You think I won't pull the trigger?' she says.

'I won't be able to do much climbing out of windows if you do.'

'I'm going to tan the skin of your arse unless you move!'

But she isn't going to do that. It would make me go, but it wouldn't stop me running away and she knows it. Dad said to Ivan, back in the house, that she had got away with murder. A woman who has killed. A woman used to violence, getting her way through violence. But now, right now, that's not going to work for her, and she knows that. She needs me to do what she wants and not what I want. If I run when I get out of here, she still needs to draw away the non-existent gang members downstairs.

'Why?' I say.

The simplest question on earth.

'Why what?'

'Why keep threatening me, Mrs Hart?'

'Because I need you to get rid of those men. And I need you to do it right now.'

'Then tell me about my mother!'

'For fuck's sake!'

She half-raises her hand to lamp me. A pathetic gesture. And she senses it.

'Shite!' she says, lowering her arm. 'Why do you want to know about your mother?'

'Because no one else will tell me.'

'Look, do me a favour; talk to your mother first! It's not for me to say.'

'I could talk to her,' I say. 'And she would probably tell me, but I don't want to ask her, just to find out something bad. I want to know what is what first. And you know what it is. You said so in my house.'

'Son, this is for your mother to tell you,' she says. 'But if you really want to know, there isn't much to it.'

She can't help glancing at the door. No doubt expecting it to fly open.

She drops a heart-felt sigh. 'I'll tell you what I know, then you need to get going and get going bloody quick. Okay?'

'Okay.'

Still no sirens.

'I wasn't involved directly,' she starts. 'It was all a long time back. Must be twenty years now. I had a guy called Gerald that ran a house for me up near the Barras. He ran three for me. We had girls that… Well let's say we had girls that… and leave it there.'

'That were prostitutes?'

'Yes.'

'And mum was one?'

'Do you want to hear the story, or do you want to guess it?'

'Sorry.'

'Anyway, as I said, I wasn't involved in the day-to-day, and this was before Spanner moved into the city centre. There were six or seven of us that divvied up the action in town. Anyway,

I'd have never remembered your mum if it wasn't for the fact that we used to have some high-profile clients. It's why I knew who she was. She was pretty, your mum, and young. Seventeen when she started with us.'

My heart falls, my mouth dries, my hands sweat as she talks. She's so casual talking about Mum. *Seventeen.*

'A right looker was your mother,' she continues. 'And she picked up a few repeat clients that were willing to pay well. And Gerald wasn't a bastard. If the girls earned well, they got a fair cut. Your mum did okay out of it.'

How could anyone do okay out of something like that?

'How did she come to be there in the first place?' I say, a quiver in my voice.

'How does anyone come to be anywhere like that? She had a bad childhood is what I heard. I hate to say it, son, but your grandfather and grandmother were both into the booze, badly from what I know.'

'I don't think your mum was looked after well when she was a kid,' she continues. Her face has softened as she talks.

'And?'

'One day she was picked up by Gerald and that was that.'

'Why did she do it?'

'Why else? Money. She needed money. You have to earn a living son. One way or another, you need to eat.'

'Was she there long?'

'Long enough. A couple of years and then the flat was raided.'

'By my dad?'

'He was part of it. They shut us down. Not that it made much difference. We were open in a new flat the following night, but your mum never came back. That's not usually allowed to happen. The girls are in for the long haul in that game.'

'Why didn't she come back?'

'Your dad. He stopped her. He wouldn't have been that much older than her back then. Maybe twenty. I don't know much more. All I do know is that if your dad hadn't stepped in, Gerald would have had your mum back at work in no time. But she never returned. And that's all I know.'

I want to ask more. Questions like: 'Who were the high-profile clients?' 'How often did she work?' Inappropriate questions that make me want to laugh. And I know that laughing now is a really bad idea.

'Now you know what I know,' she says. 'So, get moving and take those pricks downstairs with you!'

'When did you last see my mother?' I ask.

'Question time is over, son. I've told you all that I'm going to tell you, now get a move on!'

I stand up, with reluctance.

She loses patience and hauls me to the door.

'I've played your game son. Told you what you wanted to know. So now get down to it!'

She drags me into the hall, opens the door and, before she throws me out, she whispers, 'Now I know you've been threatened a hundred ways from Adam in the last few days, but I'll make you a simple promise. Screw me over this time and I still have people that will come around and chib your mum so bad that you won't recognise her. Do you get that, *son?*'

And she means it. It's written on her face in hard black pencil.

'Now go!' With that she pushes me into the hall. This time with no candle. She closes the door behind me quietly.

I stand for a few seconds, the chill from the outside wrapping its arms around me. I feel for the banister and work my way along to the first step.

Seventeen.

I was less than five years off that age. Mum was a prostitute by then. She must have known that I'd find out one day. I stood there, on that dark landing, thinking that surely, she meant to tell me at some point. Not let some stranger do it. Although how do you tell your son something like that?

I begin to descend the stone stairs and, when I reach the next landing, I hear breathing.

'Milky?' I whisper.

'Here.'

'Follow me!' I say, throwing my hands around until I find him. I grab his wrist and we move to the next set of stairs.

'What is going on?' he says.

'Shhh.'

I pull him down until we arrive on the first landing. I find the door Heartbreak told me to look for. It takes a few moments to find the keyhole in the dark before I open the door and push inside.

'Where are we?' says Milky once the door is closed.

'Shhh.'

By the echo in the hallway, this house sounds as unfurnished and undecorated as the one I've just left. But, unlike the one that Heartbreak is waiting in, this one smells of damp and little else. I open the first door on the left. There's a tiny amount of light coming through the curtainless window. I pull Milky in.

'What are we doing here, Ginger?'

'Where's my dad, Milky?'

'Your dad and I followed you when you left your house.'

'Was that you at the lane entrance?'

'It was your dad. He was flying after you. Way out front.'

'Heartbreak fired a shot.'

Milky touches my arm. 'She hit your dad.'

'Dad was shot?'

'In the arm.'

'Dad was *shot?*'

'Yes.'

'How is he?'

'He told me to follow you, that he'd be okay.'

'You left my dad when he'd been shot?'

'Not on his own. Half the doors on Magnus Crescent opened when they heard the sound of the gun. I saw Mrs Lilley come out, and she's a nurse. Your dad screamed at me that I needed to follow and find out where you went. He tried to go himself, but he couldn't get up.'

'Are you sure he's okay?'

'He said he was fine.'

'Jesus!'

'So, I followed you. When I saw you go in the close, I found a phone box and called the police.'

'Where are they?'

'I don't know.'

'And is that guy Spanner dead?'

'I don't think so. Just after you left, your dad said he was moving. What happened up in Heartbreak's flat?'

'I told her that Spanner's men were down here. I was stalling for time, for the police to arrive. I'm supposed to lead them away while she escapes. She's not stupid, she'll catch on quick that I'm lying.'

'Well, let's run.'

'We can't.'

'Why not?'

'Hart needs to be caught, Milky. She's just shot my dad, and she said she'd hurt my mum She has a bag of money. She'll vanish. Milky, whatever we do, we need to make sure she's caught.'

'What can we do about that? She has a gun.'

'If the police turn up, she has no way out. We need to keep her here. Where are the police?'

'They have to be on their way.' he says.

And then, at the very edge of what I can hear, right at the edge, a sweet sound. A siren.

'That must be them,' I utter.

'What now?'

'Back to the flat door!' I say.

'What for?'

'Heartbreak will make a run for it when she hears the sirens. She can't afford to get trapped up there.'

'But she thinks there are men down here.'

'And she'll figure they'll bolt for it when they hear the police coming. We need to stop her leaving.'

I open the door, immediately hearing footsteps from above. They are moving down. There's no light with them.

'She's coming,' I whisper.

I leave the door open. In the dark it won't be seen. Milky and I wait.

The footsteps are soon joined by heavy breathing. Heartbreak flies past. I stand up and pull Milky out of the door. I locate the banister, pulling Milky with me to follow Heartbreak down. As we hit the ground floor, I hear footsteps move towards the front of the building. Heartbreak's outline appears in the frame of the close. She's carrying the bag in one hand, the gun in the other. I still have a hold of Milky's wrist and pull him along.

Heartbreak moves out onto the path outside, we are right behind her. The siren is louder but there are no lights to indicate it is near this road. Heartbreak picks up speed, turns away from the sound of the siren. She walks quickly along the pavement.

'We need to keep her in sight,' I say quietly.

We wait until she's a little further down the road and we move out. We keep to the front greens of the tenements. If we step on the pavement and she looks back, she'll see us, power cut or no power cut. I drag Milky with me. And this is where hedge-hopping since I was four years old comes into its own. We cling to the building wall, using the shadow to hide us. We slip over hedge after hedge, fence after fence, keeping Heartbreak in sight. She vanishes around a street corner. We have to leap onto the pavement to catch her up, just as the flashing lights of the panda car light up the road behind us.

'Milky,' I say. 'Run back. Tell them what's going on. Tell them that Heartbreak has a gun and is getting away! I'll stay with her.'

Milky turns to fly towards the panda car. I turn the corner and I'm surprised at how far ahead Heartbreak is. She might have struggled to climb the grassy hill, but the appearance of the police car has given her new energy. I forget about hedge-hopping and run. She crosses the road before looking back. I freeze, but if she sees me, she doesn't stop. She reaches the next corner, disappears around it. I sprint.

I reach the corner, poke my head out. Heartbreak has crossed over to the other side of the street and is jogging along. A slow jog, but one that means I need to run again. I look back. Surely Milky must have reached the panda car by now. I hear a second siren as Heartbreak reaches a lane running between two tenements. She dives up it. I run to the entrance. It's a black hole. A siren rises behind me. I turn to see the panda car rush past the end of the street I'm on.

I walk into the lane, sticking like glue to the wall. The ground beneath is uneven. Frozen mud. Running my hand along the brickwork, I can see nothing in front. I hear a loud scraping noise. My eyes are starting to adjust to the lack of light. A squat row of small structures appears. Garages.

I move towards the scraping sound. It's joined by squeals. I think Heartbreak might be opening a garage door. And that could mean she has another car. And that means she might get away. My nerves are strung like a cattie being readied to fire. I move along the garages. A shadow ahead indicates one of the doors is open. I hear a click. A small light goes on, shining from within, casting a dim glow onto the mud outside. Maybe the interior light of the car going on as a door is opened?

There is enough illumination to see that Heartbreak has left her bag near the garage door. I don't hesitate. I run straight at the bag and lift it. From inside the garage, I hear a shout. I put my head down and run.

The bag is heavy. I have no idea where I'm going. I reach the end of the garages and stop.

'Get fucking back here!' screams Heartbreak from behind me.

I feel for the edge of the last garage then work my way to the rear. I stumble into a low brick wall, smack my shin and nearly go flying. I climb over the wall, feeling the smoothness of concrete underfoot on the other side. I begin to walk again, hand out in front of me, blind as a bat.

'I'll fucking kill you!' Heartbreak screams. 'Give me that bag back!'

My hand touches another wall. Pebble dashed. The back of a tenement. I need to find a close. I rub along the wall until my hand slips into empty space. I enter the close. The light is better here. Unlike Heartbreak's close, the stairs to these homes partly run up the outside of the building. Each home has a landing that opens to the front, looking out onto the street below. The street beyond the close stretches left and right. There's just a dark canyon of buildings on either side. If I'm caught out there, Heartbreak would have a clean shot at me. I double back to climb the stairs, rising to the top landing as quickly as I can.

'Get down fucking now!' shouts Heartbreak from below. 'I know you're up there.'

I hear her begin to climb.

There are two doors on each landing. One to the left and one to the right.

I move to my left and batter on the front door, then I cross the landing and do the same to the other door. I stand with my back to the landing railing. Behind me is fresh air, four floors down is the pavement. A cold wind blows across my back and, from the corner of my eye, I see a flashing light. The panda car rushes by beneath me.

'There you are!' says Heartbreak as she reaches the top step, heaving air as if it's going out of fashion. 'Give me that fucking bag!'

Neither front door is opening and the siren behind me is falling away.

There's more than enough light to see the gun in Heartbreak's hand.

She points it right at me.

'Bag!' she says.

I lift the bag up and, as I do so, I pull the zip open.

The lights go on. Streetlights, interior lights that had been left on, every light. All go on, as the power cut ends.

I see inside the bag.

It's stuffed with notes.

Bank notes.

In that instant, I fully unzip the bag, slinging it out over the railing, dangling it above the pavement.

Heartbreak shouts at me. 'Fucking stop!'

With a twist of my wrist, I turn the bag over. The contents pour from it like water from a tap. Bank notes fly into the chilled air. A few clumps of paper drop straight down. Later my dad will tell me that it must have been the most expensive scramble in history.

Heartbreak screams, flies at the bag as I shake it empty, money fleeing into the night. Heartbreak trips, her gun flies free, clips the top of the railing, flips over the edge. She yells, throwing herself at the railing to try to grab the bag and gun. But she's too late. I let the bag go. It spins away. I see my opportunity to escape, diving under her outstretched arms, aiming for the stairs, just as the door to my left opens.

'I've called the police,' a voice from the door shouts.

I pile down the stairs, out onto the street. A panda car appears. I wave like crazy. It screeches to halt and, as the policemen get out, I point up.

'She's up there, the Heartbreak woman,' I say. 'And she doesn't have the gun anymore.'

The policemen look up into the shower of money still raining down.

A door opens at the bottom of the close. A man in a dressing gown walks out. A ten-pound note lies in front of him. He reaches down to pick it up. More notes lie scattered around. A carpet of cash. His eyes open wide.

The policemen run for the stairs, one spotting the gun and pocketing it.

Above me Heartbreak is screaming like a banshee as more people begin to emerge from their homes.

They start to collect the money up.

The Conversation.

'*AND THAT WAS that?*'

'*Not quite.*'

'*It's light outside. We'll be out of here shortly. Was there a point to the whole story?*'

'*Let me finish and you can judge!*'

Chapter 23
'A Lazy Sunday Morning.'

MUM PLACES A cup of tea next to my bed. White, full of sugar, with a slab of cheese and toast on the side. Breakfast in bed is as rare as a rain-free day in January.

'And how is my wee ginger-haired boy?'

It's been a week since Heartbreak was arrested, shrieking at the growing hoards who had flowed from homes when they saw the street littered in cash. I'm sure a few of the polis moved some of the loose cash to their pockets as well. I know I did. Under my bed is over two hundred pounds. My payment for all the hassle. My *reward*.

'Mum, can I ask you a question?'

She sighs. I've said the same thing a dozen times in the last few days. Each time, the response has been the same. *We'll talk later.*

'Not now, Bobby!'

'Mum, I need to know.'

She lets out a deep breath, a sign of resignation.

'I really don't want to talk about it, darling.'

'Mum, I just want to know if what Heartbreak said was true.'

She sits at the end of my bed. Deke is out, Dad is at work, but will be home soon. It's a Sunday morning and I know Mum is meeting a friend in a few hours—so if ever there is a time, it's now.

'Okay, darling. What did she say to you?'

I'm almost too embarrassed to relay it, but I force it out. She listens, soft eyes that lose cohesion as I talk. When I finish, she takes my hand.

'Okay, some of that is true, but not all,' she says. 'Do you really want to hear this? I'm not sure you are ready.'

'When will I be ready, Mum?'

She moves closer.

'The first thing you need to know is that your grandpa and grandma were not alcoholics. They were the kindest people I ever knew, but your grandfather lost a leg in the war and, when he was demobbed, never got a great job. He was a lorry driver before the war but couldn't drive after. Things were tough, then your gran fell sick and lost her job. They had taken on a mortgage that needed two wages. I was about thirteen then. They struggled on for a while, but with four mouths to feed and a mortgage to pay, your grandfather did a stupid thing. Or maybe he did the only thing he could. He was so short on cash that he went to a loan shark. He ran up a big bill and, with the interest, it kept getting bigger. Until he was in so deep, there was no way out. Things were bad. I really wanted to stay at school, but we needed money, so I left at fifteen to get a job—and it still wasn't enough. We struggled on for a while, but it got worse. The loan shark had grandpa running errands. Ones that would have landed him in jail if he had kept going.'

She stops, squeezing my hand. 'Are you sure you want to hear this?'

I nod.

'It was your Aunt Joan introduced me to Gerald McEwan, and one thing led to the other. I'm not proud of what I did, but some of the clients paid well. It took me two years, but I all but paid off the loan shark's debt, then I met your dad.'

'When he raided the flat?'

'Yes. I wanted to quit before then, but you don't get out that easy. He helped me escape, then helped again by paying off the remainder of the debt to get the loan shark off our back. And that's how we got together.'

'Who knows about this?'

'Only a few people—but I always knew that would change one day. And I can't do anything about it. We just need to get on with our life.'

'And *that* was the only way you could earn money?'

'Don't you dare judge me, Bobby Bannerman. Don't you dare!'

I shrink back.

'So, why,' I ask, 'did Heartbreak tell me the story about gran and grandpa's drinking?'

'Back then, I never talked about my family. Stories grew up. I didn't stop them. I didn't care. All I wanted to do was get the money paid back. Maybe I should have said something to quash the rumours, but after a while it gets hard, and you just go with the flow.'

She slips back down the bed a little. 'Will that do?'

I nod.

'I saw Ivan Peters yesterday,' she says.

'Milky says he's left the school.'

'When they found out he was working with that man Johnston, they fronted up to his drinking and fired him.'

'Mum, one last question?'

'What?'

'Dad asked why I didn't tell him earlier about what was going on.'

'Why didn't you, son? Why didn't you come to us both?'

'Because I thought he might be taking money from Heartbreak. We just seemed to have a lot of cash suddenly. The telly, the record player, the new dining table.'

'The table is gorgeous, isn't it?'

The table had arrived yesterday. Mum has nursed it like a new-born baby. We have yet to eat on it. I suspect it may be some time before we do.

'The money, Mum?'

'I need you to promise to say nothing.'

'Blood and guts, Mum.'

'We had a wee bit of good luck,' she says. 'And not before time.'

'What kind of luck?'

'A wee win on the pools.'

'Really?' I say. 'How much?'

'Ten thousand pounds.'

'You're kidding?'

'Nope. I couldn't believe it. We got the call only a few weeks back.'

'Ten thousand pounds! What are you going to do with it?'

'Enjoy some of it, and it might even let us move into a bigger house.'

'Away from Simshill?'

'No. I like it here, but maybe we could move up to a five-room house. Give you and Deke your own room each.'

'That would be nice, Mum.'

'Yes, it would, Bobby. Yes, it would.'

Downstairs, I hear the door open, and Dad calls out. He's back from night shift.

'Mum, can you tell Dad we talked about your past?'

'Of course.'

'And I'd like him and you to know that I don't care what you did. I just want to say that I love you both.'

She smiles.

The Conversation.

'DAD CAME UP after that, just before I went to sleep that night, and asked if I wanted to go and see the football the next day. He told me he could get us into the Partick Thistle v Ferranti United game. Dad had never taken me to football before.'

'And that's the story?'

'More or less.'

'I don't get it. I mean, it was a good enough tale, but that's about it. Do you feel better getting it off your chest?'

'You know, I do. A lot of it is in the public domain if you know where to look.'

'And what isn't?'

'Hornsby and Neil.'

'What about them?'

'They must have thought they had won a watch when Heartbreak was lifted.'

'They were wrong?'

'Yip. A year later both were found in a car, up in the lock-ups where I stole Heartbreak's bag of money. A hose pipe running from exhaust to the window. Both dead.'

'Suicide?'

'Let's call it assisted suicide. Smiff and Streak were pulled in for questioning, but let go.'

'Ivan?'

'Went to work for Spanner. Died a good few years back.'

'Murdered.'

'Drink.'

'And what about my job offer?'

'I'll get to that. No more questions?'

'Like what?'

'What happened to Milky, my mum, my dad—why I'm in here?'

'Why are you in here?'

'Does my story make it sound like everything ended up like some fairy tale?'

'A little. But it didn't. Did it?'

'Nope.'

'What happened?'

'We got used to money.'

'Sorry.'

'My family got used to money. We moved up in the world. Mum and Dad got a taste for the better life. But ten grand didn't last long, not even back then. It should have, but Dad quit the force. I think he believed that he could spin out the cash, get a cushier number as a job.'

'I take it that didn't fly?'

'Correct. If we had no money before, we were soon back there, and more. I think it's genetic.'

'Really.'

'My mum's dad got in deep. Turns out my dad's dad did the same. Like father like son.'

'What happened?'

'My old man was approached by Spanner Johnston. When I was sixteen, from what I can figure. Cash in hand for jobs done.'

'And he took it?'

'Like I said, happy endings are rare. Once on the hook with a bastard like Johnston, there's no way back.'

'And you?'

'*Same ending. When I left school, Spanner approached my dad. He needed a new runner, and I was het for it. I had no choice. Dad was in a hole. Spanner asked, Spanner got.*'

'*You could have run away?*'

'*Not my style, anyway Mum was also sick by then. Heart failure. The NHS was a wonder, but it had its limits. Spanner found some drugs from the States, expensive, but they promised much. So, I began to work for Spanner.*'

'*Did the drugs work?*'

'*A little.*'

'*Johnston died an aeon back.*'

'*He did that. The bullet wound from Heartbreak didn't help.*'

'*And?*'

'*Dad stepped up and took over from Johnston. Ironic, given all his years on the other side of the street. We had money again. We moved when mum died. Dad bought me a flat in Shawlands. He moved to the city centre.*'

'*How long?*'

'*How long, what?*'

'*How long did your dad run things?*'

'*A long time. It turned out he was good at it. Played Heartbreak's game. Knew the police on the take—used it to his advantage. As they were promoted, he thrived. Top brass in your pocket will do that.*'

'*Is he still around?*'

'*No. Joined Mum. Even went in a similar way. Heart attack.*'

'*And you took over?*'

'*It was inevitable. But then again, you know that. You know who I am?*'

'*I know what you do. Know your reputation.*'

'*And does that not scare you?*'

'*Not really.*'

'*I'm supposed to be a bad bastard.*'

'No 'supposed to be' about it from what I hear. But you hardly act like one.'

'Oh, I can be a real bastard when I want to. You really don't want to get on the wrong side of me!'

'Am I on the wrong side of you?'

'Far from it.'

'You know what?'

'What?'

'I've just heard about a boy trying to do the best he could for friends and family. Is that boy gone?'

'Yes.'

'Are you sure?'

'Well, maybe not completely gone.'

'Is that why I'm here?'

'What do you think?'

'It sounded like you're seeking absolution.'

'For what I've done in the last forty-odd years? I don't think that's possible. What I did as a kid will never make up for that. Try again?'

'Because of Milky?'

'He died when I was serving a five stretch. But you know that only too well. I got him into a private hospice.'

'He appreciated that.'

'But I never got to say goodbye. I never really got to say thanks to him for being a friend. A magical friend.'

'He knew.'

'Did he?'

'More than you know. I sat with him on his last night.'

'What did he say?'

'It's your turn to guess.'

'He told you the story I've just told you.'

'Yip.'

'And was my version better or worse?'

'Worse.'

'In his version, was I the hero, or him?'

'He was.'

'Of course, he would say that. And, if I'm honest, he was. Forget how that story finished. Just count the times he dug my arse from the fire.'

'He had a good life.'

'He did that. Became a policeman and a bloody good one. Tried to nick me a few times!'

'But he didn't.'

'No. So, will you take the job?'

'I take it I can say no?'

'Of course, but I need someone. Retirement beckons.'

'You're retiring?'

'Sort of. I'm dying. My heart. It's not got long to go—curse of my family it seems.'

'So… Hang on… You're offering me YOUR job?'

'That's why you needed to hear the story—to know how much Milky meant to me. What we went through. Why I am who I am.'

'But your job is… huge!'

'I can't think of anyone better to do it. I have no kids and I wouldn't trust anyone of the idiots who work for me to take over. The vultures are moving in. You'll need to fight like hell to keep what I've built—but the rewards are great.'

'I'm no guarantee of success. After all, here I am, in prison with you.'

'You got desperate, from what I hear. You're plenty smart. You just need the resources. Anyway, if you flop, so what? I'll be gone. Anyway, the job offer is still good if you'll do me one wee favour.'

'What?'

'You were there when Milky died. Right?'

'I was.'

'What were his final words?'

'He lay for a long time after telling the story, eyes shut. I knew he was going, but just before he closed his eyes forever, he opened them one more time. Looked at me, took my hand, spoke, then he passed.'

'What did he say?'

'Son,' he said. 'Promise me something. If you ever see that bastard, Ginger, tell him he was the worst friend I ever had!'

ACKNOWLEDGEMENTS

This is by far the most personal book I've ever written. If I tell you that in 1974 I was twelve years old, had red hair (still do) and lived in Simshill on the southside of Glasgow, you'll understand. If you ever visit Simshill—the Woods are still there, as is the 'football pitch' (although I doubt anyone plays football there anymore). Simshill Primary School was knocked down an eon ago—but King's Park Secondary still stands. The lane behind the shops at Croftfoot roundabout is still there. To be fair, a lot of the of the locations in this book are, to a greater or lesser extent, based on places I knew, places I frequented as a kid. It's true my father was a policeman in Glasgow police—the father of Ginger is not based on him and Ginger's Mum isn't based on my Mum.

Please forgive any lapses in my memory that have led to geographical or historical inaccuracies. The seventies were another planet. Fifty years on things are a little blurry. Most of the events in this story never happened, but a few did—I'll leave it to your imagination to figure which is which.

As to the characters in the book—well they are all fictitious—and that's final.

I have a lot of people to thank for this book. My publisher Sean Coleman for believing this was a story that was worth sharing with the world. My beta readers/informal editors—Tracy Hall, Irene Sutherland and Gwen Jones-Edward. To my wife, Lesley, who is at this moment putting up with her husband, sitting on the floor, moaning about the edit process—I love you,

Mrs Brown. To my other informal readers, Scott and Nicky, my whip smart kids.

And, if you read the dedication at the front of this book, you'll see I've thanked a few friends, who, all being well, will be sitting at the top of Creag Bhan on the Isle of Gigha, on the first holiday weekend of every May for a while yet, toasting life—and friends.

Milton Keynes UK
Ingram Content Group UK Ltd.
UKHW041903310723
426100UK00004B/385

9 781915 433084